Praise for Hot Enough to Kill

"...the real joys in this book are the characters. And characters they are! If you enjoyed Stephanie Plum's urban New Jersey family and the quiet rural community of "Biggie" Weatherford's Jobs Crossing, give this spry first novel a read." — Margaret Baker, *Baldwin Ledger*

"...an irreverent, fast-paced, page-turning mystery. Hot Enough to Kill *is a terrific mystery, sharply drawn, cleverly plotted, dynamically presented, and pure sleuthing entertainment from first page to last."*
— *Wisconsin Bookwatch*

"If you love Janet Evanovich and New Jersey's Stephanie Plum, then you will loooove Texas' own Jolene Jackson." — *Cozies, Capers & Crimes*

"...a highly diverting tale of mystery, romance and humor. Paula Boyd has created a wickedly funny team in Lucille and Jolene and anyone who enjoys the works of Janet Evanovich or Joan Hess is going to love Ms. Boyd." — Toby Bromberg, *Romantic Times*

"This was one doggone good read and a downright funny book to boot. Boyd has an engaging writing style that grabs the reader right from the opening lines and keeps them turning the page... Excellent."
— Molly Martin, *BookDragon*

"Carl Hiaasen meets Texasville! I had so much fun reading this that I hated to have it end. Paula Boyd writes with pure Texas humor, weaving together a good whodunit and providing a backdrop that won't be forgotten. Hot Enough to Kill *is a must read for your Sherlock funny bone."* — Judi Clark, *Mostly Fiction*

"Southern charm and ambiance with heavy attitude gives you some idea of what to expect in this wonderfully humorous mystery. Highly Recommended." — *I Love a Mystery*

"...takes you on an action-packed murder mystery ride that leaves you 'shakin' in yer boots'." — *Colorado Homes and Lifestyles*

"Five plus stars, five plus laughs! ... a hoot and a half of rollicking good mystery! The best dang novel I've read all year!"
— *Midwest Book Review*

HOT ENOUGH TO KILL

PAULA BOYD

Diomo Books

First printing, October 1999
Second printing, February 2000
Third printing, December 2001

Diomo
Books

Colorado, USA
(303) 816-2521
www.diomobooks.com

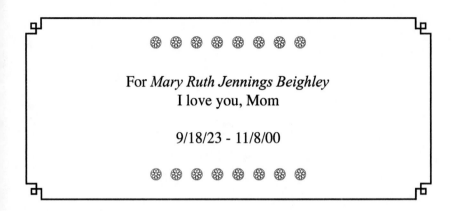

For *Mary Ruth Jennings Beighley*
I love you, Mom

9/18/23 - 11/8/00

Chapter
One

I generally find myself back in the thriving metropolis of Kickapoo, Texas, for reasons that are either beyond my control or my good sense. Sometimes both. I've come back to my hometown for holidays, so-called vacations and entirely too many funerals. The only thread of commonality in these events is that I am guaranteed to experience some level of unpleasantness. It's one of those facts of nature, like washing your car so it will rain. I show up in Kickapoo and bad things are sure to follow. Only this time, the first bad thing had already happened. Somebody had shot my seventy-two-year-old mother's boyfriend. Shot him dead. On purpose.

Now, before I explain the whos and what-fors of the murder, you need to know a few things about my mother. Lucille Jackson takes no guff off anybody. Those are her words, not mine.

No longer auburn-haired, she's still a striking woman and credits her current "natural blonde" look to a weekly dousing of a rinse called "Frivolous Fawn." But don't think I'm comparing the woman to a gentle deer frolicking in a meadow. Unless Bambi's developed a fondness for whimsical costume jewelry and wild purple pantsuits, it just doesn't work. A better visual might be a cosmetically enhanced pterodactyl with a glitter-covered chip on her shoulder and a real bad attitude. Of course I could be letting my latent childhood hostilities taint my assessment.

And to be fair, my mother holds an equally unflattering opinion of me, something along the lines of "ungrateful and man-less daughter intent on squandering her looks and journalism degree by hiding in the mountains of Colorado" covers most of the bases. We do, however, love one another in our own ways.

When my dad died of a heart attack two years ago, it took Mother a good while to come out of her shock. When she did, she did it in a big way. Or at least a scandalous one. She started dating the mayor. Unfortunately, the mayor still had a wife. Now the truth is, the mayor and his spouse hadn't lived together in years and hadn't even liked each other when they had. This is all beside the point, of course, because no matter how you sliced it, my mother's boyfriend had still been legally married to another woman. I was so proud.

Lucille, the queen of rationalization, did not share my dismay. She found Mr. Mayor's nebulous marital state to be perfectly acceptable because she didn't ever want to remarry anyway. Closer to the point, there apparently weren't many hot hunks pushing seventy to choose from in Kickapoo, Texas — population 1,024, or rather 1,023 living souls and one dead mayor. Which brings me right back to the reason I'm sweltering in 112-degree heat — and that's inside the building — waiting for my mother to come sauntering out of the county jail so I can take her home. It's not your typical family reunion spot, but Lucille is anything but typical.

That said, you can understand why I wasn't particularly surprised that I heard her before I saw her. Lucille commands attention, one way or another.

"I don't know what lies you've been told, Jolene," Mother said, bursting through the door to the county lock-up waiting area. She sashayed past a deputy, past me and toward the exit, her heels clicking out an ominous beat. "These people know good and well that I didn't kill BigJohn, not that he didn't need a what-for, the old goat." With her nose stuck up in the air and a black patent leather purse swinging from her elbow, Lucille marched out of the Bowman County courthouse and toward my dark blue Chevy Tahoe.

I dutifully followed, wondering exactly how best to handle this somewhat ticklish situation. No clear plan emerged, so I figured I ought to try to be the good and attentive daughter she'd always wished for. I clicked up the latches, opened her door, then hurried around to the driver's side to start the car — and the blessed air conditioner. I wriggled inside, hoping to keep the thin fabric of my shorts between me and the Texas-fried leather seat. The skin on the backs of my thighs sizzled as it bonded to the seat, but I started the car and said not a word, knowing Lucille would not appreciate my ugly thoughts about either the heat or her predicament. I also knew she'd spill her guts about the whole sordid mayor affair soon enough without any coaxing.

After a predictable show of climbing into "that monster truck," as she called it, Lucille settled herself into the passenger side and pointed all the air conditioner vents toward her face.

"Good heavens, I'm glad to be free," she said, patting her piled-high hair. "Nobody knows what I've been through. What took you so long to get here? Those no-account deputies wouldn't listen to a thing I said. Asking their silly questions over and over, and then talking to me like I was some dirty criminal when I didn't say just what they wanted to hear." She huffed and clucked her tongue. "I did get my own room, though."

"Your own room?"

"Well, I don't think the whole world needs to know that Lucille Jackson was put in a jail cell. Me, in jail! Why the very nerve of those people."

Technically, I was one of the "nervy" people since I'd agreed that Lucille should wait with the deputies until I arrived. It had seemed the best thing to do at the time, although I wasn't going to confess my part in her captivity or try to explain my good intentions. That sort of thing has never worked, trust me. And while we're busy setting the record straight, Lucille had spent her time in an office, not a jail cell, and had apparently been quite content to use the department's telephone and call her friends while she waited for her only child to pick her up. That was the official version. I couldn't wait to hear my mother's interpretation.

Lucille reached into her purse and dug out a tissue. After a good blow and sniff, she said, "It was the silliest thing, really. I was up at the Dairy Queen, minding my own business, having a nice glass of iced tea with Agnes Riddles and Merline Campbell, and the next thing I knew these two big old goons had jerked me out of my chair and tossed me into the back of their patrol car like some dirty criminal. It was just a crying shame, I tell you, treating me like that. Why that Jerry Don Parker wouldn't even be sheriff if it weren't for your father, God rest his soul. And what does he do to repay me? Why, he sends his big old goons out to haul me in like some thug, and right in front of the whole town."

The town was small, but not small enough for the entire populace to fit inside the Dairy Queen, particularly one with a maximum capacity sign that read 56. There were additional corrections I could make to her story, but decided to just hit the high points. "Those goons, as you call them, said you refused to talk to them and that you threatened to 'kick both of their butts' — that was a quote — if they laid a hand on you."

"Humph," Lucille snorted. "They were manhandling me and I don't put up with that from anybody."

When I didn't respond immediately, she tipped up her nose and stared out the window, suddenly enthralled by the landscape — or lack thereof.

The fourteen-mile stretch of melting asphalt from Bowman City to Kickapoo is about as straight and flat as they come, and the scenery amounts to scrub mesquite trees with more thorns than leaves. Breaking up the monotony, or adding to it, depending upon your perspective, are oil wells — lots of them — pumping like big, lethargic chickens playing perpetual tug-of-war with skinny worms of iron cable. Beautiful, really. Just makes you want to pull off the road and set up a tripod. And did I mention it's at least 125 degrees in the shade with triple-digit humidity?

But on the bright side, there are a lot of really nice folks living around here, give you the shirts off their backs and all that. Unfortunately, in the midst of these fine, upstanding, salt-of-the-earth folks lurked a rather nasty killer.

I could feel a vortex forming around me, building, ready to suck me into the madness. In my high school and college years, before I figured out I wasn't cut out to be a reporter, a story about small-town intrigue and one dead mayor would have had me doing handstands. I'd have plunged in with no holds barred to get to the truth and would have whipped out a dandy article. But not now, and especially not with my mother hanging over my shoulder. I am smarter than that, thank you very much. According to Lucille, I can't even find the right hair color (Clairol's Light Ash Brown, if you're wondering), so I certainly couldn't be counted on to ferret out a killer in the highly sophisticated locale of Kickapoo, Texas.

Nope, I was not about to get myself involved in this mess. I'd stay just long enough to be sure mother kept herself out of trouble. Then it would be back to the mountains and sanity for me. I'd call the kids (grown, but still my kids), tell them how much I missed them, meet them in Boulder for a nice dinner, mention the little problem with their grandmother and that would be that. Done and forgotten.

Then, as if my nineteen-year-old son were sitting right beside me, I heard, "Gee, Mom, I can't believe you're going to just abandon Gran, leave her down there all by herself with a murderer." The twenty-year-old daughter's voice was equally clear with "Gran wouldn't turn her back on you, Mom, no matter what you did."

Guilt and denial have tended to be the two most prominent factors in my life, and this time guilt was the indisputable winner. Okay, so I wouldn't run off right away, and maybe it wouldn't hurt if I asked a few questions here and there, just to be on the safe side. "Dammit," I muttered, shifting in the seat, highly uncomfortable on a number of levels.

"It is awful. I just cannot imagine," Mother said, seriously misinterpreting my muttering for sympathy, "how anybody could think I'd shoot BigJohn."

I waited a few beats, but when she didn't end her dismay with the expected "I loved him," I decided to get just a little clearer on the exact nature of the relationship between my mother and BigJohn. "So exactly how friendly were you and Mayor Bennett?"

"Well," she said, with an indignant sniff, or maybe it was a cocky huff, "we practically lived together for three months, not that I let him stay the night at my house, mind you. He sure as heck knew I wouldn't be washing his dirty old socks or cooking for him either. I've done my share of that and I'm not doing it any more." She took a short breath, seemed to compose herself a little, then shrugged. "It was something to do though. We went out to nice places, had a good time. Never had any problems, really, unless he brought up *her*."

"His wife?"

"Ex-wife."

"They got a divorce?"

Mother shrugged. "Same as. I saw a big stack of papers he got from the lawyer, but I didn't look at them. Didn't need to. I made it real plain that I wasn't going to marry him under any circumstances. *Any* circumstances." She sat a little taller and patted her hair. "He sure wanted to marry me though, I'll tell you that."

"Well, I guess whether he got his divorce or not doesn't much matter now, does it?" I asked, watching her from the corner of my eye lest a tear creep out when I wasn't looking. It didn't. "I might add that you don't seem overly aggrieved about his death either."

"Well, of course I'll miss him," she said, sounding mildly sincere. "He was no Bertram, I'll tell you for sure, but he did have his good points."

Posthumously, Bertram Jackson had become the perfect husband — a strange metamorphosis considering my recollection that he generally stayed in as much trouble with Lucille as I did, or do. At some point I was going to call her on that little technicality, but now didn't seem the right time. Besides, in a weird way, I was pleased that BigJohn's dying hadn't elevated him to the same sainted status my father now held.

I was mulling over the fact that my mother and I could keep a panel of psychologists gainfully employed well into the twenty-third century when she said, "I didn't advertise it, you know, but he hadn't been very nice to me lately. The old goat made me so mad I could just spit."

This was a figure of speech, as Lucille does not spit, even when she brushes her teeth, but I got the idea. The red glow in her eyes was pretty telling also. I tried to look sympathetic. "Things got kind of bad between you two?"

"I told him he ought to just go on back to his dumb old plain vanilla wife since they were both crazy as loons and ought to live in the loony bin together. Suppose that was just what he was doing since she showed up in town not three days after our set-to."

Lucille spoke with more venom than a ten-foot rattlesnake and her lips were drawn up into a terse little pucker. Apparently the wife, ex or otherwise, was a touchy subject.

"I never saw their carryings-on, mind you," she continued, nostrils flaring. "But people told me they were flaunting themselves around town, acting like newlyweds, that self-righteous, hypocritical jackass. He was over at my house every single day of the week and calling me sixteen times a day and then, poof." She snapped her fingers, a good trick considering the inch-long acrylics glued to the tips. "Just like that it was over. Not one word from him. Nothing. The way I figure it, he got just what he deserved, and I'm not about to be shedding any tears over it."

No, she surely wasn't. And furthermore, it sounded like she was quite pleased that BigJohn had been put out of her misery. Not good. Not good at all.

I drove toward Kickapoo on autopilot, trying to make myself face the unpleasant question: Did she do it? I couldn't believe it was even a possibility, but then again her mental state hadn't been a model of normalcy since she was widowed. Not a comforting thought.

In fact, about the only comforting thoughts I could find were related to my children. Specifically, since both my kids were basically grown, I wouldn't have to sit them down and euphemistically explain why Gran had to move to a new house with bars on the windows and razor wire around the yard. They'd understand just fine. And blame me for it all. Sarah and Matt, being considerate and thoughtful children, always sided with their grandmother on just about everything, and everything generally meant that whatever my opinion happened to be was the wrong one. I was tempted to call the little darlings in their dorms and tell them to get themselves down here and take over the joyous task of keeping dear Gran out of trouble. That would change their traitorous little tunes in a hurry.

Deciding that there really were no comforting thoughts after all, I wrenched one hand from the steering wheel long enough to rub my pounding temples. "Really, Mother, you've got to be careful what you say in public. You're already an obvious suspect, and talking about being glad BigJohn's dead tends to move you up to the top of the list."

"It's a free country, Jolene, and I'll say whatever I please whenever I please. Besides, I know I didn't kill the old goat, and I don't much care what that Jerry Don Parker thinks. Never knew what you saw in him anyway," she said, dismissing my concerns with the wave of an elegant hand. "I told you that boy would never amount to a hill of beans, and I was right," she went on. "Locking up an old, frail woman and treating her like dirt. Why, I never heard of such a thing. I tell you, they were all just ugly to me, Jolene. Plain ugly. And that Jerry Don Parker was the worst of the lot. You just have no idea what I've been through."

Oh, yes, I did, and it was basically nothing unless you counted what all she brought on herself. "It seems to me, Mother, if anybody was mistreated, it was Jerry. He said you smacked him in the head with your fifty-two-pound purse."

"It was an accident," she muttered. "And my purse doesn't weigh nearly that much. Besides, he had it coming."

Mother wholeheartedly believes in folks getting what's coming to them, unless of course it's coming to her.

"You're not allowed to hit the sheriff, Mother."

"I'm just glad you didn't marry that brute," she said, ignoring my comment.

I winced before I realized how much the offhand marriage comment had stung. I also recalled that Lucille was the one who threw seven kinds of fits when I told her that I wasn't marrying Jerry, and furthermore, I wasn't hanging around Redwater Falls for college but was heading to Austin, pronto. I wasn't sure which upset her most, but she always — and I mean always — thought Jerry Don Parker hung the moon, to use her words. I agreed with her on that, and maybe that had been part of the problem, not that I wanted to analyze decisions I'd made as a headstrong seventeen-year-old kid.

"Of course," Lucille said, "he'd have certainly turned out better if you had married him. Couldn't be much worse."

Shoving aside the big ball of regrets that seemed to knot up my stomach whenever I thought about my choices concerning Jerry Don Parker, I tried to focus on the grown-up Jerry of today. Regardless of my mother's melodrama, she knew very well that Jerry hadn't exactly turned out too bad, to seriously understate the facts.

He'd been the best looking guy in high school and he looked even better now. Not a dead ringer for the new James Bond, but close enough to send your basic female heart to fluttering. Texas accent rather than British, of course.

Jerry had also earned a degree in criminal justice and worked in federal law enforcement for several years before returning to his hometown to raise his kids. I'd debate the merits of that last decision, but he hadn't asked my opinion in the matter. He'd had a perfect little blonde wife to handle that task. I felt my upper lip curl and I forced it down. I needed to save my childish behavior for my mother.

"You know, Mother, if Jerry and I hadn't stayed friends through the years, he might have booked you on a whole list of offenses instead of just putting you away where you couldn't get into any more trouble."

Lucille's chin lifted another notch. "I'm not in trouble, missy. I haven't done a thing wrong. And he had no business nosing into my personal life. That's private and confidential. I don't have to tell him one damn thing about what went on between me and BigJohn."

"I'm afraid you do, Mother. Somebody killed your boyfriend. On purpose. He was murdered. That's a real bad thing. Understand?"

"Don't get smart with me, young lady. I know what happened. I'm not senile."

No, she surely wasn't, but I was definitely exhibiting some of the tell-tale symptoms. The all-night drive had done a fine job of convincing me that I was about twice as old as my forty-three years, and trying to keep up with Lucille had sent the age meter into triple digits. And it certainly didn't help that the one who should be traumatized by the ordeal looked positively perky, if seriously cranky. I opted to diffuse both our moods with a foray back to the underlying cause of both our troubles. "So who do you think killed him?"

Lucille shrugged. "Probably that loony wife of his. She didn't want anything to do with him until he started going with me, and then here she comes a running back to town. She was just pea-green jealous of me, I tell you." She twisted a manicured acrylic nail into a curl of Frivolous Fawn. "I suppose anybody could understand why."

I suppose so.

Now, I had never seen BigJohn's wife, but there's no question that my mother is a very attractive woman. Kind of a cross between Rue McClanahan, Dolly Parton and Joan Collins. And she says exactly what's on her mind. "So you really think she'd be capable of such a thing?"

She shrugged again. "It wouldn't surprise me. She probably had as good a reason as any of them."

"Them?"

"Well, there were a whole bunch of people hot over BigJohn's recent doings."

I fluffed my shoulder-length hair off my neck to try to cool off, then tucked an auburn-tinted curl behind my ear. "Like who?"

Mother frowned. "Jolene, I do not know why you insist on poking your hair behind your ears. You've always been such a pretty girl, but you really should think about a little back-combing and some hair spray. Get some lift there on the top."

I gritted my teeth and did not say that the beehive went out several decades ago, and furthermore, I thought I looked pretty decent, thank you very much. I happen to have enough natural curl in my hair that, with the right cut, it kind of does its own thing and usually turns out okay. I do not, in any way, shape or form, need any more lift to my hair. In this climate, the humidity puffs it up and out in every direction.

"And I bought you that big old tray of cosmetics for Christmas, but you don't ever use them. Why, if you'd just wear a little lipstick...."

"I wear mascara," I said, realizing as I did that I'd let her drag me into a conversation I didn't want to have — ever. "Okay, Mother, you're right, I'd look much better if I permed and sprayed and painted, but I don't, so let's get back to the point. Who all was upset over the mayor's activities?"

Lucille huffed and patted her own hair, probably wondering how she could have produced such a daughter. After another glare in my direction, she said, "Just about everybody in town was mad at him. Every single member of the city council, the mayor pro tem and a goodly number of citizens who had their water shut off in some snafu down at city hall, not to mention the secretary who had to answer all those irate calls. I'll tell you, I was so mad I could've choked the life right out of him with my bare hands over that. I didn't have a drop of water in my house for two whole days!"

I started to mention — again — that she shouldn't be spouting off her murderous thoughts regarding the dead mayor, but she was already ticking off other suspects.

"And then there's that Dee-Wayne Schuman. Why, he stood right up at a city council meeting and called BigJohn a son of a bitch, which he is, because he stopped all the house building out north of town on account of permits or something. He'd also been trying to push the city limits out around some houses to boost the tax rolls. And I never said he was a good mayor."

"Sounds like he's alienated just about everybody."

"What goes around, comes around, I always say. BigJohn wasn't nearly as smart as he looked."

Now there was a scary thought. BigJohn Bennett had been a decent-looking man, in a Lyndon Johnson sort of way, but he in no way resembled a Mensa candidate. Still, he'd been the hot catch of the senior crowd, which was most likely the reason my mother had hooked up with him in the first place. Showing her pals that she still "has it" never strays far from her mind. I shudder to think what she might have done if he hadn't wanted her. Lucille does not take rejection gracefully, trust me.

The thought jabbed at me again. I couldn't make myself believe that my mother would shoot her boyfriend, no matter how mad she got, but I couldn't short-circuit the nagging "what if" that kept looping through my mind. The fact of the matter was that Lucille wasn't acting entirely like herself, and she for darn sure wasn't distressed about the murder of a man she'd practically been living with. Her words. She'd made a fairly nice fuss about the sheriff, the jail and the abuse she'd suffered, but it wasn't a classic Lucille performance. Furthermore, she hadn't said a single word in maybe three minutes. Really weird.

I glanced at her from the corner of my eye, trying to get a hint of what was going on with her. Tears along with the silence I would have understood. In the normal scheme of things, a woman who had suddenly and violently lost a friend — much less a boyfriend — would have been crying by now. But she wasn't. She was just staring out the window at nothing. Her eyes were squinted against either the Texas sun or the workings inside her head. Unfortunately, I feared the latter. Feared it with good reason. I knew this woman. And I knew this place.

In Kickapoo, Texas, things could always get worse. And would. I had, after all, just washed the car.

Chapter
Two

W hen Mother called about the shooting, I'd been grateful I wasn't tied to a real job. The Denver area newspapers and I have an understanding that I'll send them a feature story when it suits me and they'll send me a minuscule check on a similar schedule. I have a slightly better arrangement with a couple of magazines, but none of it requires that I call in sick or fill out a form for vacation time.

And the kids aren't a panic-inducing travel issue anymore either. Usually. Being reduced to nothing but a long distance ATM machine for the college-interred offspring does have its good points.

So, unfettered and feeling a surge of importance that someone really needed me, as opposed to say, my PIN number, I'd saddled up the white horse — or more accurately, the blue Tahoe — and came charging down from the Rockies to rescue my mother.

For the first few hours of the journey, I felt really noble, heroic even. Lady Knight Jo Jackson on her journey to aid the fair queen in her hour of need. It was a large leap, but it kept me driving.

My grandiose self-image began to wilt around one a.m. when I, the would-be knight in shining armor, had to stop for my fourth Big Gulp of Dr. Pepper and stoically threw it on my face instead of drinking it so I could stay awake.

About the time I hit Amarillo — and the serious heat — I was thoroughly disenchanted with the whole notion of charging anything except the cost of a room at the nearest Hilton.

Two hours later, when I checked my messages on the cell phone and learned of my mother's incarceration, I chucked the cavalier attitude completely and went into survival mode. Embracing my dark mood, I told my sensible self good-bye and moved fully into my Kickapoo mindset.

Being of sound and logical mind in Kickapoo, Texas, is neither understood nor appreciated. It is a scientific fact that if you stay too long, your brain begins to feel like it's being sucked right out of your head. I'd learned this the hard way after returning from an enlightening four years at the University of Texas at Austin.

All aglow with youthful idealism, the cold hard truth hit me right smack in the chest while I was dutifully applying for a job at my hometown newspaper. The editor never noticed the A's on my transcript, but he did notice my breasts and offered me the job on the spot. His enthusiasm lit up his face as brilliantly as a neon sign flashing "dirty old man." I ran far and fast, and I only come back to this part of the world when I have to. And this time, I definitely had to.

So, here I am, back in my old room, too tired to sleep and too wired to stop thinking about the past, the present and the screwball mingling of the two.

Somehow it always feels like I'm stepping back in time when I come here. Maybe it has something to do with walking into a 1920s farmhouse and being hit with 1970s décor that throws me off center. Or maybe it's the fact that the farmhouse sits not on a farm but on four city lots at the fringes of a town that isn't more than a blink in the road. Or it could be much simpler: Mother's house, Mother's rules.

I ran my hand over my old, scratchy blue velvet headboard, then stared at the spongy, glitter-flecked ceiling overhead, the kind that sends clumps of white stuff down when you touch it, the kind that a kid can imagine all sort of shapes or monsters in. My room. But not. A kid's room. The kid I had been — and still felt like whenever I was here. No matter how old I get, when I'm in this house, I will always be the child. And I don't care what anybody says, feeling like you're twelve again is not a dream come true. Then again, neither is having to be the adult and collect your mother from the county jail.

I stretched out on the bed and tried to think of something besides bad old memories or bad new memories in the making. The fact that Mother was out of jail and technically off the hook was fine as far as it went. Problem was, it didn't go very far. Even in my sleep-deprived state, I was very well aware that my mother knew something about last night's murder that I didn't. Call it intuition or call it history repeating itself, but I had a very firm hunch that my mother wasn't telling me everything there was to tell about the mayor and/or his murder. Lucille's "if you don't ask, I don't tell" policy had always been a sore spot with my father and me, primarily because it was only a one-way street. Lucille's. What she was hiding this time and how bad it might be were the logical extrapolations, but outlining the possibilities was beyond my abilities at the moment.

What I did know was that Mayor John "BigJohn" Bennett had been shot in the chest with a shotgun while sitting in his den, reclining in his easy chair, feet propped up, television tuned to the station with the preacher who never sleeps. The shot shattered a window and still hit its mark. Messy, but effective. I knew these interesting tidbits because, well, Jerry Don Parker really is a good friend.

Since we parted ways in high school about twenty-five years ago, Jerry's managed to forgive me for a lot of things, childish things, like throwing a bottle at him for leaning entirely too far into Rhonda Davenport's car, kissing half the football team to make him jealous and, most especially, for not marrying him. Actually, he never held any of it against me. Ever. He even came to my wedding — and smiled. It was more than I ever did for him, and I've always regretted it.

But now, things were different. For one, we were both divorced. Eight years for me, eight months for Jerry. That we both finally wound up single again at the same time did not go unnoticed by either of us. We didn't get too starry-eyed though, having to discuss murder, mayhem and my mother's release from captivity.

I rubbed my hands across my eyes and yawned, wondering for about the fifty-third time what Lucille was hiding from her only child. I couldn't put my finger on it, but something was wrong with the whole scenario — wrong beyond the fact that a man had been sent to the great beyond by a shotgun. This was Kickapoo, Texas, after all.

And then, that funny feeling that had been nagging at me since last night gelled into a hard, thick ball.

With more energy than I thought I possessed, I jumped up off the bed and ran to the back bedroom.

My adrenaline zinging, I swung open the closet door, shoved aside the off-season clothes and saw exactly what I'd feared: a crescent-shaped indention in the carpet where my dad's shotgun had always been.

"Mother!"

●　　◎　　◎

"Yes, Jolene, I suppose I could have mentioned it, but I didn't see the point in confusing things. The gun is around here somewhere. I probably just moved it and forgot where I put it."

"Don't even start singing that song," I said as sarcastically as I could manage, considering the incredulity muddling my brain. "Your memory is better than mine and we both know it. Where's the damn shotgun?"

Lucille straightened her shoulders. "Now, there's no call for such language. If I knew where the gun was, I'd tell you. You don't have to curse at me."

I rolled my eyes and paced again. My mother could say any four-letter word she pleased, but I couldn't. Just like old times. If I didn't have worse problems I'd have pointed it out to her. But I did have worse problems. "When did you notice the gun missing?"

She shifted in her chair. "I guess it was a couple of weeks ago. I didn't think much about it." She paused and glared at me. "I am getting older, Jolene, and it isn't impossible that I moved it and forgot about it."

She was right. I've done exactly what she described on more than one occasion, and I'm three decades shy of seventy-two. Still, I knew my mother. "You've already torn the house apart looking for it, haven't you?"

Lucille tightened her lips, which was as good as a booming "yes" in Lucillese. "The gun's not here," she said, rather tersely. "And I have no idea what happened to it. Nobody's been here except Merline, Agnes, and..."

"BigJohn?" I finished for her, lilting my voice upward as if I actually needed her to answer the question, which of course I did not.

"Well, he never went snooping in my closets. And I know he didn't take the gun. Why would he?"

Yeah, why? It made no sense that I could see either, but then that was just par for the course. "I have to call Jerry."

"Well, you don't have to," she said in a superior tone. "But you will. I suppose I should have told you." She shook her head and clicked her nails on the Formica butcher block dining table. "This is certainly going to cause a stir."

I started to make some smart-ass comment like "you think?" but instead grabbed the phone and wagged the receiver at her. "I ought to make you call him. He knew you weren't telling him everything, just like I did."

I punched my finger into the rotary dial hole over the number one and began the tedious process of contacting the Bowman County sheriff's department via long distance and pulse dialing.

When Jerry Don Parker's husky Texas drawl resonated over the phone lines, I completely forgot why I'd called. I was not proud of the fact that at forty-three-years-old, I could still be frozen to the spot with my tongue tied in a knot simply by the sound of his voice. I think I might have managed to mumble "It's Jo" or something equally clever, while I mentally slapped myself into acting semi-mature.

"Hey, Jo," he said, voice rumbling in ways it just ought not. "Where are we going for lunch or do I have to wait and find a fancy place for dinner?"

Food. Just the thing to clear the brain. Fancy dinner. He remembered.

In my younger days, I had a reputation for being a lot of things, none of them cheap. I did eventually rebel from the beauty queen mentality, but I never lost my love of nice things. Besides, I spent too many years at McDonald's when the kids were little, and this was steak country. Visions of a thick, juicy filet mignon danced in my head and my mouth watered in sympathy, but I pushed aside my fantasies as best I could and said, "I'm afraid we might have to postpone our personal business for a while."

"Aw, Jo, what has your mother done now?"

As I said, Jerry is quite astute. "She hasn't done anything specific, at least that I know of, but I do have a problem. After my dad died, Mother insisted I take all of Dad's guns home with me to Colorado. I took most of them, but not all. I left one."

He groaned again. "Tell me it wasn't a shotgun."

"JC Higgins 12 gauge."

"Damn."

"It gets better."

"I can't wait to hear how," he said, none too cheerily.

"It's missing."

He let out a very long and weary sigh. "I'll be right there."

◉　　◉　　◉

I had a good half-hour before Jerry could get from Bowman City to Kickapoo, so I hopped in the car and headed to the local gathering place and official information dissemination center, aka The Dairy Queen. If Lucille wasn't going to be forthcoming with her knowledge, perhaps some of the fine folks at the DQ would. What I wanted to find out, I wasn't exactly sure, but I did want to get a feel for mood in the community. If I happened to stumble on a few little juicy details regarding my mother or the mayor, well, so be it. I could feel the reporter in me clawing its way up, but I tried to ignore it. I wasn't going to get involved, really, I was just going to ask a few questions and see if I got the same story Lucille was telling.

The DQ is located at the opposite end of town from my mother's house, which means it took me almost three minutes to get there, the speed limit being only thirty.

The place was packed, oil field pickups and big sedans lining the parking lot like matchbox toys in an overstuffed case. I was a little taken aback by the crowd. Even though I hadn't lived here in twenty-five years, I figured a good seventy-eight percent of Kickapoo's residents would recognize me immediately since I really haven't changed that much since high school, if you don't count the attitude and the wrinkles.

I wasn't all that excited about being the outsider walking into the local scene, but I forced myself out of the Tahoe and up to the front of the restaurant.

With a bravado I really didn't feel, I swung open the door and marched inside like I owned the place. Standard Texan behavior, but I've been gone a long time and am sorely out of practice.

The DQ clientele might not have been impressed with my entrance, but my mere presence zipped their lips in a hurry and there was enough neck craning to keep the drop-by doctor busy for a month of Sundays, or Tuesdays as the case happened to be.

As I waved to the crowd, which had become as quiet as Mrs. Stegal's eighth grade English class where breathing was a felony offense, it occurred to me that these folks might think I didn't know about the scene that had transpired earlier in the day. Maybe they thought I'd come here looking for Lucille. I smiled just a little at the thought, and was sorely tempted to see which one of them would get elected to tell me the bad news. But I'm really not the sadistic bitch my ex-husband claims — at least I'm not that way all the time — so I decided to let them off easy.

"Mother's home now and doing fine," I said, smiling to the gawkers. "The sheriff only wanted her to answer a few questions. Everything's just fine."

Whispers, sighs and mumblings twittered through the group.

I turned to the young clerk behind the counter, who was looking exceptionally confused, being one of twenty-two percent who had no clue who I was and obviously didn't care. Getting right to the point, I said, "Two chicken baskets to go, both with iced tea."

As she jotted down the order, I figured I was obligated to make small talk. After all, if I wanted these people to talk to me, I needed to fit in. "You know," I said, very chummy-like, "where I live, you just can't depend on getting a decent glass of iced tea. Half the time it's been there for days or they make it in the same pot they make the coffee. Sure nice to get a fresh glass here."

Clerk Jimmie Sue (I read her name tag) was quickly thinking I had lost my mind. To confirm the fact, I stuck out my hand and invited her to shake. Women in Texas don't shake hands as a general rule, unless they're passing out Mary Kay cosmetic samples.

Jimmie Sue gamely put her pudgy fingers in mine and tried to smile even though her cheeks were redder than the basket of ripe beefsteak tomatoes sitting behind the counter.

"I'm Jo Jackson, Lucille's daughter," I said, which widened her dark eyes in shock.

Jimmie Sue's hand slipped away. "Oh, my, I'm so sorry. What happened, why, it was just awful," she said, hanging onto the last word for a good six seconds so it came out sounding something like aaawwwwffuuulll. "Mrs. Jackson was mighty upset, no question. She doing okay now?"

My mother, okay? This girl was obviously new in town. To my knowledge, Lucille Jackson hadn't admitted to being okay but three times in her entire life, and all of those were times she really wasn't. "She's doing fine," I said, a real honey-sweet tone to my voice. "The whole thing's been upsetting, of course, but she'll pull through."

"Well, that's good to hear," Jimmie Sue said, putting the lid on a big Styrofoam cup of fresh iced tea. "Corrine was just fixing to call down and check on her."

I didn't know who Corrine was, but I smiled anyway. And just for the record, "fixing to" is a completely proper phrase in Texas. Essential even, particularly when used to string out getting to the actual point of the matter. I nodded to Jimmie Sue. "Lucille's just fine, and I'm sure she'll be up to visiting tomorrow."

Before I had to make up an answer for why Lucille wasn't up to it today, I took my tea and strolled toward to the biggest table of men. I am somewhat of an incongruity around here, you see. I give the illusion of being a cute little sweet thing, just like womenfolk are meant to be, but that only goes so far. Then the mouth opens and confuses the image. It is not something I have completely outgrown.

You could almost hear the eyebrows popping upward as I stepped up behind one of the men sitting around the table and rested a hand on the back of his chair. You see, segregation of the sexes is alive and well at the Kickapoo DQ, and public co-mingling is generally frowned upon. With a quick glance around the table, I recognized a few of my Dad's old friends. This was probably as good a place as any to get the real scoop — if they'd talk to me, me being both an outsider and a female. This was, after all, blatant co-mingling. I am just a scandal waiting to happen.

"So, gentlemen," I said, purring with what I hoped was just the right mix of authority and female manipulation, "what on earth happened down here last night?"

"How's the weather up in Colorado?" said a man I vaguely recalled as working at the Gulf filling station back when there was one. "Heard it was awful hot up there in Denver, almost as hot as it has been around here."

Yeah, right, and that's snow out there sizzling on the asphalt. I kept my unseemly comments to myself and smiled beguilingly at them. Rather than point out that the man had blatantly ignored my question, I played weather girl. "I live up in the mountains so it's not too terribly hot. It was actually forty-eight degrees when I left my house last night." I paused for a moment to let them wonder whether I was lying about the temperature. I wasn't.

"When Mother called me about the shooting, I just threw some things in the car and headed down here as fast as I could. She sounded awfully upset. Then when the sheriff called me this morning on my cell phone, well, I guess y'all know all about that," I said sweetly. I was warmed up and talking Texan with the best of them now, although the mewing vixen thing was wearing a bit thin. "I just can't believe what happened," I said, all breathy and gooey. "I just can't imagine who'd want to kill dear Mr. Bennett, can you?"

Instantly, the men who'd been drawn in by my sultry voice and innocent eyes became immensely interested in their coffee cups. What had gone wrong? I'd had them going. I knew I had. My ego was just starting to turn black and blue from the figurative beating when I felt a not-so-symbolic whack on my shoulder.

I turned to see a little gray-haired woman with steely eyes and a black dress ready to whack me again with her hand. Yet another of the twenty-two percent, I presumed. I might have to revise my popularity figures.

"I know who you are, girlie," the old woman said, a shrill quiver in her voice. "You better be watching what trouble you're a stirring up in this town. We're a God-fearing bunch and it was the devil's own hand that pulled the trigger on that gun. It's hussies like you and that slut mother of yours that invites the devil in. Brother Bennett was an elder in the church and pillar of this community. His death will not go for naught."

The woman was shaking, and frankly, so was I. I've never been attacked by a wiry, granny-type with fireballs in her eyes. I glanced around the table and was not surprised to see everyone staring. No one has ever accused me of knowing the best thing to say or do at any given time, but most folks know I'll do something. Actually, they expect it. I did not want to disappoint my fans.

I turned fully toward her and looked her straight in the eye, which I could do because she was about my same height of 5'4". She looked about as friendly as a caged cougar, but then I'm no shrinking violet myself. "I'll have you know, Madam," I said in my no-nonsense voice, "it's hussies like us that give biddies like you something to gossip about."

The groaning at the table told me no one was impressed with my performance. Well, fine, I could do better. I scooted closer until my nose was almost touching hers. "Are you ill or something?"

She stepped back, confusion hopping around with the balls of fire shooting from her eyes. "I'm fine. You're the one who's sick. You and that tramp mother of yours."

Tramp, slut, hussies.... The words threw up big red flags. Could this be my mother's nemesis, the little church lady who wanted the mayor for herself, and harassed my mother like a jealous teenager? Surely there couldn't be two of these types running loose in this little place. "Oh, my," I said, drawling sweetly. "You must be Old Bony Butt."

Snickers and chuckles rippled through the DQ like a finely swirled Pecan Cluster Blizzard. Apparently my mother's pet name for the witch was common knowledge. I felt a little burst of pride at my mother's dealings with this lunatic, and I couldn't help but smile.

As Bony Butt sputtered in outrage, I put on a nice fake smile and once again reverted to my youthful training. "Perhaps we should step aside and speak in private, Miz Fossy, or do you prefer Ethel?" She scowled but backed away from the table and toward a relatively open corner of the room.

She started working her jaw like she was chewing up her words, ready to spew them forth. I beat her to the punch. "Look, lady," I said, glad to speak my own language again. "My mother has a record of every single hang-up call you've made to her house. There's this clever little box you hook up to the phone that shows the name and telephone number of the caller. Just flashes the information about the call right up on the little screen, then keeps a record of it as well. Absolutely amazing." I was lying through my teeth about this, considering my mother still has rotary dial telephones and will never ever have Caller ID, although she thinks it sounds kind of nice.

"Oh, and let's not forget about the pious hate mail you sent. Don't you watch TV, Ethel? Cut and paste newsprint letters would have been better than longhand. And let's talk about gloves, Ethel. Hides the fingerprints."

You could almost see her twisting up tighter and tighter, and I kept my eyes glued to her, waiting for her to snap. "You know, Ethel, if you're going to be any good at this harassment stuff, you need to take a class or something."

Bony Butt twitched this way and that, looking on the verge of bursting a blood vessel. "You don't scare me," she said, her eyes narrowing to vicious little slits. "I'm a God-fearing servant of the Lord and He will protect me from the likes of you and that lust-crazed mother of yours. Repent or feel the fires of Hell on your heathen flesh."

Wow, this lady would be a hoot to hang around with. I started to tell her I was quite proud to be a heathen if that was the exact opposite of what she was, but decided a pop quiz might be more fun. "So where were you when Mayor Bennett was killed?"

Her mouth dropped open for a second, then started working up and down like a dying fish. "That is none of your business, and what makes you think you can ask me anything?"

I shrugged. "I guess I just figured if you were willing to harass my mother for seeing Mister Bennett that you might be willing to go a little further to split them up." I surprised myself by sort of insinuating this woman might have killed the mayor, but with that card played, I couldn't quit. "Mother thought you wanted him for yourself."

She stood there for a second, just glaring at me, then seemed to drift a little. "I knew nothing good would come of it, him sniffing around her," she said, almost calmly. "I warned him time and again how he was making a mistake with that woman. I begged him to repent. We'd prayed about it, and with my help he found the strength to stop seeing her. He was a fine, fine man, but he was weak. So weak."

I waited a few beats to see if she had anything else to say, but the glazed look was fading quickly, and with it, my window of opportunity, if you could call it that. I debated asking her another question, but since one didn't present itself, I said, "Miz Fossy, I would really appreciate it if you left my mother alone. She's done nothing to harm you, and now with Mister Bennett gone, there's really nothing to be mad at her about. Judge not — "

"Don't you dare quote the Bible to me!"

Yes, that was definitely a bad decision on my part. Very bad. Try to speak a foreign language to fit in with the natives and that's what happens. "Listen, there's really no need for — "

"I know my Bible frontwards and backwards and I understand the teachings well. I do the Lord's work and I'll not be dragged down by heathens such as you. There's only two kinds of people in this world, those that walk with the Lord and those that walk with Satan." She glared at me, apparently waiting for either a Christian testimonial or an admission that I worshipped the devil. She was getting neither. Her view of the world was kind of interesting, though, all black and white, with no gray areas at all. Dealing in pre-determined absolutes certainly would cut down on the decision-making process. Good or bad, cut and dried. Which is why I wound up in the "bad" category, I supposed, guilt by association. I smiled at the thought. Oh, that evil mother of mine. Another warm fuzzy of pride puffed up my chest. I started to give her yet another explicit directive to stay away from my mother, but her face was red, her eyes bugged, her veins pulsing, and I was seriously worried about her having an honest to goodness stroke.

"Okay, Miz Fossy, just take a deep breath and try to calm down. No need in getting yourself so upset."

Her hands shook as she clasped them together and held them up before her. I greatly feared she was going to fall to her knees and start praying for my soul, so I made a show of digging in my jean pockets, fully knowing there was nothing there but a couple of bucks, car keys and lint. "I just know I've got some of those worts in here somewhere."

She paused out of curiosity, and I hoped that meant she was going to remain standing. "Now, I'm not trying to butt my nose in where it doesn't belong, Ethel, but you look pretty stressed out and there's some stuff that could help you a lot. Ever heard of St. John's wort?" I didn't wait for her to answer. "Absolutely amazing. Really helps take the edge off those emotional surges."

Ethel was still looking a little confused, so I added, "Comes in capsules. Regular doses could make you a whole new woman."

"Why, you...you...dope pusher!" she shrieked as she spun on her heel and scurried away.

As the door closed behind her, I turned toward the crowd, figuring I'd better explain that I wasn't trying to get Ethel Fossy hooked on drugs. "I only suggested she try some St. John's wort for her nervous condition."

I waited for a nod of recognition that even one person had a clue what I was talking about. It did not come. "St. John's wort. W-o-r-t, not wart. It's an herbal mood enhancer that's been popular in Europe for years. Just catching on over here." They all still looked bewildered. "You buy it at Wal-Mart. Like Prozac without a prescription. Works wonders."

As they stewed on my latest revelation, I grabbed my carefully packed chicken baskets and large iced teas. I made a beeline for the front door and hurried outside before anybody asked me if I had any of the wonder pills. I did. A big industrial-sized bottle. It was part of my Kickapoo emergency kit, but I wasn't sharing. I had my own nervous condition to worry about, and the churning in my stomach told me I was going to need every single capsule I could get my hands on.

I hurried to my car, wondering exactly what I had accomplished other than procuring a decent supper. I wanted to ask questions, but then again I didn't. At some point I either had to pony up and get busying finding out what was going on, or just leave the state. Oddly, leaving wasn't looking so appealing at the moment. Getting some answers was.

Chapter Three

It was right here," I said, holding back the clothes in the closet so Sheriff Jerry Don Parker could see the oblong indention in the carpet where the butt of the shotgun had been. "Now it's not."

Jerry bent his tall, lean frame over into the closet for a closer look, but didn't touch anything. He straightened and swept a lock of black hair off his forehead. "How often do you open this closet?"

"Not very, and I never touched that gun," Mother said, sitting on the edge of the bed with her legs crossed. One glitter-covered gold slipper swung back and forth like a sparkly metronome, and a frosted purple nail twirled her hair, giving the accurate impression that she had better things to do than sit in the bedroom and speculate about a silly old shotgun. "I have no idea how long it's been gone. At least two weeks though."

Jerry stepped back from the closet and muttered. "I'll get somebody over here to take prints and fibers in the closet, but it's a long shot. There's no telling when the gun was moved and the interior and exterior doors are used daily so there's little point checking those." He turned toward Lucille. "I need a list of everyone who has a key to your house or who has been here to visit in the last month."

Lucille uncrossed her legs and straightened her shoulders. "Except for Jolene, nobody but Agnes and Merline has a key to my house. I have a key to their houses as well in case of emergencies, or when one of us is gone. We widow women have to take care of one another, you know."

"BigJohn didn't have a key?" Jerry asked, cutting to the chase.

Lucille's perfectly painted lips sucked up an undignified gasp. "Why, the very nerve, asking me such a thing!" she said, hopping up and stomping from the room.

I turned to Jerry. "I'd take that as a yes."

Jerry nodded. "And what do you think the odds are that her key is still at his place?"

"I guess it depends on how smart our killer is. Duplicate keys are easily made."

"Have the locks changed on every door here. Today. And don't give one out to anybody, not even your mother's friends."

Merline and Agnes weren't the problem and we both knew it, but we couldn't ignore the fact that someone had sneaked in and stolen the shotgun. "You don't really think Mother's in any danger, do you?"

"From the killer or from herself?" Jerry said, not smiling even a little bit.

Jerry wasn't being sarcastic, just realistic. I knew he liked my mother, had always seemed to like my folks, stopping by now and then over the years just to say hi. He'd always seemed amused by my mother's eccentricities, telling me I was the one overreacting to Lucille's latest antics. I had a feeling he was rethinking his stance about now.

"Jerry, you don't really think Mother's got anything to do with BigJohn's murder, do you?"

"Do I think she pulled the trigger on the shotgun? Off the record, no. But I also don't think she's telling me the whole truth about where she was the night BigJohn was killed."

My mother, not telling the whole truth? Why, who would dare think such a thing of Lucille Jackson? "She said she was at home watching television, 'I Love Lucy' reruns. She even described the episode in detail."

He ran his fingers through his hair again, ruffling the thick coal-colored mass. "Either one of us could do that. One quick look in the *TV Guide* and recollections are easy."

I had a good idea where he was headed with this and it didn't amuse me in the least. "You think she was at his house when he was killed?"

"I think it's one possibility."

"I can't believe that. If she'd seen him murdered, or even the body, she'd have been a wreck, scared to death, traumatized even. And I surely don't think she would have left him like that and not called an ambulance. She might appear cool and uncaring, but she's not, really."

Jerry leaned against the doorframe and crossed his arms. "She doesn't seem very upset that he's dead."

No, she certainly did not. I stuck my hands in the pockets of my jean shorts and tried to think of a tactful reply. Failing that, I said, "Apparently the relationship had run its course. The ex-wife showing up in town didn't help matters either. And let's not forget the 'saving face' aspect of this. Why should she shed tears over somebody who didn't want her?"

He nodded as if he were thinking over what I said, but now his blue eyes were twinkling with something completely unrelated to work. He smiled that smile I remembered from high school, the one that had made more than one cheerleader's heart melt, including mine. After a moment, his grin widened, he uncrossed his arms and relaxed his stance. "The old steakhouse is still around out on the Seymour highway. Want to skip class and make a run to town?"

Town was Redwater Falls, population one hundred thousand, give or take a few, and was situated about fifteen minutes north of Kickapoo. Ten if you took the back roads, which we always had back in the old days, for a number of reasons. The thought of replaying an illicit meeting from our youth was entirely too appealing. Unfortunately, having made it to the "older and wiser" stage of life, one has generally acquired a nagging sense of responsibility that prevents one from acting like a complete fool. Generally speaking, that is. In my case, I had a duty to my mother. "I'd love to Jerry, really...."

"But?" His smile was still there, but it was definitely forced. Obviously he didn't want to be turned down any more than I wanted to turn him down.

"If you'll recall, a certain pushy sheriff gave me direct orders to call a locksmith immediately. I try to do what I'm told."

Relief washed across his face. "Oh, yeah, you really do need to do that." He paused for a moment and then looked at me with soft blue eyes that had turned kind of gray around the edges. "I'm really glad you're here, Jolene."

That soft Texas drawl and the deep timbre of his voice rippled through me. He was the only person in the whole entire world that could call me Jolene and make me like it. "I am too," I said, although I wasn't glad I was in Kickapoo, Texas. I was simply glad to be with Jerry Don Parker again.

Lucille marched into the bedroom, startling us both. "BigJohn didn't keep my key on his regular key ring. He kept it on the one I gave him, a gold fancy thing with a "B" on it. Hung on a nail at the end of his cupboard. He hadn't used it in a while, I'll tell you that for sure. He could have thrown it away for all I know or care. Intended to ask him for it back, but it would have meant I had to talk to the old goat, and I very well was not going to do that. Not with her in town."

Jerry nodded to Lucille. "I'll go take a look around the mayor's place again." Then he turned to me. "Give me a call when the locksmith leaves."

I didn't have his home phone number, and wasn't about to ask, even if my mother hadn't been peering down her nose at me. "I'll call you at the office tomorrow."

"For crying out loud, Jolene, the boy wants you to go out with him tonight," she said as she spun on her heel and whisked herself from the room.

Jerry pulled a card from his pocket and scrawled something on the back. "Here's my cell phone number. Give me a call. Tonight. There are a few places in Redwater that stay open past nine."

I took the card but said nothing as he left, not that I could have said anything if I'd tried to, my heart having lodged itself in my throat.

It is no great news flash that I've never gotten over Jerry Don Parker. My ex-husband became painfully aware of the "Jerry" realities after our first trip back to Kickapoo less than a year after we married. I was about six months pregnant at the time.

Being a native Coloradan, Danny was more than a little taken aback with Kickapoo and its residents. In ten years of annual visits, he never did figure out how to fit in to the family or the town. Mostly, he just nodded and smiled a lot. To his credit, he never once lost his temper in the face of never-ending "Jerry and Jolene" comments whispered around.

But of all our trips to Kickapoo, that first one was the worst. I was pregnant with Sarah at the time and wholly determined to prove to everyone everywhere that I'd made the right decisions in my life. I was doing a fine job of it, too, until we ran into Jerry at the DQ. Awkward and uncomfortable sorely understates the situation. Jerry was the ultimate gentleman and managed to introduce himself and leave before Danny had time to say much more than "Nice to meet you." I don't think I said a single word. But seeing Jerry again just about tore my heart out, and it was all I could do not to sit down and sob.

I wouldn't have — couldn't have — admitted it at the time, but I think, at least subconsciously, that I knew my marriage to Danny was doomed, and had been from the very beginning. But being my mother's daughter, I stuck to my story and my choices, determined to prove myself right. It took about ten years to get over that, and another two to iron out the details of the divorce.

Now, it almost seemed like I was back at the very beginning, back at square one, or maybe it was square four, but back to having a chance with Jerry. The question was, did I want it? I was just about to settle in for some deep analysis of that question when I heard my mother rustling around in the kitchen.

"He's still got it bad for you," Lucille said from the kitchen doorway. "Never got over you marrying Danny. You know he didn't marry until about ten or twelve years ago, and that didn't last, as you can well see. She was a pretty girl, too. Sweet little thing."

Of course she was. Jerry had superb taste in women if I did say so myself, not that "sweet" ever cropped up when people were describing me. "You know Jerry and I have kept in touch over the years. I know when he got married. I sent a gift."

"Well, I don't believe you knew until now that he was available," Lucille said, a sly little edge in her voice. "I could have told you, but you didn't listen to me the first time around so I didn't figure you'd listen now either. If you'd have stayed here and gone to school, why, you'd have been a famous TV reporter or something by now."

I groaned inwardly. Oh, how I did not want to have this conversation. Mother had long ago made it abundantly clear that I had ruined my life by running off to Colorado and squandering my journalism degree when fame and fortune was only a stone's throw away in Redwater Falls. "I did what I thought best at the time, Mother. That's really all any of us can do."

"Well, yes, of course, but you know I never did approve of you running off to Colorado and marrying Danny. Everybody knew it was a mistake."

I took a deep breath. "Maybe I thought your monkey business with Mister Mayor was a mistake."

She straightened her shoulders and tilted her chin up another notch. "Well, I do believe that is my affair."

"Yes, it is. And my affairs are mine."

"Touché." Lucille patted her finely teased hair. "I suppose you're familiar with the safe-sex practices required these days, you being out carousing in a big city for eight years and all."

If you think I was shocked at this turn in the conversation, I was, but only mildly. In the last few months, my mother had made a great many comments that alluded to her being the new self-proclaimed authority on dating protocol for the geriatric set, which is pretty interesting since all I'd ever seen her do with my dad was a quick hug and peck routine. As for sex, I'm absolutely certain that my parents didn't do such things — ever. Lucille being intrigued by these activities now only confirmed the fact.

And regardless of experience, perceived or otherwise, I didn't need her telling me how to behave with Jerry Don Parker. In the eight years since my divorce, I'd had exactly two lovers, which makes a total of four in forty-three years. A loose woman I am not. Besides, I managed to do okay as a seventeen-year-old — Jerry had been plenty happy — so I was pretty sure I could probably muddle through on my own this time around as well, if there actually happened to be a "this time."

Sex was pretty close to the bottom of the list of things I wanted to discuss with my mother, so I changed the subject, quickly. "Were you over at BigJohn's the night he was killed?"

Lucille's eyes flickered a little at the abrupt change in topics, and her acrylic nails clattered against one another almost as if she were nervous about something. "What difference does it make where I was? I didn't kill him."

Nice clear answer. Actually, the only thing clear was that she'd been lying all along. "You told me, and the sheriff, I might add, that you hadn't seen the mayor privately for a couple of weeks. That was your official statement to the authorities. You hadn't seen BigJohn in a couple of weeks."

"I hadn't."

"Until that night." When she clamped her lips together and tilted her chin up, I added, "How did you know his wife wouldn't be there?"

She looked me square in the eye. "I knew she would."

◉   ◉   ◉

I parked my mother in the kitchen in a straight-backed chair by the bay window. I did not do this so Mother had a nice view of the azaleas and canna lilies, rather so I could keep an eye on her while I found a locksmith willing to drive out from the big city at four o'clock on a

Friday afternoon. Yes, there would be an extra charge, several of them, in fact.

With Earl's Locks and Safes headed our way, I replaced the phone and grabbed a Dr Pepper from the fridge. My mother really does love me or she wouldn't make a special effort to always have a six-pack of liquid tar, as she calls my favorite soda, on hand for whenever I might show up. I popped the top and took a long swig, then sat down. Facing her was a bit of a problem since she'd become terribly engrossed in the flowers and bushes in the garden.

"I'm going to have to call that Terrell boy," she said, clucking her tongue and tsk-tsking. "He didn't get all the weeds pulled from around the roses, and the zinnias are going to be choked out. I already paid him, too. He was supposed to have trimmed around the pecan trees. Did you notice if he did that or not? I'll just bet he didn't. I sure get tired of paying for jobs that don't get done. Just can't get good help anymore."

"Yes, good help is hard to find. And some people will lie to their only child when it suits them. Tragic situations, both."

Lucille sighed dramatically and turned around to face me. "Might I have a diet soda before the interrogation begins, warden?"

I grabbed a Diet Pepsi from the fridge and filled a glass with ice. Lucille Jackson does not drink from a can. When we were both settled again and our thirsts, if not our blood pressures, under control, I said, "You may as well start telling the truth right now, Mother. The whole truth. Jerry knows you were at BigJohn's near the time he was killed. For all I know, the whole neighborhood saw your car there as well."

"No, ma'am, they did not. I did not park anywhere near his place. I had gone for a walk over at the school track as I do three times a week, unless of course my knee is acting up, then I only go once or twice. But I try to not ever miss a week, you know. And I always keep a record of my mileage around the football field. Merline and I have a contest going. The one with the most miles in by Friday gets treated to a big old sundae with nuts."

I skipped the easy comeback on the nuts, rubbed my temples and tried to get back to the point. "So, you were walking around the track and just happened to stray across the back lot, past the tennis courts and down about ten blocks to the mayor's residence. Is that about it?"

"I was home by nine," she said, as displeased with my attitude as I was with hers. "And I did watch 'Lucy.'"

Okay, if she'd been out walking it had to still be fairly light out. That meant she hadn't been at the house when BigJohn had been shot because that happened around ten thirty p.m. or so. But she had been there at some point. And so had the mayor's wife.

The questions were piling up like June bugs on a porch light, but I opted for the simplest first. "Why did you go to BigJohn's?"

Lucille sipped her diet soda and clicked her nails on the butcher block Formica. "I'd just had enough of his shenanigans. I will not be made the laughingstock of this town for anybody. He was going around pretending he didn't even know me just because she showed up back in town. I went over there to keep him honest. Or at least make him spin some new lies right in front of her. She's not stupid. She knows what he's been doing."

"And just exactly what has he been doing?"

Lucille's mouth tightened into a purple pucker. "Not a damn thing, if you must know."

I wasn't exactly sure what she was referring to, but I had a hunch things weren't quite as peachy with the mayor as she'd made them out to be. Perhaps BigJohn wasn't quite the hot catch everyone had thought. "Exactly what are you saying, Mother?"

"I'm saying he couldn't get it up if he propped a two-by-four under it."

My eyes very nearly popped out of my head and my mouth hung open. Wide. I couldn't help it. This was my mother. I rubbed my hands over my face to try to erase my shock, but there were no words working their way up my frozen throat.

"Oh, don't be such a prude, Jolene. We're all big girls now. I just say it like it is. And frankly, it wasn't ever that great. Oh, for a while it was nice having everybody wishing they'd been the ones to snag him, and it was kind of fun to watch their faces as their dirty little minds thought about us in all sorts of ways. But that's about all there was to it, the thinking about it. I want more than that and it was darned clear I wouldn't be getting it from him. I'll tell you one thing, though. I will have sex again before I die."

I just kept my hands over my face and shook my head. What else could I do? This was nothing I ever needed or wanted to know about. My own mother out cruising for sex. I suppressed a shudder, and reached for my drink, finishing it in one swig. I'd seen a bottle of red wine in her fridge and I was sorely tempted to upend it as well. And I don't even like red wine.

"Okay, I think I get the general idea. You went over to his house to tell his wife there had been no hanky-panky."

"No, ma'am, I did not. I went over there to tell her she was welcome to the lying, self-righteous bastard. I just wanted her to know what all he'd been up to since she'd been gone. I figured it was only fair."

"Maybe she didn't care."

"She didn't. I think all she cared about was keeping her name the same as his so she could get his retirement and all the joint property, which I guess she's got now, not that I care. I've got my own house and it's a darn sight better than that tin can trailer house he lived in."

Ignoring the comparative housing issue, I said, "I thought you saw papers from an attorney."

"He was probably just lying to me. Lying like he did about everything, including the fact that he was still virile."

Oh, no, I'd heard way more than I ever wanted to know about my mother's sex life — or lack thereof. All I wanted to know was what had happened just before the mayor had been murdered. Simple really — unless you had to extract the details from Lucille Jackson. "The wife, what's her name?"

"Velma."

"So how did she take your appearance at her husband's door?"

Lucille inspected her acrylic nails. "She was really quite polite about it, considering the awkward situation. I don't have anything against her. Felt sorry for her really. And as I suspected, she already knew all about me and BigJohn, not that there was anything to know. Everybody in town knew about us going out, yet once Velma showed up back in town, they all pretended ignorance of the whole thing. I guess that's what set me off the most, everybody going along with his games."

"So you didn't get in a fight with these two or anything?"

"A lady does not fight, Jolene," she said, looking at me as if I were a complete idiot. "I just told them they deserved one another and I hoped they had a happy, boring life together. Velma just smiled and BigJohn stood behind her bobbing his head like the big old oaf he is, or was."

"You really don't care that he's dead, do you?"

Lucille patted her hair, then twirled a dangly rhinestone earring. "No, honey, I really don't. He wasn't a nice man. He put on a good front, but underneath the good looks and brown-nosing, he was about as crooked as a dog's hind leg. Folks were just starting to figure that out, but I was way ahead of them."

"I have to call Jerry and tell him about your little visit."

"I know. I'd have told him myself if his goons hadn't been so belligerent in front of my friends at the Dairy Queen."

I didn't argue with her or ask her what her excuse was for not coming clean about an hour ago. I figured I wouldn't like it anyway. "You need to know the approximate times you parked at the school, arrived at the mayor's house, came back to the school and then arrived home. Also, if anyone happened to see you during these times."

Lucille nodded and sipped her soda, running her nails along the sides of the glass to wipe off the beads of condensation. "I'll tell him everything this time, where I parked, where I walked, when I left, even the ugly shade of lipstick that woman was wearing. Everything."

I gave her a look that said "you better," and made the call to Jerry.

Jerry wasn't smiling even a little when he arrived back at the house, and I didn't attempt to explain or excuse anything. We both knew where the source of the trouble was.

While he grilled Mother — yet again — I supervised Earl, King of Locksmiths, who was quite friendly and chatted nonstop as he swapped out the locks and added new slide bolts on all the doors. He made a great pitch for a burglary alarm system that dialed right into a security company that would then dispatch the appropriate personnel or police and fire services to the scene. I tried to sound appropriately impressed, then terribly disappointed that I had to decline his fine offer. I didn't bother mentioning that by the time his big city security types arrived, the burglar could be in Oklahoma with the loot, never mind the fact that the local pulse dialing telephones would most likely send the high-tech burglary system into electronic spasms.

As Earl chatted away, I mumbled "Oh, really" and "wow" at various intervals but kept my ears tuned to the conversation in the kitchen. As best I could tell, Mother was finally telling Jerry the whole story, which I presumed was also the whole truth.

Earl finished the last lock with a big, hearty chuckle and grin. I figured out just why he was laughing when I looked at the bill. I wrote out a check and Earl scuttled off with enough money to make the payments on his bass boat for at least three months.

I checked my watch. Seven thirty p.m.. There was still time for a nice dinner with Jerry. I walked into the kitchen and leaned against the door frame. "How's it going?"

Jerry looked up, the strain of interviewing Lucille graphed across his face. "I think we're about finished."

He tactfully didn't mention that they would have been finished eons ago if my mother had told the truth the first time around, or even the second. Jerry really is a nice guy. And incredibly patient. A trait I sorely lack.

I was sincerely hoping that my mother's statement hadn't triggered some official business for Jerry because I had really been looking forward to going out to dinner with him. Okay, I'd been looking forward to going anywhere with him, but dinner sounded good, too. Before I could say a word, however, Lucille stood and walked to the refrigerator.

"Jolene," she said, pulling a pitcher of tea from the fridge. "Why don't you run on and take a shower. I know you've been driving all night, but a nice cool shower will perk you right up. I'll keep Jerry Don company until you get dressed, then you two can go out for that nice quiet dinner you talked about. Do you both good. I'll just have a sandwich here. Would you like a glass of iced tea while you wait, Sheriff?"

Jerry nodded to Lucille. "Yes, ma'am, I believe I would."

For some reason I felt like I'd been set up, even though we'd already planned to go to dinner. I glanced at my mother and then at Jerry, feeling like I should give him a chance to get off my mother's hook. "Listen, Jerry, if you need to work or you're tired, we can have dinner another time."

"Hurry up, Jolene," he said, that soft Texas drawl rolling across the kitchen like an electric-charged thunderstorm. "I can't even remember the last time I had a bite to eat."

Chapter Four

We laughed and talked all through dinner, chatted about old times, old spouses, kids, football games and steamy rides home after the games. We didn't talk about the specific details of those nights, but it was pretty clear we were both thinking about them.

The food was fabulous, the filet mignon so tender I'd cut it with a butter knife. And I'd had a beer, which is one beer too many for me. One little bottle of Coors Light and I was having way too good of a time. It was all the beer's fault, too. It had nothing at all to do with Jerry. Nothing at all to do with the fact that I thought Jerry Don Parker looked better than any man I'd ever seen, including Mel Gibson, Tom Cruise and any male on the cover of a romance novel. "The first time wasn't so great, you know."

He chuckled then took a sip of his beer. "I think I got the hang of it pretty quickly."

I laughed. "Yes, you certainly did."

Silence reigned for too long and I let my tongue start wagging before my brain started paying attention. "I guess you were a pro by the time Rhonda came around." Well, now, I hadn't really meant for that to slip out. Admitting that your bitter little twenty-five-year-old grudges were alive and well wasn't real great dinner conversation. I was trying to think of a tactful way to unsay what I'd just said, but it wasn't coming.

Jerry cocked his head a little, curved one corner of his lip up in a sad grin and shook his head. "I never slept with Rhonda, Jolene. I told you that about a hundred times. You just didn't want to believe it."

Even through the haze of Coors, I couldn't deny that. He'd told me nothing had happened between them, but I hadn't believed him. All I could hear was Rhonda's blow-by-blow of their so-called date, running over and over in my head. I'd thrown up. Literally. And then I'd done

the worst possible thing I could have: I pushed Jerry away and accepted a journalism scholarship to UT to get away from it all, none of which
I really wanted to do.

Within a day, for reasons that mental health professionals would no
doubt tie somehow to my mother, I'd completely changed the course of
my life. And I'd never allowed myself to talk about it ever again. Until
now. And oddly, I probably knew that it hadn't really been about
Rhonda even back then, not that it still didn't infuriate me. "She lied to
me, didn't she? God, why didn't I realize what a lying little — "

"We were all seventeen, Jo. We all made mistakes."

Some of us made a few more mistakes than others of us. "I came
out to find you, and that little twit she ran around with told me you and
Rhonda had gone to get a Coke and were then going parking. I should
have just smacked her."

He shook his head. "Rhonda needed a ride home after the game
and you were busy doing something, I don't even remember what, but
I figured I had time to run her to her house and get back to the school
before you were ready to leave. But you were gone when I came back.
I didn't see you for two days, and well...."

"By that time, I had ruined both our lives," I said, rather morosely.
This was not exactly how I'd envisioned our romp down memory lane.

"Look, Jo, I don't blame you for any of that. We were kids. And
frankly, what was between us was so intense that it scared me.
Sometimes it seemed so overwhelming I didn't know if I could handle
it. Maybe that was why I didn't really argue all that much about you
going to Austin. I think I wanted some space to see what it was
between us, if it was between every guy and girl, or just us."

"Just us," I said, but I didn't want to get all maudlin about it so went
back to safer ground: anger. "So Rhonda and her little friend set you
up?"

"I think Rhonda wanted to get back at you more than she wanted to
be with me, although she was perfectly willing to show me her charms.
I always felt sorry for her."

My hackles went up instantly. He felt sorry for her? If I saw the
woman right this minute, I knew I'd still feel like strangling her, but
only after I'd clawed her lying little tongue out of her lying fat mouth.

"She had a rough time," Jerry continued, thankfully unaware of the
evil ideas running through my head. "Family life wasn't so good for

her, you know, probably worse than any of us could have guessed. And besides all that, she was just trying to find her way, like we all were. She just went about it the real hard way."

That right there is exactly why I loved — and was often severely annoyed by — Jerry Don Parker. Even as a kid, he could always look beyond the incident to the person, the life shaped by other things, and, well, he just saw things differently. Me, I didn't give a shit about her family sob stories. I just wanted to beat the little twit to a bloody pulp for trying to steal my boyfriend. I probably would have too, if not for Jerry. Looking back, the whole thing was almost funny. Almost.

But he was right. We were just kids. I smiled, a lazy one-beer-induced grin. "I'm not sure, but I think I'm older and wiser now."

He smiled. "Does that mean you won't hang out the window on the way home and yell obscenities at any female I've ever spoken to?"

I laughed, but it was a little forced as visions of drooling little high school girls romped and squealed in my brain. "Find me one, and let's give it a try."

He chuckled. "Maybe next time, when I'm not in uniform, and you're not exhausted from driving all night plus dealing with your mother all day."

"Okay, fine, spoil all my fun." I reached for my wallet to pay the check, but Jerry stopped me, his big tanned hand resting on mine. "It's already taken care of, Jolene."

The touch of his skin against mine was about as sharp a sensation as I could experience at the moment. Words weren't forming quickly either. "Thank you, but next time it's my treat."

He just smiled and stood, then wrapped his arm around my shoulders and guided me to the car. He opened the car door for me and I had the good sense not to object.

Jerry has always been a gentleman. A tall, handsome, old-fashioned gentleman. Only he wasn't a relic of the past, more a blending of Old West marshall and New Age thinker, although I doubted he'd offer the same description of himself. Regular guy would be his words.

He started the car, then turned to me and grinned. "They've put up mercury vapor floodlights at all our old oil field parking spots."

"So where does the latest crop of lusty teenagers hang out?"

"There's a nice spot down by the creek. Willow bushes hide a car pretty good."

The image was instant and I couldn't help but remember my own times — with Jerry — in a car in the dark. "I hope you're not too hard on the kids."

He laughed. "I have to admit I've had a little fun scaring them every now and then. Making the rounds on the backroads always reminds me of you."

"Yeah, like you never went parking with anyone else."

"Never." He grinned. "At least never where I went with you."

Thinking about Jerry Don Parker doing anything with any female other than me only served to turn me into a sniping jealous beast, and I'd done enough of that for one night. I glanced at the dash just as the red LED lights flashed to one minute after eleven p.m., my old curfew. "Oops, guess I'm late again."

"Then I suppose we should make the most of it." He touched his fingers to my chin and leaned forward, brushing his lips against mine. "It's been too long, Jolene."

Oh, yes, God, hadn't it. My little heart was thumping like a fifteen-year-old's on a first date. He had no idea how much I enjoyed being with him, had always. And I felt like such a fool for walking away from him before. I wasn't likely to be feeling any better this time around either, considering the circumstances. As much — and it was very much — as I wanted to fling myself at Jerry and have my way with him, I didn't much like the possible repercussions. The headline "Sheriff Arrests Lover's Mother," or something to that effect, was not something I wanted to ever see. I reached up and ran my palm along his cheek, letting the stubble scratch against my fingers. "I'd like nothing better than to find a nice little room somewhere and pick up where we left off...."

"But?"

"But you have a job to do, and it may very well entail arresting my mother for one thing or another. She's trying awfully hard."

He sighed and leaned back. "Lucille is a character, but she's harmless. Still, you're right. Until this case is tied up, the most we'd better share is dinner."

Jumped on that one like a drowning rat, hadn't he? Not even a little argument for the possibilities. He was fresh from a divorce and I hadn't been in a steady relationship in years, which translates to no sex for us both. And in my beer-stained mind, it seemed perfectly logical that we should just take care of both our problems and be done with it.

But it wasn't really what I wanted. Sex had a nasty way of literally screwing things up at times. And I was pretty sure that I'd rather have Jerry Don Parker as a lifetime friend than a onetime lover. Not certain, mind you, just pretty sure.

"Well, my friend," I said, emphasizing my resolve to myself and trying not to be bitter, spiteful or just plain sick over the whole deal, "I guess we'd better head home then."

"After this is over, Jolene, you owe me a real date."

"Then do us both a favor and get it over with quickly."

"I'll do what I can," he said, none too optimistically. "But we don't have the staff to handle something like this. We're getting some help from Redwater on the forensics but it looks like it's going to be a slow one."

Okay, fine, I was up for a change in topics. "You didn't find Mother's key, did you?"

"No."

"From what I've gathered, there weren't many people in the county who had a fondness for Mayor Bennett."

"Which is why I'll be spending the day in Kickapoo again tomorrow interviewing."

"Interviewing, you say." I grinned. "I could help you out. I didn't get that journalism degree for nothing." Actually, it had been for nothing, but hopefully Jerry didn't know that. Rather than get a job as a reporter or glamorous TV anchor like my mother wanted, I'd started a little card company with a friend and had lots of fun. Sales were only fair, but somehow or other one of the major companies found out about us and we wound up selling out for big bucks, relatively speaking.

Danny, my ex, was kind enough — or guilt-ridden enough — to leave me my own money in the divorce. And likewise, I was kind enough to leave him breathing so he could continue acting like a fool with his twenty-something-year-old. But that's another story.

"The media here isn't known for being overly zealous," Jerry said, turning into the drive. "But we don't get many murders, and certainly not ones that involve public officials and scandals."

I knew that one of those scandals was my mother, but I didn't take offense. Lucille Jackson was actually proud of her quasi-flagrant reputation. She'd succeeded in stirring up a sleepy little town with nothing more to gossip about than who dozed through Sunday services. "I take it that means I need to keep my nose out of things."

"Your mother's in the middle of this. I'm not sure you could be objective."

He was right, I probably couldn't, but that didn't mean I wasn't getting a really big desire to help. "Mother said something about a problem with the water being cut off in a lot of homes. Did you know about that?"

He turned off the car and nodded. "Yes, but it doesn't seem quite enough to kill somebody over."

"I don't suppose that homebuilder whose project was shut down would be mad enough to kill either, but the new city permit thing sounded strange."

He shifted in the seat and turned toward me. "I hadn't heard about that one."

"Well, maybe you better quiz my mother again. She's got plenty to say about BigJohn's dealings. I think she said the guy's name was Dee-Wayne something or other. I assume that would be spelled kind of like Duh-wayne with an 'e,' but I can't be sure. He's some homebuilder who moved here from I-way Park, which I also assume is Iowa Park, but I can't be sure of that either."

"You ought not make fun of your mother, Jolene. She means well." He paused for a second then added, "Most of the time."

I didn't bother reminding him how well-meaning my mother could be. He'd already been up close and personal with Mother's purse, not to mention having to question her three times to extract some sliver of the truth. I spared him an accounting of Mother's crimes and said, "Stop by in the morning for coffee. I'm sure Lucille will cheerfully give you a whole list of people who might have been happy to see BigJohn dead."

"Including your mother. I can't ignore her, Jolene, no matter what you and I think."

No, he couldn't, particularly with Lucille blabbing to anybody who'd listen that she was glad BigJohn was gone for good. "As I said before, I haven't seen any tears, but it might be that she's just putting on a front, not wanting anybody to think she cared about him at all. It does make sense. She'd look pretty silly crying over a man who left her to go back to his 'dumb plain vanilla wife', to quote my mother. And as you know, Lucille Jackson does not look silly for anyone."

He nodded. "But it would sure be easier on everyone concerned if she'd just be a straight shooter about the situation."

Yeah, wouldn't it. "You know how she is, Jerry. Nothing much has changed, other than to get worse. My dear grandmother once said that as we age, we become caricatures of ourselves. Things that were little personality quirks in your twenties and thirties become serious eccentricities later down the road. Scary thought, but I think she was right. I'll probably make my mother look like a sedate pussycat when I'm seventy."

"Hope I'm there to see it," he said softly.

He'd done it again. Whether it was his soft rumbling drawl or the unmistakable ring of sincerity in his voice, I can't say, but something sent a warm sizzle zipping through me. It took a minute before I felt capable of speaking without my voice cracking. "Guess I'd better go in."

"I'll stop by around nine," he said, looking toward the door. "I don't figure you're any more inclined to early mornings now than you were way back when."

Less so, but I didn't say it. I'm generally quite chipper by ten o'clock, but nine is iffy. Nevertheless, I didn't want him to think I was a complete slug. "Sounds great. See you at nine."

He started to get out of the car, but I reached over and put my hand on his arm. "Please don't walk me to the door, Jerry."

"Afraid I'll kiss you again?"

I opened the door and scooted out. "Maybe I'm afraid you won't." I closed the door and hurried inside.

He waited until I turned out the porch light before he left. I watched the tail lights fade in the distance, wondering what to make of Jerry Don Parker. And what to make of myself. This was his world, not mine, and I still wouldn't stay in Kickapoo, Texas, for anything, not even him.

Closing the door quietly, I turned out the lamps Mother had left on for me and headed to my old bedroom. I flipped on the light and walked to the closet. After a little digging around, I pulled an old gray hat box from the top shelf. I hadn't opened it in years, but I knew what was in there as surely as I knew my own name. I sat down on the edge of the bed and removed the lid. Inside were the remains of a homecoming mum.

Ever so carefully, I lifted it out of the box. Miniature cowbells tinkled and clanged as I spread it out on the bed. The once-white petals were shriveled and brown, but there was still a faint musty "mum" smell about it. Loops of red and white ribbons encircled the flower and a dozen three-foot-long strands hung down like thin banners. Pieces of the gold glitter lettering had fallen away, but you could still read the words: Jerry and Jolene. Forever. 1975.

Chapter Five

"Jolene, honey, wake up."

I heard my mother's voice but I surely did not want to wake up. Not now, not this week, maybe never. "I'm awake," I grumbled.

"Jolene, you have to get up. I can't imagine why you slept in your clothes or why you didn't pull back the bedspread, but I suppose you were just so tired you didn't know what you were doing. Jerry Don's here to ask me some questions. I didn't know a thing about it, but I guess it's all right. Jolene, are you going to get up or not?"

One by one, Mother's words penetrated the fog in my brain, and when I finally realized the gist of her ramblings, I sat bolt upright in bed — or rather at the end of it. "Jerry's here? Shit. What time is it?" Then I remembered. Where was the mum? I looked down in the floor, but there was no gray hat box and no mum. There were, however, crumbled petals and sprinkles of gold glitter.

"I put it up," Lucille said evenly, no sarcasm, no nothing. "I'll go talk to the sheriff while you get ready. I'm sure he'll have me answering questions for a good hour." She smiled and left the room.

I slumped back on the bed. My mother was smiling, being nice even; Jerry was in the other room ready to quiz her on her boyfriend's murder; I felt like somebody had run over me with a Bush Hog; and there was this little twinge in my chest that I couldn't identify. Not a single thing was as it should be. "Welcome to Kickapoo, Texas," I muttered, dragging myself out of bed.

Somehow I managed to get showered and groomed in less than a half-hour. Yes, it really is an accomplishment. I couldn't do much for the bags under my eyes, but Visine did get the red out. Coffee isn't my poison of choice, but if I could suck down a couple of adequately-caffeinated Dr Peppers without anybody noticing, I might be able to speak in coherent sentences by the time I was required to do so.

I scrunched and fluffed my damp hair up off my shoulders a final time, brushed on a little mascara and tried to rub some color into my cheeks. Figuring that was about as good as it could get, I strolled into the kitchen and smiled at Jerry, who, unlike others of us, looked crisp and fresh in his uniform. As usual, Mother was, pardon the terminology, dressed to kill in a lovely azure pantsuit with matching bracelet and fingernails. Dangly silver earrings with little balls on the ends and matching necklace completed the look.

About the time my bare feet hit the cool linoleum, I fully realized I was most likely not the picture of either decorum or class in my sleeveless tee shirt, shorts and shoeless feet. It took me a full three seconds to decide I didn't give a hoot, and I proceeded to open the refrigerator door, grab a soda and pop the top. I rummaged around in the cabinets as if I knew what I was doing, all the while sipping on the liquid tar as fast as I could. By the time I slid into a chair at the table, I was feeling almost human. The key word was almost, so I just sat back and listened to the question-and-answer session. And tried not to stare at Jerry, who had fared considerably better overnight than I had. In fact, he looked pretty darn near perfect.

Jerry and I exchanged a quick glance and smile, but he went back to his note-taking as Mother continued her story.

"Dee-Wayne Schuman as much as threatened to kill him in front of the whole city council. Dee-Wayne's been in the pen before, you know, assault or something. He doesn't seem like the shotgun type, though, more of a fistfighter. Dee-Wayne looks like a big old hairy gorilla, and he knew BigJohn was afraid of him. Could have broken BigJohn in half with those big old hairy hands. I think BigJohn was ready to back off his permit craze. Just a bunch of silliness anyway."

"Building codes are handled by Bowman County," Jerry said.

Lucille set her coffee cup down and tapped her nails on the table. "This was a new city inspection. BigJohn decided the builders ought to have to come down to City Hall and buy a special project permit to work in 'his city.' BigJohn's Kickapoo Kingdom is what folks were calling it, and they weren't being nice."

"So what exactly happened to cause the confrontation?" Jerry asked.

Mother fiddled with an earring. "He and Dee-Wayne got crossways when BigJohn told him he couldn't build until he had a city permit and he wasn't going to get a permit unless he did away with all the carports and made them garages, or something like that. It wasn't a bad idea, really, but it would have cost Dee-Wayne a lot of money since he'd already signed contracts to sell three of the houses with carports, and nobody was going to pay any more than what they signed for. I wouldn't. Would you?"

I always think I can't be surprised by anything that happens around here, and I'm always wrong. And it didn't make a great deal of sense, particularly since Mr. Mayor had an oil field pipe and sheet metal carport out in front of his mobile home. And his isn't the only one by a long shot. This is oil country, and in the boom years, oil field pipe pilfering was a cottage industry. Many a pipeline job was figured to include a respectable amount for resale purposes, the aforementioned carports, pole barns, pasture fencing, flatbed trailer frames or any other creative uses for welded pipe the contractor happened to come up with. Personally, I thought the chicken coop was a little over the top, but nobody asked me. And as a final aside, the word "oil," in these parts, does not rhyme with boil or coil, nor does it exactly sound like bull or full either, but some unique blending of the two. It takes practice.

Jerry turned to a fresh page and kept writing. "What about the annexing of land west of town?"

"Oh, that went through a few weeks back. Kind of happened before anybody could really do anything about it."

"None of this sounds terribly bad for the city," I said, mildly intrigued by the small town take on big city ideas. "Why was everybody so upset?"

Lucille clicked her nails on the table. "These things might have been okay for the city, and that's what everybody thought," she said, pausing for effect. "At first. Then, it started coming out that BigJohn had his own reasons for annexing everything in sight. As it turned out, BigJohn had bought a couple of lots near the water treatment plant. By annexing all the outlying areas around the city," she said, adding hand gestures to her soliloquy, "and forcing them onto city water, it would put the rest of us down to a trickle in our kitchen faucets. We don't have much of a water system anyway, but it works, or at least it does now. But with all the new houses hooked up to the system, well, it was just trouble a brewing. And then everybody started figuring out that our taxes were going up because of all this, too. Well, I can tell you I wasn't any too happy about that. I'm on a fixed income and I don't need my taxes going up. Besides, if BigJohn had left things alone, the new houses would have been on the Redwater system. Would have been better for them anyway. Half the time the water coming out of my tap is green and smelly. Nothing to brag about that's for sure."

Jerry looked up from his notepad. "So you're saying Mayor Bennett annexed land so the city would have to buy his property to build new water services facilities?"

Lucille clicked her nails together. "That's what I just said. And it wouldn't have come cheap, I'm here to tell you. BigJohn Bennett does not give away anything. If there's a dollar to be made, he'll make two."

I sipped on my second soda. "Mayor Bennett never struck me as sharp enough to figure something like this out. That's a semicomplicated scheme."

"He wasn't a complete idiot, Jolene," Lucille said, not exactly offended, just commanding. "But no, I never thought any of it was his idea in the first place."

"So whose was it?" I asked, the small-town intrigue digging a little deeper into my resolve not to be interested.

Lucille shook her head. "I have no idea. He didn't really have any friends. Acquaintances yes, but no real friends. Have you talked to the mayor pro tem?" she asked, nodding at Jerry. "BigJohn appointed him, but they never did get along. I think Giff wanted to be mayor himself." She paused. "I guess he is mayor now. Hmmm."

Jerry flipped through his notes. "That would be Gifford Geller. Yes, he would be acting as mayor now. I haven't spoken with him yet, but Deputy Harper did yesterday."

I marveled at Jerry's tact. He didn't even glance at Lucille when he spoke of the deputy, who we all knew was the first one who Lucille had accosted.

"Well, Miz Jackson," Jerry said. "You've been very helpful today."

Lucille had the good grace to blush, but not enough to apologize for her behavior yesterday — or explain her generous cooperation today. "I'm just glad to have been able to help. Now, if you've nothing further, I'd like to be excused so I can powder my nose." She pushed back from the table and stood.

Everything seemed to happen at once. The bay window behind Lucille exploded, spraying glass across the kitchen. She shrieked, grabbed her arm and fell forward against the table. I jumped up and jerked her down behind the kitchen cabinets. Hot air gushed in from the broken window.

I heard a thump and looked back to where Jerry had been sitting at the far end of the table. He wasn't there, and neither was the chair. Below the edge of the tablecloth, I could see the overturned chair and Jerry's legs. He wasn't moving. "Jerry?" I said, scrambling toward him. "Oh, God, no."

He was lying on his side on the floor. Dark stains spread across his chest and trickled down onto the linoleum in rhythmic bursts.

"Jerry? Are you okay? Jerry?"

Oh, God, was he still alive, he had to be, had to be okay. Panic clawed at my chest, but I refused to let it take over. I leaned toward Jerry and tried to focus on the basics of first aid. The first rule was to stay calm and I was trying, God was I trying. Okay, do the ABCs — airway, breathing, circulation.

I touched Jerry's chin, ready to check for airway obstructions and he moaned a little. "Jerry?"

His eyelids fluttered but didn't open. "Jo?" he said, his voice fading in a wheeze.

Okay, he could breath, but the airway didn't sound too good, and circulation was going downhill rapidly. The pulsing blood meant arterial damage. He needed help fast. "Jerry, listen to me. You're going to be all right. I'm here and I'm going to help you. Jerry, can you hear me?"

He didn't answer. A very bad sign.

"Stop the bleeding," I muttered. "Need something...."

Glass covered the floor so I stood into a crouch and hurried to the cabinets.

Lucille was sitting on the floor where I'd left her, still staring blankly. She was in shock, and her arm was covered in blood. I scrambled to the drawer that held the dish towels and grabbed them all. She had a gouge in her arm that looked to be about three or four inches long and deep enough to need stitches — a lot of them. I quickly wrapped a towel over the wound and tied it as best I could. "Mother, listen to me. We've got to help Jerry. Go call 911."

She didn't answer, and from the paleness of her face and the glaze in her eyes, I doubted she could stand much less anything else. "Okay, Mother, listen, we need to move over by Jerry," I said, shoving as much glass out of the way as I could with my hand.

She blinked a few times and took a few ragged breaths but said nothing. She did, however, let me scoot her toward the end of the table.

I brushed aside more glass and situated Lucille beside Jerry. I knew to elevate the injured area above the heart, but in this case the injured area was the heart. A cold shiver went through me but I refused to even think of how bad it could be. I pressed a stack of towels to his chest and placed Lucille's hand on it. "You've got to keep pressure here, Mother," I said, looking directly into her eyes. "Do you understand?"

She blinked and swallowed, then took a couple quick short breaths and nodded.

"Pressure, Mother. Push down hard on the towels. I'm going to call for an ambulance. I'll be right back."

I jumped up, ran across the room, grabbed the phone off the wall and punched in 9-1-1.

Even before the recorded voice came on, I remembered: 911 doesn't mean a damn thing in Kickapoo, Texas.

Chapter

Six

Deputy Leroy Harper finally caught up with me about six hours later outside the intensive care ward at the Redwater Falls General Hospital. He'd been picking at me like a determined magpie, and after a half-hour, his charm was wearing mighty thin. Thin enough that I had gone from really annoyed to seriously pissed.

"Dammit, Leroy, I've told you at least eight times what happened. Unless you were playing with yourself instead of writing down what I said, you can read your notes. Again and again if it turns you on. Now, go away."

He closed his little spiral notebook and stuffed it into the back pocket of his brown uniform pants. "You've sure gotten yourself a filthy mouth since you left here, Jolene."

"Maybe I've just been hanging out with the wrong crowd for about the last thirty minutes."

He snorted as if he recognized he was being insulted, but not confidently enough that he knew the specifics. "You always did think you were so uppity. You and that Kathleen Jessup did nothing but make fun of me all through school. But she ain't here to pal up with you against me. No, ma'am, you ain't so uppity now. You have to answer to me, Jolene Jackson. It's the law."

I hadn't thought about Kat in ages, although I knew she was one of the few others who had escaped Kickapoo. Last I'd heard she was an attorney in Dallas. A big move on all levels, and a connection I was going to need if I became compelled to shut Leroy Harper's mouth for him.

At about six-two and two-hundred-fifty pounds, Leroy had made a fine linebacker for the Kickapoo Coyotes, but somebody needed to tell him that the game ended twenty-five years ago and he could quit mauling everybody in his path. He hadn't exactly been ugly back then, but not cute either. A big old, pale blond-headed kid with way more brawn than brains would be a kind description. If you put it that way, he really hadn't changed much, except that now he was an adult redneck on a power trip. He also carried a gun. And even after all these years, he still had me lined up in his cross hairs.

"Don't you have something better to do than stand around here and annoy me?" I said for at least the fifteenth time.

Leroy crossed his big fat arms and stepped his ham hock thighs apart. "Funny, ain't it? You thought you were such hot shit back then and now you'll be jumping whenever I say so." He grinned, exposing an amazingly intact set of tobacco-stained teeth.

A year ahead of me in school, Leroy always thought rather highly of himself. I, however, thought he was an idiot, and would have rather dated the Pillsbury Dough Boy. My mistake was in telling him so. And Leroy had not forgotten. "Tell you what, Leroy," I'm going to try this one more time, so listen real careful-like, 'kay?" I ignored his glare. "Turn around, walk out the door, get on the elevator — "

"I'm acting sheriff, Jolene. I can stay here all day if I want, and I might just do that because I think you're holding out on me."

"What exactly could I be holding out, Leroy? That I saw a man in the bushes wearing a ski mask, but he took it off after he blew out the window and said, 'Pardon me, ma'am?'"

He thought about that for a minute then said, "You sure you didn't see anything at all, or maybe hear something out the window?"

"Leroy, if I had seen anything or heard anything, I'd tell you! Now why don't you go get busy finding out who tried to kill Jerry. You don't even seem to care about him. And what about some sort of real investigation? This is the second incident in two days. There's a killer out there, Leroy. Do something about it."

He looked away for a second and I had the feeling that I'd made a slight point with him, but only a slight one. If I had, he got over his really short guilt trip and looked back at me, shaking his head. "Jerry got nailed with a thirty-eight, Jolene," he said as if talking to a two-year-old. "The mayor was killed with a shotgun. The shootings aren't related."

"Silly me. I thought 'gunshot through a window' and 'gunshot through a window' sounded sort of alike. What was I thinking?"

Amazingly my sarcasm did not escape him and he frowned. "I don't have to put up with your smart ass remarks anymore. I ask you a question, you answer it right."

I started to mention that I had just been making a comment, not answering his question, but what was the point. I rubbed my hands across my face, pushed my hair back and sighed heavily. "All right Mister Almighty Powerful Deputy Person, just what is it that I need to say or do to get you to leave me alone?"

"I'm the acting sheriff, and there's nothing you can do about it. And if you know what's good for you, you'll be watching what you get yourself into. You don't live around here anymore so you don't know how things are now. I do. Don't go stirring up trouble. You've always been too nosy for your own good anyhow. You get in my way and you'll find yourself in a worse place than the superintendent's office."

Leroy Harper was cleverly referring to my dogged pursuit of a perverted high school principal, or more accurately the removal of said pervert. I took exception to being pounced and kissed in front of the entire student council by a forty-something-year-old fool and promptly told the school superintendent. Since it was the seventies, which in Kickapoo is more relative to the Pleistocene Age, I didn't get any support from the big man, who no doubt believed that I had been "asking for it." The end result was that I had to resign as president of the student council since the pervert was the sponsor. I didn't go quietly, and as I also happened to be the editor of the school newspaper, well, it got a little ugly.

Since evolution has yet to make any major inroads around here, I knew better than to wage war on the dinosaur standing in front of me. The fact that Leroy has a penis — or at least is suspected of it — pretty much guarantees him support over me.

"Yeah," he said, hitching up his pants as much as he could around his girth. "After the way you treated me back in school, I'd like nothing better than to throw your ass in jail."

It goes without saying that Leroy Harper had not been one of my supporters in the old days, not after I'd turned him down for a date about ninety times. Somehow, while I was saying "Get away from me, you gross pig," he was hearing "Come and get me, baby." Some things never changed. And some things did, like Jerry winding up in ICU with a bullet hole in his chest. I glanced toward the steel doors and shook off a shudder. "Leroy, I'm going to try yet again to phrase this where you can understand. If it were you in that hospital room, what do you think Jerry would be doing right now?"

Leroy looked down and shuffled his feet, apparently thrown off track by a pertinent issue. "I'm going back out to the crime scene now." He paused for a moment, puffed up his chest and tried again. "I'll do my job, don't you worry yourself. But for all I know, somebody was trying to kill you and got Jerry by mistake."

"Me?"

He propped his pudgy hands on his hips. "Well, hell, yes. You come strutting back into town every now and then, acting like you're some queen bee come back to flaunt it in everybody's face that you're rich."

Rich? Me? I was too tired — and too worried — to laugh or I would have. I have a reasonable income from the card company but it doesn't allow me to shop at Neiman's. Simple economics demand that I wear primarily jeans and simple knit shirts, although I do try to "Buy American." On the way down, I splurged and bought three pairs of shorts and coordinating tank tops at Wal-Mart, my new Kickapoo Collection. Still, Acting Sheriff Leroy Harper had a different take on my financial picture for some unknown reason. I couldn't see how that would work to my advantage, but I filed the information for future reference.

"Okay, Leroy, I've had enough. Let's call a truce and — "

A high-pitched tone echoed from behind the intensive care doors. Through the windows I could see a flurry of activity in the general direction of the first bed. Jerry's. I rushed inside, but the group was clustered around him so closely I couldn't see much of anything. "Is he okay?"

"Ma'am, you'll have to leave. Ma'am...."

I felt a tug on my arm and finally realized a nurse stood beside me. "Is he okay? What's happening?"

"Are you family?"

"Yes," I answered without hesitation.

"She is not," said Leroy's gravely voice. "She was his girlfriend back in high school, that's all. I'll get her out of here."

The nurse looked at me with varying degrees of pity and contempt then turned away and went back to work.

"Could you at least tell me if he's all right," I called, but she didn't turn around. Before I could say another word, Leroy jerked me by the arm and dragged me out of ICU back into the waiting room. I jerked back the entire time but he seemed not to notice. "Let go of me, Leroy, or I'll rip off every single one of your fingers and stuff them down your throat."

"Yeah, right, like you could." He let go, however, and just stood there, glaring at me. "You get on out of here, Jolene."

I was incredulous. "Don't you even care what's happening to Jerry?"

"He's got doctors and nurses all around him. Nothing I can do one way or another about medical stuff, so I figure the best help I can give him is to keep you out of everybody's way."

"Why you sorry son of — "

"Watch your mouth, Jolene. I could arrest you for that. You just stay out of my way and maybe I won't have to."

"Now, Leroy, how do you propose that I stay out of your way when you are, so you've told me repeatedly, the big man in charge and my mother's home is the latest crime scene? You do recall that she was shot, too? A few more inches and she'd be here instead of Jerry."

"Yeah, too bad how it worked out. Nobody around here'd miss that old biddy."

Pure raw anger grabbed me by the throat. It was one thing for me to criticize my mother. It was damned different to have somebody else do it. "Don't you ever...." I paused and took a breath. "Don't you ever talk about my mother like that."

It did not escape my notice that my thoughts regarding my mother had been less than kind, but she was my mother, and mothers and daughters weren't necessarily meant to see things eye to eye all the time. We never had when I was growing up so there was no reason to think we'd start now. Still, to have this sorry excuse for a human call her an old biddy that was better off dead, well, it hurt. And it infuriated me.

My fists clenched and I trembled with fury, but I refused to raise my voice. "You know, Leroy," I said so calmly that it shocked us both. "I've always thought of you as a pig, but now I see that I was wrong. Pigs are exceptionally smart creatures and would be deeply offended by the comparison. Maybe your garden variety slug that leaves a trail of slime wherever it goes would be a closer fit."

Leroy stood there for a moment, then his face turned an ugly shade of purplish red and his eyes seemed to bulge out from their fatty sockets. "Should've put you in your place years ago," he said, turning away.

"When I do, you're gonna be wishing you'd been nice to me. I've had twenty-five years to think of what I'm gonna do to you." He stomped away, apparently forgetting that I was the one who was supposed to leave.

Leroy didn't scare me, although I know he should have. I hadn't done anything seriously embarrassing or emasculating to him back in high school — at least that I could recall. Nevertheless, he was carrying a grudge about something. If I cared, I might have tried to think back at the possibilities. At the moment, all I cared about was what was going on behind the swinging steel doors. A quick look through the window showed Jerry sleeping and only one nurse standing beside his bed.

I slipped back inside, apologized to the nurse at his bed for coming in during nonvisiting times and explained my relationship to Jerry, stretching things only in the "we'd just gotten back together after all these years" story line. She seemed appeased and gave me a quick update on his condition, then I returned myself to the waiting room.

As it turned out, the high-pitched tone that sent the staff scrambling was only a glitch in a monitor, some wire had come loose that shouldn't have. Jerry was still the same, still sleeping from the trauma and the high octane drugs, but holding his own. The bullet had done some serious damage near his heart and he'd lost a great deal of blood as I well knew. He'd been in surgery for almost three hours repairing the mess. Before it was over, he'd had every single pint of blood in his body replaced. He'd be a long while recovering, but he was alive. That was all that mattered to me. And it mattered a lot.

"Jolene?"

I turned automatically toward the voice and saw a tall, willowy blonde in a Laura Ashley dress standing behind me. Beside her were two kids. It didn't take a great leap to figure out that these were Jerry's kids, which made the woman his ex-wife, Amy.

I'd never met her, had never wanted to. And from the very strange emotions churning my stomach at the moment, I was certain I didn't want to now. Unfortunately, it appeared I didn't have a choice in the matter. I tried to smile a little while I gathered some idea what I might say to the woman.

Amy Parker was prettier than the wedding picture Mother had clipped from the paper and sent me years ago. Her long, straight blonde hair undulated as she moved her head, and the soft pastel paisley dress draped across her slender frame in true supermodel fashion, making her look wholesome, seductive and chic all at the same time.

Yes, I was just a little intimidated. You go face the latest Vogue cover girl, look her right in the chin and tell her how fine you are with being 5'4" and highly unwaif-like in a society where there are only two categories of woman: those who are tall and thin, and those who are not. And besides that, the woman was a blonde. An absolute, 180-degree direct opposite from me all the way around. I certainly didn't need anyone to psychoanalyze why any of these things bothered me, so I went back to looking for a way to save some small shred of my ego.

Amy didn't have any visible warts, moles or hideous scars, nor did she have bad teeth, complexion problems or even split ends. Fault-finding is childish, immature and pointless, but with glowing perfection staring me in the face, I was grasping at anything. Without a single glaring fault to cling to, I was further reduced to criticizing Amy's tear-stained eyes.

Her gold-flecked blue-green orbs peered out from between puffy lids, and the whites of her eyes were spider-webbed with red. Unfortunately, on Amy, the sad tearful image made her look, well, cute, sort of like a little stray kitten or puppy that you just had to hug. And even though that sort of thing is completely out of character for me, I stepped toward her and wrapped an arm around her shoulders. It felt very weird and I made it quick. "I'm so sorry to have to meet you like this."

Amy tucked her wispy, wheat-colored hair behind an ear and sniffed daintily. "It's good to finally meet you, Jolene. I've heard so much about you."

I wasn't exactly sure what she meant by that, but I had a feeling it wasn't just your typical polite thing to say. I couldn't very well recip-rocate so I did the next best thing. "Your children are adorable," I said, watching for the older boy to wince. He did, but only a little. The lit-tle girl smiled sweetly. "How old are you two?"

Amy draped an arm around the boy, who looked alarmingly like Jerry with his dark, wavy hair and kind eyes. He wore a T-shirt, tucked in, and his jeans were regular cut, not some funky fad thing. "This is Benjamin," she said lovingly. "He'll be eleven next month."

"Nice to meet you, Benjamin." I extended my hand and he shook it, trying not to look bored with the whole scenario. As I turned toward the little girl to shake her hand, I couldn't help but wonder what their mother had told them about me. "Hi, I'm Jolene. Has anyone ever mentioned that you look just like your mother?"

The little girl rolled her eyes and sighed a little, but shook my hand anyway. "Only about a million times."

"Hey, now," I said, laughing just a little. "Your mother's very beautiful, and you remember that every single time somebody says how much you look like her. Okay?"

She tipped her head to the side and nodded indulgently. "Okay."

Amy patted the girl's shoulder and toyed with her light blonde hair. "Rachel just turned eight and we're still working on being more respectful to our elders."

"Mom," Rachel groused, lilting the word into two syllables.

I wanted to chime right in with her as I was not real keen on being called an elder of any kind. Instead, I said, "Well, I'm very pleased to meet you, Rachel."

With the introductions completed I couldn't help but reflect on what I saw before me. Beautiful woman, beautiful and well-behaved children, the makings of a very perfect family. What had happened? Wise enough not to ask, I said, "Jerry's doing fine. There was a problem with one of the monitors a little while ago. Nothing serious, but it was a pretty good scare."

"But he's okay?"

I nodded, and she continued. "We were in Dallas at my mother's when they finally tracked us down. We got here as soon as we could. I still can't believe it. Are you sure he's going to be okay?"

"They say he'll be fine. He won't be chasing any bad guys for a while, but he should be good as new in a few months."

I relayed what I knew of Jerry's medical condition and a still-terrifying summary of what had happened in my mother's kitchen. Rather than relieve her anxieties, it seemed to add to them. Putting people at ease and providing comfort in unpleasant situations is apparently not my forte.

"This has always been my greatest fear," Amy said, a shimmer of tears in her eyes. "In the last twelve years, not a day has gone by that I didn't wonder if it would be the day he got killed."

That stopped me for a minute. As much as I cared about Jerry — had always cared — I surely hadn't spent every single day of my life worrying if he'd come home alive. The thought was sobering on a lot of levels.

Amy wiped her eyes and sniffed daintily. "We moved here from Houston so he wouldn't be dealing with crazies every single day. And now look what happened." She dabbed a tissue under her nose again. "Somehow, I feel responsible for all this."

I didn't want to know why she felt responsible because I didn't want to take on her guilt as my own, which I would be inclined to do, particularly in this case. Furthermore, I didn't much want to know about their married life at the moment. But denial is only good for so much, and it couldn't mask the obvious fact that Amy Parker still loved her ex-husband. And she blamed herself for their divorce.

The funny thing was, I felt responsible as well. That I had been seven hundred miles away the entire time they were married didn't lessen my guilt. In my heart, I knew that at least part of their problems had indirectly been my fault.

I glanced at Jerry's kids again, wondering at what point they would decide I was an evil witch who ruined their mother's life. I was tempted to confess and save them years of wondering, but I held back. The truth of the matter was that I had talked to Jerry maybe a half a dozen times while he was married. Maybe. And it was all very low key, boring even. Yet I still felt guilty as hell over his divorce. Irrational but true.

And for a little more truth, if I thought I could repair his family for him to make him happy, I would do it in a second. In fact, if I could go back in time and stop whatever had started the downward spiral of their relationship, I'd do that, too. I owed him that and more. Yes, I can be a jealous witch, but in the end I'd do what would make him happy. But right now, no matter how much I wanted to help, I was still the outsider and there was only so much I could do. I was also bright enough to know when it was time to bow out.

I smiled at Jerry's ex-wife and tried not to wince when I spoke. "I'm really glad you're here, Amy. I hope you'll be able to stay for the next visiting time. I really need to get back out to my mother's and check on her. The bullet took a pretty good chunk out of her arm before it got to Jerry and she has a dozen or so stitches and her arm's in a sling. I expect she'll need some help."

Amy nodded and brushed a lock of silky hair behind her ear. "Do you think they'll let us in to see Jerry soon?"

I checked my watch. "Maybe half an hour or so. I think they said the next time visitors could go in was at four. Of course, even at the designated time I had to lie to get past the Rottweiler at the nurse's station." The children's eyes bugged a little and I was just as surprised they were listening. "I was just joking, kids. The nurses will be very nice to you and your daddy will be so very happy to see you if he's awake. He sleeps a lot right now."

"Will you be back tonight?"

"I'd planned to come back, but if you're going to be here — "

"Oh, no. I won't be able to stay long with the children. They need to get home and get some rest. We'll be back tomorrow." Amy smiled, but it was more of a sad, resigned effort than an actual smile. "Besides, if he needs anybody to be here with him, it's you." She hugged her children to her. "And his kids."

There it was again, that painful stab of guilt. I hadn't had a single thing to do with either his marriage or his divorce. So why did it keep feeling like I had? Like I was somehow responsible for the misery of Amy Parker, and in turn, her children. All I wanted to do was run.

Discarding that particular option as a cowardly reflex, I spoke to Benjamin and Rachel again. "Your daddy is a very brave man. He's had a rough time. There are all kinds of funny machines by his bed with tubes and wires everywhere. They look scary, but they're helping your daddy."

They said nothing, but Benjamin rolled his eyes a little at my toddleresque delivery. I tried again. "I know you've seen all this stuff on TV, but it's different when you see it in person and it's very different when it's someone you love. I didn't take it too well myself, and I wanted you to know what to expect."

Benjamin frowned as if to say "Yeah, yeah," but I also saw him giving what I'd said some thought. Rachel for sure was.

"I want to go see my daddy," Rachel said, her angelic little face a tad less angelic. "Right now."

My heart twisted. No more. I had to get out of here. "They'll let you in to see him in a few minutes, sweetheart. You just be thinking about all the things you want to tell him. Even if he's asleep, you go right ahead and talk. He'll know you're there." I glanced at Amy as I turned to leave. "It was really nice to meet you, Amy," I said, the urge to flee shaking through me. I practically ran from the waiting room.

I arrived at Mother's house in about twenty minutes, and with each minute that passed, exhaustion weighed heavier. Between the all-night trip down and the emotional toll, the eight hours of sleep in three days just wasn't cutting it.

I went in the back door as I usually did, but I turned the opposite way from the kitchen.

Mother's house is one of the old style homes with a circular traffic area connecting every room, rather than the hallway design of later years. When I'd been overcome with a burning concern for physical fitness, I'd open all the doors and trot from room to room on my personal air-conditioned jogging track. I had been a pretty decent athlete back then, but running for any reason other than to win a short distance sprint race bored me to tears, so I didn't wear any paths in the carpet. Funny, looking back, my mother had been incredibly indulgent of my antics. Had one of my kids gone tromping through the house like that, I'd have had a fit. Okay, I'd probably indulged in a number of fits about very similar activities, but let's don't muddy the waters.

I walked through the first bedroom, trying not to make too much noise in case Mother was napping. She met me in the short hall by the bathroom, walking none too steadily, but I resisted the urge to grab her and scold her for being up. "Hello, Mother, dear," I said cheerfully. "How are you feeling?"

"Oh, I'm doing fine," she said, although I knew good and well she wasn't. When I was allowed in to see her in the emergency room, I'd counted twelve stitches in her lower left forearm. The doctor told me there were internal ones as well. They'd pulled it together as best they could and felt confident that it would heal nicely. They put her in a sling to keep her from moving it too much. They also said it was going to hurt like hell and gave her some serious narcotics.

"Are you in much pain?"

"Oh, it's started hurting a little, but I didn't want to take one of those pain pills until you got here. So much of that stuff makes me sick as a dog. I don't much want to take any at all. I was thinking I'd just take some aspirin."

"No, you probably ought not do that. Remember, aspirin is a blood thinner, and that's probably not what we want right now. Better stick to acetaminophen or the prescription."

She nodded and cradled her arm. "Well, I suppose I'll have one then."

I got her a pill and a glass of water from the bathroom and after she'd downed it, we went to the living room.

After I settled her in her favorite chair, she said, "Tell me about Jerry. Is he still in the intensive care?"

"Yeah, and will be for a while. He's pretty out of it, but I think he knew I was there."

"So he's going to be all right?"

"I hope so," I said, glancing toward the kitchen. "The police sure didn't take long in there."

"Yes, they did try to hurry, with Merline and Agnes telling them that it was just plain as day obvious what happened and how it was awful they were making me keep the place in such a mess."

I wasn't thrilled that the police could be coerced into doing a shoddy forensics job, but the ladies were right. Trajectory of the bullet was about all there was to figure out; where was the shooter, how far away, what angle, etc. Jerry had taken the bullet with him to the hospital, so there was no time wasted looking for that. Still, they'd finished up amazingly quickly, and even more amazing was the fact that the kitchen looked good as new except for the plywood on the window.

"Mother, tell me you didn't get in there and do the cleaning."

She frowned a little. "Well, I did help, but Merline and Agnes did most of it. They weren't about to leave me here alone and they wanted something to do."

I had, against my better judgment, given in to Mother's idea that I should stay at the hospital with Jerry, and Merline should come to the hospital and get her. Merline and Agnes showed up thrilled to be needed and planned to take Lucille to eat before they headed home. I doubted Lucille felt like a trip to Furr's Cafeteria, but the ladies assured me that they needed to keep her away from the house for a while longer while the police people finished up. I gave them both my cell phone number and the trio went on their way, already debriefing Lucille as they walked out the door.

"So the police haven't been gone long?"

"Oh, maybe an hour and a half, two at the most. Merline just left not ten minutes ago. She had her son come over and put up that plywood on the window. It had turned into an oven in here and the flies were just awful."

"Well, it sure cooled off pretty quickly," I said, refusing to think about what the buzzing little insects were up to.

"It has now, but for a while there I was sure thinking we'd just go stay at a motel tonight. Then again, I'm not letting some damn fool run me out of my home. Besides, I've been thinking."

"Thinking about what?"

"The gunshot." She pointed to the boarded-up bay window in the kitchen. "It's as plain as anything, but that goon Leroy Harper can't tell his head from a hole in the ground."

"I can't argue with you there, but I have a feeling you have a specific reason for saying so."

She nodded. "I've had plenty of time to think about this, Jolene, and I think Jerry getting shot was an accident."

"An accident such as some idiot was deer hunting in the neighborhood and drew a bead on Jerry?"

"No. More like the shooter was aiming at something else and hit Jerry by mistake."

I frowned. "That doesn't really make sense. Jerry's the sheriff, there are plenty of people who could be out to get him. For all we know, he could have been onto the person who killed BigJohn."

Lucille adjusted the sling, but the grimace on her face didn't ease. "I was the target, Jolene. If I hadn't stood up the very split second that I did, well, I'd be dead, plain and simple. And Jerry wouldn't have a scratch on him."

I replayed what I remembered of the incident — who was where, the shatter of the glass, the angle of the gouge on Mother's arm and the fact that she had been standing up when the shot blasted in. She was right. If she hadn't stood at that exact moment, the shot would have hit her square in the back of the head.

Shivers rippled through me. "Why?"

"The only thing I can think of is that the shooter believes I know something of BigJohn's business."

"Do you?"

"Good Lord, no. I learned early on that his monkey business was the last thing I wanted to talk about. Only way I knew what he was up to was mostly through other people or when my water got shut off."

"Well, apparently that's beside the point since somebody wants to kill you for what they think you know." I stood and walked toward the phone. "I've got to call the sheriff's department and tell them about this, then we've got to get you out of here and to someplace safe."

Lucille shook her head and pointed an acrylic nail toward me. "Sit back down, Jolene. I'm not going anywhere. I'm not in any danger right now, not with that deputy outside."

"I saw the car when I pulled up, but I waved and he sure didn't get out and try to stop me from walking right in. Not my idea of a high security program."

"Oh, well, Jolene, everybody knows who you are. No point in causing a stir when it wasn't necessary."

Fine, I'd let that slide, but not much else. "I'm still calling the sheriff. This is serious and I'm not taking any chances."

"As for the sheriff's department, Jolene, I've already tried. I've told three deputies plus the two police people who were here. A couple of them said they'd make a note of it, for all the good that will do, but they dismissed it as something they'd figure out when they got all their tests or measurements or whatever it was they were doing in my kitchen all day. Besides that, Leroy Harper's made it real clear that he's in charge of this case and we have to talk to him personally about everything."

"Well that's just peachy," I groused. "All the way around." Nasty thoughts about incompetent rednecks and backwoods police work flitted through my mind, but I tried to push them away. Leroy was just being Leroy, and hopefully the forensics people from the Redwater Police Department were just trying to get their job done fast and were ignoring Leroy like everyone else. Hope does spring eternal at times, however, I was less than willing to bet my mother's life on it. "What do you think we should do?"

Lucille sighed. "I'd like to think I can carry on with my life as usual, but I'm not an idiot. If I go traipsing off to the Dairy Queen or the Senior Center as I usually do, I'll be a sitting duck."

"Which is why we need to get you out of this place." Getting me out of this place wasn't such a bad idea either.

"I won't be run out of my home, Jolene. We do need to do something though. I suggest you call your old friend down at the *Times* and get a reporter on this."

"So do you want me to tell him about the shootings or the idiot pretending to be sheriff?"

"Both." Lucille adjusted the sling on her arm and tried to hide another wince. "As I recall, Jolene, this sort of thing is just your cup of tea."

"I like lime in my tea, not bullets. And just because I caused a stir with an article twenty-something years ago doesn't mean it will work this time, not that it worked that great then either. As you'll recall, it took them two years to fire the perverted principal."

"And nothing much has changed around here, so I suppose we'd better get started. I left you the newspaper's number over by the phone."

Gary Gammons and I had interned together at a newspaper in Austin during our final college days. We were both applying for jobs half-heartedly, and after my interview in Redwater Falls took a turn for my breasts, I told the editor I had a good friend who was a great reporter and would probably fit right in. That wasn't exactly true since Gary wasn't a leering sexist, but the position did have potential and Gary had jumped on it. And he was still there, but in an upper management position. "I haven't talked to Gary in fifteen years — at least."

Lucille shrugged. "Doesn't matter. He was crazy about you, too. Always telling me how you were the prettiest — "

"Dammit," I said, pushing myself up and stalking to the phone. "Not every male in the county was crazy about me, Mother."

"Well, a whole bunch of them were. You may not have noticed, but they certainly were. You call Gary. I just know he'll help."

I did call Gary — but not just because my mother said so — and I discovered that he is apparently a really big fish in the local media pond, which translates to darned hard to get hold of. After a few transfers and evolving explanations, I finally reached his voice mail.

Now, to be fair, Redwater Falls is technologically superior to Kickapoo in more ways than tone dialing and real voice mail. I myself can confirm that there are two actual computer stores in Redwater. One sells only DOS machines with "Winders," to quote the salesman. I was tempted to engage him in the Mac/IBM debate but it seemed pointless, particularly since he thought Mac was the name of the salesman at the second computer store in town. But educating the "Winders" man would have been easier than getting Gary Gammons to help me out and investigate the gunfire in Kickapoo. Primarily because Gary was in a foreign country, and I mean a real foreign country as opposed to, say, Kansas. In case you didn't know, the Republic of Texas is alive and well; just ask any Texan. And the particular Texan I needed to talk to was on a two-week honeymoon with his new wife in Mexico.

"It's his third," Lucille said as I explained the latest sorry state of affairs. "So I suppose he didn't want anything in the paper about it. He didn't stay with the first one any time at all. I think he was married to a girl from Nocona after that. Lasted five or six years. Haven't heard much about this one."

While it was semi-interesting to learn the life stories of my old friends, I needed a new plan on how to deal with the current unpleasant situation, namely someone wanting to kill my mother. "I could call one of the staff reporters, tell them I know Gary, see what happened."

"They've already written their little ho-hum story about BigJohn and I suspect there will be a small piece in this afternoon's paper about Jerry. The high temperature for the day will get more attention, I'll tell you for sure. It's hot enough to kill out there today and nobody's going to want to be out in it snooping around about some crazy what-if."

She was most likely right. When it got into the triple digits and stayed there for weeks, people tended to get cranky — and complacent. The level of water in the lakes and how many kilowatts the electric company was supplying were about the best you could hope for in the local lead articles. In short, chasing down a story about a crazy shooter would require someone to remove himself from in front of his refrigerated air conditioner unit and knock on doors; therefore, it wasn't likely to happen. Of course, I could be a little jaded in my assessment.

Lucille leaned back in her recliner. "There's just no help for it, I suppose. You and I will have to do the investigating ourselves. If we stick together, we can watch out for people with guns lurking in the bushes and find out who's after us all in one whack."

I'd had a nagging suspicion this might come up. "Exactly what do you mean, by 'us'?"

——➤●◄——

Chapter Seven

After a few more ineffective phone calls and another brief chat with my mother, it didn't take me long to confirm that "us" meant "me", and sticking together meant Lucille telling me what to do and me doing it. We were still glaring at one another across the kitchen table regarding the chain of command when I decided to pretend I'd won and get on with the business of deciding what I was going to do next. Besides, it was probably for the best anyway — the part about Lucille not getting physically involved, not the part about telling me what to do. Still, no matter what age you happen to be, having your mother tell you what to do can cause resentment, rebellion or just plain ridiculous behavior. Or, in my case, all three.

I have, at various times, gone out of my way to prove that I don't have to do what my mother says. These instances generally coincide with the times I'm compelled to prove my stupidity, but let's don't belabor the point. I didn't really want to have my mother either tell me what to do or go with me to do it, whatever "it" turned out to be. Still, in order to do anything, I had to get some more facts. From my mother. Yippee.

I flipped open a notepad to a clean page and began my own interrogation. Determined to be objective and thorough, I wrote down almost everything my mother said. I carefully noted all the names of the players in the various mayoral issues and their specific reasons for despising BigJohn. I made a similar list for my mother's enemies. It was no surprise to anyone that even with Kickapoo being a really small town, not a single name showed up on both lists. Things are never that easy for me anyway.

I also quizzed Mother about who might want to do Jerry harm and why. After we eliminated all the obvious criminal elements that unnaturally inhabited the area, Mother had an epiphany of sorts.

"Why, Jolene," she said, a real twinge of awe in her voice. "I never thought about it until just now. That bullet could have been meant for Jerry."

I did not see the light along with her. "So said Leroy the Slug."

"Leroy's an idiot who can't see past the end of his bulbous old nose," Lucille said, turning her own slim nose up at the very idea. "All he thought about was that Jerry got shot so somebody must have meant to shoot him. I doubt it's that simple."

I doubted it, too, although I didn't have any great alternative theories. However, from the studious look on my mother's face, I figured she did, or she was busy concocting one.

Lucille clicked the nails of her good hand on the table. "What if someone got jealous that you and Jerry were seeing each other again?"

I groaned. "That's pretty unlikely. Hardly anybody even knows I'm here, and exactly none of those care."

"Everybody knows you're here, Jolene. Word spreads fast at the Dairy Queen. Why, once when Merline let it slip that she'd not be averse to visiting with a certain new widower, the phone was ringing before she even got home. Besides all that, you went to dinner with Jerry Don. Why, that right there could have sent somebody into a tizzy."

"Because I went to dinner with him? It's not like we went to a motel and put 'Jerry and Jolene are in room 122' on the sign by the highway."

Lucille raised an artfully drawn eyebrow. "Did you go to a motel?"

"No, Mother, we did not. I was being sarcastic."

"Well, I wouldn't put it past you. I knew what all you and Jerry Don were up to, don't think I didn't."

Personally, I didn't want to think about that on any level whatsoever. "That somebody shot Jerry because of me is too ridiculous to consider, even in Kickapoo, Texas." I realized my mistake at about the same time the words left my mouth.

Right on cue, Lucille's eyes flashed and her mouth tightened into two thin lines. One did not disparage Lucille's hometown or the great state of Texas. Ever. More to the point, I needed her cooperation, not two weeks of the cold shoulder treatment such a remark would earn me. I like to think I've learned a thing or two in my forty-three years, but if I have, none of them are related to dealing with my mother.

Lucille didn't cross her arms, most likely because the sling prevented it, but she sure looked like she wanted to. "I am certainly sorry that you find all of us here such imbeciles," she said, her hackles up and bristling. "I was, however, smart enough to raise you."

This was the start of a very bad downhill slide that I'd traversed on numerous occasions. And never once had I ever been able to back-pedal fast enough to make things right with my mother. Never. Therefore, I knew better than to even try. I figured the best I could hope for was a distraction. "You know, Mother, you do have a point. But what if it wasn't one of my old boyfriends that wanted Jerry out of the way, but one of his would-be girlfriends? He's here all the time. He's a good-looking man. He's got to have women following him all over the place."

Lucille sniffed and twirled a curl of Frivolous Fawn. "That was exactly what I was trying to tell you, if you'd been so kind as to have let me finish."

Well, I felt properly chagrined, and figured this qualified for one of those "prove your stupidity" moves I'd mentioned earlier. Still, if it got me back into Lucille's good graces even a little, it would save time and energy all the way around.

Lucille stuck her nose up in the air. "It would seem to me, senile though you think I am, that his ex-wife would be the most likely suspect."

"Amy?" I said a little too incredulously. I ignored Mother's creased brow and pressed on. "Amy Parker hardly seems like a homicidal maniac. I met her at the hospital, you know. I suppose she could have some personality disorder that makes her go nuts and try to kill people, but when I talked to her, she seemed really sweet." Sweet is a highly desirable trait in Kickapoo, but it didn't look like it held any sway with my mother in this particular situation.

Lucille's nose twitched up another notch. "She may have seemed sweet to you, missy, but you don't know half as much as you think you do."

No, apparently not. But I did know things would be going a whole lot better if I'd remembered to bring along my egg shells to walk on. In truth, this nonmeeting of the minds usually happened within the first ten minutes of being with my mother, so the fact that I'd made it a full day and a half was something to be proud of. That we'd spent a good portion of that time discussing murder motives or medical care for shooting victims, namely Lucille, was beside the point.

"Okay, you're right," I said sincerely. "I'm not nearly as smart as I think I am." It wasn't so much an agreement with her as an accurate assessment. If I was smart, I'd be somewhere else, like another state.

"For your information, Jerry Don left his wife nearly two years ago," Lucille said huffily. "She didn't make it easy for him to get a divorce, though, I'll tell you that for sure."

Besides the fact that Jerry and Amy's marital history was none of my business, over the years I'd found that the less I knew about Jerry's love life, the more charitable — and supportive — I could be. Nevertheless, Lucille had baited up a fat worm of curiosity and I was compelled to bite. "So what's the rumor, another woman?"

Lucille got a Cheshire cat grin and fairly licked her lips. "I suppose I should have mentioned it before, but yes, there was talk of another woman."

Ridiculous or not, my heart twisted up in my chest, then took a plunge into my stomach. I hadn't even been here, but it hurt to think that Jerry would have fallen for someone else when he had to have known I was available. Sort of. Seven hundred miles isn't exactly around the corner, but it isn't unavailable either.

I glanced at Mother to see just how deep her self-satisfaction went. She wasn't smug, but she was snickering. Whatever the case, I didn't think it was the least bit funny. I tucked my hurt feelings and temper away as best I could and mustered up my most businesslike voice. "So who was the woman?"

"Some girl out of Redwater. I don't know her name. I don't like listening to gossip." Another sly grin. "But I heard she was kind of kinky."

Kinky? What did my mother know about that? And where did kinky fall on the latest yardstick of morality in Kickapoo? Did that mean the woman wore leather and carried a whip or that she drove the car when they went out? Don't laugh. In Kickapoo, real men do not let women drive them around.

I know this personally because before my dad died, he was, for all intents and purposes, blind as a bat, yet he continued to drive everywhere. No way was he going to be seen riding shotgun for a woman, particularly his wife. In keeping with his very macho image, he also continued to ride his Harley, without a helmet, by God. How he died in the house of natural causes rather than under a semi on the highway is still a mystery.

So, you see, kinky is a matter of perspective — and geographic location — which is why I decided to ignore the issue completely. "So how long did the relationship with the other woman last?" I asked, belatedly wondering why that particular question jumped into my head. Then again, a three-month relationship was different than a three-year one, although I wasn't feeling particularly enthusiastic about either option.

Lucille patted her hair. "Oh, they're still living together, as far as I know."

After my stomach did another free fall, I looked my mother straight in the eye and glared. "This is not funny, Mother. What exactly are you talking about?"

"Oh, all right," she said, sighing dramatically. "I understand they only live together when she doesn't have the children."

Her children, his children, what? There was something not quite right here. "So Jerry only lives with a woman when her kids aren't there, or is it his kids you mean?"

Lucille snickered. "No, honey, that's not quite it. It's not Jerry Don we're talking about here. Amy Parker's the one with the girlfriend."

I know my eyebrows raised because I felt them. "Oh."

Not a brilliant response, but the best I could manage, considering. This was definitely a new twist in the story that opened up a whole new can of questions. Amy was a lesbian? I'll admit to a twinge of relief at the prospect, as ridiculous as that is. My selfishness was short-lived, however, as the implications of the situation became painfully clear for Jerry. It would have been horrible enough had Amy left him for another man, but for another woman? That had to hurt. Bad. I wondered for a moment why Jerry hadn't told me about it, but what was he going to say: "By the way, did you know my wife prefers to sleep with women?" Not exactly first date conversation material, not that it was a date, of course. Meeting Amy, it was believable, I guessed, but only to a point. "From what I saw at the hospital, I would have sworn that Amy really loved Jerry."

"I'd heard that too," Lucille said, a little too flippantly. "Maybe she does, or maybe it's like a brother-sister thing, or maybe she doesn't at all. In any case, you can't blame him for being upset when he found his wife and her lover in bed together, doing whatever those kind do."

Those kind...kinky.... Oh, great, I knew exactly where this was headed and I didn't want to go there. Now, before the unpleasant realities of the situation set in, I do have to admit that I enjoyed a rather idyllic childhood here in Kickapoo; small school, small classes, lots of opportunities to be a big shot and very few worries. And for the most part, I was oblivious to the underlying attitude of the times, which was that anyone other than white heterosexual Protestants (Baptists being best) were regarded with suspicion, fear and outright loathing.

I was probably around eight when it occurred to me that the only person with a skin color other than white who I had ever seen was a friend of my dad's, who literally took his life in his own hands when he came over to visit us. I'm not kidding.

I'd like to believe that things are different today. And to be fair, on my last visit, I heard a kid at the Dairy Queen gleefully chattering about the two black guys on the high school football team who were, and I quote, "gonna kick everybody's butt all the way to state." Funny how an upswing in the Class AAA football rankings helps smooth out those pesky pigmentation issues. Helps a little anyway.

Armed with that little prehistoric perspective on tolerance, how well do you figure a gay person would fare in this lovely, open-minded haven, especially one that wasn't a star football player?

"Okay, Mother dear," I said, trying not to sound as weary as I felt. "How much of this stuff about Amy is hearsay and how much is truth?"

"Oh, I only gave you the facts, Jolene, but there's plenty of stories. Agnes told Merline about seeing those two out at McDonald's together. They didn't sit on the same side of the booth or anything, but Agnes said she could still tell."

No, I was not about to ask "tell what?" because frankly, the more I learned, the muddier the picture got. And while none of this appeared to have anything to do with the mayor's murder, it very well could have played into Jerry's shooting, or not. Nevertheless, I couldn't ignore this part of the equation. I scribbled a few notes then scratched out my doodle of the golden arches when I realized the only fact worth noting was that Amy had a girlfriend. "So what kind of a person is Amy's friend?"

"Oh, she's really butch," Lucille said confidently. "Real masculine looking."

I did not laugh, but I did rub my hand across my mouth to prevent it. My mother, the expert on lesbians. "What I meant was, is she a nice person?"

Lucille patted her hair. "Oh, well, I don't really know about that. Merline pointed her out to me once. Real short dark hair, thin but kind of muscular."

Again, I did not groan nor did I bother explaining that short hair and a nice physique did not mean anything whatsoever, except that the person obviously did not sit around eating chicken fried steaks with gravy and watching "Wheel of Fortune" every night as did a large percentage of the local populace.

"She works over at that new lumberyard out off the old Jacksboro Highway," Lucille volunteered. "Maybe you ought to have a talk with her."

I tapped my pen on the pad. "Why would I want to talk with her?"

"Maybe she shot Jerry."

I thought about that for a minute, and I had to admit it was a possibility, but why bother, she already had what she wanted, namely a divorced and available Amy. There were a number of other details that didn't make sense. "If she was going to shoot Jerry there are a whole lot more convenient places than in your breakfast nook."

Lucille huffed, although I could see her following along with my thinking. "Then, I guess we're just back to me. Somebody hates me enough to want to kill me. I know you find that very easy to believe."

I didn't argue with her, just sat there, trying to figure out what to do next. I couldn't see a good starting place. Either there were two separate events to unravel, or they were somehow related, which made it more complex since we didn't know if the shooter was actually after Jerry or Mother. The mayor had been the first shooter's target, and it seemed highly likely, but not certain, that the person who shot Jerry and Mother was the same one. I could link a motive for shooting Mother with the mayor easily but not confidently. And I could find a fair motive for a couple of people to shoot Jerry. The problem was that none of the motives were very strong, and there was nothing that pointed to some kind of big conspiracy.

Denial danced a jig through my brain chanting: When in doubt, block it out. Seemed reasonable. "I think I'll run back into town to see how Jerry's doing, then swing out to Bowman City and chat with Sheriff Leroy, or some higher evolved species occupying the office tonight, and see what's going on."

"I doubt he'll tell you anything."

I doubted it too, even planned on it. While denial had been grabbing my attention, another little voice was screaming "Do something, even if it's wrong." That particular voice calls to me a lot, and giving myself permission to do something wrong is not always a great plan since I can usually be highly successful in the endeavor. And no, I do not need to be reminded that it was my mother's idea to talk to the media. Right, wrong or otherwise, I was headed to the Redwater Falls *Times* newsroom to find the newest greenest kid in the place, one who hadn't been socialized into complacency yet, and lay out all the tantalizing facets of the shootings in Kickapoo, to whet his appetite for a juicy "make a name for yourself" story.

It was yet another long shot, but I didn't see how it could hurt.

⟶●⟵

Chapter
Eight

T he next morning I forced myself out of bed at the obscene hour of seven a.m., threw on my standard uniform of shorts and a T-shirt, and set about my mission of snagging the newspaper before my mother did. Stumbling into the kitchen for my daily infusion of liquid tar, I saw that I was too late. Way too late.

Lucille Jackson sat at the kitchen table, newspaper spread out in front of her, bifocals perched on the end of her nose and steam coming from her ears. Apparently, intern Kimberlee Fletcher had written an article on the unseemly activities in Kickapoo.

Without a word, I grabbed a can of Dr Pepper from the fridge and sat down at the table. Stupidly, I said, "Anything interesting in the paper this morning?"

Lucille shoved the newspaper at me. "You should know. Every other sentence in this trashy little piece ends with 'Jolene Jackson said.'"

Uh oh. A sick feeling settled over me, and it was like I was being called into the office again for writing my "Fire the Pervert" editorial in the school paper. "It really says that? 'Jolene Jackson said?'"

"You have no idea the can of worms you've opened up, Jolene. And why on earth they printed this mess is beyond me."

"Slow news day?" I said, trying to be halfway amusing, lighten the mood, that sort of thing.

Lucille stood and glared. "You've made this mess, Jolene, now you're going to be the one fixing it. Not that you can unsully my reputation."

I watched her stomp out, but got the feeling she wasn't all that mad. If she had been, she'd have already dragged me out of bed accompanied by the phrase "Jolene Janette Jackson, look what you've done." So, I figured it couldn't be too bad.

I was wrong.

The more I read, the sicker I got. If Kimberlee Fletcher had been to even one journalism class, it was not readily apparent from the words printed on the page. It goes without saying that she didn't know the first thing about investigative reporting either, like the fact that you don't just print everything some moron off the street tells you. The moron in this case, of course, being me.

The highly informative and speculative article detailed every little trivial thing I had told Kimberlee, including the fact that my mother, an eccentric, flamboyant type (yes, she used those words), had been dating a married man who was now dead via unnatural causes, specifically the mayor whose obituary, she dutifully noted, appeared on page twenty-three. Kimberlee Fletcher was right on top of this story.

And furthermore, the "highly esteemed sheriff of the county, Jerry Don Parker, former high school sweetheart of the very same Jolene Jackson, was critically wounded during an early morning visit to the elder Ms. Jackson's home." The little snot had made it sound like we were both sleeping with him.

After I quit hyperventilating, I read on. Kimberlee had told every little bit of hearsay and speculation about all the goings-on at city hall. She even hinted that the mayor's wife had been having an affair also, but nobody knew for sure who with, and what did anybody really know about the mayor pro tem and what is a pro tem anyway? All in all, it reflected rather tackily on the populace of Kickapoo, not to mention the sleazy informant.

And I had to agree with mother. How on earth did this piece of yellow journalism get published? This wasn't typical of news stories, even in this paper. The *National Enquirer* would have passed on this one.

Then it hit me. When I'd been doing my internship, I'd had to beg and fight to get assigned to anything other than a feature story on a homecoming queen. And in those stories you didn't have to check out anything, just write what you were told, and, true or not, everybody was happy.

I flipped through the rest of the paper looking for little Miss Kimberlee Fletcher's byline. It didn't take long to find it, right beneath the headline that read: Greenbelt Bowl Queen Nominees Announced. A dozen or so photos of smiling high school girls lined the sides of the article. Pretty much the same headline and format as when my picture graced the page twenty-odd years ago. And then, at the bottom, I did see my high school picture with the words: "Former Bowl Queen Involved in Recent Shooting."

"Mother!"

Now, I was the one with steam coming out my ears. "Did you see this?" I said, pointing at the article as she walked into the room.

She put on her glasses and peered over my shoulder. "Why no, I didn't. I always did like that picture of you. It's one of my favorites. I paid a fortune for that dress but it surely did look good on you. Look how that lace vees down over your bust. You surely did have a nice figure back then, of course it's not bad now. In fact, I bet you could still fit into that gown. It's in the closet, you know."

Yes, I knew. And I knew I couldn't fit into the thing if my life depended on it. I'd been sixteen years old then, for godsakes. And now every person in the county and the next would be commenting on how I'd aged, and how I used to be such a smart and sweet girl, on and on ad nauseam. It was all stuff I didn't care about under normal circumstances, but here, that kind of thing just plain makes me nuts. And what would the killer think about all this?

Don't think I hadn't thought of that aspect. I had. A lot. My plan had been to stir enough interest so the idiot reporter would investigate and put pressure on the killer, maybe make him back off a little. More than likely the killer had just added my name to his hit list on general principles.

"Okay, Mother, I admit it. I screwed up." I folded up the newspaper and shoved it aside. "So what do we do now?"

"It seems to me, Jolene, that your newspaper article puts all the cards on the table, so to speak."

"It's not my article, Mother."

"Whatever," she said, with a flick of her nails. "The point is that I doubt the killer and/or the shooter is going to be thrilled. I suppose one choice is to just sit back and let the sheriff's department handle it."

Handle what? They hadn't handled anything at all that I could see, and with Jerry barely alive, I had no hopes that his troops would pull themselves up by their bootstraps and become efficient criminal-catching machines here in the next ten minutes. "You're right about the article, but I have no faith whatsoever in the current leadership of the sheriff's department."

Lucille wandered over to the cabinet and got a glass, then filled it from the jug of water in the fridge. When she finished, she set the glass aside and turned toward me, rather haughtily. "Well, Jolene, it seems to me that all Leroy's said to the newspaper is 'No Comment.'"

She was implying that Leroy had more sense than I did, and I didn't appreciate it, although I couldn't argue with her point. I had made a really dumb mistake and I was rightfully obligated to fix it. I stood. "I'll take a quick shower and head up to the hospital. Jerry was awake for a few minutes yesterday, so I'm hoping he'll be awake when I'm there today."

"No visits with the reporter?"

"Oh, yes, I'll be visiting with little Miss Fletcher, and her boss as well. I think they both need a lesson on responsible journalism."

"Well, you go on and have a good time, dear. Merline's coming over around eleven and we're going to the Dairy Queen for lunch."

I stood, frowning as I thought about her plans. "I don't think so, Mother. Somebody might be trying to kill you. We agreed you would stay home until this was over, with the nice deputy outside to see to your safety."

Lucille waved her good hand in dismissal. "Well, I've thought about that, and nobody's expecting me to be out so they can't very well be waiting in the bushes with a gun. Somebody would have seen them by now."

I started to point out that nobody had seen the shooter before either, but instead I used a different tack. "What about that article in the paper?"

"Well, really, Jolene, I hate to say it, but you'll be the one taking the heat over that."

Or a bullet. I didn't say a word, just smiled.

"Besides, I'll not have anyone disrupting my lifestyle for any reason. If I want to go have a hamburger and a glass of iced tea with my friends, I'll certainly do so. Like Merline said, I'm kind of a celebrity now."

Oh, so that was it. A celebrity. "So you're not mad at me anymore?" I asked hopefully, willing to take my "get out of jail free" cards where I could get them.

"You ought not have told that little girl to print all of Kickapoo's dirty laundry."

"I didn't tell her to," I said, obligated to defend myself. "I made it crystal clear that I was just giving her some tidbits to help with her investigation, which was no investigation at all as it turned out. In the real world, the eager reporter gets a tip then starts digging into public records, does interviews and tries to get to the truth of the story. Remember Watergate? Kimberlee's rambling piece of nothing shouldn't have been printed. A decent attorney could retire off the potential libel suits in that article."

"Well, it's all water under the bridge now," Lucille said, turning and heading toward her bedroom.

"You're one of the ones who could sue her. I'm another."

She stopped at the doorway and turned toward me, sling swinging and free hand perched on her hip. "Well, Jolene, I believe there is entirely too much suing and countersuing going on in this world and I do not want to be a part of it. Besides, I can hardly sue somebody else for what my daughter said."

With no good response to that one, I turned myself around and marched off to the bathroom to ready myself for yet another trip to Redwater Falls *Times* and General Hospital, two stops.

As I was drying off after my shower, I heard the doorbell ring. My first instinct was to turn the shower back on and hide as I usually did when Lucille's friends came calling. Then I realized that nothing about this was usual. For all I knew there was a lunatic at the door with a gun this very second, pointing it at my mother. I grabbed a towel, wrapped it around me, ran down the hall and peered into the living room.

There was a lunatic with a gun all right. Leroy Harper stood in the middle of the room nearly nose to nose with my mother.

"What do you want, Leroy?" I called, peeking out from behind the door.

"Why, Jolene, you look right fitting for a trip to the jailhouse."

While I was mentally reciting every profanity I could think of, Mother said, "You get out of my house, Leroy Harper, or I'll smack you in the head with my purse again."

Only then did I notice her weapon of choice clutched in her good hand. "Leave my mother alone, Leroy. It's me you really want to harass. Wait outside. I'll be out in a minute."

He made a childish face at Lucille then walked to the door. "Either you're out in five minutes, Jolene, or I'm coming back in and taking you out of here. If you want to be nekkid, that's fine with me."

Leroy left and I hurried myself in dressing. The last thing I wanted was to be even half naked, or nekkid as it's called here, around Leroy the Slug.

When I walked outside in a plain white T-shirt and jeans, the first thing I noticed was the paralyzing heat. The second was the wind. Blowing at about twenty-five miles per hour, it felt like being surrounded by a thousand blow dryers on hot and high. And with the humidity in the air and the instant sweat that drenched my just-showered body, I could just imagine how fast and high my hair was frizzing. I ran my fingers through the wayward bottle-brown mess, which had the effect of fluffing the curls higher and causing Leroy to lick his lips as he got out of the running, and air-conditioned, patrol car.

Gentleman that he is, he walked around to the passenger side and opened the rear door. "Get in," he grumbled, still licking his lips. He looked like he was trying real hard to pretend that he wasn't distracted by being within two feet of a real live female. He was failing miserably.

I was neither dressed provocatively nor acting it, although Leroy tends to get confused about these issues. The truth of the matter was that I was melting from the heat, and my patience with Leroy, which is never high, was wilting right along with me. "I'm not getting in your little patrol car, Leroy, so get over it. You either produce a warrant for my arrest or you just toodle on back down the road and do whatever it is you do when you're not being a jerk to me."

He frowned and lifted his hat off his head, then wiped his forearm across his pale forehead and thin hair. Setting his hat back in place, he said, "That write-up in the paper's got you in big trouble with the commissioners."

"Is that so?"

"You don't just go spoutin' your mouth off and not expect somebody to notice. 'Specially when you don't even know what you're talking about. You've done it for sure now."

"I expected that so-called reporter to have half a brain and do some investigating on a real story. That article was junk and you know it. My only mistake was in talking to a brain-dead Barbie doll instead of a real reporter."

Leroy's face flushed a bright red that had nothing to do with heat. "Don't you talk about Kimberlee like that. She just wrote what you told her. You're the one at fault here."

I stepped over into the limited shade of a mimosa tree and leaned against the smooth trunk. "So am I to deduce that you and Miss Kimberlee are, um, friends?"

He took a menacing step toward me. "She's a real nice girl. Real sweet and kind."

Unlike me, was a given. "Well, she won't last long as a reporter if all she does is write down what anybody tells her."

"She'll do just fine, Miss Know-it-all," he said, closing the space between us.

I leaned away from the tree and took a few backward steps toward the house. I figured I'd slip inside and slam the door in his face before he realized what I'd done. I kept backing and wiping the sweat from my face. Not having eyes in the back of my head, I misjudged where the edge of the house was and the sharp corner of brick caught my arm, scraping off what felt like several yards of skin. I might have muttered a curse or two, but I didn't stop backing toward the house.

Unfortunately, Leroy noticed my slinking and followed, pacing me step for step, and very nearly nose to nose.

"Now, Leroy, if you have some legitimate questions to ask me, why don't you come back inside where it's cool and we'll have us a nice little chat," I said, lying through my teeth. "I even promise not to call you too many appropriate names, Slug."

That was evidently the wrong type of enticement because he puffed up like a toad and leaned even closer toward me. "Why, you little — "

The screech of tires and a pop like a firecracker. A piece of brick shattered off the house between us, sending puffs of dust and rock into our eyes. We both dropped to the ground, but the car was already squealing away.

Leroy cursed and rubbed at his eyes. I rubbed at mine, too, although I tried not to be stupid about it. I was coherent enough to realize that pieces of brick could do some serious damage.

Although tears poured down my cheeks, I tried to force my eyes open to get a look at the retreating car. I blinked several times, but couldn't keep my lids open long enough to really see anything. There was a ball of white in my vision but I couldn't tell if it was a car, a house, or just a cloud of dust. A shiver went up my back. Somebody must have taken quick offense to the newspaper article. I'd made a mental wisecrack about courting a bullet, but I hadn't really believed they'd come after me. But they had. And if Leroy hadn't been back-ing me up to the door, the bullet would have skewered me in the tem-ple, dead center, so to speak. "Dammit," I said, stumbling up to my feet and trying to pretend that I wasn't totally and completely petrified. "Did you see anything, Leroy?"

A blurry glance at the acting sheriff told me he hadn't seen anything and wouldn't be for a while. Leroy was on his knees, his hat in the dirt beside him and his balding head gleaming as he rubbed his fists into his eyes with frenzied enthusiasm.

"Stop grinding rocks into your eyes, Leroy." I blinked away my own tears and tipped my head to the side to wash out the debris. "Stop rubbing or you're going to be in eye patches for a month."

"Shut up, Jolene," he said, bracing himself against the house as he stood. He held one hand to his face and staggered in the general direc-tion of the patrol car. "Goddammit, I can't see shit. Jesus this hurts."

I followed along and opened the car door and handed him the radio so he could call in our latest little incident.

Lucille had heard the commotion, but was wisely standing inside the screen door. I waved to Mother that we were okay, then said to Leroy, "Just tell them I'll drive us to the hospital in your car. It's the quickest way. I'm probably okay, but you're not."

"I'm fucking fine, Jolene," he said, tears and blood streaming down his face.

That's when I noticed the piece of brick about an inch long lodged in his forehead, just above his left eye. I turned to my mother and hollered. "Need some dishtowels. Grab your purse — and mine. Lock the house. We've got to get to the hospital."

She nodded and disappeared into the house.

I maneuvered Leroy into the back seat and sat down beside him. "Is that deputy still here?"

"No. I was gonna be here so I sent him on a call out by Mankins."

Well, swell, there'd be no help from any official types. Once again I had to play EMT, like it or not. And I did not. The rule of thumb was to leave any foreign object securely in place until professionals could remove it. Unfortunately, I didn't much think that was a good plan in this case — and I surely didn't want Leroy fooling with it, or whining about it. The wound was also bleeding pretty good, and I wasn't going to mash down on a piece of brick to try and stop it. They were going to be digging rocks out of his head for the next two weeks regardless, so, right or wrong, that slice of brick was coming out.

"Leroy," I said, preparing to give him the bad news about the projectile lodged in his face. "I need to, um, well...." As I searched for just the right words to convey my news, it occurred to me that maybe he didn't need to know what I was going to do. He wouldn't handle it well either way, but having him not know until the deed was done would be easier for both of us, but mostly for me.

At that moment, Lucille reached the car with an armload of hand towels, the dishtowel supply having been depleted. "Thanks," I said, grabbing one and laying it across my lap for quick access.

Lucille glanced at Leroy and grimaced in sympathy.

I signaled her not to say anything then tried to coax Leroy's hands away from his eyes. "You're going to have to move your hands so I can see what's wrong."

He grumbled and growled, but his hands dropped away. I put my fingers on his cheek and worked my way around his eye to the chunk of brick. "Hmmm," I said cleverly. "Looks like..." Then I grasped the end of the brick piece and yanked it out.

"Owww!" he yelped, swinging his meaty fingers up to his face. I managed to slip the towel over the wound before he got his hand up. "What did you do to me!"

"You had a chunk of brick in your head, Leroy," I said, not so sweetly. "Well, now, that's no great revelation, let me rephrase. You had an exterior chunk of brick stuck in your face. I graciously pulled it out. You can figure on a few stitches at least. And patches on both eyes would be my guess. Should have listened to me about rubbing them so hard."

I scooted out of the back seat and mother scooted in. I situated myself behind the wheel, snapped my seat belt and turned on the whirling lights. I've always wanted to do that. The siren was tempting, but I didn't want to attract any undue attention. The lack of a warning siren did not prevent me from exceeding the speed limit to the hospital, however. I did drive carefully, though.

Leroy moaned and groaned and whined the whole way to town, and didn't shut up until Lucille threatened to whack him with her purse. Knowing she was as good as her word, he piped down a little.

When we arrived at the hospital, medical personnel swarmed the car and whisked Leroy into the emergency room. They tried to whisk me as well, but I declined their insistent offers. I was fine. More shaken than I was ready to admit, but physically fine. My eyes had quit watering and didn't sting so I knew there wasn't any real damage. I leaned myself against the front fender of the cruiser and refused to budge so a doctor peered into my eyes there and pronounced me both obstinate and "probably" okay.

I was still holding up the fender when an army of deputies spilled out of the emergency room doors. In this case, an army meant four, but that was quite a few, considering. With Jerry and now Leroy out of commission, the ranks were dwindling rapidly and it appeared there was a little nervousness running rampant through the remaining soldiers.

One of the deputies, an attractive brunette about my size, stepped toward me. She looked to be in her late twenties or early thirties. "I'm Deputy Marshall," she said, narrowing her eyes just a tad in warning in case I wanted to comment on her name. "Are you the one who drove Deputy Harper to the hospital?"

"Guess that depends on whether I'm going to get in trouble for it or not." She frowned at my half-attempt at humor. I started to tell her I could do better, but she didn't seem inclined to smile, much less laugh. "That was a joke," I said. "Stress does that to me. Some people freeze, some people cry, I crack jokes, or try to."

Deputy Marshall nodded to me and then to Lucille, who stood a few feet away. "Would you ladies follow me."

I fell into step beside Mother and muttered, "The woman has the sense of humor of motor oil."

Mother scowled me into a highly unfunny mood so I just kept my clever thoughts to myself and marched along.

We followed Deputy Marshall down a series of hospital halls until we came to the cafeteria. She motioned us to sit down at a table in the corner. "Coffee or soda?"

"I'd like a Dr Pepper and a visit to ICU."

She didn't even blink. "Sheriff Parker is not allowed visitors."

I blinked rapidly, and my heart fluttered at a similar pace. "Is something wrong? Is he okay? What happened?"

"His condition is stable, but they are keeping him sedated. He's under guard until further notice."

Her detached spit-out-the-facts manner was getting annoying fast. Not that I wanted Leroy back, mind you, but he was easier to read. "Why is Jerry under guard?"

Deputy Marshall looked at me like I was a complete idiot. "For his protection. Someone is shooting our officers. We do not take that behavior lightly."

"So that means I can't see him?"

"Yes." She turned a steely eye my way. "No one other than immediate family and official personnel can see him right now."

I was sorely tempted to make a juvenile remark accompanied by a childish la-te-da face. I really do want to be like Deepak Chopra, wishing everyone well in my thoughts and heart no matter how much they piss me off, or something like that. Unfortunately, I'm still working on the kindergarten lesson of not letting every thought that enters my brain come out my mouth. But I think it counts that I think about being a better human being.

"Miz Jackson," Deputy Marshall said, slightly less monotone. "I have worked with Sheriff Parker for four years now, so I am well aware of your relationship with him."

Was that so? And just how did she know something I didn't know? I started to ask, but managed to restrain myself.

"He's a good man and an excellent sheriff. I will do everything in my power to see his assailant brought to justice."

"I hope that happens soon. But I still want to see him."

She gave me a quick, curt nod that did not scream "rival," and I am pretty good about picking up on that sort of thing. "I will make a request for an exemption on the visitation restrictions."

After our chatty little group had sipped about half our drinks, Deputy Marshall pulled out a notebook and began the pop quiz portion of our show. Nothing terribly enlightening emerged from the grilling, but I did at least feel this particular public servant would follow up on all the leads we'd given her — unlike Leroy or Kimberlee. It wasn't much, but it was something.

◉　　◉　　◉

We arrived back at Mother's house to find the place crawling with deputies and other official nonuniformed types. Deputy Marshall tried to rush us into the house, but I lingered behind, trying to overhear what the people digging in the side of the house were saying. I didn't catch much except the words "probably thirty-eight caliber."

After Deputy Marshall made an obligatory sweep of the house and pronounced it clean, I decided a little casual conversation was in order. "Wonder why our shooter isn't using the shotgun anymore?"

Deputy Marshall stopped and turned toward me with her unemotional stare. "A pistol is both easier to conceal and hold, particularly while operating a vehicle. Logical choice of the two, although a higher caliber automatic weapon would be more effective than either a twelve-gauge shotgun or thirty-eight caliber pistol."

Well, I'd had my lesson in logical thinking for the day. "So, Deputy Marshall, what next?"

She checked her watch. "A deputy will be assigned to stay here with you."

I could have mentioned that having a deputy or sheriff here with us hadn't been a real great help so far, but to my credit, I did not.

"My shift here ends at eighteen hundred hours," she said. "That is approximately two hours from now. I will be monitoring all phone calls and visitors. Other than that, you should behave as if nothing is amiss."

"Nothing is amiss?" Lucille shrieked behind me. "I did not ask for a babysitter and I don't want you people lurking around my house spying on me. I want you to go lock up whoever's doing these awful things!"

"Ma'am," Deputy Marshall said, without a hint of emotion or fluster, "events of the last two days indicate that one or both of you are at risk of injury or death from an unknown assailant."

"It seems to me," Lucille said, just as logically if not as unemotionally, "it's the deputies who are winding up in the hospital."

"That contingency is also allowed for."

Lucille pointed a fingernail from her good hand in Deputy Marshall's direction. "Well, I'll tell you what, missy, there had better be somebody actually working on solving this case. I don't plan to live the rest of my life in a prison camp."

"Yes, ma'am," Deputy Marshall said simply, turning toward the kitchen to set up shop at the kitchen table.

I almost smiled. I liked it when somebody besides me was getting a what-for. And I did admire my mother, giving them a dose of reality.

Plywood still covered the windows so the risk of another bullet coming through with any precise intent was unlikely. My stomach growled and I realized that not only had I missed breakfast, I'd missed lunch as well. I was more than a little lightheaded and nauseous to boot, so knew I had to get some food quickly. My mother isn't known for being a gourmet chef, or even a semi-enthusiastic cook, so I ate a whole lot of TV dinners when I was growing up. Just one more facet of the "good old days" that I didn't want to relive now. What I really wanted was one of those tasty chicken baskets. Yes, with gravy, and every blessed fat globule and calorie it contained.

It took a little expert negotiating with Deputy Marshall, but I managed to recruit a deputy, who was sweltering outside in day number thirty-seven of triple-digit heat, to scurry up to the DQ for me. When he returned, he was much more cheerful and I suspected he'd had his own snack and iced tea while he was at it. With food and drink in hand, I was also feeling better, at least until he told me the temperature outside, and I quote: "One hunnerd seventeen and hot enough to kill."

This local phrase was not my favorite at the moment, for obvious reasons. "What happened to the old 'fry an egg on the sidewalk' thing?" I asked, just a tad peevishly.

The deputy grinned. "Kickapoo doesn't have any sidewalks."

Well, no, it didn't. But it surely did have a killer.

Chapter
Nine

I awoke the next morning to the nostril-burning smell of fingernail polish and hair spray. The spray hovered in the hallway like a cloud, raising the urge to cough, as well as my suspicions. Lucille was hauling out the big guns in personal care products for a reason.

I dragged myself out of bed, sauntered down the hallway and leaned against the bathroom door to watch her layer on another coat of helmet-in-a-can. Frivolous Fawn wasn't moving a micrometer today.

"I'm glad you're up," Lucille said, setting the can of hair spray back on the shelf. "I've convinced the deputy that came on duty this morning, his name is Tim and he seems like a very nice young man, to take us to the funeral this morning."

Funeral? Oh, BigJohn. I felt a little foolish — and guilty — that I'd forgotten all about the very reason I'd been summoned to Kickapoo. The man had been murdered in his own home and I'd just forgotten about it. No, I hadn't for a minute forgotten the event, but I surely hadn't thought much about the man, at least in human terms.

"There should be a huge turnout," Lucille said. "Not that they're coming for the right reasons, of course, but I expect most of the town will be there. A good many from Bowman City and Redwater, too."

She'd made it sound like going to BigJohn Bennett's funeral was some grand outing, an exciting date that I should just be all aflutter over. I wasn't. Even if I hadn't developed the nasty habit of shaking at even the thought of attending a funeral, I wouldn't be interested in going to this one. "I don't care anything about going to BigJohn's funeral. I didn't even know the man. And you probably shouldn't go."

"Nonsense, I'm determined to go. Not that I'll shed any tears, but I don't want to sit in this house all day doing nothing. At least at the funeral I'll get to see some of my friends."

"And cause a stir."

She shrugged. "It should make things interesting."

"I'll say."

She patted a curl and it held firm. Selecting a pencil and tube from her collection, she expertly lined and filled her lips in a deep cherry color, then snapped on matching red earclips, which, incidentally, also matched the new color of polish on her plastic nails. It looked like an awfully good paint job to have been done with her "bad hand," but I didn't mention it. Satisfied that she was ready for the ball, she slipped off her housecoat and hung it on the rack. Wearing a cherry-red, two-piece suit with white trim and a shiny belt, she looked quite spiffy.

"Wow," I said, words being my forte. "You look terrific."

"Why, thank you, Jolene. I guess your mother still has it when she needs to." Waving me into the other room, she said. "I've laid out my sleeveless navy dress with the gold belt. It should be just about right for you. Help yourself to whatever jewelry you want. I have a pair of navy pumps that should fit. They're too small for me and I've been meaning to give them to you anyway."

Right then and there I thanked whatever superior being watches over me that she didn't offer me one of her wild purple things and glitter sandals. "Thanks. I'll hurry." Then I paused. "Wait a minute. I just told you I don't want to go."

"Sure you do, Jolene. How else are we going to figure out who's trying to kill us? You're supposed to be asking questions, remember? What better place?"

"I can name several better places to interview possible suspects."

"Killers always go to the funerals of the people they killed. Happens every single time. I guess they come just to make sure the job is really done."

I groaned. "Maybe on television, but — "

"I know the killer will be there, Jolene. I'm just sure of it. I don't get these intuitions often, but when I do, I'm always right. Now hurry up."

I have my own share of intuitions and the meter had been set on disaster since I reached the city limits of Kickapoo. Still, I guessed she had a point. It would be good to get out of the house, and it might even be better than sitting at home watching the thermometer rise.

◎   ◎   ◎

Once again, I was wrong. I would have rather watched the little red line of mercury until my eyes crossed than endure a military funeral. I jabbed my mother with my elbow and growled, "Why didn't you tell me he was a veteran?"

Lucille lifted her hand to her mouth and whispered, "Because I knew you wouldn't come."

She was damned right about that. I glanced at the casket with the American flag draped over it. Oh, she was going to pay for this one. She very well knew I wouldn't take this well. And I wasn't. In my mind, every single casket with a flag on it was my dad's. Just looking at the thing was making my throat choke up. At least I'd had the forethought to wear dark glasses to hide at least part of my face. "I'm leaving," I muttered.

Lucille let out a little sniff and grabbed me by the arm as if she needed me for support. Oh, please, like anybody who even casually knew Lucille would buy that. "Let go of me, Mother. You know I don't do well at these things."

"Of course, I do. I also know it's past time you got over it, Jolene. Funerals are a part of life."

Oh, I was not happy. Not at all. Not only had she tricked me into coming to this thing, but now she was telling me it was for my own good. The only saving grace in this whole thing was that if I was mad, I wasn't crying. Still, it was just a matter of time. I couldn't stay mad and distracted throughout the entire funeral. I never could.

The only funeral in the last two years I hadn't cried at was my father's. I couldn't. I had to be strong for my mother, who was nuts enough for us both. So, I just kept my eyes off the flag-draped casket and counted flowers. There were sixty-seven red carnations, forty-three white ones, thirteen lilies, nine blooms I couldn't identify and six blue spider mums. Let's not forget the eleven potted plants, two of them ivy. I don't remember that much about Dad's funeral, but I remember the floral arrangements. I felt myself choking up again and knew a different distraction was in order.

Rather than sort and count the present floral arrangements, I began estimating crowd size. There were probably more than two hundred people present at the elaborate graveside service that the grieving widow, in her infinite wisdom, had chosen to have.

I suspected that having the funeral outside during the hottest part of the day was most likely a spite-related decision, and I kind of had to admire her for that. She was showing everybody she was in control, if only for a few minutes. Still, if several attendees didn't drop dead from the heat it would be a major miracle.

The cemetery people had set up three big tents for shade and they'd turned on two high pressure sprinklers upwind from the service to cool the air blowing in our faces. Best I could tell, the makeshift swamp cooler was about the only heavenly thing present.

The preacher was probably fifty-something with steel-rimmed glasses and a graying ring of fluff encircling his head. Apparently, he was from the mayor's church, but he was no dummy. Knowing full well that he'd go straight to hell for lying, he hadn't tried to canonize BigJohn. In fact, he didn't spend much time at all on the eulogy. He just stepped right up on his rather high and mighty soapbox and delivered the loving and forgiving message I remembered all too well from my childhood: Come to Jesus or rot in hell.

He could have been insinuating that the former mayor was currently aflame for his wickedness, but I tuned out rather quickly as this type of preaching has the effect of a bucket of ice water on my emotions. Or maybe that's a box of matches. I tried to suck in a deep breath and hold it, hoping that would stave off my tendency to hyperventilate in such situations.

I have good reason for this reaction. Reasons, actually. Many of my fondest childhood traumas surround the First Baptist Church of Kickapoo. I vividly recall a stern Sunday school teacher who terrified me more than all the fires of hell and devil business they could think up, although I still look for horns to pop out of the ground every time I dig a hole. You know, I don't think that old woman ever smiled. She did, however, get a gleam in her eye when she rapped my knuckles for not knowing the assigned Bible verses.

But I digress.

Wishing I had a paper bag in case I really did start to hyperventilate, I turned my attention back to my conniving mother who had gotten me into this mess, make that messes. Not that she was concerned about me and my little hysterical mental escapades. Oh, no, she had other things on her mind. Like having a glaring war with the supposedly grieving widow. Even behind her dark shades I could see where she was staring. Lucille was giving Velma Bennett the eye. Make that the evil eye.

"Just look at her," Lucille hissed, covering her mouth with her hand and leaning toward me. "Sitting up there like a queen in her old plain black dress and that silly-looking basket hat, acting like she cared about him. That woman never cared about anything but his money and his name. They never even really lived together. I think she was out doing more carousing than he was. I wonder if her lover's here."

I scanned the crowd, looking for what, I'm not sure, but I looked. Getting worked up over religion was a little better than getting worked up over the be-flagged casket — and unresolved grief — but taking a wild guess at who Velma Bennett had taken for a lover was almost amusing.

"Jolene," Lucille whispered, distracting me from my almost-fun. "Look over there. That's Dee-Wayne Schuman standing in the middle of that little group." She bobbed her head in the general direction of a crowd of men and I picked out the one who looked most like a gorilla. It wasn't as easy as it sounds. "That white-haired old man next to him is the mayor now, Gifford Geller," she added. "I didn't know he and Dee-Wayne were friends, but they sure are looking chummy."

Yes, they surely were. Gifford was the acting mayor now and Dewayne was the one needing a certain city permit issue forgotten. "Is Gifford still making Dewayne change his carports to garages?" I whispered.

"Good question. Maybe you ought to go ask him."

"Maybe I will," I grumbled back. "Maybe I'll ask them both separately. You sure they don't know each other."

"Well, I'm sure they know one another, Jolene. Everybody around here knows everybody else. But that doesn't mean they'd be hanging around together."

Somebody behind us cleared his throat and I took that as a definite sign somebody actually wanted to hear what the preacher was saying. Not one to inflict my personal opinions on others, I mumbled my apologies at being raised in a barn and nudged my mother toward the edge of the tent where a little pocket of empty space waited. We didn't have as good a view of the pulpit, but I wasn't complaining.

"Look there," Mother said, nodding back at Dewayne and Giff. "They're laughing about something."

Probably us looking at them, but I didn't say so. Finally getting my wits about me, sort of, it occurred to me that the white car that had been nothing but a blurry cloud in my vision might very well be parked here somewhere. The cemetery was laid out in random-shaped patches of plots with circular loops of pavement leading from one to the other and around. Cars lined the snaking roads as far as I could see. At least half of the vehicles were white. White sedans, a few white compacts and plenty of white pickup trucks — all with gun racks. "What kind of vehicle does Dewayne drive?" I whispered to Mother.

"I think it's one of those pickups with the four doors and a big old toolbox in the back. I see him at the Dairy Queen sometimes."

"What color?"

"White."

A shot cracked out across the cemetery.

I jumped, snapped around toward the sound and managed to catch myself before I fell to my knees. Apparently while I'd been busy looking for my assailant's vehicle, the preacher had finished his sermon and the honor guard had been called to arms. I turned and watched the smartly dressed crew with shiny shoes and white gloves finish their snappy drill. Impressive, always. I made certain I didn't even flinch for the next two volleys.

Lucille looked a little shaken by the gunfire also, but she was doing a fine job of not letting it show. She straightened her lovely red suit, this way and that, smoothing it down over her shapely hips with great dignity, or at least as much dignity as she could with her arm in a sling and her nerves on edge.

A couple of old ladies in the seats next to where we stood were snickering behind their Bibles and I was highly tempted to tell them that they might be a little gun-shy themselves if they'd been shot at a time or two in the last few days. I mean really. My mother had stitches in her arm from a shot through her window and I'd had a bullet an inch from my nose, not to mention that I'd seen my oldest and dearest friend nearly killed in my mother's kitchen. It was a wonder we both hadn't hit the dirt instantly. And in truth, I'd been closer to doing just that than I wanted to admit. Deciding they needed a little lesson in manners, I took a step in their direction.

Lucille caught my arm. "Don't waste your breath, Jolene."

She was right. There was no point. No matter what I said to the self-righteous biddies, it wouldn't change a thing. I turned back toward the front of the tent to see the honor guard present the flag and bullets to the official widow.

I was trying to peer over and see if she'd mustered up a tear or two when, off to my right, I noticed Dewayne Schuman edging away from main attraction and toward the back of the crowd. Then I realized there was someone in front of him, a woman, with her back to me. The dark curly-haired woman had Dewayne's full and undivided attention, and he was shaking his head "no" and backing up quicker by the second, so quick in fact that he looked in danger of tripping over himself. She wasn't a physically large woman but she was sure putting the fear into Dewayne. Interesting.

I started to get Mother's attention and tell her we should go check it out when I saw a flutter of ebony bobbing through the crowd. When it finally broke out into the open, I could see that it was a little gray-haired woman dressed all in black, scurrying from the funeral like a roach fleeing light. She had a dogged brisk step that rang a familiar bell, but not loudly enough for me to put a name to it. I made a quick look back for Dewayne and couldn't find him, which was curious. There'd be time to ask about that one later so I nudged Mother and nodded in the direction of the black apparition hustling away at Mach nine. "Who's that?"

Lucille glanced at the woman and said, "Oh, that's just old Bony Butt. Good Lord, I bet she's hot in that get up. Wonder why she's running off before it's over. That's rather rude, even for her."

Yes, why. And what was going on with Dewayne Schuman? Where did his pal Gifford go, and how did any of it relate to the shootings?

I watched Ethel Fossy, aka Bony Butt, double time it across the freshly cut grass and flat headstones, not bothering to see who she was stepping on. For an old lady, she was really moving fast. Faster than I could have in this heat, that was for sure. Bony Butt kept up her brisk pace until she reached the driver's side of an old Chevrolet Caprice four door, late seventies model, but still in decent shape. White.

Ethel tried to kill me? It made perfect sense, and it didn't. Even considering Bony Butt's fanatical bent, she wouldn't have shot me for what I'd said at the Dairy Queen, would she? Lucille, sure, but probably not me, and definitely not BigJohn. Bony Butt was his biggest fan, and she was also bosom buddy to Velma . Still it seemed like there was a link to something here that I couldn't quite grasp. Just for curiosity's sake, I turned back to Mother. "What kind of car does Velma Bennett drive?"

She bristled at the name, but answered anyway. "The old goat bought her a brand new Lincoln Town Car not two weeks ago — as a coming home gift, I guess. Or maybe as a bribe for putting up with his sorry self."

Before I could ask, Lucille said, "Yes, Jolene, it's white."

Well, now, weren't they all.

—————————

Chapter
Ten

The rest of the funeral had been fairly routine, which was plenty fine with me. I'd had enough excitement to keep my unruly emotions in check, although I did get a little teary on the way out when we passed near my father's plot with the tasteful bronze marker and military emblem. Naturally, I did my best to make certain no one noticed my traitorous leaking eyes. Naturally, I failed.

Mother had very kindly asked if I wanted to stop, and I'd very kindly said my usual "no." She'd just shaken her head and lectured me on denial and growing up and being mature. All in all, it was about the same speech she had used on me when I was an obnoxious fifteen-year-old. It was no more effective on the obnoxious forty-three-year-old, but I nodded and made sincere statements about doing better next time. We both knew I was lying. Some things never changed.

One thing that did change, however, was the deputy sentenced to watch us on the way home. They all seemed to like the job just about as much as we liked having them there, which was not at all.

Mother and I were pretty worn out from the funeral so neither of us had felt like harassing the night crew. I did get a little snippy when they told me I could not go to see Jerry nor could I call to check on him because nobody was going to tell me a single solitary thing. I went to bed early and fell asleep trying to make sense of the snippets of weirdness I'd experienced.

When morning rolled around I was no clearer on much of anything, but I was wishing for another distraction, as long as it wasn't a funeral. As it turned out, there were several other things I could have omitted in my wishing, the first being the delivery of the daily newspaper.

"That idiotic little twit," Lucille said, shoving the newspaper across the kitchen table. "Never in my life have I heard of such a thing. It's not like BigJohn was the King of England or anything. Why on earth would they put his funeral on the front page of the paper? And why would anybody in their right mind spend their time watching every move we made and then writing it down for the whole world to see."

I peered over Mother's shoulder and read, my blood pressure thumping higher with every word. "Whispering and pointing throughout the service!"

I read on, but not out loud. "There was some speculation as to who and what they were discussing during the service as neither appeared interested in the memorial for the deceased."

"I can't believe she wrote that, about us, in this so-called news story!" My voice was neither calm nor even.

"This is just not right," Mother said, glaring at me as if I had either a clue or control over any of it. "How is she getting away with this, Jolene?"

My stock response to this sort of thing is usually "Welcome to the Bubble City," meaning Redwater Falls. I've had various theories about the mentality of the place, which ranged from "it's something they put in the water," to suspecting the city fathers (there are no city mothers) of a Stepford wives kind of thing, to a plain old "we do what we want around here" attitude. To my credit, I again kept my traitorous thoughts to myself.

The truth was, Redwater was a generally friendly and down-to-earth kind of place, but the world here worked in a predetermined manner, and nothing was going to change that — most especially not me. Nevertheless, I was obligated to try to rein in the loose cannon I'd lit a fire under. Kimberlee Fletcher needed her unprofessional little fuse dipped in a bucket of cold water — and fast.

Obviously there was no point in complaining to a higher-up, either in the cosmos or at the newspaper, since somebody had to approve the printing of these articles. Maybe a Dallas paper would be interested in the situation. Yeah, and maybe they already knew — and were laughing their big city heads off. Redwater has a rather dubious reputation in the state, so I'm not the only one who picks on them.

Fresh out of possibilities for a personal friend to don a cape and mask to make a quick and dirty rescue, I moved on to official options. That didn't last long because I couldn't think of a single reason that anyone with any sense would get involved. The FBI, the CIA, the police in the Bubble City, nobody.

I could certainly make the calls and explain the situation, but I knew good and well nobody was going to listen to a lunatic who told a stupid reporter every piece of gossip she ever heard. The snooping during the funeral episode wouldn't help either. So there was only one thing to do.

"Well, Mother, I'm just about starved for one of those tasty chicken baskets. How about we go make a run up the street?"

Lucille glanced around to where the officer sat in the living room, reading a NRA magazine with a look that could only be described as lust. "What about him?"

"What's he going to do, pull a gun on us? If he's a good boy I'll buy him lunch too. Otherwise, I'll leave him here. Either way, I'm getting out of this house."

As it turned out, the deputy didn't take too much coaxing, and we loaded up in the patrol car and took the three-minute, nonscenic drive to the one and only eating establishment.

There was a merry little throng at the DQ, at least until we three waltzed in. A quick study in the Lucille Jackson school of nonchalance, I sauntered up to the counter and placed our order.

The deputy, who was now looking like he regretted his decision to spring us, was scanning the room for either a killer or a place to hide. I suspected the latter. Lucky for him there was a booth in the corner open. He ushered Mother over to have a seat, and she went, but very slowly, stopping at each and every table to speak and nod to those in her favor. The queen and her court. That makes me, what, the jester? Well, yes, and I take my position seriously.

When Mother finally settled herself at the royal table, I paid the tab, collected the drinks and paper tag number and wandered back to the assigned seat. Maybe I'd been cooped up too long or maybe it is just inherent in my personality, but I was possessed to say something to these people, particularly since the only sound in the place was the deep fryer crackling behind the counter.

"Y'all having a nice day?" I said, smiling stupidly as I sat the tray on the table. "We are too. Just hope we don't get shot at again. I'm getting a little annoyed with this guns and bullets stuff."

"I am too," said a thick gravely voice. Leroy Harper stood up. He had a big thick bandage taped across his forehead and a patch over one eye. The uncovered eye was red and puffy. He wasn't acting all that mad though, relatively speaking. Maybe he was going to express his gratitude for me heroically plucking the brick from his face.

"How's the head?" I asked, fairly sincerely.

He frowned and reached up to his forehead. "Took them about two hours to dig out all the chips of brick. I've got eight stitches under here, Jolene," he said, point to the bandage and implying that this was somehow my fault. "Eight."

"I guess I could have left that big chunk in there, too, Leroy, but I was afraid somebody would think you were losing your mind and try to pound it back in."

Nobody laughed — except my mother.

"Tough crowd," I said, waiting for Leroy to get a clue or sit down. "No, really, Leroy, glad you're up and around and doing better."

"I'm still officially in charge," he announced. "But I'm supposed to take it easy until next week. Then I'll get to the bottom of this. Nobody's gonna get away with what they done to me." Leroy sounded quite threatening, apparently deciding this whole thing was really serious since he was the latest unfortunate victim.

As I sat down to have a sip of really good iced tea, Leroy shimmied up closer to the table.

"Deputy," he said to our uniformed keeper across the booth. "You have orders that these women are not to the leave the old lady's house until the shooter's under arrest."

"Old lady, my hind foot, why, you..." Lucille started to sputter.

I nudged Mother gently lest she sputter out something really good to annoy Leroy. It was my turn for that, thanks. "We're not staying in that house every single minute, Leroy, particularly when I don't see anybody with even a guess at who the killer is. We're not under arrest, you know."

"No, we surely are not," Lucille said, trying to wedge her purse up from beside her. Considering that I was between her and her intended target, I figured it was best to stop her. "Don't whack him, Mother, you'll get your purse all dirty."

Leroy narrowed one eye, the patch keeping me from seeing if he narrowed the other one at the same time.

"I'm not a pervert, Jolene, and I've had enough of you treating me like one."

I hadn't called him a pervert, and it was news to me that I was treating him like one, although I'd rightfully admit to treating him like a self-important, puffed-up toad. Not wanting him to explain how he'd come to this pervert conclusion, however, I decided to cut the chat short. "Okay, Leroy, whatever you say. Bye-bye now." I settled my attention on the big Styrofoam cup in front of me and took a long swig of iced tea, crunching on some of the soft little slivers of ice that you hardly ever find anymore.

As Leroy spun on his heel and stomped away, Mother tried to engage our deputy in light conversation. "How on earth can you work for that fool?"

The deputy got a pained look on his face and shrugged. He was wise enough to see that any answer he gave would get him into trouble one way or another. "How about I go see if our order's ready?" he said, zipping from the booth as if it were a downhill bobsled run and scuttling toward the safety of the front counter.

I was in no hurry to chase him down and he was in no hurry to come back, so Mother and I sat sipping our drinks, waiting for the chicken to fry.

I was still savoring my tea and ice when only minutes later Leroy came back inside the DQ, his big old arms waving wildly and his face flushed with excitement. "Looks like this thing is all but over. We got us a suspect in custody!"

The DQ turned into a buzzing beehive of gossip, and there were more than a few sighs of relief accompanied by "I wonder who it is" and "It must be so and so."

"So who did you arrest?" I asked bravely.

Leroy lost a little of his enthusiasm. "Now, Jolene, you know I can't tell you that. That there is confidential information."

Well, I knew that, but I didn't know if he did. "Did you find the murder weapon?" I felt like the reporter I once was and whispered "pen" to mother as I grabbed for a napkin.

"Yes, ma'am, Miss Hotshot Know-it-all, we sure did. We found a shotgun in the suspect's closet."

I took the pen from Lucille, but I didn't rush to make a note. "Minor detail here, Leroy, but there's probably a shotgun in the closet of every male in this county, maybe even the state."

"We're not worried about quail and dove hunters, Jolene," he said, rather sarcastically. "We had reason to search the house and plenty good reason to make an arrest. That's all anybody needs to know right now."

The deputy escort turned from his post at the counter and asked the acting sheriff if he still had to guard us. Leroy, in a flush of victory, promptly released him from duty. The babysitter was relieved, but not nearly as relieved as babysittees.

Lucille fairly leaped out of her seat. "Get our order to go, Jolene, and let's get out of here. We'll finish it at home while we're getting ready. I haven't been to the mall in nearly a week."

I did as I was told, at least about grabbing the food, although I had been looking forward to not having to unwrap my meal this time. Nevertheless, I took my pleasant moments where I could. I had, after all, gotten to sit at a real restaurant table for a few minutes. It was something.

After a not so leisurely lunch at the kitchen table and no refills on the iced tea, we bid our good-byes to the deputy and headed to our respective vehicles. I'd argued with Mother about driving and going to the mall alone but she'd huffed away and told me not to baby her. Besides, she didn't want me going with her. She wanted time alone.

I didn't necessarily think it was a good idea, even if the deputies did have a suspect behind bars. Mother, however, did not want to hear about it and told me in no uncertain terms that she was going out and there wasn't a thing I could do about it. I like to think I'm in charge every now and then, but clearly I am not.

I cranked on the air conditioning in the Tahoe and locked the doors. I'll admit it was good to be behind the wheel again. At least I could be in control of the vehicle, for the most part.

Mother headed for the mall and I headed directly for the hospital. If we were free, Jerry would be, too.

◉   ◉   ◉

When I arrived at Redwater General, I was shocked to find that Jerry had been moved to a private room. I was even more shocked to see him propped up in the bed, "Hogan's Heroes" on the TV. I hoped his move from ICU was because he was making a miraculous recovery and not because somebody screwed up. Medical care is somewhat iffy in these parts, although I had to give them credit for saving Jerry's life. They'd sure come through with flying colors on that one.

His eyes were closed so I watched the inmates bring a beauty queen up out of the floor, then hide her and put the floor back before Sargent

Schultz came marching in. We'd watched the show together after school on many occasions. That and the original "Star Trek." I guess Jerry was always my Colonel Hogan and Captain Kirk: strong, virile, sexy and a different woman chasing him every week. Whoa. Rewind that. I should have stopped while I was ahead.

Trying to vanquish an all-too-clear image of my hero with a certain gorgeous blonde, I noticed he'd opened his eyes and was staring at me.

I walked over to his bed. "Hey, you look great," I said, forgetting everything except that he really did look good. Healthy, strong, handsome and alive. I'd spent so much time away from Jerry that I never realized how much I missed being with him until we were together. And this had so much more attached to it. He had very nearly died — in my mother's breakfast nook. The concept was still hard to come to terms with.

We had never really been physically together over a few minutes at a time in the last twenty-five years, but he was still always "there" if I needed him — or if he needed me. For the most part it had always been a mutual give-and-take friendship, and I never wanted to lose that — or him. "I was pretty worried about you, cowboy," I said, trying to smile away the mist that had gathered in my eyes. "They wouldn't let me in to see you there for a while."

"I know," he said, his soft Texas drawl rumbling across the room like a tornado, sucking me in as it always did.

I took the hand he held out to me and leaned over and kissed his cheek. "I'm glad you're okay."

His smile faded just a little. "I'm glad you're okay, too, Jolene. Leroy told me what happened. Crowed about it, actually. He was quite impressed with your first-aid skills."

I couldn't imagine Leroy being thrilled with me for any reason so I moved on to the latest development in the case. "They arrested Dewayne Schuman a little while ago."

He nodded. "I think it was a mistake, but the commissioners are pushing for some kind of action on the case." He shook his head and it was hard to miss the disgust. "I've got to get out of here so I can handle things, otherwise we're going to have an even bigger mess on our hands."

I wasn't sure what he was hinting at, other than the fact that Dewayne shouldn't have been arrested. "Does that mean you don't think Dewayne killed the mayor?"

"I think it's too easy. Schuman's no saint, and his list of illegal dealings is getting longer daily. We're also fairly certain that Bennett was blackmailing Schuman."

"But?"

"Schuman's not completely stupid. He wouldn't have kept the murder weapon in his closet. If he's guilty, he had a twelve gauge in there for the sole purpose of proving his innocence. We all know he's a big bird hunter. It would be odd if he didn't have a shotgun. I have no doubt that the residue tests on the gun are going to come back that it hasn't been used since last year during dove season and they're going to have to let him go. He'll laugh all the way home and we'll still have a killer on the loose."

I didn't disagree with anything he said, but I couldn't get a gauge on what he really meant. "Whose idea was it to arrest him?"

"Apparently there was an anonymous tip called in to the department. When the deputies went to check it out, they made the arrest."

I figured it must have been a pretty elaborate tip to get Dewayne arrested. I also had to wonder about the identity of the tipster. Scenes from the funeral flashed before me, but without any real information to connect the dots between the pictures, they didn't mean much. "So you don't think he did it, or you do?"

"I don't think we can prove it." He sighed and shifted around in the bed, wearing down quickly and looking a little peeved about it. "I've got to get out of here, Jolene. This is making me crazy. I'm feeling fine, but they won't let me go home. It's just ridiculous. I'm a grown man and I know what I can handle and what I can't."

I smiled at him, amused to see the always-calm Jerry getting a little cranky. And while I empathized with his plight, I was also relieved that he was here where he wouldn't be hurt again. I could surely see how a wife would worry about a husband who did what Jerry did for a living. I've never been very good at compartmentalizing my life, and I'm afraid I'd worry worse than Amy, probably to the point of being psychotic. "I met Amy." The words had just slipped out before I realized I'd said them.

I hadn't said a word about any particulars, but his eyes darted away and I knew he assumed I'd found out about Amy and her friend, and thus, the reason for the divorce, which of course I had. Even an idiot could see it was still a sore subject.

Jerry stared down at his arm and studied the IV line that ran into a thick vein. "I didn't know how to tell you."

I leaned a hip on the bed and scooted up next to him. "We've been friends forever, Jerry. I would have been there for you. No matter what. I wish you'd have let me help."

"I couldn't."

I understood. This was something he himself didn't want to face, a perceived blow to his manhood that I couldn't possibly fathom. And it was further complicated by the fact that Amy still loved him. How did that fit in? Hell, how did I fit in? I had the feeling that even in absentia, I'd factored into the equation somewhere. An unpleasant tangle no matter how you looked at it. I couldn't begin to imagine what Jerry had lived with these last few years. I said the only thing I could think of. "Your kids are great. Benjamin looks just like you, and Rachel is just a little doll."

"She looks just like Amy. Hard not to notice that."

Yes, impossible, in fact. "Rachel is gorgeous, just like her mother." I noticed his lip curl just a tad. "Amy seems nice," I said, trying to smooth things over a little. "I don't know what happened — and don't need to unless you want to tell me — but I did get the feeling that she still cares for you very much."

He grumbled and looked away.

I hadn't intended to steer the conversation back to this topic, but since it had happened I figured we might as well get it over with. "What she is or isn't has nothing to do with you, you know that. She seems like a good-hearted person and that's what counts. I can't believe she'd deliberately hurt you."

"No, she didn't mean to hurt me. I knew years ago that she needed more than I could give her. I just didn't think she'd find what she needed with another woman. Good Lord, Jolene, how could I have not noticed something like that?"

I had no answers for him. In fact, about all I could come up with were more questions, specifically what couldn't he give her and why. "She seems like a good mother and you have two beautiful children. You can beat yourself up forever about something you had nothing to do with, or you can move on. Those kids need you. Don't let your resentment of her interfere with that. In time, you might even wind up being friends with her."

The look on his face said that was as unlikely as fluffy snowflakes falling from the one hundred and eleven degree cloudless sky, so I let it drop.

He smirked, very un-Jerry-like. "So how's Danny?" he said, turning the tide of emotional bullshit toward me. "Still married to that blonde?"

I laughed, although I'll admit it was forced. I've had eight years to find my ex-husband humorous, and time has helped a lot. But I'd be lying if I said the old resentment didn't flare up every now and again. I was doing better, though. I didn't even take it personally anymore that he'd latched on to a series of brainless twenty-somethings to make him feel young and virile.

"Bambi turned twenty-five a month or so ago," I said with no rancor whatsoever. "I heard he threw her a big party with balloons and pony rides."

Jerry grinned a little. Almost laughed.

I shrugged. "Hey, who am I to cast stones? Danny is losing his mind right along with his hair, but it seems he'll die a happy man. What more could a guy want than youth, beauty, big boobs and a Baywatch body? That she can't speak in full sentences and giggles as a second language is kind of a non-issue."

He did chuckle then. "Still a little riled, are we?"

Okay, he'd caught me. Maybe I wasn't as evolved as I pretended. "It really doesn't bother me except in the general sense of things. I don't care if he has fifteen bimbos to play with. I made a mistake with Danny, a big one, and I've paid the price for it. But I'm older and wiser now. I wouldn't go back and be twenty-five again for anything. Besides, I don't want to be anywhere else than where I am right now."

He smiled and reached toward me.

A knock on the door and a shuffle of feet put an end to the almost-tender moment. And when I saw who had just barged in, I was neither surprised nor amused.

"Sorry to interrupt, boss," Leroy said, hauling himself across the room.

I didn't move from my intimate position next to Jerry on the bed, but I did turn to half-smile at Leroy. "Long time no see, Deputy Harper." I am always quick with the clever lines.

"Should've known you'd be here climbing all over the sheriff."

"What now?" Jerry said evenly, although I could hear the anger bubbling just beneath the surface.

Leroy huffed and shuffled to the end of the bed, oblivious to his boss's thinly veiled anger. "Had to turn ol' Dee-Wayne loose."

"Are you expecting me to be surprised?"

Leroy frowned. "Well, it seems there was a spider's nest in the barrel of the shotgun and ol' Dee-Wayne had some kind of story for being somewhere during every single one of the shootings."

"We'll be lucky if Schuman doesn't sue us for stupidity. If he does, I'll testify for the plaintiff."

Leroy scratched his head, apparently trying to figure out if that was a good thing or a bad thing. Giving up, he said, "I still think he's guilty. I'm gonna be keeping an eye on him."

"Leroy, you are supposed to be on medical leave until next week. Go home and stay out of everyone's way."

"Nah, I refused leave. I'm needed on the job and that's where I'll be."

Jerry closed his eyes and sighed. After a minute or so of strength-gathering, he looked up at Leroy and said, "Bob Travers is in charge of administrative issues while I'm off duty. Pam Marshall is handling scheduling. Any leads on the shootings need to be shared with Detective Rankin in Redwater."

Leroy puffed up. "The commissioners made it real clear they want me on this case, Jerry, and I sure don't need no Redwater city boy looking over my shoulder."

"I've got to get out of here," Jerry mumbled.

"Look, Leroy," I said, turning from Jerry just a little. "The sheriff needs to rest right now. That he's been able to talk this long is amazing to me, but I know it's not doing him any good. He thinks he's superhuman, but he's not, and I don't want any of this causing him any setbacks in recovery."

Leroy scowled. "Well, I guess that's all I got to say anyway." He turned and waddled to the door. "But if I gotta leave, you ought to have to, too."

The door closed behind him and I turned back to Jerry. "He's right. I've talked too much, and worse, I've made you talk too much. I better go."

Jerry sighed. "In a minute," he said, exhaustion heavy in his voice. "Don't jerk Leroy's chain too hard."

I gave him a "what gave you that idea" kind of look. "Me?"

"I know you, Jolene. And I know Leroy. You just have to remember that he's as big as a horse and not nearly as bright. He's not second in command because he's the best person for the job. He's there because his uncle is a county commissioner. That would be Calhoon J. Fletcher. Remember him?"

"Oh," I said, nodding as old history burrowed its way up. I don't remember much of anything about this part of the country unless I'm forced to, and now it was coming back in painful little bursts. The unavoidable fact was that everybody was related to everybody else around here in one way or another, and some of them got a little cranky when the lesser-connected types, like me, got confused about the matter. Things were clearing up rapidly. Fletcher. Calhoon. Kimberlee. The not-so-clever spellings were a giveaway. "And this Kimberlee Fletcher that writes so brilliantly for the *Times* is related how?"

"Fletch's granddaughter, which makes her a second cousin to Leroy, or something like that," Jerry said, politely. "Go easy. He's got a big crush on her."

In certain circles, marrying one's first cousin was somewhat frowned upon, but a second cousin, well, that was just keeping things in the family. "Heaven help us if they reproduce. Don't they know they're both idiots and inbreeding only producers bigger idiots, although that's hard to imagine."

He took my hand again. "There are some things you just have to accept if you're going to live around here, Jolene."

I jerked reflexively. "Which is one of about four thousand reasons why I can't live around here." I instantly regretted my outburst, but I didn't retract it.

Jerry squeezed my hand and looked away. "I can't leave my kids, Jolene."

I knew that. And had I asked him to anyway? He was going to stay here with his family and I was going to run back to Colorado just as soon as I put gas in the car. Some things never changed. So why did I always feel like our non-relationship was all my fault? No matter how much we wanted it, things just never seemed to work out to where we vaulted past the really good friends stage. It didn't seem fair, but then it wasn't fair that Jerry had almost been killed either. That too, I figured, was somehow my fault, although I couldn't see exactly how just yet.

With nothing more to stay about the sorry state of affairs in our life-long attraction, I figured I could quiz him about the sorry state of affairs with the lunatics in Kickapoo. "So if Dewayne is free again, am I going to be under house arrest when I get home?"

"You should be, guarded that is. And I wouldn't have approved of dismissing that deputy assigned just because Dewayne Schuman was in custody. And Leroy had no authority to do it either. He's supposed to be on medical leave."

"You don't think Dewayne did it, do you?"

"I think it's possible, but I don't think it's a certainty. And even if he did kill Bennett, that doesn't explain who shot me or who shot at you. Frankly, I can't come up with a single good reason Schuman would shoot any of us other than BigJohn."

Neither could I, but I had given it a good try or two. "What if Dewayne thought my mother knew something, that maybe the mayor had confided some scheme to her or something. I don't think you were meant to get shot."

He frowned a little. "I'd thought about that, and I certainly haven't ruled it out. Still, shooting Lucille with a sheriff in the room is not only bold but a little ludicrous."

I didn't mention that the goings-on in Kickapoo, Texas, were, more often than not, ludicrous. "I still believe, for whatever reason, the intended victim in the breakfast nook was Lucille. The fact is, if she hadn't stood up at the absolute precise moment that the bullet came through the window, she would be very dead right now."

"Just like the mayor."

"And just like me if the shooter hadn't been in a moving vehicle and Leroy hadn't been backing me up the sidewalk."

I sighed, not thrilled at having to examine the realities of my own near-death thing. Denial is my friend and I have embraced it. Besides, I'm jumpy enough without having people shoot at me and my loved ones. Rehashing it over and over just makes matters worse. Besides, thinking of my own mortality makes me highly nervous, a luxury I couldn't afford at the moment. No, with Jerry in the hospital and Leroy in charge, I knew I had a better chance of figuring out who was doing what and why than any of the official types on the case. Redwater police were stretched thin with their own troubles, and Leroy didn't really have the sophistication to tie his shoes much less do any cogitating on multiple murder motives or suspect analyses. This was something I was going to have to do. I already had gathered the basics. I'd made notes on the various players and games afoot, but none of them seemed to mesh yet. A little tingle of excitement buzzed up my back. I'd figure this out.

His frown was deepening. "Why you?"

He caught me off guard and it took a minute to figure out that he was referring to the shooting. Mr. By-the-book Sheriff would not be pleased to know that I was going snooping into an official case, of this I was very certain. I curtailed my comments to that of being a shooting target. "I've asked myself that at least a thousand times. All I can come up with is the Kimberlee Fletcher fiasco. I spouted off a whole cassette of speculation and innuendo to her, which she promptly printed for the whole world to read."

"I can't see somebody trying to kill you over that. It was a ridiculous fluff piece that nobody could possibly have taken seriously."

I started to remind him that we were talking about the highly sophisticated populace of Kickapoo, Texas, but the glare in his eyes told me he didn't need that reminder. "If the killer thought BigJohn had told Mother something, then it's perfectly plausible that Mother would have told me, at least it would be plausible in a normal mother-daughter relationship."

Jerry just shook his head.

"All right then, let's take another approach. Since we have a published article with the words 'Jolene Jackson said' in it seventeen times, maybe the killer thought I was going to tell on him in the next story. Who knows."

Jerry rubbed his untethered hand across his face and I knew this was wearing him out. "It still doesn't fit just right. Schuman's dirty, but we haven't found anything dirty enough that would seem to be a motivation for all of the incidents. Still, I'll pass your ideas along to the detective."

I didn't know I'd actually had any ideas, only questions, but I didn't argue. "Who is this detective? Nobody named Rankin has talked to me."

Jerry sighed. "He was out during the forensics work, also handled by Redwater personnel. Rick has my notes from the initial interviews, but he's working directly with Pam Marshall on this. I expect he'll be getting in touch with you soon."

I was a little taken aback that Jerry had come up to speed on things so quickly, and even though he was fading fast, I was possessed to ask. "How are you so well-informed on all this?"

"Pam Marshall, you talked with her I believe, is my unofficial second in command. She's sharp and professional, and she briefed me yesterday and again this morning."

Okay, I admit it. A nasty little twinge of jealousy bit me.

"I'd sure feel better if she were calling the shots officially, but that's out of my hands. The minute I became incapacitated, politics took over."

I didn't need any explanation for that one. In these parts, blood is definitely thicker than either water or common sense. "I guess it's good then that Ranger Rick from Redwater is handling things."

"No, it isn't necessarily a good thing. Rick moved here from California a few months back. He's good at his job, but dealing with the small-town mentalities takes a special approach."

"Meaning a big city detective might think everyone in Kickapoo is a moron and couldn't possibly be smart enough to talk to them?"

He grinned. "Easy enough to understand, right, Jolene?"

Touché. Effectively chastised, I tried to keep my ugly thoughts to myself. "It seems to me that the physical evidence in all three cases is almost nil. If they don't start talking to the locals, they aren't going to know anything."

"I didn't mean to imply they weren't working on it, but it's not going to happen fast. And until I know for sure that the right person is in custody, I want you protected. I've already made the calls."

"Aw, Jerry, I really wish you hadn't done that. I'll be okay."

He reached up and ran his fingers along my cheek. "I know. You've always taken care of yourself just fine. But just once I wish I could do it for you."

I could tell his strength was long gone and he was running on bravado. And since the conversation kept steering back to highly intimate ground that neither of us really wanted to explore, I decided it was time to get us out of it. I felt guilty for not leaving twenty minutes ago, but knowing he'd be asleep as soon as I walked out the door helped ease a little of my guilt for talking so much.

I took his hand, gave it a quick squeeze and scooted off the bed. After a quick peck on the cheek, I said, "I'll be back later tonight to check up on you."

His eyelids drooped down, but he managed a weak smile. "No, Jolene, you won't."

Chapter
Eleven

A s I pulled out of the hospital parking lot — air conditioner on max — I replayed the bits and pieces of what I knew about the various situations. The information from Jerry about small-town politics taking over wasn't a great revelation in and of itself. But when you started linking Commissioner Fletcher and his apparent power to Leroy, who couldn't spell nepotism but certainly understood the concept, it did bring up some interesting possibilities, not the least of which being was Leroy Harper somehow involved in the shootings.

It made sense, and it didn't. Then again, I only had a smattering of facts and details. Having a few more would no doubt cast yet a different light. But where to start?

I mulled over several interview possibilities from Calhoon to Dewayne to Gifford to Leroy, but why would any of them talk to me? This, I fear, is the reason I eventually deemed myself poor reporter material. Writing a story I could do well enough; getting a good interview I could not do at all, primarily because I never really wanted to go talk to anybody. Hand me the facts, and a fine article I would write. Tell me to go fetch the details and I tended to freeze. Kind of like now.

But that wasn't completely true. I had a bucketful of really good questions I was perfectly willing to ask each and every one of the afore-mentioned people. The real problem was actually twofold. The most obvious being that there was no good reason for them to tell me anything, but there were plenty of reasons for them not to say one word. I'll spare you the list, but everything pointed toward the "keep your mouth shut" side. Two, I didn't necessarily want any of them to know I was snooping. Call me silly, but if one of those people had tried to kill me — or since Leroy was also in the line of fire, have me killed — I surely didn't want them to think I knew any more than they already assumed. Self-preservation does rear its head when necessary.

My options of what to do next being severely reduced, it occurred to me that if I was back under house arrest, so was my mother. If they could find her. I was ahead of the game in that department as I knew where to look, not that Lucille being at the mall was an anomaly.

Not overly eager to visit the mall myself, and since it was a relatively safe haven for her, I opted to take a quick cruise down the current drag in Redwater Falls, which coincidentally is the same drag as twenty-five years ago.

Today, however, there are a few more stopping spots — or less, depending upon your point of view. More fast food places, fewer vacant lots. I drove through Burt's BBQ and got my old favorite chopped beef sandwich, along with an essential iced tea. (I tend to limit my Dr Pepper consumption to reliable and unwatered-down cans.) I wove the Tahoe through the lot and parked at the edge of the street where I could watch the traffic.

In my younger days, my best friend Kat and I spent a lot of nights on this particular street watching the cars go by. Kat was also watching the boys go by — and fearlessly flagging them down. I didn't much think it was a good idea, but she didn't much care and insisted that I not act like a stuck-up prude. I didn't exactly think I was stuck-up, just shy. I chuckled, remembering how she laughed hysterically when I tried to explain my inherent shyness. After that, she made it her mission in life to embarrass me. She'd say things to guys that made me wish I could hide in the trunk, and they all just seemed to find her the most charming little thing on the block. She got us into some interesting double dates, but darned if we didn't have a good time at it.

I was still smiling when I polished off my authentic and tasty Texas-style BBQ sandwich. As much as I like to poke fun at my hometown, I really do have a lot of fond memories of the place. While I could certainly take another trip or two down memory lane, I had to face reality sooner or later. Like it or not, it was time to locate my mother, which meant I was going to the mall. Yippee.

I backed out of Burt's parking lot and headed toward Redwater Falls' one and only indoor mall. The mall is fair-sized with one big fountain and three anchor stores. It does not have an upper level, but it makes up for this deficiency by having two, highly popular cafeterias and three cosmetics stores. I doubted I'd spot Lucille on my first walkthrough, but the place was small enough that I figured I'd run into her eventually.

I turned into the north parking lot and noted the place was packed. Middle of the day in the middle of the workweek and it was wall-to-wall cars. Shopping is, I recalled belatedly, the number one physical sport around here, not to mention that it's nice and cool in the mall. I wound my way around to the south side, hoping the parking lots there would be a little more sparsely populated. They were, but apparently some shoplifter was being subdued in front of the side entrance and it was drawing a hefty crowd. I turned to swing wide of the commotion when I saw a bobbing ball of Frivolous Fawn and a black handbag swinging in the air.

"Oh, shit."

I slammed on the brakes, backed up and headed for the scene of the crime, meaning an assault on someone, likely a law enforcement official, by my mother. I parked illegally by the yellow curb, shut off the car, jumped out and ran toward the center ring of the circus. "Let me through," I said, shoving spectators aside. "That's my mother. Let me through."

By the time I got to the head of the pack, I saw that my mother did not need my help so very much. Others, however, certainly did. Lucille's weapon of choice was swinging this way and that and folks were giving her a wide berth. There was one uniformed security officer and one man in regular clothes trying to get a hand on her, but neither was having much success.

I edged as close as I dared. "Mother! What are you doing?"

Lucille stopped in mid-swing and looked at me, giving the uniformed security guard an opening. He grabbed her purse and the other man gripped her good arm. She tried to jerk away, sling flinging this way and that. "Now, look what you've done, Jolene. They've got me trapped," she howled, sounding not so much like a wounded animal as an enraged one.

I hurried up to center stage, noting that none of the three stars looked pleased about being in the impromptu production. "What's going on here?" I asked the security guard.

Mother answered for him. "This goon was following me," she said, nodding to the man in plain clothes as she tried to pull away again. "Creeping around after me like I was some hoodlum."

"Miz Jackson," the man in question said. "I'm Deputy Bob Travers. Sheriff Parker sent me over to protect you. I was just giving you a while to shop before I told you. I was trying to be nice."

"Nice, my hind foot," Lucille sputtered. "Just how'd you know I'd be out shopping at the mall anyway? Nobody knew I was going to be here except Jolene."

She shot me an evil glare to which I responded with an appropriately innocent shake of my head. This was not my fault and I wasn't willing to take the wrongful blame. "Hey, I didn't squeal."

"Then you had to be stalking me," Mother said, turning back to Deputy Bob. "I've been stalked by that bony-butted fool Ethel Fossy long enough to know when I'm being stalked. I also darn well know it's against the law. Now get your hands off me."

I was torn between trying to help my mother and protecting the rapidly thinning sheriff's department employees from their captive. But seeing a third option, namely that somebody needed to disperse the masses, I settled for being the designated crowd controller. I held my hands up like a seasoned evangelist and called out to the swarm. "Listen up, people. This was just a misunderstanding. You can all go on about your business. Move along, now."

Not a soul did.

I glanced at Mother and grinned — sort of — then turned back to the crowd. "You folks better get on out of here. This woman has Alzheimer's. And AIDS. And she bites." I've never been that great at extemporaneous speaking. "You've seen what she's done already. Nobody can predict what she'll do next. We won't be held liable for any bites or infections."

The crowd evaporated instantly.

When I turned back around, Lucille was scowling, but luckily not at me, probably because she hadn't heard what I said. Luckily, she was dividing her glares between the security guard and Deputy Bob. "This is a violation of my civil rights. I know it is. Now you ought to have to leave me be. It's a mighty sad case when a little old woman who wouldn't hurt a flea can't go to the mall for a little recreation without being trailed around by a goon. Why, it's just horrible, and I'm gonna file a complaint with somebody. If that Jerry Don Parker weren't shot to pieces, he'd give you two a what-for about this."

I was amused that Mother was throwing Jerry's name around, particularly since her earlier reference to him involved an unflattering comparison to a post. Jerry was apparently not hanging the moon quite as high as he did in the old days, but he still had his good points.

"Jerry Don's the one who sent me out here, Miz Jackson," said Deputy Bob, trying to soothe her. "I'm here as a personal favor to him. This is my day off."

Lucille didn't soften even a little at his above-and-beyond the call thing, but before she could tell him about it, the mall security officer stepped back a little, rubbing his shoulder. "You need me anymore, Bob?"

Deputy Bob looked at Lucille, then at me, then back at the guard. "Now that her daughter's here it should be okay." He'd said the words but he didn't look very convinced. I had a good idea he'd rather be at the golf course, or probably even home cleaning toilets, than be here dealing with my mother.

We eventually made a three-car caravan and dutifully followed Deputy Bob back to our assigned quarters in Kickapoo, but only after Lucille had finished her shopping. I'd had no idea she was completely out of fingernail polish, lipstick and cologne, not to mention the fact that she needed a new slip and bra. I had a nagging suspicion that these last two purchases were for pure spite, but I had the decency not to say so. Besides, I wasn't looking forward to being imprisoned again either. I was also wishing I'd decided to do pointless interviews with suspects who didn't want to talk to me. I would have at least been free. Or dead, a little voice in my head nagged.

When we got back to Mother's house, however, we didn't rush right in and bolt the doors. For one, we couldn't get to the doors for all the cars and yellow tape. Yes, new tape and new flock of cars.

Mother pulled up into the driveway like she owned the place, which she did, leaving the back half of her car sticking out in the road since there was a sheriff's department vehicle already there. Our keeper, Deputy Bob, had parked a few cars down the street and was sprinting toward Lucille. I muttered and cursed as I maneuvered the Tahoe into a small spot across the street and killed the engine. I know I should have raced over to see what was going on, but my pesky friend, denial, was perched on my shoulder screaming, "You don't really want to know."

Gathering up my ever-present paper cup of tea, my keys, my bill-fold and courage, I flicked the pesky voice from my shoulder and hustled myself toward the fray. Yes, it had occurred to me that nobody was sprinting out to escort me inside, and it did kind of hurt my feelings.

By the time I got to the house, Deputy Bob had already zipped Lucille inside and was back talking with another deputy. He turned toward me with a grim expression. "There was a package left on the back porch while you were gone, Miz Jackson. We'll need to talk to you about it."

"I assume it was not a floral arrangement, a fruit basket or a box of cosmetics." Yes, I'd managed to verbalize my little snide remark, but my heart was not in the sarcasm. I knew good and well we weren't having a deputy convention over FTD, Chiquita or Avon, which meant it had to be bad. Really bad. Visions of dead bodies and sundry body parts danced before my eyes, and my stomach did a triple somersault at the gory image clips. I swallowed hard, my bravado sliding down as fast as the bile was surging in my throat. "What is it?"

"A shotgun."

"Dad's?" I said, relief and shock swirling around, mucking things up until I didn't really know what I felt.

The shotgun's reappearance brought a whole bunch of the old unpleasant issues right back into the foreground. Specifically, did this confirm what we had all guessed? Had my father's favorite shotgun been used to kill my mother's boyfriend? And why was it now being flaunted in our faces? The killer's boldness scared me almost as much as the bullets. Almost.

"You ain't gonna want that gun back, Jolene," Leroy's gravel-like voice said from behind me. He marched up and broke into our cozy group, his usual leering grin in full slobber. "Bertram would be fighting mad, I reckon, seeings as how the stock on that thing is just plumb ruined."

I looked to Deputy Bob. "Tell me."

"It would be best if I didn't," Deputy Bob said apologetically, then turned to glare at Leroy. "This new piece of evidence is vital to the case and we need to keep it out of the newspapers."

I didn't take offense at the remark, at least from him. I kind of liked Deputy Bob, and I knew he wasn't implying anything about the moronic article I'd been an unwitting, or maybe that's witless, party to. He even started to say as much, but I waved away the concern. He was also right about keeping the facts of the case out of the paper, but I still wanted to know what had been done with and to my father's gun. And why.

"Slut," Leroy chirped.

My head snapped toward him. "What did you say?"

Leroy tucked his thumbs in his belt loops and snickered. "Slut. I said slut."

What stupid thing was he up to this time? "Good for you, Leroy, you learned a new word. Are you wanting me to help you spell it or give you the definition?"

He scrunched up his good eye and puffed out his chest. "The word slut was carved into the stock of your old dad's gun, Jolene. Bertram's probably turning over in his grave." He paused and got a smug look on his face. "Guess we all got the message pretty clear, huh, Jolene. Slut," he repeated, laughing. "Kinda funny, ain't it?"

Lucille, who I hadn't seen walk up, didn't think it was funny at all and promptly whacked him in the head with her purse. The blow landed in the vicinity of the bandaged stitches, and I didn't much care if every single one of them ripped out on the spot.

Apparently neither did any of the on-duty deputies since they promptly turned their backs and left Leroy screaming in the driveway while they escorted us into the house.

⸺⊷●⊶⸺

Chapter Twelve

T he Redwater forensics guys did their thing on the gun, the back porch and outside areas. Mother and I chatted with the deputies on hand, but from the questions they were asking, I didn't see that we were any closer to having any idea who was after my mother and me than we had been. The unofficial opinion was that the killer and the shooter were one in the same even though the thirty-eight caliber pistol had yet to surface. Wow, where'd they ever come up with a crazy idea like that?

The return of the shotgun had renewed the issue of matching up someone on the mayor's hate list with someone who would equally hate my mother — or me. I still couldn't see how I'd had time to offend too many people in four days. I'm good, but generally not that good, although I supposed it was possible. Still it was heartening to see them officially pursuing something.

And, of course, there was the slut thing. Carving up the gun in order to slander my mother wasn't a prank or a joke, it was premeditated viciousness. It sort of discounted a heat-of-passion killing as well. Somebody had gone to great lengths to steal the gun, plan and execute a murder, hack up the stock on the shotgun, then return it while no one noticed. Very clever. Or at least very determined to make a point.

The Redwater Falls detective Jerry had told me about was the latest arrival on the scene and he gravitated toward me like a flaming meteor. Having already chatted with Deputy Bob and Deputy Marshall, I was less than enthused about covering the same ground again, particularly with the blond-haired beach boy headed in my direction.

Detective Richard "you can call me Rick" Rankin was probably in his late twenties or early thirties, tall, lean, well-tanned and very blond with a stylish cut that just screamed "waiting to be discovered by Hollywood." Detective Rick looked like he belonged at the beach perched on a surfboard rather than in my mother's kitchen flashing a detective's badge.

After dispensing with the introductions and "nice to meet yous," we got down to the business of rehashing what was obviously old news for us both.

"Look, Rick," I said, after about fifteen minutes. "This is getting us basically nowhere. How about I tell you what I know, have heard rumored or have just plain guessed at, and then we'll get back to the old news, okay?"

Detective Rick Surfer Dude set his pen aside and leaned back in his chair. "Okay, Jolene," he said, sounding just a little too friendly — and arrogant — for my tastes. "Just what has your investigative reporting uncovered?

I declined to mention that I actually hadn't investigated much of anything, but I was ready and willing to do so, and in fact had several darned good theories on the various crimes.

I ran down my own list of suspects, dutifully noting that Velma Bennett's name seemed to crop up in conversation an awful lot and there was that new white Town Car to think about. I cited motive and opportunity for shooting both her late husband and my mother, but my theory couldn't explain why the grieving widow would want to kill me or Leroy, whoever had been the intended target in that incident.

Not knowing the intended victims hampered my extrapolations just a tad, but it did not deter me. As I rattled off my ideas, Detective Rick nodded and smiled like a politician who didn't give a damn about your issue but wanted you to think he did so you'd vote for him. Rick did perk up when I mentioned the fact that the brick to Leroy's head had loosened his tongue, and the trip to the hospital had been amusing if not particularly coherent. I'd jotted down what I could remember of his ramblings and meshed them with Mother's information to come up with a general state of affairs for the first official suspect, Dewayne Schuman.

Apparently, Dewayne's arrest for murder had triggered, or maybe accelerated, other ongoing criminal investigations, and now the Bureau of Alcohol, Tobacco and Firearms had swooped in with guns blazing, so to speak. It seemed that Dewayne Schuman, homebuilder and former felon, was buying and selling things he ought not be. The materials shed out behind his house held more than surplus lumber from his construction projects. Behind some sheets of waferboard and vinyl siding, Dewayne had stacked about forty wooden crates that held a fine and varied assortment of weaponry.

That in itself was plenty bad enough for a convicted felon, but Dewayne was doing a little modification of his inventory as well. And being somewhat of a thinker, he had quite efficiently labeled each modified box with the words "full auto." In layman's terms that means fully automatic and seriously illegal. It seemed Dewayne had a whole lot more to worry about than a spider-webbed shotgun in the closet or the carport/garage issue. Not being an expert on either construction or arms dealing, I still suspected that Dewayne's profits from selling guns were considerably more than from selling houses. There was a pretty good motive for murder lurking in the tangled web somewhere, even if I couldn't make it play out in every corner.

Detective Rick seemed interested in my assessment, but I was afraid he was mostly concerned about how I obtained the information. This told me I'd managed to piece things together pretty well. His curt "you're not to discuss this information with anyone" comment was a pretty good clue as well.

I took a turn, leaning back in my chair with an arrogant little smirk. "You know, Rick, I've been thinking."

He didn't groan, but I suspected he did so internally. Professional types such as Rick do not appreciate amateur types such as myself attempting to "help" them with their work; therefore, I did not wait for him to ask me what it was that had been weighing on my mind.

"I know you've already talked to Gifford," I said, not knowing that at all but figuring it was a good guess. "He and Dewayne were awfully chummy at the mayor's funeral. I guess you know all about that."

He made a quick note on his pad, then looked back at me. "I'll follow up on that."

"It's also common knowledge that Giff didn't care for either BigJohn or Lucille. That doesn't make a huge ripple in the cesspool of suspects, but it sure is something to be aware of. On the surface, being mayor of Kickapoo, Texas, is hardly worth killing for. The job pays a whole dollar a year. It has been rumored, however, that the kickback potential is in the mid-five figures, which ups the possibilities considerably."

Rick was back to scribbling on the paper, and I figured he could just keep at it.

"You do remember about the mayor's wife's new Town Car, right? The grapevine says BigJohn paid cash, and those things aren't cheap."

Rick seemed to think about that for a while then made a comment of his own. "The Bennetts were not divorced, you know. It is certainly not unusual for a man to buy his wife a car."

If he was saying this stuff to insinuate anything, he was wasting his breath. "I am well aware that the Bennetts were legally married at the time of his unfortunate demise. The mayor previously told my mother a rather different story, however, going so far as to show her something he called divorce papers. You might want to check on that. He said he'd officially filed, but then the wife showed up in town and subsequently so did a new Lincoln."

I let him stew on that for a few seconds, then added, "Could be important to know the exact sequence of events. I don't know what Mayor Bennett had in the way of assets, but if the grieving widow was still legally married to him, then she'd retain control of all the community property, including a tidy lump sum distribution from his retirement plan, not to mention the Lincoln."

That was the end of my soliloquy, and I figured Rick could make the necessary leaps to the conclusion that Velma Bennett was far better off with BigJohn out of her way than if he'd stayed alive and divorced her. Ample motive for murder if you asked me. Follow that down the pike with the spite motive for mother, which could trickle down to me as well, and you had yourself a fine suspect.

Rick looked up from his writing and thumped his pen on his notepad. "You certainly seem to know a lot about all of this." He sounded kind of impressed and was smiling just a little strange.

In a different situation I would suspect he was flirting with me. I decided to ignore his grin and shrugged. "I'm in the middle of this whether I like it or not. And when people start shooting at people I love, not to mention shooting at me, I tend to get interested in details." I nodded to his legal pad. "I also take good notes."

"I didn't see you referring to any."

"No, I've got these stories down pretty well by now. Amazing how staring death in the face can help refine a memory. Tends to put quite a few things into perspective." I paused for a minute, trying to assess Detective Rick's intentions. "Sheriff Parker said you'd be helping his department out on this case, but exactly what is your role?"

His eyes twinkled just a little more and his boyish grin went on in earnest. "I get to interview all kinds of interesting people."

The look on his face was drifting farther into the non-business realm and I was not amused.

"I've learned a great deal about you over the last few days, Jolene, and I have to say I'm impressed on quite a few levels."

Oh, please. I didn't want to know what he'd heard about me or inquire as to what it took to impress him, and I surely didn't want to get into some idiotic flirtation thing. I was, however, definitely flattered that he seemed to find me attractive enough to sidetrack an official interview. I don't get too many of the young studs making fools of themselves over me anymore. That honor generally falls to guys with AARP cards and pacemakers.

"I don't know what you've heard about me, Rick, but one thing I promise you is true."

He waited like a patient puppy expecting a treat. "What would that be?"

"When a woman gets to be about forty, she realizes that she doesn't have to put up with the same bullshit she did when she was twenty. She begins to care less about offending people and more about just getting to the point."

His brow wrinkled a little. He was beginning to see where I was headed with this and was deflating accordingly.

"At the moment, Rick, two major points jump right out at me. One, no matter how cute you grin, I'm not going to be the older woman that you remember fondly for teaching you something or other about love, meaning sex."

A tell-tale band of red was creeping up his bronzed neck and he tried to sputter out a denial.

I didn't let him. "Secondly, we've got a killer on the loose and you, Rick-the-big-city-detective, may be about the only chance we've got, under the circumstances, to catch him."

He hung his head and toyed with his pen. "Yes, ma'am."

"Oh, save the 'ma'am' business. I'm not your mother. Furthermore, if I were five years younger and you were five years older, I'd zip you off to some sleazy motel and give you something to tell your pals in the nursing home about forty years from now." Okay, maybe I am still a sucker for salvaging male egos. Besides, he apparently had exquisite taste in women.

With his head still bent, he looked up at me and grinned again. "I bet you could. If you change your mind...."

I laughed. "I know where to find you."

While he cleared his throat and tried to figure out how to finish the interview, I decided to help him off the hook one more time. "I guess you know about Ethel Fossy, the geriatric stalker, also known as Bony Butt. Besides lurking outside Mother's house and following her around, Ethel also indulges in hang-up calls and hate mail."

Rick, looking relieved to be back in business, so to speak, flipped through his notes. "Isn't she a friend of Mrs. Bennett's?"

"Yes, that's the one. Also a big supporter of the late mayor, which muddies up the obvious motive. Fossy went to the same church as the Bennetts so there shouldn't be any wild religious overtones or undertones, although the little lady is pretty firm on the fire and brimstone business."

Detective Surfer Dude nodded and wrote. "She is kind of a character."

"Aren't we all," I muttered.

"Anything else?" he asked, smiling just a little.

Well, yes, I could sit and speculate all day, but I didn't want to. "I think that's about it for me."

He pulled a business card from the side pocket of his notepad, jotted something on the back and slid it across the table to me. "If you think of anything else...." He let the statement hang just a tad too long. "Give me a call. I put my home number on the back."

I said not a word, just slid his card to the side and waited while he packed up his notepad and stood. He promised to give old Bony Butt a good scolding and tell her it was not okay to harass people, even if she could find scriptural justification. He also said he'd check her activities against those of the Bennetts to see if anything looked suspicious. That was at least something.

"Thanks, Rick," I said, standing and extending my hand. "Give me a call if you have any more questions."

Rick was back to stumbling over his tongue when Lucille came hurrying into the kitchen, a strange look on her face. "Calhoon Fletcher. I don't know why I didn't think of it sooner."

Rick released my hand and turned toward Lucille. "Miz Jackson, are you referring to Commissioner Fletcher?"

Mother nodded, her face pale. The bing cherry lipstick she'd so carefully painted on didn't help matters at all, the contrast making her face look all the whiter. "Oh, my, I just don't know why I didn't think of it sooner. Everybody knew Fletch was trying to get rid of BigJohn because of all the problems with the builders and water plant and what not. Well, just about everybody in town was thinking we needed a new mayor. But Fletch took it personal about trying to stick the city for those lots. He'd even gone so far as to tell BigJohn he was going to condemn those lots for the water plant rather than pay BigJohn's price. Personally, I think Fletch was just jealous he didn't think to buy the lots first."

Rick flipped open his notepad and went back to work.

"Okay," I said, trying to link this up with any of the other situations, issues or gunfire. Nothing jumped out at me. "So we add his name to BigJohn's hate list."

Lucille nodded then sighed heavily. "You may as well put Fletch on my hate list, too."

Rick looked up, brushed a blond lock from his forehead. "Why is that, Miz Jackson?"

"As you're probably aware, I'd started a recall petition against Fletch the day before BigJohn was killed." Rick didn't look aware at all but that did not deter Lucille. "I'd just had enough of his picking on BigJohn, not that the old goat didn't need it, mind you. But Fletch's hands were just as dirty as anybody's, and I didn't think it was fair that he got off scot-free."

My mother had started a petition? My mother? Spouting off was one thing, but doing something official about it was quite another. I was highly impressed. "Wow, Mom, that must have taken some effort."

She looked at me, obviously missing the point that I was proud of her activist activities. "Well, Jolene, I'm not helpless. Granted, it wasn't an easy thing to do, what with getting all the i's dotted and t's crossed so the petition would be official, but it was something that had to be done, and I did it."

"May I see a copy of the petition?" Rick asked.

Lucille pulled a folded copy from her pocket. "I hadn't gotten but a dozen or so signatures, but everybody in town knew about it. It was just a matter of time before I had what I needed for a recall. After the shooting, of course, I didn't keep up with getting people to sign."

I'd heard Lucille say Fletch was dirty before, but I didn't catch any specifics. Condemning land is legal, if exceptionally unpleasant for the owners, so that couldn't be the main issue. "What were your specific reasons for the recall?"

Lucille patted her hair. "There were plenty of them. Fletch had pulled so many shenanigans it was hard to know where to start. There were a lot of things that we couldn't prove, but it wasn't for lack of working at it, I'll tell you for sure."

I have to admit that I was completely and totally shocked at my mother's involvement in politics and her resulting activism. When I was growing up, the closest she came to caring about politics was casting a vote for president that was guaranteed to cancel out my father's vote.

"Did you uncover illegal activities?" Rick asked.

"You're mighty right we did. Merline and I had been snooping into some of the deals going on in Bowman County for quite a while. We began to piece things together and figured out that Fletch had set up a planning and zoning board that was supposed to manage the so-called growth in the county. Supposedly this was to make sure some big, smelly plant didn't get built in the smack dab middle of a neighborhood, that sort of thing."

Rick pulled out a chair, sat back down and motioned us to do the same. I debated leaving him with Lucille, but her story was getting a mite intriguing, if I did say so myself.

"The zoning board, you see," Lucille continued, "was just a front. BigJohn learned about it first somehow, but Merline and I confirmed it kind of sneaky-like. Anyway, the way Fletch set it up, if you wanted to put in a building in this county, you had to get it approved by this board first. And this was easy to do as long as you greased the right palm. Darn near impossible if you didn't. We knew this for a fact because Merline's daughter and son-in-law wanted to build a house out on the road to the lake and it took almost six months to get approval." She blinked at the detective. "Dewayne Schuman got approved for six houses all in the same day."

"Is that so," I muttered, trying to link Dewayne to Fletch. I could, but only through Leroy or maybe Gifford and neither of those roads were paved with any real facts.

"Now, this is a different permit program than what the mayor instituted, correct?" Rick asked.

Lucille nodded. "BigJohn had a city permit; this was county, started it up maybe a year ago. Like I said, dirty, dirty. It's like there's this big old bucket of mud and every one of them is seeing who can get their hands in the deepest. It seems to me they were all just trying to out-do one another."

"If you don't mind, Miz Jackson," Rick said to Lucille. "I'd like to go back over some of your statements and make sure I have a clear picture of the various situations you're familiar with."

"Why, of course, young man. That'd be just fine." She was being quite gracious and that worried me. I wasn't exactly sure why, but it did. Maybe it was because it had taken Jerry three "chats" to get to the truth about where she was the night BigJohn was killed, or maybe it was just because Lucille was involved in general. She was volunteering to elaborate on Dewayne and the garage/carport thing as well as the water scandal. Since I'd already heard these songs, I stood and took a step toward the living room. "Excuse me."

"Jolene, honey, I know you must be hungry." Lucille pointed to the refrigerator. "I believe there's some pimento cheese spread in the icebox and a whole fresh loaf of bread in the cupboard. How many deputies and police people do you suppose are out on the porch?"

I didn't know how many official types we still had lurking about, but I knew darned well I wasn't going to be making pimento cheese sandwiches for them, and that was exactly where Lucille was headed. My mother was about a nail click away from saying: Jolene, honey, why don't you fix these nice men a sandwich? And she didn't intend for me to answer the "why don't" part either. Besides the fact that I'm not the Betty Crocker type, her beloved pimento cheese is not my favorite variety of sandwich — spread or otherwise. "Thanks, Mother, but I'm not really hungry," I said, then scurried from the kitchen and into my room before she could catch me.

I actually hated to miss learning any new details on the cases that Lucille might impart, but I had heard these stories before and sometimes you just have to make hard choices. Besides, I had another source of information that could update me on the shootings and then make me forget I even cared. In fact, he had a lovely way of making me forget about almost everything but the sound of his voice.

After settling myself on my old bed with two equally old pillows propped behind me, I relaxed a little. I couldn't help the smile that curved my lips as I grabbed the phone, dialed up the Redwater Falls General Hospital and asked for Jerry Don Parker's room.

In the old days, two hours on the phone was just getting started. I hoped he felt like talking even a little this afternoon.

I was still smiling when he came on the line.

When he said my name, I was pretty sure he was smiling, too.

Chapter
Thirteen

After a long and pleasant trip down memory lane with Jerry, I hung up the phone and stared at the ceiling. There was no way this could work out. No way. But darned if it wasn't fun pretending it could.

The phone rang. Two rings. By the fourth ring, I had to assume that Lucille was still enthralled in storytelling and couldn't be bothered. I picked up the receiver.

"Is this Jolene Jackson?" a steady feminine voice said.

I didn't recognize the voice, but I scooted up in bed to clear my ears, my voice and my fantasies. "Yes, this is Jolene."

"You don't know me, but I'm Amy Parker's friend."

She paused and let that information sink in. It did, like a floating fifty-five-gallon oil drum shot full of holes. As various interesting thoughts and questions trickled in, the biggest one bubbling to the top was: Why would Amy's friend be calling me?

"My name is Susan Miller, and I take it you've heard about me."

"Well, yes," I said, always quick with the clever replies. The next words out of my mouth were going to be "So what do you want?" but it sounded a little snotty, even for me. I mentally stuttered for a few seconds and nothing tactful leapt to my tongue so I just blurted out the untactful version. "Why are you calling me?" Just to make it clear that I wasn't being rude, my voice was adequately laced with puzzlement rather than sarcasm.

"There's something I hope you can help me with."

Help her? Me? Do what, and why? I groaned, if only in my mind. I did not, in any way shape or form, want to get involved in the personal affairs of Jerry Don's ex-wife's girlfriend. That's a little weird on any level.

"Amy said you'd be the best person to contact," Susan said, unperturbed by my silence. "I couldn't very well ask Jerry Don for help, even if he wasn't in the hospital. Under the circumstances, my options are few."

I mumbled in a noncommittal way and waited for her to get to the point.

"I know this is awkward," she said. "But I'd like to meet you in person and talk about a few things."

This was becoming stranger by the second. I certainly didn't want to meet Amy's girlfriend, but what was I supposed to say, "No, go away and leave me alone" or "Sure, hon, just what can I do for the woman who broke up my best friend's marriage, not that I'm all that sorry he's divorced?" Geez.

"I know this is a bit unusual," Susan continued. "But I really don't know what else to do. I can be there in fifteen minutes."

"Well, I'm not sure the guard dogs out front would let you in. This place is swarming with cops at the moment."

"Really? Did something else happen?"

"Well, it seems —" I caught myself. "It seems the deputies and other law officer types just can't get enough of us over here. I've answered the same questions at least thirty-five times, and yet they keep asking."

"Do you think they'll be leaving soon?"

I leaned over to the window by the bed and pulled back the curtain. Most of the Redwater officers were already gone or in the process thereof, including Rick who was just pulling away from the curb area, there being no actual curbs in Kickapoo. Two deputy cruisers were all I could see that were left in the area. One was blocked in by Lucille's car and the other was out front. Another stellar investigation finished in record time, I supposed. "Things are calming down over here, looks like only one or two deputies left, but I can't leave the house without an escort and nobody gets in without being frisked and fingerprinted."

"I'll be there in fifteen minutes. Just tell them I'm a friend."

She hung up before I could say anything, specifically that I didn't want her to come over here, but it was too late. She was coming to chat about something, whether I wanted her to or not.

I slid my feet over the edge of the bed and into my sandals, figuring I'd better warn my mother and the deputy in charge of her arrival.

After I relayed the sketchy details of the impending visit to my mother, she frowned. "That is very strange, her calling you out of the blue like that and then inviting herself over. Why on earth would that woman want to come out here and talk to you? She has to know about you and Jerry Don, not that I can see how that matters to her. She's got Amy...." Her voice trailed off, obviously as confused as I was about the whole thing.

"I can't make any sense of it either. I guess we'll just have to wait until she gets here and see what she wants."

Lucille shook her head and rubbed her bandaged arm. "I just don't know about this, Jolene. You really think we ought to let her come barging in over here?"

No, I really didn't, but for different reasons than I suspected were flitting through Lucille's mind. I didn't agree with her probable worries, however, since lesbianism wasn't contagious as far as I knew. "I'll just chat with her outside and hope she makes it quick."

Lucille looked highly relieved. "That would probably be best."

"I guess I'll go inform our latest guard. Do you know who's been assigned to watch over us this time?"

"No, but Stalker Bob and that Deputy Marshall woman both left. I don't know who's out there and don't much care," she said, wandering to the living room.

I didn't much care either and I was also not so eager to leave my little air-conditioned haven. I opened the fridge, pushed aside the Dr Peppers, grabbed a jug of water and poured myself a cool glass of Ozark spring water, which Mother purchases by the case as she refuses to drink what flows from the tap. After chugging the water, I decided to treat myself to another small inoculation against the god-awful heat and stuck my head in the freezer until my nose froze. Blinking frosty lashes, I marched outside into the furnace to look for the guard.

Only one official vehicle remained so I suspected my selection of deputies was limited as well. It took me a minute, but I finally spotted a lawn chair in the shade of the big pecan tree by the garage. And in the chair sat a sweaty deputy in an equally sweaty brown uniform, sipping on an extra large drink from the DQ and looking less than pleased with his assigned duty. As I walked toward him, the face began to look familiar — in a sickening sort of way. Then it registered. It was a Harper face parked under that tree in the lawn chair. But not the most familiar one. This had to be Leroy's younger brother Larry. Great, there were two of them with guns and power.

"Hi, Larry," I said, rather chipper-like, considering the person, the heat and the mission. "Didn't know you were a deputy, too."

"Off and on," he said, not bothering to stand. "Leroy called me in since they were short-handed. Most of the time I'm out in the oil field."

Which might explain why he looked like such a greaseball. Or not. I smiled and mentally chastised myself for my ugly thoughts. "Well, I figured I should let you know that I have a friend coming over in just a few minutes. Nothing you need to worry about."

Larry Harper grinned, his brown teeth stained as badly as Leroy's although there were definitely fewer of them. He had a big wad of chewing tobacco stuffed inside his lower lip, which made him look like a slobbery old bulldog. He spit into the grass. I started to go right back in the house to get my mother and her purse so she could give him a good whacking. Lucille would not tolerate spitting in her grass.

Larry stretched his bulky legs out in front of him, but didn't attempt to stand, which was a good thing since the chair would probably have come off the ground with him. "Still have to check out anybody setting foot on the place," Larry said, spitting again. "Them's Leroy's orders."

I started to argue with him, then heard gravel crunching as a car slowed out front.

"Man, oh man, would you look at that!" Larry said, jiggling this way and that as he wedged himself up out of the folding chair. "That is one fine looking Vette!"

I turned to see a bright, shiny, cherry red Corvette pulling up in front of the house. Susan drove that? "That must be my guest, Larry, you just stay here. I'll go up there and talk to her."

"Hell, no, Jolene. I'm going to look at that car. Ain't every day somebody drives one of those babies right up in front of me."

There was no stopping him so we walked — I walked, he lope-jogged — up toward the car. He was considerably more eager than I was.

The low slung door opened and a slim, muscular woman in shorts and a T-shirt unfolded herself from behind the wheel and got out. She had black curly hair that just touched her shoulders and her face was unpainted, but reasonably attractive, although not by Texas standards.

Standby Deputy Larry Harper stopped dead in his tracks and swung himself around toward me. "Her? She's the one you're so all-fired hot to trot to talk to?" He didn't wait for me to answer, just huffed and puffed and started marching himself back to his spot in the shade. "You and the dyke have yourselves a real good time."

Well that was just great. Harper number two had made what already promised to be an unpleasant situation all the worse by his antics. And what was I supposed to say? Sorry, he's an idiot? That sort of went without saying.

Susan strode toward me, a wry smile on her face. "Don't sweat it, Jolene. I'm rather used to it. I didn't want to talk to him anyway. The Harper boys aren't real fond of me."

"Yeah, well, I can relate to that."

Susan nodded toward Mother's front porch. "Could we sit for a moment and talk?"

"Sure," I said, relieved that she didn't want to go inside. I started to volunteer that Lucille was resting and we really shouldn't bother her, but I managed to keep my lame excuses to myself. It wouldn't have served any purpose anyway.

We each selected an old-fashioned solid-metal yard chair, green for me, yellow for Susan, and settled ourselves down on the striped plastic chair pads. The thing about the heat in these parts is that you can't really hide from it. It's still plenty hot in the shade. I was guessing somewhere around 146 degrees. Okay, maybe a 108 was closer to reality. But it felt darned hot, stifling even, considering I was supposed to have a normal conversation in a highly abnormal situation.

"I know you're curious as to what I want," Susan said, seriously understating the issue. "It's my brother. I'm very worried about him. I've tried all the regular channels, but as you might guess there's no one at the sheriff's department who will even talk to me about it, much less do anything."

"Your brother? Do I know him?"

"I'm sure you've heard of him. Dewayne Schuman. He builds houses around here."

This time I did groan. Out loud. Amy's girlfriend Susan was the sister to murder suspect and ATF-most-wanted Dewayne Schuman? Small world. Entirely too small, if you asked me. "But your name is Miller," denial said. I had a bad feeling that this was going to make nasty complications for somebody, most likely me.

"Yes, Miller was my married name," Susan said pleasantly, brushing a curly strand from her cheek. "I decided to keep my former husband's name for business reasons."

Married. Another curve ball. Both Amy and Susan had been married — to men — but were now attached to one another. And in the open-minded capital of the world, no less. Wow.

Being bold enough to make that choice and live with it in this county was amazing enough, and I admired them for following their hearts. But honestly, being public about that kind of relationship around here was like enrolling in the kamikaze school of pilot training. The intent might be admirable, but the end result was going to be painful, to say the least. Not that I could say things would be that much better for them where I live. As much as I like to believe folks in Colorado are, for the most part, a higher evolved species, the various national headquarters for intolerance down in Colorado Springs prove over and over that it's just not true. I guess the difference is that I can live my life without ever having to deal with it directly. Not so in Kickapoo.

Getting back to the presumed point of the visit, I said, "So why are you worried about Dewayne?"

"You probably know he was arrested."

"And released, but yes, I happened to be at the Dairy Queen when Leroy made the announcement."

"That idiot," she muttered, and I wasn't sure if she meant Dewayne or Leroy, although they both apparently qualified. She sighed heavily. "Then I presume you know about the ATF problems as well."

If Leroy's delirious prattle could be believed, yes, I knew a few things. Maybe I knew most things since Detective Rick hadn't seen fit to correct any of my assumptions. "I've heard a little, primarily just that they were called in."

"Well, the feds aren't here for alcohol or tobacco reasons, in case you missed that part of the story." She frowned and tapped her fingers on the flat iron armrests. "Dewayne certainly isn't the only one involved, but he's going to be the one to take the fall for it."

"Sounds serious."

"The feds don't waste their time otherwise. I think they'd been watching the house for a while. Who knows what they would have done if he hadn't been arrested. I'm actually surprised they didn't just storm the place and shoot him."

Well, now, that did not sound good at all but did it play into anything else, specifically the various shootings and twisted politics in Kickapoo? If not, I wanted to be as far removed as I could from any

Ruby Ridge or Waco kind of thing that might be brewing. Still, I had plenty of questions for Dewayne Schuman. "This really sounds bad, Susan, but I don't know what I can do about any of it."

"No, there's nothing anyone can do about the guns. The feds are going to nail him on something, that's a given. He's not the only one who's guilty, but he's guilty just the same. But he did not kill Mayor Bennett. I'm certain of that."

Susan sounded wholly convinced, emphatic even, so I decided to see what else she had strong convictions about. "I guess he didn't shoot Jerry or at me either then."

"Somebody shot at you?" Her voice lilted upward in surprise.

I really figured gossip moved faster than that, and I was truly amazed that she didn't know about the brick-shattering incident. "Well, it was nothing really," I said, not wanting to say something that official types would take exception to. "Now then, why do you think I can help Dewayne?"

She looked at me for a minute, apparently debating whether to ask me about the shooting, then said, "Dewayne isn't acting like himself lately. Getting arrested for murder and having the ATF confiscate everything he owned has made him a little crazy. I'm afraid he's going to do something stupid. Frankly, I think he's suicidal."

I had to think on that one. The last time I'd seen Dewayne, which was also the first time I'd seen Dewayne, he looked quite jovial. Those two psyche classes in college didn't qualify me to make any mental health evaluations, but chuckling away at a funeral did not point to take-your-life despondency. I suppose it didn't preclude it either. Of course if he was the killer and a possible lethal injection was in his future.... Still, he'd been let go so he had to know there was no good evidence against him, at least so far, but maybe he knew it was coming. So did that mean he was the killer? Maybe. Or maybe getting crossed up with federal gun laws might have been the last little straw that broke the carbine's back, so to speak. Maybe. There were entirely too many maybes.

"I realize things don't look so great for your brother about now, but what makes you think he'd kill himself over it?"

"My brother is not a strong man, Jolene. Physically, of course, he's a bull, but he can't stand up to much mental pressure. When his wife ran off with a hairdresser from Redwater, he slammed his fist through every wall in his house, then piled her things in the yard and had a bonfire. Sat on the front porch with a cooler full of beer and his chin propped on the barrel of a shotgun for three days. He finally got over it."

Lovely. Just lovely. Susan was painting a very demented picture of her brother, and frankly, I didn't doubt a word of it. Still, I had a little trouble mixing that image with what I'd seen at the funeral. Dewayne had looked reasonably normal, if a little crass, for chatting and chuckling with Gifford during the service, although I was one to cast stones on the chatting business.

"When I talked to him a couple of hours ago," Susan continued. "He was going on and on about wishing he was dead, and how he'd rather die now than be dragged through a trial and locked up on death row. Swore he wasn't going back to the pen no matter what. He was drinking too. Heavily."

I didn't feel too many pangs of empathy for the demented drunken arms dealer who specialized in automatic weapons, but I had to agree it sounded rather grim for old Dewayne. Why that needed to be my problem was beyond me. Finally, I got to the main thing that bothered me about this situation. "Why don't you go check on him?"

Susan sighed and shook her head. "Oh, I've checked on him several times, but we had a fight. Big one. I might be the older sister, but he's not going to listen to anything I say. He made it clear I better not come back unless I changed my tune. I don't really think he'd shoot me, but when he's drinking, he gets kind of weird. He absolutely refuses to let me help him. And, as you saw with that Harper creep, the sheriff's department isn't going to do anything."

Nobody else will go see about poor old Dewayne so dear sweet Amy sends her girlfriend to me for help? When did I give the impression that I was Mother Teresa or even Doctor Laura? "Look, Susan, I'm no good at talking anybody into or out of anything. When my kids were little, I couldn't even convince them to wear matching socks, so talking somebody out of killing themselves is a little out of my league. This sounds like a job for one of the police shrinks. Have you talked to Pam Marshall? She seems pretty professional and competent."

Susan snorted. "You mean Deputy Spock? She listens to logic and reason, and there's not much of that to go around where Dewayne's concerned. Besides, being Jerry's right-hand man, I don't think she likes me very much."

I nodded, that little biting jealous bug asking me just how close Jerry was with his "right-hand man." I put aside my petty doubts, telling myself Jerry wouldn't be so thrilled to see me if he were involved with his deputy. Besides, I was certain — pretty certain, anyway — that he'd consider an intra-office fling unethical. Didn't mean he wasn't attracted to her, the nasty little bug chirped. Telling myself that I am entirely too mature for such childish speculation, I made a mature — and helpful — comment. "I could try talking to her about the situation. She seemed professional when I spoke with her earlier."

Susan shrugged. "Do what you want, but I'm telling you nobody takes this seriously, including Deputy Marshall. I've called everyone I know to call. Only a couple of them actually laughed in my face, but they all might as well have. Besides, I think you have a chance with Dewayne. He might listen to you since you're not from around here, well, anymore anyway."

"That's a great theory but there's one little problem. I don't want to get shot, thank you very much. I've developed a nasty aversion to gunfire of late."

"Dewayne's not going to shoot you. He doesn't have any guns. The feds took them all. He couldn't shoot if he wanted to."

Yeah, right. And just how long would it take a local black market arms dealer to find a gun? Three, four minutes?

Granted, it kept occurring to me that if I did go over and talk to Dewayne, and actually lived to do so, I could ask him a few questions about the shootings, the garage/carport fiasco, Gifford, Fletch and whatever else I had on my list. The opportunity to get some answers was enticing, but only to a point. I am nobody's idea of a hero or a martyr, but I pretty much earned the "all around sucker" award because in spite of how deranged Dewayne might be, I wanted to talk to him. Had wanted to talk to him since the funeral. This would just give me a good excuse. Now, if I could come up with something equally believable for Gifford Geller and Calhoon Fletcher, not to mention Velma Bennett....

"Okay. I'll go check on him. Where does he live?"

"On Walnut Street. Go past the Dairy Queen and turn left. Then go about six or eight blocks. It's on the right. Shabby looking place with a big elm in the front yard and a rickety shed in the back. Can't miss it. Sits between two mobile homes."

I nodded. "If he kills me, I'm coming after you."

She smiled and stood. "Don't worry. He's harmless." She trotted off the porch and hopped into the Vette. "Thanks a million, Jolene. I really appreciate it."

She closed the door, started the car and was zipping down the road before I could ask her if she wanted me to call her after I talked Dewayne out of killing himself. Guess not.

I turned back toward the house and wandered to the side by the garage where Larry sat. Maybe Susan was just exaggerating about Dewayne. It couldn't be as bad as what she was making it out to be, but just in case it was, a guard dog couldn't hurt. Okay, it could, but it seemed better to have one than not. "Here's the deal, Larry. I need to go check on somebody and I need you to go with me."

Larry laughed, a course, wet chuckle, then spit again. "That dyke got you convinced old Dee-Wayne's ready to kill himself, didn't she?"

I didn't say anything, just frowned. This was going nowhere and I knew it. I wasn't going to get anything but trouble from Larry and I might as well not waste my breath trying.

Larry worked his chaw around in his mouth a little, then said, "She's been calling in to dispatch every other hour, whining about wanting somebody to check on her little brother. Like anybody gives a shit. Hell, I wouldn't walk across the street to check on either one of them, much less drive across town."

That famous Harper compassion gave me warm fuzzies all over. Make that hot prickles. I suddenly wished I carried a purse — or perhaps a baseball bat — with which to smack him. Since I didn't, I kept my hands occupied with rubbing my temples. Obviously Larry was not going to mobilize the troops and check on Dewayne, so that left but one alternative. Meaning me. Big surprise.

Without another word, I tossed my good sense aside and left it in the shade of the pecan tree with Larry, then went back into the house and got my car keys. By the time I got the Tahoe's door open, Larry was at my side. He'd moved pretty fast considering his size and the heat.

"You ain't to leave the place, Jolene," he said, spitting for emphasis. "I got my orders. I'm guarding you and you ain't going nowhere."

"You know, Larry, I am. Now, you can hop in and go with me or you can step aside and leave me alone. I really do prefer one option over the other, but I'm willing to compromise."

"You ain't leaving," he repeated, sliding his hand down to his gun.

I laughed. "Oh, right, you're going to shoot me for driving my car out of your sight. I don't think so. I'm not under arrest here, so get out of my way."

I climbed inside the car and jerked the door closed even though he was standing in the way.

As the door slammed against him, he yelped and jumped back.

I locked the doors, started the car and backed up. Larry waddled-ran over to his patrol car and got on the radio to tattle on me. I was soon to be a hunted woman, a protective custody escapee run amok. "Dangerous outlaw on the run" had a nicer ring to it, but since I'd left my mother and her purse at home, I couldn't really be considered armed. Or very dangerous. My romantic notions flickered out and I got on about my business.

As I drove toward the DQ, the landmark needed to locate Dewayne's house, second thoughts — and third and fourth ones — bombarded me. What was I thinking? I had a better chance of getting information out of Ethel Fossy, and I wasn't nearly as likely to get shot in the process. What would Dewayne think when a strange car — a dark four door "could be the feds again" type of vehicle — pulled up in front of his house? "Shoot," I muttered to myself. I didn't mean it in the "oh, darn" sort of way either. I meant shoot, as in bang bang, he'd shoot me.

With the Dairy Queen looming ahead as an oasis, I headed straight for the last spot of shade on the east side of the building. I figured if I had to face death and Dewayne, I at least deserved a last drink of good old Texas iced tea.

As I moseyed inside, I noticed there weren't but four other cars in the parking lot. A white oil field truck that was mud-red from the hood down, a blue Chrysler sedan, a white Lincoln Town Car, and an old white Chevy Caprice. I didn't have a clue as to who owned the muddy truck and the Chrysler, but the other two I had a real good handle on. Velma Bennett and Ethel "Bony Butt" Fossy were inside.

Well, now, wasn't that an interesting turn of events. Why, it just wouldn't be right if I didn't drop by their table and say howdy-do, now would it?

With a slightly evil smirk on my face and clever opening lines running through my head, I walked inside the moderately cool DQ, marched right up to the counter and said hi to Jimmie Sue.

Jimmie Sue did not looked overjoyed to see me. She just nodded a little, grabbed an order pad and pencil, tapping the latter annoyingly on the counter. Apparently this was her new sign language for "May I take your order, please?" Miss Jimmie Sue was not being nearly as friendly as she had been before, so I suspected she had been listening to ugly gossip about me. Tsk, tsk.

"Good to see you again, too, Jimmie Sue," I said, truly trying to not sound like a smart ass. Okay, maybe only half-trying.

Tap, tap, tap, tap tap, tap....

After I ordered a large iced tea — without comment on the fine quality to be found in the establishment — I decided it was time to leap in with some subtle snooping. Just because Jimmie Sue wasn't being very friendly, didn't mean I couldn't pick her brain, such as it was. I smiled as if she'd been treating me like royalty instead of a royal pain. "Things sure have been turned upside down around here since all this started," I said, clucking my tongue and shaking my head.

"Yes, they have," Jimmie Sue snapped, breaking her silence rather curtly. After giving me what a less forgiving soul might have called "the evil eye," she then turned and jammed the Styrofoam cup into the ice bin. She usually filled the cup with the handy metal scoop because the fancy ice was so dense it would break chunks out of the cup, or at the very least bend the top so a lid wouldn't fit on. I didn't get much ice that way either, and the hot tea was going to instantly melt what little ice made it in the cup. Yes, it sounds whiny and that's exactly how I felt about the whole thing. Jimmie Sue might not like me, but golly, gee, couldn't she make my iced tea right?

Jimmie Sue smacked the cup down on the counter, a half inch of tea slopping out. I caught a glimpse of the last ice bits as they melted in the puddle.

"Um, well," I said, wondering how to get a little more ice into the cup. I wasn't going to drink iceless tea, for goodness' sake. "Could you, I mean, if you don't mind, could you put a little more ice — "

Jimmie Sue leaned around, grabbed the metal scoop, gouged out some ice and plopped it into the cup, sending more tea splattering out on the counter. "I think it's high time everybody just went on back where they came from and left us all alone," she said, glaring at me as if I were an idiot and might miss the inference.

I kind of liked the old Jimmie Sue better, but I tried to pretend she was still acting just as sweet as pie. "Yes, all these various investigations sure seem to be upsetting things. I heard Dewayne Schuman's been kind of down lately." Okay, maybe it wasn't a great leading line, but I haven't been to the "say this to get people to spill their guts" school of question making.

"Don't know nothing about Dee-Wayne except he ought to be feeling bad over all the trouble he's in plus what he's causing around here. We sure don't need no more snoopy government types nosing around here. Or outsiders."

I ignored the obvious and tried to think of something to ask that she might answer, otherwise standing here listening to Jimmie Sue was pointless. "Guess Gifford's not too happy about any of this."

Jimmie Sue's eyes darted across the room. "Not my place to say who's happy or not about anything."

I turned to where she had glanced. In the corner booth sat a stocky man in a light blue-gray business suit that I suspected was made of old-fashioned polyester and might have been called a leisure suit in a previous life. He had a thick, short neck, a couple of chins and a large fleshy nose that looked like it might have been broken a couple of times. With a head full of thick white hair, cut in a one-inch buzz on top and nearly skin close on the sides, he made a memorable impression. And I knew I'd never seen him before. I remembered my dad grousing about Gifford Geller from time to time, but this was my first visual.

I knew I should go talk to him, the opportunity being tossed in my lap, but I am not all that gregarious, really. Yet again another fine example of why I was not cut out to be a reporter. I am basically a shy and unobtrusive person who doesn't want to bother anyone. Yes, I really am, dammit.

But I couldn't be this time. I had to suck up my fears and go talk to the man. "I can so do it," I muttered to myself.

Jimmie Sue looked at me like I had lost yet another screw, so I just took my tea and turned away before she could make a nasty comment about my habit of talking to myself.

Giff sat in the back corner booth. Velma and Bony Butt sat in a middle table just a few feet away. I couldn't get to Gifford without walking past the nongrieving widow and the wiry zealot. I did not want to be whacked again, or preached to, thank you very much, but the options were definitely limited.

Even though it would have been a whole lot easier to just leave, I forced myself to take the proactive approach and walked directly to them. "Good afternoon, ladies. My it's hot out there."

Velma Bennett looked as bland as her gray plaid dress, but she did glance my way and nod. Bony Butt looked a little more lively, wearing brown stretch pants, a gold floral shirt and a wicked scowl. "It's long past afternoon, missy, and if you don't like the heat, why don't you just run on back up to your mountain cave and sit yourself in the snow. Just enjoy it while you can because there won't be any snow saving you from the eternal fires."

I couldn't comment on that eternal fires business, but I could have mentioned that it is almost guaranteed not to snow at my house in July, but that would have spoiled her fun. Speaking of fun, I checked my watch and realized Ethel was right about one thing. It was almost six. Where had the day gone? Time flies and all that, I guess. I turned from Bony Butt and nodded to Velma Bennett. "I don't believe we've been introduced. I'm Jolene — "

"She knows who you are, hussy," Bony Butt said, wagging a gnarled finger at me. "It's because of that slut mother of yours that Velma's beloved husband is dead."

Beloved husband? Oh, please. And his death was my mother's fault? Anger prickled up my back and curled my lip. "Don't you dare blame my mother for any of this," I said, dropping any pretense of being willing to put up with her abuse. "My guess is, Ethel, that you've got a mouthful of sour grapes since Lucille is the popular one and you're not."

Bony Butt's head started twitching and fireballs sprayed from her eyes. "I'd never go with a married man, and I'd surely not parade myself around like a tramp."

"No, I can see you're having way too much fun being a fire and brimstone nut case."

"Now, see here," Velma said, almost forcefully. "That kind of talk is uncalled for. You might have taken your schooling here, Miss Jackson, but surely you realize you're not one of us."

Yes, that much had been abundantly clear for many years.

A burst of laughter from the back booth saved me from further explaining my disdain. I turned to see Gifford Geller waving a hand in my direction, motioning me over to his table. "Ethel," he hollered to

Bony Butt. "Leave the girl alone. She doesn't have to put up with your caterwauling. Everybody in town knows you're jealous of Lucille."

While Bony Butt sputtered and Velma patted her hand, I marched on back and slid into the booth across from the acting mayor of Kickapoo, Texas. I didn't need to introduce myself because he obviously knew me, but I didn't know where to start the conversation either.

"I knew your dad pretty well," he said, eliminating my initial problem. "We worked together out at the county."

Yes, I knew that much, but I also knew Dad didn't think much of Giff. Called him a loudmouth with a big ego and a little brain, or something along those lines. I couldn't quibble with the assessment, but I could sure add mean to the list. The set of his pudgy jaw and the coldness in his eyes, even when he laughed, made me think he could be cruel if it suited him.

"Yeah, sure do miss ol' Bertram. Don't have nobody leaning over my shoulder telling me what a dumb ass I am, if you'll pardon my talk."

I nodded and shrugged all at the same time. This was not exactly where I'd figured this conversation would go, and saying ugly things about my father wasn't bowling me over with good will. "So," I said, resisting the urge to agree that he was a dumb ass, "what's it like being mayor now?" This seemed to catch him off guard and change his thoughts to something other than how awful my dad had treated him. I doubted Dad had done or said anything to Gifford that I wouldn't have. Actually, I'm sure he would have been a whole lot nicer. "Is it everything you hoped it would be?"

After a few more seconds, he took a sip of his coffee and shrugged. "Ain't much to it. BigJohn made it a big deal when it didn't have to be. I'm mostly just trying to straighten out all the things he messed up."

That statement pretty much jibed with what Lucille had said, so I followed it out a little more. "So you're dropping the city permit thing?"

He snorted. "First thing I did when I walked in the door. Dumbest thing I ever heard of."

"I guess that made Dewayne pretty happy."

"I wouldn't know about that." He fiddled with the handle on his coffee cup and drummed his fingers on the table. "Don't think he probably even knows about it. Guess I ought to tell him."

"You mean you didn't tell him at the funeral?"

Gifford shifted in his seat just a little. "Nah, didn't figure it was really the time for business."

Then it must have been the time for cracking jokes because they'd both sure been having a grand old time. "I'm headed over to Dewayne's in a few minutes," I said. "I'll mention it to him if it's okay."

"Oh, sure. No secret. That's one thing I'm not gonna have is a bunch of secret deals going on like that dumb shit Bennett. Pardon again."

Yes, well, that remained to be seen. "Too bad the city water deal's already gone through though. Sure would have been nice not to have to build a new treatment plant."

"Well, now, that's a whole 'nother issue. Can't say that we don't need a new plant." He lowered his voice to a near whisper. "But I'm figuring on getting a better deal from ol' Velma on those lots."

A variety of questions hit me at once, some of them not really fully formed, more bits and snippets of whys and what-ifs. Okay, I'll admit it. I did wonder if Giff might have killed BigJohn so he could get the lots cheaper from Velma. The theory didn't fly too well, but maybe it was only one feather on the wing, so to speak. And that was the real problem. I had plenty of theories available, but none of them were quite ready to soar with the eagles. I tried again. "So, say you get the lots at a good deal, won't you still have to hold a vote on a bond issue for the water plant?"

He rubbed a weathered hand across his equally weathered face. "That's one way of doing it, sure, but taxes are going to go up no matter what. Seems better to save the city the cost of an election and just figure out how to pay for it now."

"Aren't you required to put something like that to the people for a vote?"

"Not necessarily. There's ways around these things." He paused a minute and frowned. "How come you're so interested in all this? Planning on moving back?"

Oh, no. Hell no. I forced my hackles down and leaned back a little in the booth. "Just curious mostly. But, like everyone else around here, I'm wondering who killed BigJohn and who tried to kill my mother and me. The former mayor had created so many controversial issues with the city, I thought that might figure into it somehow."

Giff took another sip of hot coffee. "Don't waste your time on political matters. That don't play into the killings, er, killing, I mean. The goings on at city hall didn't have nothing to do with it."

"You sound awfully certain. How can you be so sure?"

He chuckled. "Because ain't nobody trying to kill me."

Yet. Or maybe he didn't have to worry about that because he was the killer or at least knew he was safe from the killer since they were in cahoots on all of this. The scenario had potential. I stood. "Nice to meet you, Mister Geller."

He stood also. "Call me Giff. Now, you need anything, little lady, you just give me a call up at the city hall. Do whatever I can to help you and Lucille out. Always liked Lucille." He winked.

I shuddered and gave him an "in your dreams, buddy" kind of chuckle. Then, without further ado or adios, I hurried from the room. About the time I turned the key to start the car, it occurred to me that something was missing that I should take note of. I glanced around the parking lot and noticed we were short a couple of white sedans. Specifically, a Lincoln Town Car and a Chevy Caprice.

Bony Butt and Velma the nongrieving widow had vanished.

<hr>

Chapter
Fourteen

W hen I finally located Walnut Street, I didn't have to guess about which house was Dewayne's. Odds were pretty darned good that it was the one with the sheriff's car parked in front and a crowd of people clustered in the yard. I had highly unpleasant feelings about the reason for the activity, but held out a glimmer of hope that I was wrong. Maybe Dewayne was just having a going away party or something. Or something would have been my real guess.

The house was little more than a square box with a drooping two-post porch on the front. The weathered gray clapboard siding showed a few hints that it might have been covered in white paint at one time, but that time was probably twenty or thirty years ago. And this was where a prominent arms dealer and homebuilder lived? Not exactly lapping up the luxury with his earnings.

I took my time wandering up to the crowd, looking for a semi-friendly face to quiz. Unfortunately, a decidedly unfriendly Harper face spotted me first and came waddling through the weeds in pursuit. Larry was not smiling. He was, however, spitting.

"Guess you were right about old Dee-Wayne," he said, shaking his head and working his lump of tobacco around in his mouth.

"What do you mean?"

"Poor bastard hung himself."

That familiar sick feeling swelled up in my stomach. "He did? Are you sure?"

"Well, I'm pretty sure he hung himself since there was a rope still around his neck."

I'd seen enough old photos of outlaw hangings to have a general idea of the end product, and it was nothing I wanted to see firsthand. Just the imagined image did nothing for my already-queasy stomach. I turned away, hoping I didn't embarrass myself by throwing up. This was the very thing I was supposed to have prevented. Aside from all the personal guilt, and there was a staggering amount of that to be dealt with, how was I going to break the news to Susan? She'd blame me for not coming sooner. Hell, I blamed me for not coming sooner, amongst a thousand other things I'd probably done wrong. While I pondered what I should have done, and what I had to do now, my mood got blacker by the second. I had really blown it this time. And I was literally sick about it. I shouldn't have allowed myself to be dragged into this, but no, I'd jumped right on the chance to talk to Dewayne — at any cost. Dammit all.

Part-time deputy Larry Harper stood beside me, seemingly oblivious to my inner turmoil as well as the fact that a man had just killed himself. "Yep," he said between spits. Expectorating was apparently his emotional outlet. "It's a good thing Miz Bennett and Miz Fossy overheard you telling Gifford you were headed over to Dee-Wayne's. Of course, it ain't really all that good since he'd already hung himself before we got here. But it was good they called."

I turned back toward him. "They called you?"

He nodded and spat again. "Called into dispatch. I met them here. They was afraid you'd say something to Dee-Wayne and get him all stirred up. With him being upset and all, well, they figured I ought to check it out."

"And you did. For them." My dark mood was broiling into a nice bright crimson. He wouldn't listen to me, but one call from the Wicked Witch of the West and he was falling all over himself to check things out. If I hadn't already been sick, that would have gotten the job done.

I turned on my mental censor and fast-forwarded through most of the ugly stuff, mainly omitting the "you stupid, stupid son of a bitch" introductory line that was just begging to be said. I even took a deep breath and tried to speak calmly. "If you would have just gone with me like I asked, Larry," you moronic stooge, "we could have stopped Dewayne and he'd be alive right now." I exhaled slowly. Having to say what you should instead of what you think takes some work and was just not worth the effort. "If you hadn't been so busy being an arrogant jerk on a power trip, you'd have seen the good sense in pulling your tobacco-stuffed head out of your ass for a measly five minutes and driving over to Dewayne's, but nooooo. You wouldn't listen to me."

Larry narrowed his buggy Harper eyes and his jowls quivered. "Ain't no way you're blaming this on me. Leroy's on his way over to talk to you."

Lovely, just what I've always dreamed of, being tag-teamed by the Harper brothers. I rolled my eyes and crossed my arms. "I don't have to wait for Leroy and you know it."

Larry spit in the dirt then wagged a fat finger at me. "You stay right here until Leroy shows up. I've got enough problems without you running off again. No telling who'd show up dead next."

I resented the implications and would have cheerfully slung gravel in his face as I sped away in my car except for two things: curiosity and stupidity. Actually, in my case, those terms tend to be interchangeable, so I selected two more tangible items: Velma and Bony Butt.

I hadn't noticed them when I first arrived, but there they were, front and center in the crowd, kneeling beside the porch of the shack, just outside the single line of yellow police tape Larry had haphazardly strung from post to post. The ladies were praying, I presumed, for Dewayne's recently departed soul.

I have to confess that public religious displays always strike a chord with me, something like one of those pulsing dissonant chords that sound real scary in a haunted house. My gut reaction is usually to turn tail and run, but today I was overcome by either morbid curiosity or, as my old ruler-wielding Sunday school teacher once said, the hand of Satan. It's kind of hard to walk hand in hand with the devil when you don't believe in such things, but I decided to give it my best shot and moseyed on up to the two-body prayer circle. Besides, it beat standing out in the sun feeling guilty about dead Dewayne.

Respectfully waiting until the final duet of amens had been said, I stepped toward them to be the kind and courteous person I really am. I held out an arm to each and said, "Let me give you a hand, ladies."

Bony Butt's head snapped up and her beady eyes locked onto me like a heat-seeking missile. Then, her hands started waving and slapping, and her lips sputtered unintelligible noises. "You, you, heathen! Get away from us! Git!" She leaned toward Velma. "Lord protect us and keep us safe."

Meaning from me, I had to presume, and it peeved me just a tad. I stepped back a little. "Hey, I was only trying to be helpful."

Ethel quit swatting long enough to grab onto Velma and start them shuffling to their feet. "We don't need your kind of help around here," Bony Butt said, scrambling and weaving with Velma. They made it to a standing position rather ungracefully, and both looked like red-faced plums by the time they got the job done, Bony Butt being the shriveled tough variety. I would have been glad to help them, but no, that would have been a sacrilege or something.

Velma Bennett dusted off the front of her gray dress, and looked at me blandly, no scowling, no nothing, nor did she speak. Bony Butt, on the other hand, had gotten her nice brown slacks all covered with dirt and weeds, but she had her attention focussed elsewhere, namely on me.

I sighed rather heavily, having a pretty good idea what was coming next.

"You, you, heathen!" she screeched, right on cue. Her face was all screwed up and she was shaking a fist at said heathen. "We knew you were up to something when you starting quizzing Jimmie Sue and then went right over and told Gifford you were going after poor old Dee-Wayne. And now just look what's happened."

Trying to make sense of Bony Butt gives me a headache, but best I could tell she was going to blame me for "poor old Dee-Wayne's" death, not that I wasn't doing the same thing, but for less dubious reasons. "I've never been introduced to Dee-Wayne," I said, using the local pronunciation because I kept hearing it so darned often. "And I surely never have talked to him, so I don't know what you're trying to imply, Ethel, dear."

She apparently doesn't much care for me calling her Ethel as her eyes tended to flame a little brighter at my impertinence. Fossy was kind of hard to get my tongue around, however, and I suspected it would come out as "fussy" if I tried it in the heat of the moment. Then again, it was kinder than the "bony-butted bitch" option that was crossing my mind at the moment.

Ethel edged closer and wagged her fist again. "Nothing good has happened since you set foot in this town." Velma nodded beside her, but not with much enthusiasm. "I just knew something bad was going to come of this. I just knew it."

I could have asked her just how she "knew" these things, and drummed up what would no doubt be an interesting conversation regarding psychic abilities and/or Satan's charms, but I decided to pass. What I really wanted to know was exactly when Dewayne had done this to himself. Or, more specifically, had he already killed himself before Susan showed up at my mother's? That would at least lessen my guilt over going to the DQ instead of directly to his house. Lessen it a little anyway. "So, you were the ones who found Dewayne?"

"Well, of course. We came right over after we heard you talking," Ethel said. "We were coming to witness to him and turn him to the ways of the Lord."

"But we were too late," Velma intoned matter-of-factly. "He was already dead. Nothing to be done for it."

These two were taking this pretty well. If I'd been the one to find him, I doubted I'd be so nonchalant about the whole thing. Shouldn't they be a little traumatized by finding Dewayne dangling from a rope? Or maybe it had been an electric cord, or some kind of construction material? What had he hung himself with? And did they cut him down or leave him hanging there? I had a ton of questions I wanted answered, and then again I didn't. The less I knew the easier it would be to deal with. Yes, I needed to distance myself from the guilt.

"Deputy Harper, Larry that is, called Redwater for an ambulance," Velma volunteered evenly. "It should be here in about twenty minutes, or maybe fifteen now."

"You get on out of here," Bony Butt butted in, swatting her hands around as if shooing flies. "We don't want the likes of you around here stirring up trouble. This is just one more awful thing that's happened since you showed up."

I started to mention that the trouble had been stirred long before I arrived, but didn't waste my breath. "Okay, you're right, Miz Fossy. I should go home. But since I can't, why don't you tell me what made you two sneak out of the DQ and scurry over here?"

"Because when I heard what you said to Mayor Geller, I knew something awful was bound to happen, and I asked the Lord what I should do. He told me you were up to something and I should get over here right away." Bony Butt's face screwed up a little tighter. "And He was right. Just looked what happened."

"Amen." Velma didn't have the zealous rage of her bony-butted friend. In fact, I couldn't see that widow Bennett had much emotion at all. And my mother was right. She was very plain looking, kind of a frumpy Aunt Bea with a really tight perm. I was not impressed with either the woman or her choice in friends. And she hadn't really answered my question, not that I knew exactly what I'd expected her to say. People were doing things for reasons, but those reasons didn't seem to make much sense. Surprise, surprise.

Ethel Fossy turned toward Widow Bennett and her scowl lightened into a concerned frown. "Come on, Velma, honey," she cooed. "You haven't been yourself lately, and this is all just too much for you." Bony Butt took her friend by the arm. "Let's get you away from all this, this, commotion."

Meaning me, I presumed, so I smiled.

"You ought to be ashamed," Bony Butt hissed back. Then, she dragged Velma away toward their cars.

"Yeah, Jolene," said another familiar and unpleasant voice. "You ought to be ashamed."

I let out a long and weary sigh and turned to face my accuser. "Leroy. How not nice to see you again. How's the head?"

Acting-sheriff Leroy automatically rubbed at the bandage, which was mostly hanging just below the band of his official brown deputy hat. "My brother says you took off from the house to go looking for Dee-Wayne, and the next thing he knows Ethel Fossy's calling saying Dee-Wayne's dead."

There was no point in explaining anything, I'd at least learned that much, but I felt compelled to respond in hopes of circumventing at least one stupid question. "Apparently, Leroy, I was at the Dairy Queen while Dewayne was busy doing himself in, or maybe he'd already done the dirty deed before I left the house. I don't know. But you're not going to listen to a thing I say, so just move along to the next idiotic thought that leaps to your tongue."

He frowned a little harder. "Just what did you say to old Dee-Wayne to make him want to kill himself?"

I got the stupid question anyway. "Even you are smarter than that, Leroy. The pecan tree is smarter than that." I paused for a minute to let him catch up. "Nothing I've ever said has made you jump up and run kill yourself."

Leroy recognized that I was insulting him and squinted his eyes real mean-like at me. "Just answer the question, Jolene. This here is yet another official investigation you've got yourself mixed up in and you better start talking or I'll haul you over to Bowman City and let you sit in the jail for awhile."

Yeah right. I suppressed the urge to roll my eyes. "Okay, Leroy, here's the deal. I've never spoken to Dewayne Schuman in my entire life. Not today, not yesterday, not the day before, not a year ago, not five years ago."

He adjusted his hat a little against the sun and wiped a little sweat from his eyes. "I ain't gonna listen to your smart-alecky talk, Jolene, just answer the damn questions like you're supposed to."

I was grateful I had stayed in an errant patch of shade from the house, but I didn't move over and offer to share. "I answered the question, Leroy. I have never spoken with Dewayne Schuman in my whole entire life."

"Then what were you doing coming over here out of the blue?"

I debated how much I should tell, but Larry already knew Susan had been by Mother's so Leroy would also know it, eventually, maybe. "I was coming over here to check on him because his sister asked — "

"Holy damn," he muttered, shaking his head. "She talked you into checking on him, didn't she?"

I was getting just a little tired of these guys acting like I was an idiot for trying to be helpful. Further, I didn't appreciate the insinuation that Susan had conned me into doing something I didn't really want to do. The woman was worried about her brother, for godsakes, and I had tried to help. Not exactly a crime, but if I thought about it very long, I sure felt pretty darned criminal, although not in Leroy's sense of the word. True, I didn't know Dewayne, or Susan, for that matter, but this was a very sad deal no matter how you looked at it. A man was dead because nobody wanted to listen to his sister's concerns. Growing up, I'd always wished for a brother or sister of my very own. I know my own kids fought like crazed panthers when they were little, but now they really seemed to like one another. And they'd have each other as they grew older. Other than my mother and a few aunts, my kids were my only family. Family. And exactly who was going to break this news to Susan?

"As it turned out, Leroy. Susan was right. And if I were her, I'd be thinking of what number I wanted to put before the word million in a lawsuit I'd have my attorney fast and furiously working on."

Leroy snorted, a really pig-like sound. "That dyke won't be suing nobody, not if she knows what's good for her."

The wail of sirens kept me from asking him for an explanation of his terse statement, not that he would have given me one anyway.

From the sound of the siren, the ambulance was closing in, maybe only seconds away, which meant it was time for me to make a discreet and rapid exit. I didn't want to be here for any of what was about to transpire. I nodded to Leroy. "If you had any sense whatsoever, you'd get these people out of here before the paramedics come in. And, by the way, don't crime scene or forensics people need to go through the place first? I'm not an expert or anything, but since Dewayne was involved in an ongoing murder investigation, shouldn't you be considering this death just a little suspicious?"

Leroy looked a little taken aback, and I was sure if he had a deputy's handbook, he'd have been rabidly flipping through it. But since he didn't, he was forced to wing it and pretend he knew what he was doing. "This here ain't a murder, Jolene, and you don't know what you're talking about. Larry said it was plain as day that Leroy hung himself and that's that. Besides, Ethel Fossy said the same thing. No need in dragging out the Redwater boys for something cut and dried like this. I don't go around making up trouble where it don't exist."

Unlike me was the obvious continuation of that thought, but I didn't bite. No, I just nodded, thinking of how Jerry was going to hit the roof when he heard about this little breach of protocol. Or maybe, he'd just hit Leroy. I smiled, sort of. "I'm going back to my mother's now, Leroy, and you're going to leave me alone, got it?" He didn't look like he was getting much of anything except heat stroke, so I added, "I sure hope I'm around when Jerry finds out how bad you've screwed things up."

With Leroy sputtering behind me, I marched to the Tahoe, fired it up and headed it toward my mother's.

I made it back to Lucille's driveway before the air conditioner had even started cooling the baked interior, but the few short, sweltering minutes in the car had given me plenty of time to come to a variety of conclusions. The main one being that I'd had enough of this place and wanted out. Now. I left the car running — and the blessed air conditioner on high — and ran into the house. I gave Mother a brief synopsis of Dewayne's supposed suicide and Leroy's crime scene contamination, causing her to shake her head and cluck her tongue at the absurdity of it all. But when I told her to grab her purse, she didn't leap to her feet and race through the house. In fact, she just sat there, staring at me.

"Well, Jolene, what you said about Dee-Wayne is just awful, but why does that mean we have to run off right now?"

I had about a thousand reasons, but at least half of them concerned being fed up with the present locale and its residents, so I decided to skip those. I relayed my concerns, sticking to the basic fact that people were dropping like flies for one reason or another, and bullets were buzzing faster than that, and well, I'd just had enough of all of it.

She didn't look ready to chime in and agree with me so I tried another tack. "Right now, we don't have a guard in the yard. Let's get out of here while we can."

She reached for her purse, opened it and dug through, checking to see that she had whatever it was she deemed essential. "I certainly wouldn't mind a little break from being locked in the house. It was certainly refreshing to go to the mall. How long do you think we'll be gone?"

"A month at the most."

Mother's perfectly drawn eyebrows shot up. "Now, Jolene..."

The more I talked, the better it sounded, and the more eager I got to hit the road. I could almost smell the pine trees, not to mention the freedom. "After I stop by to see Jerry, I'm packing up and heading back to Colorado and you're going with me."

Lucille turned toward me and narrowed her eyes. "I most certainly am not. This is my home and nobody's going to run me off from it. Besides, I don't take that mountain altitude well at all, and you know it."

"Well, it's a hell of a lot easier to take than obtuse rednecks on power trips and homicidal maniacs with guns. People are dropping like flies, Mother."

"Enough about the flies, Jolene. I get the point. And I don't know why this thing with Dee-Wayne has gotten you so stirred up. It's not like somebody shot him. You said he killed himself."

"So said Ethel Fossy. Do you believe anything she says? She's the one who found him. How do you know she didn't make Dewayne shoot the mayor, shoot at us, and then make him hang himself for his sinfulness. Or maybe she hung him herself. Or maybe he was dead before she strung him up. Shit, I don't know!" I knew I'd gone a little overboard, but if you'd been in my shoes, you'd have been diving pretty deep, too. The fact of the matter was that this was getting to me. I just couldn't help it. And the thought of fleeing the place made me just a tad hyper, if I were to be objective about the situation, which I saw no need to be.

Lucille stood, grabbed her purse, clutched her bandaged arm and started walking toward the door. "Well, Jolene, I think you had one good idea mixed in there somewhere. Let's drive on in to town to the hospital." She clicked her sandals haughtily across the linoleum toward the back door. "I'm sure they've got some kind of medication that'll settle you down."

"Is that so?" I clopped along right behind her. "Well, then, Mother, since we're going that way anyway, maybe we should stop by and check out that nice new nursing home out on the highway, hmmm?

"Just get in the car, Jolene."

"Just get in the car, Jolene," I mimicked childishly, snagging a Dr Pepper from the fridge as I hurried by.

———⟫●⟪———

Chapter Fifteen

We drove in silence toward Redwater Falls, both stewing for different reasons. I do not enjoy fighting with my mother, but I'm also not real fond of having to muddle my way through this alternate universe that she calls home.

We arrived at the hospital without saying a single word to one another, but we did arrive safely. I made several passes through the parking lot until I spied one slot that had a sliver of shade from a gangly tree in the median. I squeezed the Tahoe between two compacts, shifted into park, but left the car running. "Look, Mother, I'm sorry about being cranky. This hasn't been the most pleasant of situations to deal with, and you know how I get sometimes."

"I know exactly," she said rather tartly. "I've lived with you for forty-three years."

I was compelled to mention that I'd lived with her for an equal amount of time but gritted a little enamel off my teeth instead. "So, are you going in with me to see Jerry?"

She shook her head and patted her hair with her good hand. "No, I'll just sit here for a few minutes. If you're not back shortly I'll turn off the car and sit in the lobby where it's cool."

I nodded and opened the door. "There are some CDs in the console if you want to listen to any."

"Zoloft."

I leaned back inside. "Who?"

"Zoloft. It's not a who, it's a what. Little tiny blue things. I think it takes a while to build up in your system, so the sooner you get started on it the better."

It dawned on me what she was talking about and I was not amused. "Sure, Mom, and while I'm inside getting all antidepressed, you can skim through my latest copy of Kevorkian Quarterly. It's in the backseat there."

"That's not the least bit funny, Jolene," she said, tipping up her chin.

"I'm not laughing," I said, closing the driver's side door. I marched around the back of the Tahoe, opened the cargo doors, and fished out a bottle. I held it up over the seat and rattled it. "St. John's wort, Mother, will that do?" She didn't answer. I unscrewed the bottled and poured myself some. "I'm taking three of them. Are you happy now?"

Lucille did not turn around. "I will be if they work. You're just entirely too wound up."

Wound up? Okay, maybe a little. And truth be told, I kind of hoped they'd work, too, but I didn't tell her that. Maybe things would appear rosier through wort-colored eyeballs and my deteriorating attitude would improve as well. Maybe I'd even start thinking dodging bullets and guessing who was going to wind up dead next was great fun. Or maybe I wouldn't just rip the throat out of the next person who looked at me crossways.

I said an overly sweet bye-bye to mommy dearest and hustled myself into the hospital. After a quick stop by the water fountain in the lobby, I was herbed-up and ready to go. If I was lucky, I might have calm and peaceful thoughts in less than half an hour.

I headed up the elevator to the fourth floor and made my way to Jerry's room. The door was propped open, so I peaked inside before barging in. It took me a couple of blinks to realize that not only was the bed empty, the room was empty as well. No flowers, plants, balloons or IV rack. Panic grabbed me by the throat. He wasn't well enough to leave the hospital. He'd just gotten out of intensive care. What was going on? I checked the room number again, twice. There was no mistake. Jerry Don Parker was gone.

Trying to stay reasonably calm and sane, I forced myself to walk, or at least not to sprint, down to the nurses' station and discreetly inquired of the two women on duty as to the status of Mr. Jerry Don Parker. The look on their faces did not allay any of my fears, nor did the fact that they both started scrambling to find out what had happened to their patient. The registration office provided an official time of departure, eleven-o-eight a.m., but no doctor's release. And nobody had any personal knowledge of any of it. Great.

The issue was still being hotly debated when I stomped off. It was either a big-time staff snafu, a planned escape or an abduction. In any case, I knew the identity of his accomplice because, to quote several eye witnesses, Jerry had been taken away — very sweetly I might add — by a charming and exceptionally pretty blonde woman. Golly gee, do you think it could have been Amy?

And that was the real rub. If he needed somebody to spring him, why hadn't he asked me?

I sat in the hospital parking lot with the car running and my face smashed against the air conditioner vent by the door. I felt like pounding something or crying. Both, actually. I knew I had no right, but I was just flat furious. To my credit, I just kept my face in the cold air and gritted my teeth, not making even one snide remark. I didn't want my mother to know how mad — and hurt — I was.

She knew anyway.

"You may as well rant and rave, Jolene. Bad for your blood pressure to keep it all in. You did take your pills, didn't you?"

I growled in response. Yes, I had, but I darn sure wasn't taking another one of the stinking things. I wanted to be mad, thank you very much.

"Whenever you're up to it," Lucille said evenly, maybe even compassionately, although I wasn't up to recognizing it. "We can just drive on out to Amy's place and see what's going on. Jerry Don built a nice big house out on the Bowman City highway, about two miles out of town. He's done real well for himself, you know, although she did get the house in the divorce."

I didn't say a word, just pried myself away from the vent and put the car in gear. Fine, I'd go see Amy's nice big house, yes, indeed I would. What I did after the look-see, well, I couldn't say, we'd all just have to be surprised. I might have punched the gas pedal a tad too hard because Lucille yelped and her head kind of bounced back against the headrest. I muttered a sincere "sorry" as I sped out toward the Bowman City highway.

When mother pointed out the house, I hit the brakes and swung into a long driveway that curved up in front of the house. Amy lived in a fancy, Texas-style brick model with a huge, crown-like roof that seemed almost as big as the structure beneath it. The house was upscale for the area, or even the county, and I had to wonder just how Jerry's salary had funded the project. Then again, he hadn't always been a small-town county sheriff. Still, any way you looked at it, Amy Parker had done right fine in the divorce settlement, and I was not at all happy for her.

I left the car running with Mother inside and walked, okay maybe trudged is a better word, up to the front door, the two-sided door with custom leaded glass. I say custom because you generally don't buy double doors with an etched scene of whitetail deer spread across both sides and surrounded by beveled glass pieces of various shapes and colors off the rack at Home Depot.

No, I was neither bitter nor jealous. I'm not the type.

After ringing the doorbell, knocking and playing peeping tom at every custom-covered window I could reach, I finally accepted the fact that no one was home. If Amy had picked Jerry up at the hospital, and really, who else could it have been, she surely hadn't brought him home with her. It would have been the most logical option, so naturally it hadn't occurred.

I felt a not-so-gentle stab of fear. Why wasn't Jerry here, really? And furthermore, where was he? Something wasn't right. Not right at all. Maybe Amy took him to his own place, the location of which was not on my mother's list of knowns, or mine for that matter, although I knew he lived in Bowman City. We didn't send cards and letters to each other, just talked on the phone. I hopped back in the car, relayed the obvious and grabbed my cell phone. I punched in Jerry's number and waited. After four rings, the message machine picked up. A little shiver ran up my back at the sound of his voice, my usual involuntary reaction to that deep Texas drawl. His message was brief, but when the tone sounded, I hung up. What was I going to say anyway?

"Why'd you hang up?" Lucille asked, clicking her nails on the armrest.

"Well, I don't know. What did you want me to do, say 'Sorry you decided to run off with your ex-wife. Call when you have time?'"

"You don't know the situation. Assuming the worst isn't going to help. Regardless of what's going on with Amy, we need to talk to him if it's at all possible."

"Fine." I punched redial and waited for the tone. "Jerry, this is Jolene." I tried to sound real cheery, like I wasn't worried sick or sickly jealous, which of course I wasn't. "If you get this message, please give me a call on my cell phone." I gave him the number, said I hoped he was feeling better and hung up before I blathered on about things that did not need to be said.

"I suppose we should drive on out to his house, just to be sure," Lucille said. "Do you think you can find it? I don't know my way around Bowman City very well."

Aside from the obvious telephone book source, I was fully confident that I could ascertain directions to Jerry's house at the Bowman City DQ — I have a way with folks, you know — but I didn't think that would do much good. I had the distinct feeling that even after I found his house, I still wouldn't find Jerry Don Parker.

I rustled around in my billfold until I found Jerry's card. I grabbed my cell phone again and punched in the number for the sheriff's department. "I'm going to try Pam Marshall. Maybe she knows what's going on."

Lucille nodded. "That's a good idea, Jolene. Real good. You be sure and tell her we're out and about after running off from her deputies while you're at it."

Yikes. Good point. I started to hang up, but I really had to know that Jerry was okay. When the phone answered, I asked a lady, who sounded like she didn't much like her job, if I could speak to Deputy Marshall. The answer came quick and sharp. No, I couldn't speak to Deputy Marshall because she was not on duty. And no, I couldn't talk to Deputy Bob either. I'd almost called him Stalker Bob, but managed to admit I couldn't remember his actual last name. The lady on the phone remembered just fine and curtly informed me that Deputy Travers was on a call and wouldn't be available for quite a while and, well, just exactly who was I and what did I want anyway?

Before I could think of Plan C, Acting Sheriff Leroy Harper came on the line. "Jolene, is that you? Where are you?"

"Hi, Leroy," I said with a very heavy sigh.

He seemed not to notice my displeasure and continued on in a highly enthusiastic voice. "We've been looking everywhere for you and your mother. You okay?"

First, I wondered why he didn't sound his usual hateful self, and secondly, why wasn't he still out at Dewayne's place? That couldn't be over with this soon. My only hope was that Deputy Bob had taken over in Kickapoo and things were getting handled correctly. One could always hope. "We're fine, Leroy."

"Where are you?" he repeated.

I did not answer the "where" part specifically, but explained that we had gone to visit Jerry in the hospital, although we had hit a little snag. "So where is he, Leroy?"

"Now, Jolene, if he's left the hospital, there's no telling where he's gone off to. I didn't go get him or anything." He paused and I could almost hear his brain clicking away at his thoughts. "Have you been over to his house?"

"No, but I called there and no one answered."

"Hmmm," Leroy said, mulling over what I'd said. "Well, maybe he's there at the house and just not answering the phone. Couldn't blame him for that."

No, I couldn't, but I also couldn't imagine him being there, hearing my message and not calling me back. Unless of course sweet Amy was screening calls. "I thought about going over there, but I don't really see the point," I said, although the point had just come to me clear as a blonde bell.

"That's a great idea!" Leroy said. "Heck, I'll even meet you there just to be sure everything's okay. It's real important that you and your mother are kept safe and sound. That's my job, you know, taking care of you two."

Thrown off balance by his abrupt change in demeanor, I didn't really know what to say. He sounded friendly and pretty darned sincere and that scared the living daylights out of me. "Mother and I are just fine, Leroy. No need to worry about us."

"Glad you're fine, but you sure did make a good point about checking out Jerry's house. The more I think about it, the more I'm sure we ought to go over there and see what's going on. But he's gonna be madder than an old wet hen if I show up and you're not with me."

I frowned. Something was very fishy. Very. "So you know for sure he's at the house?"

"Well, I reckon that's where I'd go if I went home from the hospital. I'd go to my house, wouldn't you?" He did not give me a chance to answer, just rattled off directions to Jerry's house and signed off with a hearty "see you there in fifteen minutes."

I hung up the phone and looked at Mother. "Is Leroy a drinker?"

Lucille stared out the window at Amy's fancy red brick house, pursing her lips this way and that. "Leroy's an idiot. I don't know the particulars. What's he trying to pull now?"

"I don't know for sure, but something. He was extremely nice to me on the phone, eager to help."

"Nice, you say. Eager to help." Lucille picked at a curl of Frivolous Fawn, her eyes fixed on the road. "Well, then, I'd have to agree that something's wrong. He's been nothing but trouble through-out this whole thing, and now he's being extra nice? Has to be a reason."

"Maybe he's just trying to win me over so he can arrest me or something because of Dewayne."

Lucille continued to stare out the window and it wasn't likely she was making a list of the shrubs in the flower bed. "That doesn't feel right," she said. "You had nothing to do with that and even he knows it. No, it's something else."

"I'm listening."

"Well, I don't have all the answers, Jolene. I'm just trying to fig-ure this out same as you are." She rubbed her bandaged arm. "It seems to me, we're going to have to go to Jerry Don's place and see what Leroy's up to."

"Oh, I don't think so. Just because he's acting nice now, doesn't mean he really is. A leopard does not change his spots within the span of two hours."

"He does if somebody tells him to," Lucille said, staring at nothing, but the wheels in her mind spinning at a ferocious pace. "We both know that when Leroy thinks for himself, stupid things result. Like accusing you of having something to do with Dewayne's hanging. That's a stupid Leroy thing."

I tapped my fingers on the steering wheel and studied the deer on the leaded glass front doors. One of them was staring straight ahead, ears all perked, at full alert, trying to figure out what was going on. I could certainly relate. "Okay, I follow that much. Go on."

"I'm only making suppositions, of course, but if we go meet Leroy, it seems we might have a little chance of finding out what's really going on, depending on what he tries to do, and who's pulling his strings, and why."

This plan of my mother's had "sitting duck" written all over it and that wasn't one of my favorite games, particularly when it was highly likely gunfire would be involved. "You know, Mother, maybe we ought to limit your input to things like 'Everything's going to be just fine.' Or better yet, 'You just do what you think's best, Jolene.' Yes, I really liked that last one a lot."

Lucille huffed, but otherwise basically ignored the fact that I'd said a word. "It seems pretty clear to me that something has changed since we left Kickapoo, something that made a new man out of Leroy."

She was right, I just didn't want to face the nasty extrapolations that naturally came with the revelation. Leroy had been determined jerk, just looking to cause me trouble. If he hadn't been right beside me when the bullet hit the brick, I could probably find a reason to blame him for just about everything. Then again, if someone was giving him orders, then that meant there were at least two of them involved. Maybe they were taking turns at the targets. And now Leroy was up at bat again.

I turned toward Mother. "What if he's one of the ones behind all this? It makes sense if you add Uncle Fletch into the equation. Leroy shoots BigJohn for Fletch and Fletch nails Jerry for Leroy. I was just the bonus round, I guess."

Lucille nodded. "It's possible, I suppose, although why bother shooting you?"

"Leroy hates me?" I offered, but not with enthusiasm. It was possible I'd asked too many questions or made too many stupid comments to a certain related reporter. That stopped me. "Kimberlee. I threw out all kinds of possibilities as to who killed BigJohn and why. Maybe I got one right."

Lucille went from nodding right along to shaking her head in a highly negative way. "Oh, my, this is bad."

Yes, it was. And sitting here in Amy's driveway chatting wasn't really helping matters. "So do you want to go through Amarillo or cut over to Albuquerque and then head north?"

"We have to go to Jerry Don's house, Jolene," Lucille said. "We've got to get to the bottom of this one way or another. If Leroy's going to try to kill us, we should know pretty quickly, and you'll simply have to outrun him."

I did not see great promise in trying to outrun bullets. "Now that is one heckuva plan, Mother," I muttered, a nasty swarm of butterflies invading my stomach. "But wouldn't it be easier if I just called him back and asked him where he planned to kill us so we could avoid that street?"

"Don't be sarcastic, Jolene, it's unbecoming. Now, hurry up, I'd like to get to Jerry Don's house before Leroy does."

I made the loop around Amy Parker's circular driveway, pulled out onto the highway and headed toward Bowman City. I saw no particular need to hurry, and this apparently did not sit well with my mother.

"You better get a move on it, Jolene, or Leroy's going to beat us there." She craned her neck over and looked at the speedometer. "How fast does this thing go, anyway?"

I accelerated just enough to break the speed limit and shrugged. "I've never had it over about eighty, so I don't really know."

"Hmmm," Mother said, shaking her head again. "My Buick had a governor on it. Just plain quit at a hundred. Hope yours doesn't have one of those things."

I did not ask my mother how she knew her car "just plain quit" at one hundred miles per hour nor did I ask her to elaborate on the past tense she so deftly used. The answers were obvious and I didn't need to dwell on the visual of my mother flying her Buick down the highway at 110 miles per hour. I also did not put the pedal to the metal to see if my own vehicle was equipped with auto-kill, figuring that was something I preferred not to know.

Following Leroy's directions, we wound up near the edge of town a small white house with forest green trim. Not even a distant relative to the upscale place Amy lived in, but neat with a big yard. He'd chosen it for the kids, no doubt.

A maroon sedan pulled up and parked in the street a few houses down, but there weren't any other suspicious-looking vehicles cruising the neighborhood — if you didn't count the blue Tahoe.

My stomach growled, reminding me that I hadn't eaten, being preoccupied with various other issues. I also hadn't realized how late it had gotten. It was getting dark quickly, and when I looked at the clock on the dash, I knew why. Eight fifteen didn't allow for much time to use the sunlight. The night closing in didn't do anything to ease my worries, but it did pretty much guarantee no one was in Jerry's house. All the curtains in the house were drawn closed and I couldn't see a flicker of light or any signs of movement inside. "So what now?" I said to Lucille.

"Well," Lucille said, glancing around. "I'll bet you dollars to donuts that Jerry Don is not in that house nor has he been since he was shot in my breakfast nook, if indeed this is the right house."

"I agree."

"I've got a funny feeling," Lucille said, her eyes still scanning this way and that. "Maybe we ought to get on out of here."

I caught a flash of white in my rear view mirror. "Too late. Leroy's here."

Lucille eyed the patrol car moving steadily toward us. "Turn around and head toward him."

"You want me to talk to the moron or should I just stop in the middle of the road and be real still so he gets a good shot?"

Lucille frowned. "He's not going to shoot us right here in the middle of the neighborhood, Jolene." She paused and I swear I heard her mind say "I don't think." "Besides, we don't have much choice now. This is our chance to see what he's got up his sleeve."

A forty-four mag would be my first guess, but then maybe he was a thirty-eight kind of guy. Someone out there sure was. Nevertheless, I whipped the Tahoe around in the middle of the street, ever grateful for the short turning radius. Facing the sheriff's cruiser sent my stomach to fluttering again, but I crept toward Leroy anyway, determined to play the hand we'd dealt. "I'll try to smile real pretty so he won't shoot me right away, okay?"

"You do that, Jolene," Lucille said, clutching her purse with her good hand and otherwise ignoring my sarcasm.

I stayed on the right side of the road and pulled to a stop beside the cruiser, which had also stopped, so my window was directly across from Leroy's. To give him a really good shot, I supposed. Trying not to shake, I rolled down my window, putting me less than two feet from the grinning acting sheriff. He was wiggling around in his seat like he had a nest of fire ants in his underwear and he was hugging the steering wheel like it was a life preserver. His obvious anxiety pulsed out in shivering waves, and I was getting more uneasy by the second. He was worried about something, so therefore I was worried — and just as nervous. Unfortunately, this condition tends to compel me to make either smart ass comments or inane chatter. Feeling highly unclever at the moment, I jumped right in with the inane. "Doesn't look like Jerry's home, Leroy," I said, shivering as if I were chilled. "Guess we drove all the way over here for nothing."

Leroy rubbed his trembling fat fingers across his primary chin, wriggling the extra chins beneath. "Well, maybe we ought to go take a look-see inside just to be sure."

I smiled and tried to cough up a believable chuckle. "That's okay. I appreciate you trying to include us in this, but we need to get on back to the house. But knowing you're checking things out makes me feel better." I almost choked. I'm not a very good liar or a suck-up. "Give me a call and let me know what you find out, would ya? I'm really worried about Jerry." At least that last part was one hundred percent true.

Leroy shifted in the seat and blinked rapidly. "Now, Jolene, don't you go running off. Jerry might be in the house and need our help."

He didn't sound very convinced of his own theory, and I had long ago discounted the possibility of Jerry being anywhere near here. No, Leroy wanted to get us in that house for a completely different reason, and I was positive it was not a good reason. "Maybe you should call for backup or something. I'm just no good at this kind of thing. Why don't you give Deputy Bob a call, see if he's finished with his call. I bet he'd be just pleased as punch to go in with you. I'm not a professional, you know."

Leroy's smile vanished, and I finally noticed he no longer had a patch over his eye, although the newly uncovered one was twitching fiercely. "Pull on back up to the house, Jolene," he barked. "Hurry up, now."

He was getting serious and that was not a good thing. I had to do something. "Hey," I said as cheery as I could, and seemingly oblivious to the fact that he was as jumpy as a cat and I was the mouse in the crosshairs. "You got your patch off. How's that eye feeling? Still got stitches?"

Leroy rubbed a significantly smaller bandage on his forehead, but didn't comment on his medical condition. "Jerry'd want you to do what I said, Jolene." Sweat trickled down his face. "Come on, now. Just do as I said."

This was bad. Really bad.

"I'm not doing anything that goon says," Mother hissed. "Get us out of here. Now."

I kept my eyes on Leroy, and I did not like what I saw. He looked more worried by the second, and itchy, maybe even ready to panic, which meant he was likely to make a move quickly. I didn't know if he was about to leap from the car and grab me, or just point and shoot, nor did I want to find out. I tried to smile a little. "Okay, Leroy, whatever you say. Let me make the block and I'll meet you at the door. I know you're right." I tried to smile sweetly. "If Jerry is in there, he'd be really ticked if I didn't stop and say hi."

Leroy's eyes widened and he smiled widely, wiping the sweat from his twitching eye. "That's right. Mighty ticked." He let out a big whoosh of air and reached down toward the floorboard.

I had already decided I didn't want to know what he was grabbing at, but when I saw his arm come up, along with a reflection of metal, I knew it was time to leave. Quickly.

"Did you see that?" Mother whispered, having apparently seen the same flash. "He's going for his gun. Step on it."

I tried not to panic. I just smiled, hit the button for the electric window and pulled forward. I resisted the urge to leave rubber on the road and drove slowly away, watching my mirror to see what Leroy was going to do. Then, I turned at the corner like I'd said I would. I did not, however, make the block. As soon as we were out of Leroy's sight, I punched down the gas pedal, headed straight for the highway and hoped like hell I didn't have a governor on the Tahoe.

Chapter
Sixteen

Lucille was wedged around, leaning between the bucket seats, watching out the back window at the patrol car following along at Mach nine behind us. "You've got to go faster, Jolene," she said, a quiver of either panic or excitement in her voice. "He's gonna catch us."

I kept my eyes on the road, sparing only an occasional glance for the speedometer. I had no idea where we were headed, but by golly I wanted to live to get there. Another glance. Ninety-six. Geez. I'd never gone this fast in my whole life. And it was not that much fun. "I'm not going any faster, Mother. I just can't. This road does curve every now and then and we're not gonna curve with it."

"Well, Jolene, you've got to do something or he's going to be right on our bumper in about two minutes."

My nerves were wired just about as tight as my grip on the steering wheel. Damned worthless worts. "If he wants to catch us, I just don't think I can keep him from it."

I'd already had about six minutes of pure terror, wondering if I was going to make it around the next curve in the road, and consequently, my fear of Leroy was beginning to pale. Body parts strewn amongst crumpled pieces of Tahoe was my primary fear of the moment. I wasn't sure, but I didn't think blood would do the gray leather seats any good at all. "I've got to slow this thing down before I kill us."

"No, ma'am," Lucille said, turning back around in the seat. "You just keep driving and don't let off on that gas pedal. You just drive and I'll do the thinking."

I thought we'd already covered that chain of command, but I didn't have time to restate the rules, not that it would have made even the tiniest bit of difference to my mother.

Lucille clucked her tongue. "I don't know what on earth is going on here. I swear that Leroy was gonna pull a gun on us back there and shoot us dead. That boy has completely lost his mind."

"Well, Mother, we're going ninety-six running from the sheriff. I don't think that speaks highly of our own mental health."

"I don't see that we have a choice. We got out of there just in time. Another three seconds and Lord knows what he would have done." Lucille reached down, grabbed her purse from the floorboard and plopped it into her lap. After a few seconds of digging, she pulled out a cell phone and started punching in numbers.

And just exactly when did Lucille leap into the wireless information age? "I didn't know you had a mobile phone. You've been using mine the whole time I've been here, acting like it's something out of 'Star Wars.'"

"Well, Jolene, I don't have a fancy one like yours. Mine's very simple. And it's only for emergencies. I'm using it now because I believe this qualifies as an emergency. Besides, I'm on a fixed income and I don't need some outrageous phone bill to upset my budget. I'm sure you have all kinds of free minutes on your phone."

If I hadn't been driving ninety-something down a strange — take that anyway you want — road, I'd have sputtered a little indignation and explained the concept of roaming charges to her. As it was, the best I could do was grit my teeth, hang on to the wheel and keep my eyes peeled for a stray cow, coyote, possum or sharp curve. Any of them would do us in, except maybe the possum, although I'd probably kill us trying to miss it.

I was still occupying my mind with these cheery details when Mother's party apparently answered.

"Hello? Hello, Merline? This is Lucille. What? No, Merline, this most certainly is not Agnes. I told you this is Lucille. Merline, what on earth is wrong with you? Have you been drinking? What do you mean you haven't seen Lucille? I'm Lucille and I know you haven't seen me because I'm right here in the car with Jolene going about a hundred miles an hour out on the highway trying to get away from that goon Leroy Harper. There's a deputy there? Oh, my Lord." She covered the phone and said to me, "There's a deputy at Merline's place. They're looking for us!"

I had to wonder why they'd be looking for us when we had the acting county sheriff on our tail. The head man knew exactly where we were. So Leroy didn't have his department out after us, or did he? "Shit. This makes no sense. Why are they looking for us there?"

Mother frowned, then turned back to the phone. "Merline, what does that deputy want? Yes, I know they're looking for Lucille and her daughter! Can't you tell me why? Protect us, my hind foot! Yes, Merline, it certainly does look bad for Lucille," she said huffily. "And no, Merline, I will not call back if I hear from her."

"Hang up, Mother, she can't help us."

Lucille started to click off then snapped the phone back up to her ear. "Merline? You still there? Well, good. Now, if I don't make it, you be sure and water my canna lilies and azaleas. Yes, I remember when we all went down to Dallas for the fair and you ate yourself sick on that funnel cake...."

"Mother, hang up!"

Lucille glared at me. "Well, yes, you really should go lie down for a bit. Oh, Merline, I almost forgot. You and Agnes divide up the pecans. It looks like it's going to be a good year. Oh, and be sure to have all the trees sprayed, those old bag worms killed that elm out by the back fence, you know. I'd sure hate to lose my pecan trees."

"Mother!"

"I better go now, Merline, my daughter is about to have a hissy fit. Sure hope you get to feeling better. I'm just as sorry as I can be about all this — "

"Hang up!"

Lucille pushed the appropriate buttons and set the phone down. "I might not ever get to talk to my best friend again and I don't think it's too much to ask to let me say my good-byes. Besides, I think she was trying to talk in some kind of code."

"I don't plan on either of us dying, Mother," I said, none too friendly. "And Merline Campbell can't scramble an egg, much less relay any secret messages."

"Why, Jolene Jackson, that is just plain ugly. Merline thinks you hang the moon, and look how you're talking about her. I'm sure not going to ever tell her you said such a thing."

Merline and my mother were two peas in a very eccentric pod. Neither cooked and both were intensely proud of the fact so I couldn't see that I was saying anything so off the wall. They also worked real hard to outdo one another in the hair and costume arena. Agnes was the only normal one of the trio, and I always enjoyed her infusion of sanity. In fact, I could use a nice dose of it right now.

"Okay, Mother, now that you've tidied up all your gardening issues, perhaps we could focus on what we're going to do here. Why don't you find a way to call the State Patrol or the FBI or somebody, for godsakes, that can help us. Does 9-1-1 work out here?"

I figured she was scowling at me, but I didn't dare look. We were coming into a patch of trees and I needed to watch what I was doing, although I was getting a little more comfortable with flying. A little lift on the fenders and we could be dusting crops.

Lucille picked up her phone and punched in the three little numbers that were supposed to make us all feel confident and in control in an emergency. "Hello? Redwater? This is the police department? Well, good. Yes, I darn well do have an emergency. I'm here going about a hundred miles per hour trying to get away from a lunatic with a gun. Yes, I do know who it is."

"Hang up, Mother."

I guess she figured out how ridiculous it was going to sound about the same time I did. She clicked off and huffed. "That was a dumb idea, Jolene. Who's going to believe us about this? He's the sheriff, for pete's sake."

"Maybe I could call Rick directly. He's met Leroy. He might listen."

"Well, that's just fine, Jolene, you do that. In the meantime, you've slowed down and Leroy is getting close enough to get a good bead on us."

As I glanced down at my speedometer, I heard a loud pop behind me. My eyes darted up to the rearview mirror. "Shit!"

Leroy was hanging out the window, waving a gun in his left hand, motioning me to pull over to the side of the road.

Like hell, I thought with a flash of bravado. Then that reality thing again. "You don't really think he'll shoot us, do you?" I was sounding whiny, I just knew it.

"Well, Jolene, I saw a gun and I heard a shot. What do you think?"

I gripped the steering wheel tighter and pressed my foot down a little harder on the accelerator. "Jesus."

"Why, Jolene, are you blaspheming or preparing to return to the flock?"

"Not funny, Mother. Not even a little."

"Oh, I know," she said, apparently unconcerned about the moron with the gun behind us. "Spirituality and religion are two different ducks, so you say. As for myself, I'm not quite as tense as you right now, me being right with my maker and all that. I think everybody ought to go to church."

"And I think everybody's mother ought to mind her own business." I didn't have a whole lot of brain cells to devote to one of my least favorite topics, being otherwise occupied with driving ninety miles an hour and trying to keep us from getting killed all at the same time. I loosened my grip on the steering wheel, hand by hand and tried to work out the cramps. Too bad I couldn't ease the pain in the seat next to me as easily. "Okay, Mother, since you have all the answers to the questions of the universe, what exactly do you think we should do now?"

Another pop.

"Well, I never." Mother whipped off her sling, flung it to the side, yanked open her purse and started digging again. "This is just the most ill-mannered, ridiculous thing I've ever heard of. He should have just left us alone when he had the chance."

"Mother, you think you ought to be moving your arm like that?"

"I'm fine, Jolene. Besides, I'm not about to let that Leroy kill us dead, or shoot out the tires and then kill us dead, if we don't die in the car crash first."

I wished she'd knock it off with the morbid options. I was about to tell her to do just that when, from the corner of my eye, I saw a flash of what looked like a wiggling stream of red light from one of those laser pointer pens. Then I saw my mother pulling, not a pen light from her purse, but a compact black pistol. "What is that!" I shrieked.

"It's my Little Lady," Lucille said affectionately as she rolled down her window.

"It's a gun!"

"Why, yes, Jolene, it is. Specifically, a Glock nine millimeter semi-automatic." She snapped the clip into place with the heel of her good hand. "Nice and compact. It's just a dream to shoot. Merline and I go to the range at least twice a month. She's got a Beretta that's kind of nice, too."

"You...you...you've got a laser sight on that thing."

"Why, of course, I do, Jolene. How else would I be able to hit a burglar in the dark?"

I didn't know what to say, but unintelligible groans and moans were coming from my mouth nevertheless. My mother owned a gun, with a laser sight, for godsakes, and carried it with her in her purse. The fact that she was a regular at the shooting range was kind of anticlimactic. There were a multitude of issues to be addressed but I hit on the big one first. "Do the words 'concealed weapon' mean anything to you?"

"Why, yes, Jolene, they most certainly do. I believe those very words are on my permit."

Permit? If I hadn't already put my jaw muscles into spasms by clenching my teeth so hard, my chin would have dropped down to my knees. My mother had a permit to carry a concealed weapon. I was not heartened by this news. I vaguely recalled reading somewhere that you had to have a class or something to get a permit, but I wasn't going to bet my life on it. "You put that thing away. Right now."

"I most certainly will not. That Leroy Harper needs somebody to teach him some manners. I've had enough of his monkey business, and I'm not about to let him just drive up and kill us." Lucille contorted herself around until she could lean out the window. "Tire or radiator?"

"Shit, Mother, sit down. You can't shoot at the sheriff."

Bang.

"Stop that!"

"This laser sight doesn't work worth a darn in the daytime."

Bang.

"Looks like he's backing right off," Lucille hollered, still hanging out the window. "I don't think I hit him though. I could try the clip of hollow points."

"For godsakes, Mother, would you put the goddamn gun away and get back in the car!"

She did and I checked the mirror again. We were indeed leaving Leroy behind. Probably because he'd called an entire army of deputies to cut us off at the next pass, wherever that might be. We were going to jail, for real this time, no question about it. No matter what Leroy might have done back at Jerry's, we hadn't given him the opportunity to actually do anything, like say, kill us, so technically he hadn't done anything at all wrong. Not so for the Jackson gang.

As with most normal people, my entire education on how to be a criminal on the run came from television, movies or books, and not the true crime stuff either. Oh, no, it was fiction all the way for me, and any idiot knew what worked in a stupid made-up story never ever worked in real life. Never. So I could just forget any ideas about Carl

Hiaasen or Elmore Leonard helping me out of this mess. Mel Gibson wasn't going to come to my rescue either so I had to just get myself together and figure out the best thing to do. And if I didn't hurry up about it, Dirty Harriet was looking like she'd do it for me.

Lucille had her eyes glued to the side mirror and the gun clutched in her good hand. I eased off the gas a little and when the speedometer crept down to eighty, I felt like we were crawling. "We've got to get off this road. Where do we go? Hell, where are we?"

Lucille looked up from the mirror and surveyed the landscape. Huge expanses of flat land peppered with clusters of scrub mesquite whizzed by but there were also getting to be more and more areas of real trees. The road was even beginning to have a little up and down to it. We hadn't met a single car yet, but I knew we would. I just had to hope when we did it wasn't somebody Leroy had called in to catch us.

"I believe we're not far from Olney," Lucille said, pointing out the window. "If I remember right, there should be a little road here before long that cuts west across to Megargel. Take it, then we'll head toward Seymour."

"Sure, fine, then what? You do realize we are official felons, which does not put us in prime shape to go skipping back into Kickapoo to get us a chicken basket at the Dairy Queen, you know."

"There's a Dairy Queen in Seymour," Lucille said reasonably.

"Look, Mother, we are in really big-time trouble here. We need a place to hide." I hadn't really thought about hiding until the words slipped out, but realistically that was all we could do.

"I suppose you're right." Lucille said, begrudgingly. "We'd better find us a hideout."

She didn't look flustered or even mildly perturbed, and I was getting just a little tired of shouldering the hysteria for both of us. I took a deep breath and tried to speak slowly and calmly. "You know, Mother, you don't look the least bit concerned about any of this. In fact, I'm getting the disturbing notion that you find this whole fiasco fun."

She sucked in a breath and straightened her shoulders, having the good sense to at least appear offended. "Why, I can't believe you could even suggest such a thing."

"Well, if you don't mind, I'd kind of like you to be a little worried right along with me. Or at least pretend to be, okay?"

Lucille huffed and puffed but didn't say anything, she just went about the important business of cleaning her gun.

After a bit of strained silence, I heard a click and metallic sliding sound.

I snapped around to see exactly what she was up to, trying to prepare myself to see a red dot flickering about my nose when I did so. But no, Mother dear, had just popped the clip from her Glock in order to give it a good once over, or whatever you did to a clip in a gun that had just been fired at a sheriff. I said not a word, just gripped the steering wheel a little harder and stared straight ahead, looking for a sign that pointed the way to Megargel.

"You know," Lucille said, still doing something with her gun although I couldn't see what and didn't want to. "Jerry could be at his Mother's place. I was going to suggest we drive by there before Leroy interfered."

"I didn't know Jerry's mom was still living out at her place. Why didn't you mention this earlier?"

Piece by piece, Lucille replaced the Glock and its accessories reverently back in the case and slipped it into her purse. "I didn't say Miz Parker was living there. She's not in good health, you know. Had to be put in one of those homes. But she was real bad." She shot me a wicked look to emphasize the extreme difference in conditions of Jerry's mother and the mother sitting across from me. "Out of her head, didn't know anybody, couldn't take care of herself. Real real bad."

My mother does not truly harbor any fears about winding up at Shady Pines, or Semi-Shady Mesquites, or whatever the name of the most-feared nursing home is in these parts. We just like to keep one another on our toes, one of those weird family traditions, I suppose. I just nodded and murmured a clever "hmmmm."

"It was just another place to look," Lucille said. "Jerry Don must keep the place up because he takes her out there every now and again, not that she knows where she is, the poor old thing. But he's a good son." She let the statement hang there, and I figured that was a fine place to leave it.

The light was fading fast now, but up ahead I saw a break in the mesquite trees. I caught a glimpse of a little tiny sign that blurred as we passed it, but I thought I saw a capital "M" and an "L" at the end. I hit the brakes. "Hang on." I took the turn on two wheels.

Lucille grabbed for the hand bar above the window with her good arm. After overcoming her initial shock, she let out a very unladylike whoop. "My that was fun!" she said, breathless and with more enthusiasm than I could ever recall her having. "I do believe I kind of like this riding shotgun business."

I sighed. "Yes, I know."

"You know, I just never imagined myself in a getaway car!" Lucille said gleefully.

Yes, indeed, the getaway car. I would have groaned and sighed and groaned again, but it would have only reinforced my rapidly darkening outlook on life. The idea of wearing handcuffs does not turn me on — for any reason. My mother did not appear encumbered by such worries as being arrested, and no, I did not want to know her opinion on handcuffs. One thing was perfectly clear, however — she was having fun, which to the best of my knowledge didn't happen very darned often. That it took guns, specifically hers, and high-speed car chases to make her smile was a little unsettling. I, obviously, did not share her enthusiasm for criminal mischief — or committing felonies — having been spared that particular genetic flaw. "It's real swell that you're having fun, Mother, but this is not some "Thelma and Louise" lark we've got going here. And even if it were, you know what happened to them in the end. It wasn't a good thing, remember?"

"Oooh, I hadn't thought about that," she said breathlessly. "That's such a good movie, one of my all-time favorites. I finally bought it for myself about a month ago, although it would have made a nice birthday or Mother's Day gift for me, if anybody actually ever thought about what I liked before they just sent any old thing that happened to be handy."

I did not acknowledge her not-so-subtle hint. I just kept driving as if I knew where I was going. To hell was probably the general consensus in and around Kickapoo, but that was not my most immediate concern.

Lucille continued, "Merline and Agnes watched it with me again one night last week. That real cute Pitt boy's in it, you know, although he was such a little stinker. Of course, I just love the part where that old rapist gets a what-for."

"Don't we all."

"That Susan Sarandon sure could drive, making a run for it here and there. No governor on that convertible, I'll tell you for sure."

"I'm not driving off a cliff, Mother, even if we did happen to find such a thing around here."

"Oh, for goodness sakes, Jolene, I was just making conversation. You get the silliest ideas. Off a cliff, indeed."

"Okay, then, you tell me our options because I don't see too many. If we get stopped, we're both going to be arrested. Handcuffs, fingerprints, the whole bit." I got the feeling I was beginning to sound like a broken record, but she didn't seem to grasp the seriousness of our situation. "Being arrested and thrown in jail is kind of guaranteed when you discharge a lethal weapon at a sheriff, particularly when you're running from him at the time."

"Haven't I taught you anything, Jolene?"

That caught me off guard and I had no clue to what she was referring, my lack of education being vast and sprawling.

When I didn't comment, she continued, "There's a time to keep your mouth shut and there's a time to fight. Now's the time to fight. We tried letting those goons handle things and look where it's gotten us. We've both been shot at, Jerry Don's been shot bad and now he's missing entirely. And that Leroy Harper is up to no good about something. I don't see how letting him get his paws on us is going to help a thing. Good Lord, he might have even killed us before we got hauled to jail. Now wouldn't that be something?"

My brain felt like a sloe gin fizz, but for yet another time, I had to agree with my mother. Letting Leroy catch us wasn't going to help anything.

Lucille rustled around in her purse again, dug out her emergencies-only cell phone, along with pen and paper. After punching in some numbers and waiting for an answer, she said, "Agnes, this is Lucille. Is there some goofball deputy at your place? Well, that's good. Merline's got one breathing down her neck looking for me so don't go over to her house. Jolene and I are trying to get away from that oldest Harper boy. He shot at us. Can you imagine such a thing?"

My mother did not mention that she shot back.

"Well, Agnes, it seems we're in a bit of a bind. This whole murder and shooting business is just getting uglier and uglier. I tell you, I don't know how much more I can stand. I know it. Yes, I've got my medication with me. Oh, well, don't worry about the azaleas today, Agnes, what I really need is Calhoon Fletcher's phone number, if you don't mind." Mother jotted down the number, thanked her other best friend, and started to make the next call.

"Uh, exactly why are you calling Fletch when we pretty much decided he's got to be the one in on this with Leroy?"

"That's exactly why I'm calling him." She kept dialing. "Hello, Fletch, this is Lucille Jackson. Well, not so very fine at the moment, Fletch. It seems your nephew has taken it upon himself to shoot at me and my daughter. No, I don't have any idea why he'd want to do that, but Jolene was thinking you might want to kill me because of that recall petition."

I sucked in my breath and flopped open my mouth like a shocked bass.

"And you know, Jolene was shot at, too. I tell you what, Fletch, I've had just about enough of this shooting business."

Lucille paused for a second and ventured a furtive glance in my direction. "The radiator, you say. Well, he ought not have shot at me first." Her face turned slightly crimson and her aristocratic nostrils flared widely. "I am not going to jail, Calhoon Fletcher. I don't care what you or your stupid nephew says." She punched the hang-up button and huffed. "That sorry old buzzard. I'm gonna get him thrown out of office, you mark my words."

"Unless he kills us first," I mumbled. I was only a little surprised that Leroy had immediately informed his uncle. My best guess was that Leroy was playing both sides of the fence, that is, alerting Fletcher for nefarious reasons while sending his deputies after us for legitimate ones. "So, you did hit Leroy's radiator after all. I guess that explains why he slowed down. This is good, really good."

She lifted her chin. "You should be proud of me for helping us escape."

"Oh, and I am, I am," I said, with no sincerity whatsoever.

"I've got it!" Lucille said as we sped past another road sign. Turn right at the next intersection. "I know just where we can go. It's perfect. Nobody will ever find us at the lake."

"Kickapoo?"

"Of course, Kickapoo. I certainly don't have a cabin at Possum Kingdom, although your father was always trying to buy one down there. But we wouldn't have gone down there and I very well knew it. We hardly even went to Kickapoo after you got grown."

"You still have the cabin? I thought you sold that thing twenty years ago."

Lucille nodded. "You're right, we did, but the people who bought it couldn't make the payments so we got it back in just a few months.

We figured it was fate and kept the place. You and your dad always seemed so fond of it out there. I preferred a less primitive getaway myself, but you two were happy so I went along. Guess that's why I haven't sold it."

She was right. I did have fond memories of that place. The little rectangular box of a house on a knob hill overlooking the reddish-brown lake wasn't much more than one big room, but it had seemed quite grand to me back then.

I could still see the place clearly, the ancient faded pink sofa with scratchy nubbed fabric, the old dining table with a red checkered plastic cover, and a black and white console TV with rabbit ears that couldn't catch a signal from across the room, much less anywhere else. But that was thirty years ago. I suspected the vision would be slightly deteriorated from that and accented with and lots and lots of dirt and cobwebs, all aptly accompanied by an old dusty, musty smell. And let's not forget the outhouse. It was there for a reason.

Yes, my happy little jaunt down memory lane had ended up in the toilet. Literally, the kind without running water. The cabin had sat unused for at least twenty years and was probably falling down around itself by now, but it was probably the last place anyone would think to look for us. If I didn't know she had the cabin, I doubted anyone else did.

I was not atwitter with excitement at the prospect of walking into this place, however. Fond memories were one thing. Spending the night or the week in a run-down shack with all manner of vermin and no running water was quite another. I think I preferred to remember things as they were. But then, what were the options, really?

Making the appropriate twists and turns, we made it to the lake in less than twenty minutes. My fast-forwarded visions of the present-day cabin had become clearer and creepier the closer we got. I was not looking forward to trudging into twenty years of dust and disintegration. The thought was enough to choke a dust bunny. Maybe I'd just sleep out by a mesquite tree, or down at the crappie house.

We were almost to the little dirt road that wound around the east side of the lake. "Is there still a little store and bait shop on the corner up here?"

Lucille nodded. "Yes, I believe so."

"You know the people who run it?" I caught myself. "Better yet, do you think they'd know you?"

Lucille sighed. "Not everybody in the entire county knows me, Jolene. I'm not quite that popular."

"Well, I'm stopping there to get a few things. We can't just go out to the cabin to hide without food and water."

Within a minute, I saw the sign, not a neon variety, but a painted one with a bulb shining over the top. The paint had flaked off in a number of spots but I could still read "Bud's Beer and Bait Shop." "Says they're open until ten." It didn't give us long to shop, but I wasn't complaining. In fact, I was starving.

I parked and Lucille wisely stayed in the car, just in case someone recognized her. I didn't bother mentioning that the Colorado plates made it hard to be incognito — even if you didn't account for my accent and my attitude. The attitude you know about; the accent is a bit of enigma. Here, my voice gets me pegged as an outsider to be wary of; in Colorado, it labels me a Texan in a heartbeat — and you don't want to know what that means. Either way, I'm in trouble. I'd just have to do my best though. I'd rein in the attitude, try to go native and hope like hell nobody looked outside at the plates on the car.

I walked in as Texan-like as I could and said howdy to a burly bald guy that I suspected was Bud.

"What can I do for you, darlin'?"

Darlin'? My skin crawled right up off the bone, but I swallowed down the sarcastic comebacks flowing freely to my tongue and said, as darlin'-like as I could manage, "So, how was the fishing today?"

It wasn't the question he'd expected and he chuckled as if humoring a three-year-old, a moron or a woman. "Oh, fishing's pretty good." He chuckled again, a very wise and knowing cackle. "Sunfish are hitting on top pretty good."

Six-inch sunfish had been quite thrilling when I was four, but I wasn't four anymore, and I wasn't really interested in fishing either. Was I? "I was thinking more along the lines of crappie, bass, catfish."

He shrugged. "Pulling in some nice cats on trot lines. You and the mister going out tonight?"

Ah, of course, I'd have to have a husband, now, wouldn't I? I certainly wouldn't be chugging around on the big old scary lake all by my little old female self, much less baiting out a big old, heavy trot line. I did not humor him with an answer as to my marital status, but acting like I was going fishing was turning out to be a pretty darned good idea.

"I'll take two dozen minnows," I said confidently. I'd free the little fish once I got to the cabin, although my daddy said minnows were trash fish and not to be worried over. I worried anyway. "Tell you what," I said, just as Bud lumbered into the next room to dip his net into a big metal tank. "I'll just grab a couple boxes of worms instead." Worms didn't weigh on my conscience nearly as much as little fish. Of course, I fully intended to kill and eat whatever I caught, meaning big fish, so the whole thing was kind of ridiculous anyway.

Despite his inherent chauvinism — and my reneging on the minnows — Bud seemed nice enough, watching me with both a brown and a blue eye. But then he got extra friendly when I started stacking my non-fishing selections by the register, these items being marked about triple what they were worth. Bud was going to be knee-deep in profits after I left.

I bought the best of what was to be had in the food section, if indeed bean dip and Cheez Whiz are considered food items, along with two jugs of water, the appropriate soda essentials, and a six pack of beer, bottles, thankfully.

Keeping my head amidst all the manly gear and the gleeful Bud, I also bought the necessary toiletries, paper towels, a can of Lysol, and some Raid. Deciding one can of instant insect death might not be quite enough, I grabbed another can that emphasized its lethal nature to eight-legged creatures. I was racking my brain for what else we might need for our little excursion when a dusty green Coleman lantern caught my eye. I moved my gaze to the hand-written price tag of fifty-three bucks and tried not to choke. Twenty dollars at Wal-Mart, easy.

"That there has an automatic lighter," Bud called from behind the counter. "Only way to go,"

I smiled. "Sounds great. I'll take it. It'll be good to have...out on the lake...at night...while we're fishing."

Before I was possessed to buy some other outrageously overpriced thing, I lit up Bud's life with every bit of cash I had in my pocket. He grinned wide enough that I could see all six of his teeth as he handed me back four ones from my hundred. Ninety-six dollars would have bought a more than decent hotel room and a really nice meal, but I tried not to dwell on it. Truly, I was just having the time of my life.

It was pitch dark by the time we snaked our way down the narrow dirt roads to the cabin. Pointing the headlights toward the door, I grabbed my sacks of essentials and followed Mother inside.

To my surprise, she flipped on the light switch, and I saw fifty-three dollars go up in smoke. Not only was there electricity to the place, but the mice hadn't chewed through the ancient wires and the place was brightly lit. While I marveled in half-shock at having power and light, Mother moved from in front of me, and what I saw then sent me into sputtering spasms.

The place was spotless — and totally refurbished. Very recently. It smelled of fresh paint, new carpet and duplicity. Lucille had really pulled one over on me this time. I stumbled to the dining area and set the bags down on a new glass-top dining table next to an expensive-looking vase with silk flowers. Through a newly installed door, I saw another little modification that could only be an added-on bedroom. After processing that development and gawking for a good three minutes, I turned toward my mother and asked the very most important thing on my mind, "Does this love nest of yours have a bathroom?"

Lucille huffed and opened what had been a closet door. "If you must know, BigJohn had it put in. I'd always wanted a real bathroom out here and I finally got it. It's no big deal."

The hell it wasn't. This remodel had to have cost twenty grand if it cost a dime. "When was this done?"

Lucille turned on the new refrigerated air-conditioning units sticking out of two windows, then put the drinks and perishable food items in the new refrigerator. "A couple of months ago, I suppose. We hadn't been going together very long when we drove out here. Next thing I knew he had the whole thing redone and new furniture delivered. He did care for me, you know."

Whatever BigJohn's reasons for turning the spider-infested old place into a cozy little hideaway, I was deeply appreciative, at least at the moment. "You could have told me," I said, vacillating between being annoyed and hurt. "I spent at least sixty bucks on junk we don't need."

Lucille shrugged and stashed the insecticides in a cabinet. "Oh, no, it's just fine. I didn't have any bug sprays out here at all. And it's always good to have a back-up lantern around."

I was not terribly proud to have been of assistance. Who was this woman, anyway? She looked like my mother, she talked like my mother, but this woman had a secret life that I knew absolutely nothing about. I felt like I'd come in during the middle of a bizarre movie, one that you had to see the beginning to understand. Then again, even if I'd seen the opening credits, I doubted I'd ever understand how my very own mother had wound up with a laser-sighted Glock in her handbag and a love nest at the lake. "I'm going to bed," I said, my hunger having evaporated into some form of shock.

"Well, Jolene, I'm just about to faint from hunger and you did buy all that food. Besides, it'll be time for the news in just a few minutes. You don't mind if I turn on the TV, do you?"

Yes, I did mind. I minded a lot of other things, none of which made any difference to a single living soul that I could tell. I minded having to race down to Texas to get my mother out of jail. I minded having my mother and her house being shot up. I minded my dear friend nearly getting killed — and now stolen. I minded being shot at myself, and I also minded my mother shooting at the sheriff. "Yes, I do mind, Mother. I think we have enough bad stuff of our own to deal with that we don't need to hear about everybody else's. I don't want to watch or listen to the news."

"I suspect we are the news, Jolene," she said, rather snottily. "And I'd like to see just what tales are being told about us right now."

"Oh, that," I said, sheepishly. I just hate it when my mind spirals downward like a really good flush on an old-fashioned five-gallon toilet. "You're right. Turn it on. We need to know what they've said about us so we know what to do."

"That was my thought, yes," Lucille said. "I'll fix us a snack, too."

With instructions to yell if our would-be mug shots had made it to the silver screen, I investigated the new bathroom in the closet, intending to avail myself of each and every one of the fixtures, especially the shower. I have to admit that whomever BigJohn had do the work did a first-class job. The sink was one of those little triangular in-the-corner types, but it wasn't a cheapy, and the shower was small but was nicely tiled rather than covered with some tacky plastic-coated fiberboard. I was impressed.

I was just finishing up my nice, hot shower when Mother banged on the door.

"Jolene!"

I grabbed a towel and raced out to see just how bad the story being broadcast across the county was, more specifically if "armed and dangerous" were used in the description of the mother-daughter menace running amok.

"Dee-Wayne's not dead! Can you believe that? That idiot Leroy, or Larry, whichever fool Harper went in the house, didn't even bother to check to see if he was breathing. It seems the board Dee-Wayne looped the rope over broke, but not before he passed out. With all that fat around his neck, sounds like he wasn't even hurt."

I'd left the scene before competent law enforcement or medical personnel arrived to assess the situation, so I hadn't actually witnessed the removal of the body. But I had seen the ambulance drive up, so they were likely the first to figure things out. I also suspected Deputy Bob had arrived fairly quickly to take over for Larry & Moe, or Curly. Whatever.

I'll admit I felt a huge relief that Dewayne was alive and well. Even though I didn't know the guy, and his self-destructive yearnings were not my personal issue, his self-demise would have weighed heavily on my conscience for the rest of my days. But Dewayne hadn't died, and the blame for screwing up the situation fell squarely on Harper shoulders, with a little help from Ethel Fossy.

I listened to the rest of the TV news story, which amounted to speculation and innuendo — an apparently contagious disease sweeping the media in the area. As the report wound down, I breathed a sigh of relief. We hadn't been mentioned at all.

While I was reveling in that small victory, one last detail caught my ear and sent a shiver up my back: Dewayne, the resurrected, had disappeared.

⇒►◄⇐

Chapter
Seventeen

I slept reasonably well for a while, but by four a.m., I gave up all hope of ever going back to sleep and got up off the sofa. I dutifully folded the sheets and set them at the end of the couch, did what needed doing in the bathroom, then wandered into the kitchen area to see what sounded good for breakfast.

After a can of liquid tar and a Snickers — the breakfast of champions that had gotten me through college — I had a good hour or so before sunrise. Considering what difference that made provided about a fifteen-second distraction, then I moved on. The new color TV — with its roof-mounted antenna — was ready and willing, but television was never my first choice in alleviating boredom. I didn't have a book and I'd thumbed through Mother's magazines last night trying to nod off, so that didn't leave many options. Too bad I couldn't really go fishing.

Could I? Was Dad's pier and crappie house still down there?

I fired up my new prized lantern, grabbed my boxes of worms, and an extra can of Dr Pepper, then headed down the hill to the lake.

The rock steps I'd built when I was a kid were still there in spots, but the trail was overgrown with knee-high grass and weeds. It didn't look like the lovebirds had been fishing or swimming or anything else that you generally went to the lake for.

Near the bottom of the hill, the wooden pier met up with the trail and I stepped cautiously out on the old boards. The creaks and cracks weren't encouraging, but they didn't turn me back either. At worst, the thing would collapse and I'd fall into the water. Really red muddy water. How fish lived in this lake had always been a mystery to me.

The door to the crappie house wasn't locked — and never had been as far I knew — so I turned the handle and let myself in. I realized I'd been holding my breath, and let it out slowly. The place smelled old and dusty with a hint of decomposing foam rubber, probably from the stuffing in the bench pads.

I set the lantern on the bench and took in the room. Everything was just as it had been twenty-five years ago, only older, more weathered. Relieved didn't even begin to describe how I felt. I hadn't really thought about the possibility that BigJohn might have redone the fishing hut, too. If I had, I surely wouldn't have come down here. This was my dad's place. Always would be.

When I was little, he'd bring me out here on the weekends to fish. We'd sit here in this little room for hours, staring down at the water beneath the lift-up hatch in the floor, watching the red and white bobbers bounce on the incoming waves. Sometimes talking, sometimes not. Just being.

I wanted to do that again. Just like before.

I looked up to see if things were as I remembered, and sure enough, fishing poles still hung around the room, bobbers, swivels and hooks still in place, as if they'd been waiting for me to come back. I edged my way around the trapdoor and set the worms on the bench. My foot bumped against something and I jumped. This sort of thing was happening a lot lately, and it was not fortifying my delusions of being a fearless, courageous and heroic independent woman. I bravely ventured a look under the bench to see what I had bumped.

A coffee can. With dirt inside. Scary business.

Feeling like a complete idiot, I started to kick the can farther under the bench for scaring me, then stopped. That coffee can wasn't old and rusty like it had been left here on Dad's last fishing trip. No, that can was a bright new blue color. The dirt wasn't a dusty, dried-up clump either. I bent down and poked my finger through the crusty top layer. I churned up a little moist earth — and a dandy ball of night crawlers. Somebody had been fishing here, very recently.

Someone had invaded my father's private space. Had just made themselves at home like they owned the place. I felt a rush of fury that balled up in my chest like a tight hot balloon. Images of people sneaking down the hill and creeping into the crappie house bombarded my mind. What made people do such things? Didn't anybody have respect for others anymore? This was probably another case of what I meanspiritedly call the California mentality: What's mine is mine and what's yours is mine, too. I don't really mean to pick on Californians, but those "Don't Californicate Colorado" bumper stickers were made for a reason.

Being a transplant from Texas, I didn't have any room to cast stones at the hordes of people moving into the state. And I didn't, at least in the physical sense, until some escapees from Orange County built a house on one acre of steep rocks up behind my property.

Not content with their little patch of cliff to dwell on, they decided all the land below them — namely my five acres — was free land and theirs to do with as they pleased. You see, they just really loved my little trout pond, and well, their kids wanted to fish, or just sit by the water, and they weren't hurting anything. What was my problem anyway? It took more than one visit from the sheriff to convince them that they really did have to respect private property, and buying a one-acre plot on the top of the hill did not entitle them to everything below it. So, yes, I get a little sensitive to trespassing. And somebody had very well been trespassing in my Dad's crappie house.

Trying to put my past and present anger aside, I flipped open the trapdoor, grabbed the dipper kept for just such a use and scooped up a little lake water for the old night crawlers and added my new ones to the can. I took down a Zebco rod and reel that looked in good shape, nabbed a fat worm and set to work.

After a less than artful start at skewering, I managed to get most of the worm on the hook. I pointed the tip of the pole over the hole and mashed my thumb against the button on the reel. The line dropped down into the water with a plop, the bobber settling itself on the surface. I sat down and cut the light to the lantern. It would be getting light soon and I didn't need to see the bobber to know if I had a strike or not.

I tugged the line out a little and held it between my thumb and middle finger then turned the crank once to lock the reel. Then, I tried to relax.

I hadn't fished like this in years. All I ever did anymore was throw out a lure now and then to snag a trout from my little pond. Not a difficult task.

Still, I knew how to fish in a real lake. Or at least I had when I was ten years old, when I hadn't yet discovered boys, when I'd loved being Daddy's little fishergirl. I couldn't remember catching many fish out of this hole, though. I know for a fact we never ever pulled a big fat catfish up through that trapdoor. But we could sit for hours staring down at that little square of lake beneath the trapdoor, little red waves, bigger waves and an occasional white cap sloshing by beneath us. Why we looked at the water like that, I don't really know. The water has always been so red and thick that you can't see an inch below the surface. But we did look, Daddy and me.

I felt a little catch in my throat and a twitch in my hand. Maybe this hadn't been such a grand idea.

Then my fingers twitched again.

A strike. I had a fish checking out the worm. I blinked a few times and sniffed, but kept myself stone still and waited for just the right moment to make my move. When the strike came again, I jerked back quick on the rod and set the hook. Got him.

After wiping my hand across my eyes, I turned the crank and reeled the fish up, then grabbed the lantern and turned it on. Bud was right — it was the only way to go.

The light confirmed what I'd guessed, I had myself a really nice crappie, at least fifteen inches. Fish sounded good for lunch — as opposed to, say, bean dip. If recollection served me correctly, crappie were fine-tasting fish. They were also about eighty percent bones. I sincerely hoped Mother still had a fillet knife around. A sharp one. I eased the fish back in the water while I hunted around for a stringer.

Luck smiled on me again, and I found the stringer under the bench in a corner, covered with cobwebs. After giving it a good shake to displace any multilegged creatures, I hooked the chain end to the latch on the floor. I unsnapped the bottom metal clip, which looked like an overgrown swivel or a mutated paperclip. After reeling up the fish and moving it away from the trapdoor, I tried to get my hand around it so I could get it on the stringer.

The crappie was not so very happy about being caught and flailed this way and that, intent on jabbing its spiny fins into me. For lack of a better idea, I used my foot to hold the thing down until I could work my left thumb into its mouth to hold it the official way. With my right hand, I squeamishly worked the bottom clip through the fish's gill and out its mouth. I hated this part, although smacking them in the head before you cleaned them wasn't much fun either. But it had to be done. Freeing up the pole had to be done as well. When the fish swallows the hook, there's nothing to do but cut the line and start over. I did, then plopped the fish and the long chain of stringer back in the lake.

Now, I needed another swivel and hook. Looking under the bench again, I didn't see a tackle box or much of anything else, so I glanced toward the bench on the other side. No tackle box there either. But there was something catching the light. I worked my way around the trapdoor for a closer look.

The edge of a manila envelope stuck out from beneath the cushion of the bench.

I wasn't overly surprised by the find, because things were always being stuck under the bench in the crappie house for one reason or another. Dad had made it a point to keep a stash of Outdoor Life magazines and JC Whitney catalogs for when the fish really weren't biting and it was too hot to nap. Or, as that song Mark Chestnut sings goes, "Too hot to fish, too hot for golf, and too cold at home." I always liked those lyrics, even if they had hit a little too close to home a time or two.

Humming the aforementioned tune, I speculated that the envelope was something my dad had left here before he died, and therefore was something I didn't need or want to look at, these things tending to send me on emotional journeys I could very well do without. Before I knew what I'd done, however, I had slipped the envelope from beneath the cushion and had it clutched in my hot little hands. I am definitely a sentimental when it comes to my dad, and while I'd been worried about not getting myself all weepy, I'd managed to overlook the fact that my dad wasn't a manila-envelope-hiding kind of guy.

So whose was it?

There was no writing on the outside and it wasn't licked shut, only clipped. With no clues forthcoming, I worked the little metal ears up and opened the flap. Inside, was a stack of papers. Not a single neat stack, but random neat stacks mixed with what looked like business envelopes, newspaper clippings, receipts and crumpled scraps of something.

The sun was coming up and the lighting was getting better, but I still needed the lantern to see much of anything, like words. I slid the papers carefully out of the envelope and heard a clank on the floor beside my foot.

There, not three inches from the trapdoor — and the hole down to the deep red water — was a shiny silver key. I picked up the key and closed the hatch as best I could considering the stringer snapped to the latch. I hadn't seen the fish's white belly floating along the surface so assumed the crappie was still alive.

With the floor relatively secured, a quick glance over the papers did not send my emotions sloshing down memory lane again, although I'll admit feeling the urge to cry when I saw the word Bennett sticking out from the top edge of one paper. Not only had BigJohn made himself at home in my dad's private fishing hole, he'd used it as a hiding place for a hefty stack of what looked like legal papers and receipts. And if there wasn't something fishy about them, then why were they hidden in the crappie house? It just figured.

As for the mysterious what-can-this-go-to key, well, that just figured, too. With a murder investigation, two attempted murders, gun running, and a long and weary list of improper political activities, it was perfectly reasonable that a mysterious key would be involved.

If this was your typical safety-deposit-box-surprise-evidence thing, then I had to be a good citizen and turn it in. This, of course, required that I make nice-nice with the Harper-Fletcher gang — and get an attorney. None of it sounded terribly exciting. And it had completely ruined my enthusiasm for fishing.

I put away the rod and reel and gathered up everything else. With my still-gasping crappie on a stringer in one hand and the envelope in the other, I trudged back up the hill to the cabin and sneaked inside.

As it turned out, the sneaking was a waste of time since Lucille was sitting at the table already freshly showered, painted and poofed, sipping coffee from a china cup and flipping through a current *Redbook* magazine. She did not look at all like she was roughing it, although I knew she considered staying at the cabin exactly that. After all, the Dairy Queen was a good fourteen miles away. She looked up at me, scowled, then tried to hide the fact that she had. "I see you've been fishing."

Feeling like a first-grader again, I held up my stringer and proudly displayed my crappie, which in the light of day looked a few inches shy of my optimistic fifteen. If we got a deep fried snack out of the little bony fish, we'd be lucky. Nevertheless, I smiled broadly and said, "See what I caught, Mommy." I tried to sound little and cute. "I'm so proud."

Lucille sighed dramatically, wholly unimpressed by my childish attempt at lame humor, or maybe that's a lame attempt at childish humor. Either way, it kind of hurt my feelings that she didn't play along — or even chuckle. She just kept looking at her magazine. "It goes without saying," she said flatly, "that I'm not cleaning it. I'm not cooking it either. I don't cook crappie, Jolene. It's entirely too much trouble.

Too many bones. But there's a skillet and oil in the kitchen if you want to try it for yourself."

I didn't want to try it for myself, but I didn't have a great deal of choice, particularly since the crappie was now dead. "I'll take care of it, Mother. I'm sure I can figure out how to fillet a crappie. I do reasonably well with trout. How different can it be?"

Actually, very different. Even so, except for two close calls when the knife slipped, I managed to get the thing filleted, skinned and sliced just fine, meaning I still had all of my fingers fully attached and no Band-Aids binding gaping wounds. Having accomplished these amazing feats, I was determined to fry my little chunks of fish come hell or high water. On the bright side, it wouldn't take much cooking oil.

With half a plate of the morsels draining on paper towels and the grease turned off, I dished up the rest of my cleverly thrown-together meal. I'd helped myself to a can of whole kernel corn and French cut green beans from the love nest's pantry and opened a bag of chips to round out our fine almost-lunchtime feast.

"Why, Jolene, this fish is right tasty," Lucille said, with more shock than was necessary. "I'm quite impressed."

Keep in my mind that my mother can be impressed fairly easily with anything she doesn't have to fix, and the rest of us are equally impressed that she doesn't try to cook much of anything herself.

Growing up I had more ravioli, canned stew and TV dinners than I care to recall. I'm not complaining, mind you. It was far better than the home-cooked meat dishes that appeared on the table at luckless times. Believe me, you can't fully appreciate a finely grilled sirloin unless you've had a not-so-finely fried round steak. And I'm not talking chicken-fried either. I'm talking skillet-fried. My mother's steaks were so tough the dog thought they were rawhide chew toys. So did my dad and I, for that matter, although we were not stupid enough to say so.

To be fair, I'm not that great of a cook myself, but I had managed to get the fish fried to a nice golden brown, the batter cooperatively staying stuck to the fish, not the pan, and the grease not igniting a household fire. I can come through in a pinch. Sometimes.

"This fish does taste pretty good," I said, pulling a bone out from between my teeth.

Lucille reached for another piece and dusted it with salt. "It's definitely better than Cheez Whiz."

My mother is never free and loose with her compliments. "Thanks."

We ate in silence for a few seconds, which gave me time to get over the processed cheese spray insult. It also gave me time to look around the room.

Last night, I had thought the remodel job to be first rate, but being dark, I couldn't really tell that much for sure. In the daylight, it was obvious that my first impression was correct. The lake cabin didn't look like a cabin at all, but a really nice apartment. "Whoever gave this place a face lift did a great job. He obviously cared about his work."

"Yes, he did, although BigJohn would have rung his neck if the job hadn't been perfect. BigJohn was like that, you know." She patted her hair, the Frivolous Fawn not moving even a little. "He insisted on only the best."

I let the personal reference slide because a realization was dawning on me and I wondered why I hadn't thought of it sooner. "Dewayne Schuman did this, didn't he?"

Lucille nodded. "I don't know for sure, but I suspect so. I never was out here while the work was being done, but I was real pleased to see such a fine job. I've heard rumor that Dee-Wayne's sister does all his plumbing and electrical work on his houses. I guess she did this work too."

"Susan?"

"Yes, I believe that was her name, or is it just that you told me. Hmmm." Lucille clicked her nails on the table. "You know, now that I think about it, I bet she did the tile work, too. I sure can't see either BigJohn or Dee-Wayne picking out those trim pieces with the little blue flowers. I don't know why he didn't just tell me she was out here, or Dee-Wayne, for that matter."

I frowned. It was perfectly acceptable to know everybody's business in a small town, to know who did what with whom and how all those stories tied back into one another sooner or later. "Seems strange. BigJohn and Dewayne pretending to be at odds, but working together. And Susan working with them, yet everybody in town seems to have nothing but disdain for her."

"That would have included BigJohn as well, I'll tell you for sure. Wonder why he let her work out here." Lucille tipped her head and toyed with the silk flowers in the leaded glass vase. She'd gleefully

abandoned her sling yesterday in order to shoot out the window at
Leroy and seemed to be doing just fine without it. The bandage over
the stitches was still in place though. "Amy's friend does work in town
at the lumberyard, like I told you before, so maybe this is just a part-
time thing. Maybe BigJohn didn't know. Hmmm."

I didn't have a thing to add on the subject of Dewayne's sister —
or the sister's girlfriend who left her husband. And thinking of Jerry
only made me worry. Since I had yet to think of any way to find out
about either Jerry's condition or his whereabouts, I decided, a la
Scarlet, to think about it later and moved on to the more recent development. "I found an envelope full of papers stuck under the seat in the
crappie house. I haven't looked at any of the stuff closely, but I think
it has to do with BigJohn. Know anything about it?"

Lucille raised a well-drawn eyebrow. "No, I surely don't. What on
earth would his papers be doing in the crappie house? BigJohn wasn't
a fisherman at all. As far as I know, he didn't even own a rod and reel.
I can't imagine him sneaking off to hide papers. He never even wanted to walk down to the lake just to look."

I'd already deduced that moonlit walks on the pier weren't a part of
their routine, and I politely did not ask her for any lurid details of what
actually had constituted their sort-of affair. It wasn't any of my business, but I have to admit I was a little curious. BigJohn had dumped a
bundle into a love nest, presumably with high hopes of something, but
couldn't physically come through with the main event. You'd think
he'd have at least indulged himself in some fishing.

"So let's see these mysterious papers, Jolene." Lucille clucked her
tongue. "This could be very important. Why on earth didn't you rush
right in and tell me about this first thing?"

"Because I was hungry" didn't sound very nice, and saying I was
fed up with the goings-on around here and just wanted to ignore it all
wasn't much better. Besides, I knew it was time to dig in, draw conclusions and piece together some very slimy pieces of a very crooked
puzzle in order to get me, myself and my mother out of this mess.

I stood and retrieved the manila envelope from the kitchen where
I'd put it next to what remained of the crappie (that's pronounced crop-
pee, not...well, you get the idea). I needed to get rid of the fish guts and
various leftover pieces sooner rather than later, but moving on to the

current gore, I wandered back to the table. I dumped out the envelope contents — including the key. "This is it."

Lucille picked up the key. "Oh, my, isn't this interesting? I wonder what this goes to."

"Safety deposit box would be my guess."

"Well, it wouldn't be mine," she said, rather snottily. "My goodness, Jolene, everybody knows what a safety deposit box key looks like. They're flat. This is a regular key like you can have made at Wal-Mart."

Well, yes, I knew that, too. But this was Kickapoo, Texas, after all, and I figured that bank keys might be different here — God knows everything else is. "So maybe the key goes to a diary, or a briefcase, or a fireproof box or something."

"We could guess all day about that, now couldn't we?" she said, with a grandiose air. "And we still wouldn't know if we were right or not. Let's look at these," Lucille said, grabbing the papers and digging into her task with the eagerness of a kid hunting Easter eggs. She rummaged through the pile and came up with a stack of legal-looking documents. "This looks like the divorce settlement." She flipped to the last page. "Just like I suspected. He never even filed this mess, the lying ass."

While Lucille muttered and huffed about who was supposed to get the muffin tins and the toilet brush, I took on the rest of the stash. I selected a thick business-type envelope and opened the flap. Inside were real estate deeds. Three of them. The town of record was, of course, Kickapoo, and the addresses to the properties were in sequence. "Where's Myrtle Street?"

Lucille looked up from her papers. "East edge of town. Why?"

"By the water treatment plant?"

She nodded then frowned, getting the idea where I was headed. "BigJohn's lots."

"Not exactly," I said, probably a little too smugly. "These deeds are in Velma's name."

Lucille's eyes widened and nostrils flared. "That deceitful, conniving son of a bitch. He bought them for her."

I felt a little guilty for the way I'd handled that one, and I still didn't really know any more than I did before. "The only reason I can think of that they might be in Velma's name is if this was sort of a pre-divorce agreement or something."

Lucille snatched up the divorce papers. "There's not a word about it in this that I can tell, besides, these papers were drawn up back in January. He bought those lots after he met me."

Oops. I was sorry I had brought it up. Very sorry. "Well, I guess we should keep it in mind. It might mean something."

"It means something, all right. It means BigJohn Bennett couldn't tell the truth if his life depended on it. And I guess it did. Just serves him right."

"Well," I said, trying to think of a way to claw my way up out of the hole I'd dug. "Let's keep going through the papers and see what else we can come up with."

"Yes, like what else he lied to me about," Lucille said, flinging the divorce papers aside and grabbing another stack. "We'll just see what all he was up to."

Finally realizing that I wasn't going to make things any better by talking, I kept my mouth shut and grabbed an eye-catching canary yellow receipt from the stack. Printed in block letters across the top was D Bar S Construction. Dewayne Schuman? Had to be. I scanned the invoice — several things snagging my attention, the first being that it was neatly typed and there were no misspellings. Dewayne had somebody doing his invoices for him. The second point of interest was that this was the bill for the cabin remodel. And it was for fifty-one thousand dollars.

Fifty-one thousand dollars?

Even if Bud from the Beer and Bait Shop had been setting prices, you could have built a whole new cabin — twice as big and twice as nice than the original — for that amount.

I tried to recall exactly what the relationship was between Dewayne and BigJohn — or at least what I thought it had been. There was the carport-garage thing, and suspicions of BigJohn blackmailing Dewayne, neither of which explained why the blackmailer was paying the blackmailee more than double for a remodel job on a lake cabin. And if they were enemies — as they'd publicly appeared — why were they doing business together? The web of shenanigans was wide and tangled, and somehow, mother and I were in the center of it. I had a lot of questions but none of them were making sense to me so I certainly couldn't articulate them. I set the yellow sheet aside and took what was next in the stack: a newspaper clipping.

I scanned the nice big photo that had run in the *Redwater Falls Times*, trying to see if I recognized anyone. I did. Several someones. Besides BigJohn, grinning like a fool, and a variety of official officials, I saw Dewayne Schuman and Gifford Geller — along with my mother. The caption told me the photo was taken after the mayor's swearing-in ceremony. It was a unanimously smiling group. I wasn't even surprised to see the name of the man standing right next to BigJohn: County Commissioner Calhoon Fletcher. Imagine that.

After reading the article, which was mercifully short, I didn't know much more than I had, except that these same people kept showing up over and over. They all had to be connected one way or another. This, of course, included my mother. How I figured into the equation, was anybody's guess. I was grasping at very thin straws and trying to make a basket when a knock on the door made me jump very nearly out of my skin. My theory-making was replaced with panic in a matter of milliseconds.

"Go in the bedroom," I said to mother, who had developed a definite paleness to her cheeks. She didn't argue, but she did grab her purse as she went. I eased over to the window beside the stupidly unlocked door, the knob of which was jiggling this way and that.

"Miz Jackson," said a low voice that would have no doubt been big and booming in a normal tone. "It's me, Dee-Wayne Schuman. I need to talk to you."

Oh, shit. Dewayne. How did he find us? The options all pointed to Leroy and/or Fletch and I did not like the way that was playing out. Who else was out there with him? The questions played free and loose with my fear, revving my heartbeat into the red zone, and making it difficult to take a good breath. Schuman was not here to see how the new toilet was working. He was here for us.

With the mush for brains I had left, I wondered if I could lunge for the door, lock the deadbolt and be on the carpet below average firing level before he noticed. Ditto to grabbing the fillet knife.

"What is it you want, Dee-Wayne?" my mother said, scaring the living daylights out of me since I had very forcefully told her to get to the other room. But there she stood, right behind me, directly in front of the door, holding her pistol, the little red laser dot wiggling, but only a little. "I'm sure you can appreciate me being wary, Dee-Wayne, what with considering all that's happened lately."

"Oh, yes, ma'am, Miz Jackson, I surely can," Dewayne said, rather cordially. "Truth is, Miz Jackson, ma'am, I'm in a bigger mess than you are, and I think we might can help one another."

"How do I know that idiot Leroy Harper's not out there with you, putting you up to this so we'll come out and he can kill us?"

I peeped out the window and didn't see a vehicle of any kind. That wasn't necessarily a good thing since Dewayne had to have gotten here somehow. I whispered my observations to Mother, who frowned in response, but didn't have any more clue than I did what significance it held. Either he'd parked his truck a ways off and walked, or somebody dropped him off and was out buying more bullets since Dewayne's supply had dried up. I rubbed my hands over my eyes. My brain was whizzing thoughts by at an alarming rate and none of them were making any sense.

"I'm all alone, Miz Jackson," he said, a hint of confusion in his voice. "About the last person I want to see right now is Leroy Harper. Why, I can't show my face anywhere any more than you and your daughter can. But I'm not guilty of nothing except trusting the wrong folks. I figure you better know who those folks are. We're kind of in this together, you and me."

Lucille didn't look ready to huddle up for a big "go team" with Dewayne. "You listen here, Dee-Wayne, I've got my 9 mm Glock pointed right square at the door. You come in and try anything, or I see another living soul with you, I'm firing off ten rounds just as fast as I can pull the trigger. And then I'm popping in my clip of hollow points."

"Yes, ma'am," Dewayne said, a definite quiver in his voice. Apparently he knew my mother better than I did. "May I come in?"

I stood there for a few seconds, looking at my mother, the 72-year-old female Dirty Harry. She hadn't said the words, but I could see it in her eyes. She'd be just pleased as punch if Dewayne tried to make her day.

And that was certainly a distinct possibility. There was nothing keeping Dewayne from just barging on in, in which case Mother would shoot him. Besides being messy, we'd get no information at all, assuming he had any to give, and I assumed he did. If he stayed outside, Lucille might shoot him anyway, and I knew it was best to have the bloodletting done on the interior of the house instead of the exterior, for self-defense purposes anyway. "Let's get him in here so we can torture him," I whispered to my mother, figuring that sort of thing would appeal to her. I didn't mean it, but I was catching on to what appealed to my mother.

I figured right because Lucille nodded and said good idea.

I let Dewayne in and closed the door behind him, locking it this time, just in case there was someone else waiting out in the mesquites.

The big old hairy gorilla mother had pointed out to me at BigJohn's funeral wasn't laughing now. In fact, he looked genuinely nervous. Or scared maybe. The bruises around his neck — and knowing how they got there — added an eerie touch that sent a shiver up my back. He wasn't the walking dead, and I had to remember that. He was very much alive and well and quite able to overpower both of us. From the hunted look on his face, however, I had to believe his comment about being on the run. But why, and from whom? Aside from the obvious official types, there were only a few living possibilities, Fletch and Leroy being the most obvious. I guess one way was to just flat-out ask him. But where were my manners? Having made the decision to get him in the house, I figured we ought to make him feel right at home. It might even make him amenable to telling us who was on the loose in the mesquites with a pistol and a bad attitude. That plan assumed, of course, that the lunatic on the loose was someone other than Dewayne. I motioned to the glass table. "Have a seat, Mister Schuman. Can I get you a drink?"

Lucille followed us to the table, keeping her gun pointed at Dewayne, social niceties not being her main concern at the moment. "I thought you said we were going to torture him."

I glanced at Dewayne who was looking even more nervous. "So, did you want something to drink?"

He sat down, his big dark eyes darting between Lucille and the little red dot from her gun that danced around the table and his chest. Dewayne apparently had a healthy appreciation for a Glock with a laser sight. He swallowed and looked at me rather pitifully. "I'll take anything you've got."

I ran down the list of beverages, saving the best for last. He looked a little uneasy requesting a beer, but I had one on the table before he actually had to say anything. He unscrewed the top and downed the thing in one long swig. After he finished, he set the bottle on the table and said, "I don't know where to start with all this."

"Well, I do," I said, determined to cut to the chase. "Who's after you and is it the same person who's trying to kill us?"

Dewayne's big gorilla eyes got bigger and he shook his curly head furiously. "I swear, I don't know who's after you two."

"Now, Dee-Wayne, that's not what you said before we let you in."

"I know, Miz Jackson, but I had to get in here. I just had to."

"Why is that?"

He looked down at the table. "I guess you know I'm on the run from the police."

"Because you faked your suicide?"

He shook his head. "No, I meant to kill myself, but I didn't count on that board breaking. I got my share of troubles, you know."

Yes, and they'd be significantly worse if murder was involved. "Did you kill BigJohn?"

Dewayne frowned and shook his head again. "I ain't a killer. Oh, I get riled up now and again, but I usually just punch something and feel better. I ain't never killed anybody that I know of. Besides, me and BigJohn were partners."

"Partners?"

"We had several deals going." He sighed and caressed the empty bottle of beer. "It's kind of a long story."

And complex and convoluted, no doubt. I had seen the canary yellow invoice, which was no doubt just the tip of the lettuce, iceberg variety. "Okay, we'll get back to your deals in a minute. Why did you try to hang yourself?"

Dewayne expelled a burp and then another big long sigh, and rubbed his huge hands over his face. Aside from the fact that the guy had tried to kill himself, he looked like he hadn't slept in days. Not a healthy combination in anybody's book. "They were gonna frame me."

I wanted to ask who "they" were again, but if I got pushy, I might get nothing. "Somebody was going to frame you for BigJohn's murder?"

"And other stuff."

"The gun dealings."

He nodded. "And I knew once they started snooping into things, they'd find out about my partners."

"Partners? Who besides the dead mayor?"

"I don't know exactly." He glanced at me, saw my skeptical expression and continued on. "BigJohn dealt with the main man him-

self. I never met him and never wanted to. All I did was get the ship-
ments in, sell some to my friends when I felt like it, and send the special orders on where I was told."

"What kind of special orders?"

"Nothing that bad, really. I fixed up a case of SKSs now and again,
but mostly just regular stuff."

"Fixed up meaning modified into automatic assault rifles?"

"It can be done, all legal-like if you want."

I didn't know whether you could or couldn't, but if having an automatic assault rifle was legal it had to involve reams of paperwork. I
took the generic route. "Except you didn't have a license."

He shrugged. "Kind of hard for an ex-con to get one."

No kidding.

Now, as best I could tell, BigJohn and ape-man here were about as
sharp as eggs. I just couldn't see how either of them, alone or in tan-
dem, could have set up or managed such an elaborate scheme. "It
seems to me that you were sort of the distribution center for this deal."

He nodded.

"What did that make BigJohn? He wasn't a saint in anybody's
book, but this sounds a little bold for a small-time mayor to try to pull
off."

"Well, maybe, but I think he was more of a go-between. I kinda
think he was just doing what he was told, just like me. I think he was
afraid not to."

Another blackmail? Sounded like it, and frankly, it was beginning
to put my brain on spin dry. I couldn't tell the blackmailers from the
blackmailees, primarily because they took on both roles, depending
upon who they were in bed with at the time. "Was Calhoon Fletcher
involved in any of this?"

"Fletcher? Man, I don't have nothing to do with Calhoon Fletcher.
I ain't real bright, so folks tell me, but I'm smart enough to know better than to mess with a county commissioner, I'll tell you for sure."

I had no idea if he was lying or not, but I proceeded onward, in case
he said something that sounded semipertinent. "What about Gifford?"

"Me and Giff go way back. I do work for him every now and again.
Little jobs mostly."

I decided to take another approach. "Exactly who is after you,
Dewayne?"

He scrunched up his face and shook his head. "I don't know for sure. I think it may be BigJohn's partner."

Why, was my next question, but I didn't think he was telling the truth anyway so I mulled the situation around until I came up with another random question from my mental list. "So what was the deal with the carports? Why was it so important that they had to be turned into garages?"

His scowled lightened a little and he almost grinned. "That was mostly BigJohn's idea. We was getting worried that we looked too chummy in public. Folks might get suspicious. Besides, them carports are kinda ugly."

I did not groan, but I did sigh, heavily. The tag-team screw-ups had just made things harder for themselves. "Thing is, Dewayne, that carport-garage fiasco was that very thing that made people suspicious of you after BigJohn was murdered."

"I know," he said sadly, kind of like a little boy who'd broken a window with his baseball and knew he had to fess up. "But it did seem like a good idea at the time. I never figured it'd just make people think I killed him. Over stupid carports."

He sounded like he was getting teary, but I really wanted to get all the information I could while I had somebody willing to talk to me. "Do you remember anyone coming in the house yesterday, while you were upset, and, well, when you were, um..."

"Trying to hang myself?"

I nodded. "Yes."

He snorted. "I surely do. I hadn't no more than hit the floor when that Miz Bennett and Miz Fossy came storming into the house. I wasn't out or anything, I was just laying there on the floor, thinking about what a screw-up I am, if you'll pardon my French."

I nodded even though I'd never ever understood why profanity — or in this case pseudo profanity — was euphemistically called French. Didn't want to know either. "So what did the ladies say and do?"

"Praying and wailing, mostly. I was going to stop them until Miz Fossy started in saying what an awful person I was and how I deserved to die, God's will, and all that. Miz Bennett didn't say much except 'amen' and 'Jesus saves' or something like that.

"I was getting a little upset that they didn't even come over to check on me, or notice I was alive. To tell you the truth, I got kinda mad. I was thinking about hopping up and telling them that I'd risen from the dead to see how they'd like that, but Larry Harper came strutting in, so I just laid real still and kept my eyes and mouth closed. Gotta wonder about folks sometimes. He didn't even check on me either."

I didn't know what to tell Dewayne about the merry little crowd that had come to his almost-hanging. None of them sounded too concerned about a fellow human being, but maybe you had to be there.

Lucille, who had apparently been silent long enough, lifted the gun from her lap, where I guess she had been holding it pointed at Dewayne, and propped it gently on the glass table. "Why are you really here, Dee-Wayne? And don't give me any fool nonsense about partners and carport crap."

He looked at Lucille. "I need a place to hide."

Mother tapped a long plastic nail on the Glock. "Staying with us isn't gonna help you much. I shot at Leroy yesterday."

Dewayne's big old bushy eyebrows shot up and his black eyes widened. "You shot at Leroy? With that gun?"

Lucille nodded. "He was chasing us all across the countryside and I'd just plain had enough. He just kept coming and coming, and Jolene was going just as fast as her car would go. They have governors on them now, you know. Mine shuts right off at a hundred."

Dewayne frowned. Apparently he didn't know about this shutdown thing either. Either that or he was trying to envision Lucille hanging out the window shooting at Leroy. It did sort of leave one speechless.

"I got no place to go, Miz Jackson," he said to Lucille. "I came out here, thinking it ought to be safe for a while. I figured nobody even knew about this place except BigJohn, me, my sister, and of course you two. But I didn't even think about you being here. BigJohn's dead so he sure wasn't going to show up, and I figured you two were still being guarded by deputies, and my sister's got her own troubles to keep her busy, so no reason for her to come out here, not that it'd matter about her."

"So Susan did do some of the remodeling work out here?"

"Oh, yeah, that Sue, she's real smart. Best electrician and plumber I ever had working for me. Dang good with tile, too. "You know of her?"

"I met her yesterday. She was worried about you. Wanted me to ask a deputy to check on you since they wouldn't listen to her. They wouldn't listen to me either so I went over to your place to see if I could help. But I was too late, or so I thought."

"Sue's always worrying about me for one reason or another. I worry about her, too, even though she don't think so. I think she just don't want nobody nosin' into her affairs."

He looked at me as if he wanted to say something more. If he was going to try to convince me that it didn't matter about Susan's preference in mates, that she was still a good person, he could save his breath. I'd given that speech so many times in the last few days I knew it by heart.

"You don't have to explain a thing to me, Dewayne. I've met Amy and I know the story. They seem happy about their situation and I don't see that it's anybody's business but theirs."

He nodded. "Most folks don't look at it that way. But Sue's got lots of good things going for her. She works on all my houses, doing whatever needs done. Helps me run my business, too. Heck, I wouldn't be in business if it weren't for her. She's got a knack for working things out."

He was obviously proud of his sister's talents, and rightfully so. "She also works at the new lumberyard, right?"

"Yes, ma'am, that too. But just part time." He winked. "She works there so we get a discount on supplies."

Oh, well, wasn't that clever. A discount. Silly me, I was still grappling with the human terms in all this. "You do know that Jerry Don Parker and I are old friends, don't you?"

He nodded. "Yeah. I think everybody knows that. Sue said Amy sure did. Kind of a funny triangle or maybe a rectangle, everybody wanting who they ain't got. Amy wanting Jerry, Jerry wanting you, and Sue wanting Amy, but Amy wanting Sue too. Kind of just squirrels up your head if you think about it."

No kidding. And I had been thinking about this stuff way too long. My brain was twisting up in knots directly behind my eyeballs. I turned to Mother. "Do you have any aspirin or something?"

"In the bathroom cabinet, honey. Help yourself."

Dewayne got a funny look on his face, so I felt obliged to ask him if he wanted a pain reliever as well. He declined but asked to use the facilities when I'd finished.

I excused myself, grabbed a glass from the kitchen and went in search of serious headache relief. I opened the mirror-fronted cabinet and hit the jackpot. I had my choice of acetaminophen, ibuprofen and back pills.

My mother had a long and varied list of ailments that cropped up when necessary, but she did not have a bad back. Out of what can only be a perverse streak, I picked up the bottle to see how many pills were in it. And yes, I couldn't help but wonder if the back pills were a pre or post almost-event medication. I set my ugly thoughts aside and the bottle back on the shelf, then grabbed the ibuprofen. When I moved the bottle, a rounded edge of shiny chrome caught my eye. I pushed aside the next bottle and saw a lock. A little shiny lock that looked like it might fit just right with the little shiny key on the table.

On closer inspection of the cabinet, I realized that the thing was not recessed fully into the wall as it should have been. And furthermore, the side nearest the door — and less likely to be noticed — was hinged. It looked like if you put the key in the lock and unlatched it, the whole cabinet would swing out of the way. To reveal what? Money was my first guess. Lots of money was my second. And that, was the first reason for him being here that made any sense at all. Damn.

I got that sick feeling again, and with it, a really bad shiver of fear. More than likely, Dewayne had put the box in and that was where the bribe or gun or other illegal funds were kept.

Drugs! Maybe they were all into drugs.

I discarded the notion quickly. I couldn't imagine that either of these guys would last long with that kind of rough crowd, at least the old Miami Vice version of such things. No, it had to be money. But who had put it there? Or did that matter?

The main question that kept zipping through my head and sending panic up my spine was very simple. Would Dewayne kill for the money in the box? I turned on the water, tossed the pain killers aside, my headache now a pounding throb of fear that nothing was going to ease. I had to go back out there and pretend that nothing was wrong. I could do it. I had to. I took a deep breath, opened the door, and stepped out into the main room. Then, I froze.

Dewayne Schuman had my mother's gun and was pointing it straight at me, the little red dot defining his aim. "Leroy was right. You're too smart for your own good, Jolene. I know you found the safe."

I tried to look stupid, and I'm sure I succeeded admirably, but I did not look innocent. I knew, and he knew I knew. "There's nothing in it."

He narrowed his eyes and stood. "There goddamn sure is," he growled, marching his big old hairy gorilla self toward me. "Get out of the way."

I did, and with amazing agility and speed, but the table prevented my escape. He squeezed past me anyway and stomped toward the bathroom.

Not fully in charge of my faculties, but adrenaline pumping stupid thoughts through my head, I grabbed the really expensive vase of flowers off the table. Mother sucked in her breath, but I ignored her, and smashed the vase on top of Dewayne's head.

The effect was not exactly like in the movies because you see, in the movies, the vase conveniently shatters and the bad guy conveniently falls down, instantly unconscious. The lovely leaded glass did not shatter. It did, however, smack against Dewayne's head with a solid cracking thud that reverberated back up my arm and into my shoulder. And I dropped the vase.

Lucille shrieked and lunged.

I figured she was going for the vase, but she didn't. She snatched her beloved Glock right out of the old gorilla's hand. I'd stunned him enough to loosen his grip on the gun, but not enough for him to hit the floor in a heap. Movies ought not confuse people like that. I was kind of intent on seeing him crumple to the floor, the lying conniving bastard.

"Now, Dee-Wayne," Mother said slowly. "You turn your big old hairy self right around and get on out of here. Right now, you hear? Are you listening to me, Dee-Wayne? You git, or I'm gonna have to shoot you."

Dewayne shook his head and rubbed a huge hand across the back of his skull where I had whacked him. I left the pretty silk flowers scattered across the carpet and grabbed the vase again. I held it steady in case I had to bop him again. "Give me the key, Mister Schuman. Just toss it on the floor over here."

Dewayne turned from the bathroom, his eyes a little glazed over. Maybe I'd done more damage than I thought.

He held out his left hand and unfurled the long thick fingers, then sort of just let the key fall from his fingers.

I maintained my death grip on the vase and nodded to Mother to grab the key, which she did handily. "What were you looking for in the safe?" I asked Dewayne, keeping his attention on me rather than Mother.

He swayed from side to side, but seemed to comprehend what I was saying. He took a couple of steps toward Lucille, who pocketed the key and prodded the addlebrained monkey toward the door with the end of her Glock.

"Just wanted my money," Dewayne muttered. "That's all I wanted. It's my money. I want my money."

"How much money?"

Dewayne kept stumbling along. "Supposed to have twenty-two thousand coming when it was all over with. Was gonna move back to I-Way Park. Get myself on the straight and narrow. No more under-the-table dealings for me. This was it."

Nice try, not likely since I was pretty sure the ATF people could find him in Iowa Park, even if it was a good fifteen miles away. I doubted he'd appreciate my realistic assessment of his situation so I did some really simple math projections instead. Assuming I was close on the cost of the remodel, the twenty-two thousand could be what BigJohn owed him for the legitimate work. Then again, maybe it was payoff money from the gun sales, some kickback scheme or any number of other idiotic activities.

I kept getting more tidbits of information but none of them were really giving me any clear answers. And at the moment, all I really needed to know for sure was that Dewayne was going far, far away.

Lucille waved her gun at him. "You get out of my house, Dee-Wayne Schuman, and don't you ever come near me again. You do, and I'll have your big old fuzzy face on my wall for decoration. Now, git."

I trotted around and courteously opened the door for him.

Dewayne blinked, rubbed his chin and lumbered out. "Durn fool women. All I wanted was my money."

In a few minutes, I heard the roar of an engine and the spew of gravel from his tires. I watched out the door until I saw his white pick-up truck go lurching down the road.

A few seconds later, I saw a white sedan trailing after it. Coincidence? I don't think so. I turned back to mother. "We've got to get out of here. Right now. I don't know where we're going, but we're going somewhere. Canada sounds good to me."

Mother clucked her tongue as she gathered up her purse and essential firearm accessories. "You're awfully obsessed about running off to some godforsaken place, Jolene. There's no need for that. This will all work out fine. You'll see."

I did not see. And she might not have seen things so optimistically either if she'd had a peek at the car zooming along behind Dewayne's truck.

It was Velma Bennett's Lincoln.

———◦●◦———

Chapter Eighteen

Within seconds we were headed toward the Tahoe. Within a few seconds more, we knew we wouldn't be going anywhere because every single tire on the car was flat. And it had not been just an innocuous air-letting either. The sidewall on each tire had a nice, long, vicious slash in it.

I rushed Mother back inside the cabin and bolted the door. I made sure the curtains were pulled tight over the windows and I jammed a chair under the doorknob. It wouldn't stop a gunshot or even a kick, but it was all I could think of at the moment. "All right, Mother, now what do we do, just sit here and wait for Dee-Wayne to come back and kill us? And how could he have had time to slice all our tires, anyway?"

Lucille did not seat herself at the dining table as would be her usual bent. She paced and repaced a small oval in the kitchen, arms crossed, making mumbling noises. My mother was as scared and clueless as I was, and that was not a good sign.

"We have two cell phones, Jolene," she said, her voice a little quivery. "My battery is almost gone. Where's yours?"

"In the car. Why?"

"I think you should go get it."

"Sure, I'll go get it. Just as soon as you find me a bulletproof vest and a baseball bat."

Lucille rummaged around in her purse. "You go on, I'll get the Little Lady and cover you."

"A lot of good that would do. I'd be about the only thing you'd have a clear shot at."

"Well, I'm not going to shoot my own daughter," Lucille said. "I'm not blind, you know."

"Just put the gun away, Mother. I'll be fine."

Lucille sighed and finally settled herself at the table. "Whatever you think best."

I glanced at the door, then back at my mother. Gun or no gun, I wasn't in all that big of a hurry to go outside. It was entirely possible that someone was waiting for us out there. "Do you think Leroy's in on any of this?"

She shrugged. "He did try to trap us and shoot at us."

Dewayne had told a variety of tales during our quizzing, but the one snide comment about me aside, I didn't get the feeling that he and Leroy were very tight.

"What do we do, Jolene?" Lucille said, a little edge of fear in her voice.

Yes, what? Best I could tell we had about two options. One, we could go walkabout and die from the heat or the riff-raff tailing us. Or we could use the one remaining tool we had available to us. "While I'm getting the phone out of the car, you be thinking about who we can call to help us. I'm going to try to call Jerry again, for all the good that'll do, but after that we need some serious help. Maybe we can call Deputy Marshall or Bob."

"You really think they'd listen to us?" Lucille shook her head and clucked her tongue. "You know good and well that Leroy has told them about the, um, radiator problem. You think they'd take our word over his?"

"They might."

"Yes, and they might also trace our call and come haul us in."

"Can they do that?" I frowned, trying to remember anything I'd read on the subject. "I don't think they can do that. I remember something about not being able to trace 911 calls on a cell phone. But maybe they can now. Geez, I don't know."

"I don't think it's worth the risk."

Going out to the car to get the phone was a risk, too, but I didn't see a choice in the matter. Better to have the phone than not. I mentally plotted my course across the mine-strewn battlefield to the foxhole, or rather the ten steps across the grass burrs to the Tahoe. The only tree on the place was on the far side of Tahoe, so slinking behind trunks was out of the question. No, the options were definitely limited, and it didn't take a great thinker to figure out that I had to run to the car and back just as fast as I could. Complex plan, that.

I peeked out the cabin door, made sure the coast was clear, pointed my remote at the car, clicked open the latches and made a dash for the

Tahoe. I snagged the phone and was back inside the cabin within seconds. And nobody shot at me.

The unit had been plugged in and was fully charged so I turned it on, sat down at the table across from Mother, and checked for messages, something I hadn't done in a while. I had five.

The first two were from my daughter, who was all of a sudden desperate to talk to me. Over the limit on the credit card would be my first guess, but she could just really need some fine motherly advice. Hey, it was possible.

The third call was from my son, who really had just called to say hi. I smiled.

The fourth was from Leroy, who had somehow found my phone number." His message wasn't anything earth shattering, just your typical turn-yourself-in-or-die kind of thing that declined into a "I know where you are and I'm coming to get you" scenario. Mixed in there was also some gibberish about losing his job over this, and how Uncle Fletch was hopping mad. Old news.

The last call was from Jerry.

My heart leaped and fluttered all at the same time. I was thrilled to hear his voice, thrilled he was doing okay. I got over it rather quickly when he declined to tell me where he was. "In a safe place" was what he said, "with Amy and the kids" was what I heard. My stomach churned and I felt my skin turning green. I am not proud of this reaction, and to be fair, it doesn't crop up except in certain circumstances, most of which involve Jerry Don Parker.

The fact was, eyewitnesses said Amy had picked him up from the hospital. I certainly didn't know where she'd taken him, but I suspected she'd high-tailed it back down to Dallas. At least that's what I would have done. Park him at her mother's where he'd be safe and where she could take care of him. I wanted to throw up.

"Something wrong, honey?" Lucille said sincerely, tapping her nails on the glass table top.

I tried to look like everything was just peachy, but I do not have a poker face. And, I've always been a lousy liar so I didn't bother trying that route. "I think Jerry might be at Amy's mother's house in Dallas. I suspect his kids are there, too. One big happy family again, I guess."

Lucille thought on what I'd said for a few seconds then shook her head. "If Jerry Don did go with her, I'm just sure he had a good reason for it. You're just being silly again. You've got to quit thinking of yourself for a minute and think about what Jerry Don might be going through. You think he'd just run right off with his ex-wife after what she's done to him? And just what about that friend of hers? How does she fit into this? I sure haven't heard anybody saying they aren't seeing one another."

No, I hadn't either. And my mother was making some sense. The green monster had calmed down some so I tried a little half-smile, but it didn't feel that great. I was being a selfish bitch and I wanted to revel in it. "Jerry didn't mention any of the previous unpleasantness concerning his wife and her lover. He sounded absolutely robust and cheerful in his message. Could be he's forgotten all about Amy's little dalliance. Forgive and forget for the kids' sake. Happens all the time. Probably for the best anyway. Get the family back together at all costs. I'm happy for him, really I am."

Lucille snorted and rolled her eyes. "Good Lord, Jolene. Why don't you just open a bag of chips and a Coke and have yourself nice little pity party."

Yes, I was wallowing, but I didn't care. If I allow myself a good bout of self-pity, I get over things pretty quickly. I buck right up and become a generally decent human being. I propped my elbows on the table and my chin in my hands and hoped that the metamorphosis hurried itself along.

"I'm just sure you're wrong about all this," Lucille said. "Now sit up straight and don't slump."

I automatically straightened before I caught myself doing what I was told. Just to show that I did what I wanted, I leaned back in the chair and crossed my arms. So there.

"He's not making a fool of you, Jolene. I know what it's like to be made a fool of, kind of like somebody jabbed an ice pick straight into your heart."

"Yeah, that about covers it," I muttered.

"Speaking of ice picks," Lucille said, her voice noticeably perking up. "Did you see that "Basic Instinct" movie?"

I scowled. "No more movie trivia, please."

"Oh, well, that's not the point anyway, is it?" She paused for a moment and pursed her lips. "But you know it kind of is. That Michael Douglas sure didn't know if he was being made a fool of or not, of course he could have been in the end, what with that ice pick under the bed and all. But he just kept right on acting like nothing was wrong. Only thing you can do. You have to hold your head up high and put on a good front even though you know good and well people are snickering behind your back. You just never let on how horrible you're feeling. And in your case, you shouldn't be feeling horrible at all."

Well, that made me feel a whole lot better. Now, not only am I a fool for mooning over Jerry Don Parker, who was now presumably back with his wife, I was becoming my mother. That we shared this commonality in being made fools of did not blanket me with warm fuzzies. In fact, it made me mad. Really mad.

I uncrossed my arms with more spite than I intended and banged my elbow on the edge of the table. It was not funny. In fact, nothing was funny at all, especially the tingling spasms emanating from my elbow. And when I lose my sense of humor about things, it's time to get serious and play hard ball.

There was one really good thing about getting to this point. When I'm mad, I'm not afraid. That does not equate to sanity, mind you, nor does it guarantee that I'll behave in a prudent and rational manner. It does, however, guarantee that I'll do something besides hide out in a cabin shaking like a rabbit.

"Mother," I said, shoving the chair up against the table. "I'll grab us a couple of drinks, you get your purse, gun, phone and whatever you think we'll need. We're outta here."

Lucille did not move from her chair. "We can't go anywhere, Jolene, your tires are all hacked up. I can't walk in this heat, not that there's any place to walk to."

I couldn't walk in the heat either, nor did I intend to. "We're going in the car, Mother, now get in. I can't drive fast, but I can get us down to Bud's."

I had no idea what good that would do, but I was going there anyway. "Oh, and hand me the key to the wall safe. I'll be taking Dee-Wayne's money with me. Seems like he owes me a new set of tires. Wheels maybe, too. Hell, I may get myself a whole new car out of this before I'm through."

I grabbed the key from Mother, and marched into the new bathroom. It took only seconds to swing open the false fronted cabinet and drag out stacks and stacks of cash, mostly hundreds and fifties. I didn't take the time to count it, but it sure did look like more than the twenty-two thousand Dewayne had been expecting. I was neither amused nor intrigued by the new little clue. I was just plain pissed at the whole situation and had no qualms whatsoever about claiming the cash. That it was probably evidence in a number of crimes was not going to be my problem. Right or wrong, I'd do what I needed to do.

With our essentials in the car, I started the engine. Only when it kicked over did I realize it could have been vandalized too. Then I would have really been mad. I put the car in reverse and rolled back enough to where I could pull straight onto the road. I figured the less sharp turning I did on the tires, the better.

Mother buckled up and clutched her purse in her lap. "So what happens if somebody comes up behind us. With those cut up tires we can't outrun them."

"Shoot 'em," I said, not joking even a little.

I kept my foot on the brake, the normal pull of the engine making us go faster than I dared. I dropped the transmission into second and rolled along, the rubber thumping and grinding beneath the wheels.

Lucille's eyes were big and her terse little mouth was in a pucker again, although this time it was more likely to keep her lips from quivering than from her usual attitude. I think I was making her a little nervous. Going a hundred down the highway is a thrill, but three miles an hour on a dirt road is terrifying. Or maybe it was my remark about shooting people. Either way, she didn't look to be having quite as much fun as yesterday.

"I'm not kidding, Mother. You get the Little Lady out and line up all your clips. If somebody comes after us, it's not because they want to ask us for dates. We're going to have to creep down to Bud's," I said, although creep was kind of a speedy word for what we were doing. "And I want to know the second you see anything coming toward us, even a cow. Bud's is only a mile or so. We should make it okay."

"Then what, Jolene?"

"Well, I'm going to try to rent Bud's car or pay him to take us to Redwater Falls so we can turn ourselves in, preferably to Detective Rick. I'd sort of forgotten about him, but I think he could be coaxed into listening to our story. It's the only chance we've got that I can see."

My phone rang, and we both jumped. I fumbled for the unit and hit the button. "Hello."

"You're in big trouble, Jolene."

Shit, it was Leroy. I tried to pretend nothing was wrong. "Leroy, I don't have any idea what you're talking about."

"Cut the crap, Jolene. I ain't got time for your bullshit. You and that mother of yours better get yourselves into the courthouse right now."

The gravel crunched under the flat tires making noises like they were all about to grind to pieces, which I guess they were. Worrying about the tires was tops on my list, but I managed to respond to the genius playing sheriff. "I haven't done anything wrong, Leroy, other than be stupid enough to set foot in Bowman County, Texas, which is pretty damn bad, I'll tell you for sure."

Mother snorted and huffed at my disparaging comments. Leroy ignored them and I ignored my mother.

"I got me a killer on the loose," Leroy said as if he were king for the day. "And he's most likely after you and your mother. Ought to just let you get yourselves killed. You sure wouldn't turn a hand to help me."

I started to mention that I had removed brick from his head and hauled him to the hospital, but I saved my breath. "Here's the deal, Leroy, Dewayne Schuman has already tried to kill us today, about a half hour ago to be precise. Mother and I took exception to the notion and sent him on his way. Last I saw of him he was headed toward town with Velma Bennett tailing him."

"Miz Bennett? Are you sure?"

"White Lincoln Town Car. Didn't see the driver."

"Where are you?" Leroy said, excitement twittering in his voice.

"Why, so you can come arrest me?"

"Yeah, and keep you from getting killed."

"Like you care, Leroy. For all I know you'd kill me first. You and that uncle of yours are probably up to your eyeballs in one or another of the scams going on around here anyway. I'm thinking there's not much you wouldn't do."

"You got no right saying something like that, Jolene. You don't know a damn thing about anything that's going on around here. Not a damn thing."

"I know that Dewayne Schuman and the dead mayor had some sort of blackmail deal going, but I don't know why, or who else was involved. Was it you, Leroy? You and Uncle Fletch?"

He kind of growled. "Why don't you come on in, Jolene," he said, his voice getting sickly sweet as if trying to coax a toddler to eat peas. "We'll straighten all this out, and everything will be just fine."

I had some serious doubts about that. And Leroy could pretend to be nice all he wanted to, but I wasn't going to meet him no matter what he said. Besides, we were almost home free, metaphorically speaking.

Up ahead, surrounded by scraggly mesquite trees was Bud's Beer and Bait, its peeling clapboard siding and crooked sign calling to us with open arms. "Gotta run, now, Leroy. Things to do, people to see." I clicked off before he could respond.

As I fumbled for the off button, the phone rang again. I answered. "Listen, Leroy, I'm not talking to you anymore. Got it?"

"Um, Jolene, this is Susan. Susan Miller, Amy's friend."

Had somebody printed my cell phone number in the paper or on a wall somewhere, what? I glanced at Mother and covered the phone. "It's Susan. Amy Parker's friend."

Mother's eyebrows went up, but she just shrugged. After all, what was there to say?

"How'd you get my number?" I said, trying not to sound completely hateful.

"Amy. Well, actually from Jerry Don. Amy was going to call, but, well, I figured I should talk to you myself."

She was making about as much sense as everyone else around here. "This really isn't such a good time."

"I need to talk to you about Dewayne."

"Sorry, Susan, but he's not on my list of favorite people at the moment."

Susan sighed heavily. "Mine either. I do appreciate your going over to check on him yesterday. I wanted to know if there was anything I could do to pay you back for trying to help him."

I could hear the tires thumping harder and I knew we were ready to start slinging chunks of rubber in all directions. Bud's was less than three hundred yards away now, but the closer we got the more distinct the big white car parked in front of the store became. "Dammit."

"What?" Susan said.

"Listen, Susan, I'm kind of in a bind right now. I don't mean to cut you off, but we're having a little car trouble and I need to take care of it pretty quickly."

"That's okay, I understand. I just wanted you to know that Jerry's all right. I hate to see it happen, of course, but Amy was just really confused about things. I guess things all work out for the best. Of course, maybe not for you and me."

Whoa. What was going on? I did not like the sound of this not even a little. "Are you saying it's over between you and Amy?" And therefore between me and Jerry as well, my mind screamed.

"Afraid so. I'm doing okay with it, I think. I'll miss her, of course, but these things happen."

I was getting back to that really sick stage. "It was one thing for me to guess at this stuff and quite another to have it thrown directly into my face. What reason would Susan have to lie about any of this. Like she said, she was out on the cold just like I apparently was. I just sat there, creeping along, with the phone to my ear, completely dumbfounded.

"Jolene," Lucille said, shaking my shoulder. "Get off the phone. We've got to do something."

I grabbed a few of my wits about me and made an abrupt sign-off with Susan. "What is it?" I asked Mother, trying to see the problem, other than the obvious.

Lucille pointed to the obvious. "I think there's someone sitting behind the wheel in that car."

"I know," I said, not wanting to tell her whose car I thought it was, or that it was the same one I'd seen tailing Dewayne away from the cabin. We had little choice but to drive right up to Bud's and park beside the big white sedan. "We have to go on. If I stop here, we're on foot. We're at least twelve miles from town and I've already ruined the wheels on the thing as it is."

"Pull up right beside her."

"Her?" I said, getting a little nervous at the gleam in my mother's eyes. Apparently she recognized a Lincoln Town Car when she saw one too. Just in case she hadn't, I said, "Her who?"

"Miz Mayor."

I groaned. Lucille was back to her assertive self and it wasn't necessarily a good thing. "Now, Mother, there's no use getting all upset."

"I'm not upset, Jolene," she said, sounding exactly as if she were. "I just think it's time me and Velma had us a real nice little talk."

I did not agree — for a number of reasons — one of which was that we didn't really have time for a cat fight, and furthermore, I didn't want to be held liable for anything my mother happened to do. But I had to pull up to the store whether I wanted to or not. "Exactly what do you plan to say to the woman, Mother?"

Lucille unbuckled her seat belt. "Any damn thing I please."

I groaned, loudly, but it didn't faze her. She was out of the car before it rolled to a stop. I hopped out and followed her over to the white sedan, which was running. I just hoped Velma Bennett didn't get peeved and either shoot us or run over us.

Mother tapped on the darkened window with her fingernail and it began to lower. As the dark glass slid down, I was more than a little surprised to see a man in the driver's seat. A man I recalled having a nice little chat with at the Dairy Queen.

"Gifford Geller," Lucille said, a little shocked. "What on earth are you doing driving around in Velma Bennett's car, and chasing after Dee-Wayne to boot?"

Gifford rubbed his chin with wrinkled weathered fingers and frowned. "Why, Lucille, this is my car. Well, to be precise, it's the wife's, but I drive it every now and again. And as for Dee-Wayne, well I almost hit the fool boy out on the road by my lake house, but I weren't following him per se. He was in such an all-fired hurry, though, that I figured I ought to see what was wrong. Never did catch him. Needed to though. Kinda wanted to talk to him about doing some remodeling for me on the lake house."

"He's not cheap," I muttered.

Gifford held his hand up above his eyes to shade the sun and looked in my direction. "He does good work," he said seriously. "And he's been right fair with me."

I nodded. "Still enjoying being mayor? Getting all those pesky details cleared up?"

He cleared his throat. "Like I said before, everything's going fine. Just fine."

Lucille, who was showing signs of wilting in the heat, rallied enough to point a clawed finger at the now-mayor. "Fine my hind foot. You wanted this job from the minute BigJohn named you pro tem, Gifford Geller, and everybody in town knows it. BigJohn thought you were his friend, but you weren't. You were just using him. I want to know why."

"Now, Lucille," Giff said in a placating tone. "It weren't like that at all. You know as well as anybody that BigJohn just got plumb goofy here about four months back. Nobody wanted him doing nothing as mayor."

"So you just up and shot him," Lucille said, rather daringly.

His leather-like face scrunched up a little, although it was hard to tell with all the wrinkles and lines already there. "You've no call to be saying something like that, Lucille Jackson. I don't know what's come over you in the last year either. Why, I expect Bertram's been turning over in his grave for weeks."

Lucille's eyes flashed and her painted-on eyebrows flattened into two straight lines. "You leave my husband out of this, God rest his soul." She leaned back from the car and wagged her finger. "I'll tell you one thing, Gifford Geller, I'm gonna get to the bottom of all these shenanigans going on. And when I'm through scraping up the dirty laundry, I figure your shorts will be right on the top of the pile."

"I don't have to listen to this," Giff said, slamming his wife's car into reverse.

"Oh, wait a minute," I yelled belatedly, since Giff had powered up his window and sped off down the road. "We could have used that car, Mother."

"I don't need his stupid old car," she said, then she spun on her heel and marched into the swamp-cooled dimness of Bud's Beer and Bait.

As I watched an escape opportunity disappear around the corner on four inflated tires, I tried to think of a better option than using Bud's Taxi Service. I suppose I could give Mother the go-ahead to pull her Glock on him and we could force him to drive us to town. The idea had some merit so I headed into the bait house to offer the option.

When I stepped inside, I saw that Mother was already in the midst of an animated conversation with Bud, so I wandered down the snack food aisle, which was also the only food aisle. Within minutes, Lucille came marching back to where I stood admiring a rack of potato chips.

"Bud's gonna drive us to town, Jolene," she said, sounding none too pleased. "I ought to just highjack him and be done with it."

I shrugged. "Go ahead. What's one more felony?"

"Are you being sarcastic again?"

"Only a little."

"Well, then, I guess I'll do just that if it comes to it. But right now I told him our car broke down and we needed a way into town. I told him you'd pay him for his trouble so he seemed willing enough. Of course, for two hundred dollars he ought to be dancing a jig as well as driving us."

Two hundred dollars was nothing. Nothing at all. And I was quite happy to pay for a ride into town. Technically, BigJohn and Dewayne's stash of money would pay, but I wasn't in the mood to pick nits. "You know, we've got plenty of money. Can't we just buy his car or something?"

"He won't sell us his car I've already tried. Offered him twice what that junk heap is worth."

Ah, there was the problem. Bud's profit margin is more in the 300 percent range. "So does he have somebody to run the store for him or are we going to have to pay him to close up shop, too?"

"He's called someone to come in, but it's going to take them a few minutes to get here. He said we could just get ourselves a Coke and have a seat back in the bait house where it's real cool. It shouldn't be long."

Waiting around made me seriously nervous, but kidnapping Bud and/or hijacking his car didn't evoke calm and serene feelings either. I'd give it a few minutes and see what happened. If worse came to worst, I'd turn Lucille and her Little Lady loose on him and we'd get to Redwater Falls just fine. Still, if there was a chance at doing things without committing another felony, I tended to lean in that direction.

I walked on into the back room, where the smell of fish was overwhelming, but not putrid. Just fishy. The room was sparsely furnished with a few chairs lining one wall and a wooden workbench lining another. Bud had assorted mounted fish and fishing paraphernalia nailed up here and there, but the main attractions in the small room were the bait tanks. Bud had himself four big metal troughs, lined in twos in the center of the room, to house his various minnows, crawdads and sundry creatures. Each trough had a bubbler and some sort of circulating pump to keep the water cool and fresh. You could see through the water a little bit to glimpse movement, but not much else.

I'd always been fascinated by these tanks as a kid and could stand staring down in the water for what seemed like hours. I moved up to the tank and stared. I still kind of liked it.

Then I saw it, on the bottom of the tank, not moving at all. It looked like a big-headed green club with whiskers. A catfish. A really big catfish. Bud had most likely nabbed this prize on his own personal trot line and put it on display for his pals to see. It was the traditional sportsman-type thing to do around here. That and hanging the head on a fence post.

Mister Whiskers looked plenty unhappy in that trough, and I didn't want him blaming me for his incarceration. Catfish are highly skilled at self-defense, which I always took as being downright mean. They'd just as soon stab you with their nasty old spines as look at you. I was worried that the back fin on this big rascal would stick right up out of the water if he were so inclined to fluff it up, so I moved myself along to the next tank.

The second I stepped up, a swarm of little fish shimmered to the far side of the tank, the living mass shifting as a single unit. I moved to the middle and watched them, lined up like fat brown toothpicks, wiggling this way and that, yet staying in one place, doing what little fish do. My mood improved a little and I lost myself in the perfection of the minnows, moving together as one.

"Afternoon, ladies."

That gravely voice shattered my complacency. Leroy. What was he doing here? Had Bud the baitmaster called him? I glanced around and didn't see Bud, not that it mattered much. I should have opted for the felony kidnapping since there was no getting away now. I couldn't see a darn thing we could do, so that's what I did. Nothing. Just kept staring at the little fish, wishing I were anywhere but here. Well, maybe not anywhere. The morgue was not on my gotta-go-there list.

"Leroy Harper," Lucille said, not at all reticent about speaking. "I've had my fill of you and I've a mind to call some fancy civil rights people and tell them what all you've done. Harassment's against the law, and you darn well know it."

"What's against the law, Miz Jackson," he said huffily, "is running from the acting Bowman County Sheriff, not to mention shooting at him."

From the sound of his voice, I could tell that Leroy had positioned himself somewhere behind me and in front of my mother. I could both feel his presence and smell it. Leroy was sweating like a pig, so to speak.

"I can't very well overlook your shooting at me, no sirree. You're gonna have to answer for that." He chuckled, but it sounded more like a bullfrog coughing. "And I'll be taking that gun now, Miz Jackson. You're liable to hurt somebody with that thing."

"Wrong thing to say, Leroy," I muttered. I could feel my mother's tension pulsing across the room like a force field. She was going to blow. Big. Nobody, but nobody, touched her Little Lady. I turned around in time to see her getting a good grip on the purse. "Oh, shit."

The purse hit Leroy square on the side of the head and he spun around like a big, fat top, then flopped butt-first into the trough with the big old catfish. This was going to get ugly fast.

The tank erupted into a churning splashing frenzy. Leroy screeched loudly and leaped up from the tank, grabbing his backside with both hands. "Something bit me! Something bit me!"

Leroy lurched about the room rubbing and cursing. I didn't suspect he'd actually been bit. More likely, Mr. Catfish had taken exception to the company in his tank and had put his spines at full mast. Leroy continued to scream and hop and curse and drip and curse and scream.

Mother grabbed me by the arm. "Come on, Jolene. We'll take his car."

I glanced at the hopping, howling Leroy. "Good idea. Should I ask him for the keys or do you want to?"

While my mother considered her choices, Leroy yelled louder, and I could have sworn I heard a couple of "how could you do this to me" whines amidst the howls.

"Shut up, Leroy," I said, out of patience with everyone and everything. What to do, what to do.... Then it came to me. Being my mother's daughter, I grabbed his gun, which if he'd had any sense he'd have already pulled on us, and promptly handed it to my mother who likes being in charge of such things. "I really don't want you to shoot him," I said to Mother, although I was looking at Leroy. "Unless you have to." Then to Leroy, "Hand over the keys to the car, Mister Acting Sheriff. My mother and I feel the need to go for a little ride."

"You can't take my cruiser, Jolene," he sputtered, still howling in intermittent bursts. "This one's on loan while mine's being fixed." He shot my mother a wicked glare. "I get this one messed up and I'm done for."

"Give us the keys, Leroy, and don't try anything stupid," Mother said, a scary twinkle in her eyes, "if you can help it."

As Leroy moaned and sputtered some more, I glanced around to see if anyone else was in the store. Apparently not. Bud was long gone, and I could only hope he was calling in some official police types, good guys in white hats would be my preference, not that we could wait around for them to arrive. "The keys, Leroy."

He tried to wedge his fat fingers into the wet and stressed fabric of his trousers, but with little success. "This is all your fault, Jolene. Every durn bit of it. I try to help you and look where it gets me. My backside is burning like fire and I'm probably bleeding like a stuck pig. All on account of I came to help you."

"Help me? I don't consider letting you kill me to be of much help, particularly to me."

"Kill you? Why that's the dumbest thing I ever heard of. I've been doing nothing but working night and day trying to find out who murdered BigJohn and who shot at all of us. I'm doing my darndest to put a stop to these shootings, and I'd just appreciate it if you'd quit giving me grief about it."

Uh oh. This was beginning to have a prickly ring of truth to it. And while I value honor and truth above all else, this was blowing some big holes in my conspiracy theory, which promised to leave me with no theory at all about any of this mess. "Okay, Leroy, if you're so innocent, why did you try to trick us into going to Jerry's house?"

"All I was doing was trying to get you and your mother to a safe place like I was told. Then you run off and start shooting at me."

"You shot first," contributed Lucille from her spot by the bait room door.

"I was just trying to get your attention. I was afraid I couldn't catch up to you, and I didn't think you even knew I was back there trying to catch you. Next thing I know, she," he bobbed his head in Lucille's direction, "is hanging herself out the window and shooting at me. For real. And with a laser sight. Scared the holy shit out me, if you don't mind me saying so. And then, she blew a hole right through the radiator. She could've killed me!"

Well, yes, there was that. "But since you didn't die, you immediately called your uncle and told him about it."

"Well, hell, yes. I needed help, and I didn't want it blabbed around the department that I'd let two women shoot up my car and then leave me stranded on the side of the road. I'd have looked like a fool. Besides Uncle Fletch lives not far from where I was. He came and got me."

This was not sounding good. Not good at all. "So you don't have some warrant out for our arrest?" I asked, cautiously. I was leaning heavily on the side of believing Leroy, specifically that he hadn't intended to kill us at all. And that meant we were in big trouble for a number of reasons. One was the obvious jail thing, but worse, if Leroy wasn't the one who'd been trying to kill us, who was?

He scowled at me. "I should'a just called your crimes into dispatch and had a whole patrol out after you. That's what I ought to have done. Might've made me look stupid, but you'd a been locked up long ago and I wouldn't have half my back end ripped off."

I though he was being a little melodramatic, but there was no denying that he was making sense. Furthermore, there was one little phrase he'd said a while back that had raised a large red flag, one that was now ready to whip around and slap me in the face. He'd said "like I was told." I doubted Fletch was the one concerned for our welfare, which left maybe Deputies Marshall and Bob, but more likely Jerry. But how?

"So," I said cautiously. "Yesterday, when you tried to get us to go inside Jerry's house, you were trying to protect us?"

"Hell, yes. I was supposed to keep you there until this thing got wrapped up. Jerry Don told me he didn't care whose nephew I was, if anything happened to you two I'd be back in the oil field fixing pipeline."

Bingo. Jerry Don was involved. Okay, maybe things weren't as bad as they seemed. Leroy wasn't going to kill us, or at least he hadn't been going to, although the way he was scowling and clutching his backside now made the odds lean back in that direction. But he wasn't going to do us any harm, not if Jerry had threatened him with being demoted to the salt mines, or flats, as happens to be the case.

I searched my brain for all available options and came up with only one. Since having an official deputy on hand might be helpful, I figured I should repair the one we had available, then all hop in his cruiser and head for Redwater Falls, where Mother and I would readily cooperate with the authorities. I relayed this information to Mother, who was leaning against the wall, taking in Leroy's true confessions.

"If you hadn't been such an idiot, Leroy, none of this would have ever happened. Terrifying an old woman like that. Why I thought you were out to kill us both dead. You could have given me a heart attack. How'd you be a feeling then?"

Leroy worked his mouth up and down, ready to replay his previous explanation. "I done told you — "

"Leroy," I interrupted, debating how to best go about this first-aid business. "There's only one thing to do." I stood in the bait room, arms crossed, staring at the sopping wet blob of man clutching his rear end. "It sickens me to say this, but, take off your pants."

He didn't leer at me, his eyes just bugged out then narrowed into a mean little glare. "The hell I will."

With his eyes rolling back and forth, his mouth quivering, and his tan uniform stuck to his blubber, he looked a lot like his nemesis. The fish, not me.

I sighed heavily, uncrossed my arms. "Believe me, Leroy, if I thought there was any other way around this, I'd leap upon the idea like fire ants on a floating log. But I can't, so suck it up, and let's get this filthy business over with."

Mother settled herself down in a folding chair by the wall, crossed her legs, and propped Leroy's gun on her knee. I could tell she wasn't as comfortable with Leroy's weapon as she was her "Little Lady," but she'd set her purse on the chair next to hers for easy access. "May as well do what she says, Leroy. Those catfish spines are poisonous, you know. You're liable to die if she doesn't get you fixed up here real soon."

I didn't know if that was true or not — I suspected not — but I felt obligated to see what kind of damage we were dealing with, considering that once again my mother was the perpetrator of the incident.

I glanced around the room and saw a big fillet knife hanging on the wall over the cleaning sink. I pointed in the general direction of the wicked-looking thing. "I could get them off for you, if you're not able. I'm pretty good with knives. Hardly ever slip."

He scowled, grumbled and unbuckled his pants, then turned around and pointed his rather hefty posterior in my direction. He didn't drop the pants much, but enough that I could see a strip of pasty-white skin with a thickening red scratch that led downward into unpleasant territory.

I was wishing — real hard — for one of those surgical drape things that only has the part you need to see cut out, and the part you wished never had to see covered up. "Like it or not, Leroy, and I promise you I don't," I muttered, "I'm gonna have to follow this scratch down and see how bad it is. You hang on to the left side of your trousers and I'll sneak a peek."

In theory, it was a good idea, but the actual execution left a lot to be desired. I got to see way more of Leroy Harper than any human should ever have to. "Lucky you," I said. "It's a cut. Pretty bad one, even, but not a puncture wound. I was sure afraid you'd fallen right on top of a spine. Stay right here and don't move. I'll go find something to put on the wound."

I scurried to the other room and grabbed all the medical supplies on the shelf. Which means I got a bottle of peroxide — I would have preferred alcohol or some other stinging product — and a box of bandages.

Walking back into the bait room, I heard my mother say, "You know, Leroy, with that big old butt of yours, you could have a right nice bulldog tattoo. I mean the kind with the big old jowls that sort of snarls when you move just right. Or, one of those pretty ladies with the big boobs, whatever suited your fancy. Plenty of room to work back there, I bet you could have you a real nice picture of something, yes indeed."

I cleared my throat and it was not trivial gesture. I was trying not to throw up. And no, I did not want to know when, how or why my mother had developed her interest in tattoos. I walked on in like I hadn't heard a single nauseating word. "This won't take but a minute, Leroy, and you should be just fine."

I set about my work, trying to keep my mind on the task rather than the territory. On the positive side, his clothes were drying up pretty quickly. Other than being almost finished with the patch job, it was the only other positive thing I could think of. "So, Leroy, just how much trouble are we in?"

"You're both in big trouble, Jolene. More now," he said, wincing as I smacked a bandage in place just a little harder than I should have. "What you two done is serious. Real serious."

That was no great news flash. Unlike Leroy, I could spell both felony and jail time. But since doing so didn't sound like much fun, all we had to do was keep Leroy from telling on us. "Well, Leroy, if you look at it from my point of view, we didn't know that you weren't involved with whoever is trying to kill us, therefore, self-defense comes in to play, and all that."

He cocked his head around to look over his shoulder at me, apparently thinking on how that scenario played out. It didn't play out that well, but it didn't have to, really. Leroy's desire to not look stupid — as if that were possible — in front of his peers was our best bet.

"You ain't suppose to have to defend yourself from the sheriff," he said. "Everybody knows that."

Ah, he was waffling. "That's usually true, Leroy, but in this case we thought the sheriff was the bad guy. How were we to know you weren't?"

As he frowned and scowled to assist his thinking, I slapped on another bandage and did some thinking of my own. Whatever had been going on behind the scenes, I couldn't guess. But one thing was very clear: Jerry cared. I got a little warm fuzzy feeling, but it faded pretty fast when I realized that while he had cared enough to try to keep us safe, we had promptly tried to shoot his safety manager. Leroy was to blame for some of the confusion. Maybe most. I stuck on the last bandage. "This is really just a silly misunderstanding. If you'd have just been honest about what you were up to, Leroy, none of this would have ever happened."

With the patch job finished, Leroy pulled up his pants, zippered and buckled then turned toward us. "That woman," he said, pointing at Lucille, "has hit me in the head with her purse more times than I can remember, and she's shot at me. That's a little more than a misunderstanding."

Lucille shook her head and tsk-tsked him like he was a two-year-old. "Now, Leroy, you shot at me first. How's that going to look like in a silly old report?"

Leroy frowned. "I was just trying to get your attention. You were really trying to shoot me."

Lucille laughed. "I was just trying to get you to back off and leave us alone. I believe it was a sound plan."

I didn't believe it was too sound, but Leroy the not-so-bright was thinking it over. Or thinking over how the story would sound when he told it to Jerry. In my opinion, none of it pointed to brilliance on the part of any involved, and I wasn't too excited about having to confess my role.

I was debating how to make my actions sound perfectly plausible when the door in the front room creaked open, then banged closed.

Either somebody needed some bait awfully bad or Bud had returned. I glanced toward the front room, but I couldn't see anyone for the rows of overpriced canned goods.

"Somebody's coming," Leroy whispered, then glanced at Lucille. "Give me my gun back."

"Are you going to arrest us?" I said, sounding suspiciously like a blackmailer.

"In all the years I've known you, Jolene," he said, still rubbing his bandaged bottom, "you never ever been nice to me."

Geez, I'd just doctored his butt, how much nicer could I be? "Okay, Leroy, I'm sorry. I guess it's just part of my nature, but I'm trying to do better. From here on out, I promise to be a complete angel to you. Swear." Personally, I couldn't hear a single tonality that remotely resembled honesty, but Leroy was nodding thoughtfully.

He hitched up his pants and puffed out his chest. "I am feeling better."

I smiled, hoping he'd forget that he wouldn't have been feeling bad at all if my mother hadn't knocked him into the fish tank. I did not ask how his head felt.

"Give me my gun." Lucille did and he holstered it right up. "But one more misstep out of either of you and the deal's off." He turned toward the front room. "I'll go talk to Bud."

I grinned, widely, not even realizing we'd made a deal. Mother and I were getting off the hook, so to speak, and things were looking up, cheery even. Why, it was almost worth having to doctor Leroy's butt.

⟶➻◆≺⟵

Chapter
Nineteen

Leroy came walking back into the bait room, holding his hands high in the air. And he was not preparing to give me a double high-five. His eyes blinked rapidly and he looked a little green around the gills. And under the circumstances, I surely couldn't blame him. Dewayne Schuman stood behind him with a rifle muzzle pressed against his back.

Dewayne prodded Leroy along into the bait room, finally backing him up against the catfish tank. The sheriff looked more worried about the fish than the gun.

"Sorry about this, Leroy," Dewayne said rather congenially. "But them two took my money and I aim to get it back. BigJohn owed it to me. We had a deal." He scowled for a minute then added, "I give him an invoice just before he got killed."

"You mean before you killed him," I said, trying to watch his face for some hint of the truth. I was out of theories and was ready to throw out any possibility and see what stuck.

Dewayne scratched his gorilla head with his free hand. "I done told you I didn't kill BigJohn. We were partners."

I groaned inwardly. "Okay, fine," I muttered, seeing no promise for an upswing in the situation. "If I give you your stash of illegal money — and we all know it is — you'll go away and leave us all alone?"

Dewayne nodded. "Would've left you alone earlier if you and your mother there hadn't been so pushy. I thought about what to do for a long time. I gotta have that money. I was heading back out to the cabin when I saw your car here."

"Should have shot you when I had the chance," Lucille muttered, her hand slipping over toward her purse. "And I want to know why Giff was chasing you around the lake out by my cabin."

"Gifford? Never saw him today." He was watching Mother as if he were going to say something, probably "give me that Glock," or something to that effect. He also hadn't asked for Leroy's gun. Only a minor oversight I feared. Mother was the one he needed to watch. And apparently, he was remembering that.

Before his thoughts gelled too much, I decided to get him thinking of other things. "Did you know Gifford Geller was here when we rolled in, and I do mean rolled in since you slit all four tires?" He turned back toward me — and away from Mother — so I continued, "Giff said he'd been trying to catch up with you, followed you around the lake for a while."

"Well, I durn sure never saw him." Ape-man shook his scraggly head. "And I didn't touch your car, woman. I got better things to do than fool with your tires. You and that mother of yours get the craziest ideas."

The thought turned his attention back to Mother and I figured he was about one thought away from remembering what it was he should be watching Lucille for. "All right, fine. I'll get the money. Let's go out to the car. You can leave from there. Go to Mexico, go to France, I don't care, but leave us alone."

He nodded and motioned me toward the front room with the tip of his rifle.

As I marched past Leroy toward my mother, that familiar sick feeling swooped down upon me once again. Lucille was digging in her purse. I didn't know whether to tell her to sit still, keep walking or prepare for the worst. Knowing my mother as I have come to, I prepared for the worst. And the worst that I could think of was that she'd try to shoot Dewayne, and thus me in the process. Or else we'd just have an old-fashioned wild West shootout.

Right on cue, I caught a flash of red from the corner of my eye. A little glowing dot began to dance around on the front of Dewayne's shirt then work its way down his arm. Laser sight. Gun. Shit.

Without really thinking, I jumped away from Dewayne and back toward Leroy, ramming my shoulder into him, sending us both sprawling across the floor.

Dewayne swung around toward us. A gun shot boomed. Dewayne screamed. A clatter on the floor.

"Oh, my," said my mother, completely unflustered and innocence oozing from her lips. "I didn't realize this little thing was loaded."

Like hell, I thought, scrambling across the floor for Dewayne's gun. I nabbed the rifle while Leroy lumbered to his feet, pulling his own recently returned weapon. It wasn't really necessary, considering Mother and I both had guns pointed at Dewayne, who was rolling around on the floor, clutching his hand and shrieking. I turned to Mother. "Were those hollow points?"

"Oh, no," she said, wiping down the gun with the corner of her blouse. "I just used regular loads. I felt bad about doing too much damage to the big old dumbbell. Those hollow points would have just exploded his hand. This way, he's only got a hole. I do expect I hit a few bones though."

I shoved Dewayne's rifle under the fish trough and glanced at Leroy, who was holstering his own gun. He stood over Dewayne, staring down like he didn't really know what he should do, or either he was in shock himself.

"Go call for an ambulance, Leroy," I said, looking around for a towel or something to wrap around Dewayne's hand. Leroy didn't move, so I figured I'd just get Dewayne situated and handle the job myself. I quizzed Dewayne about this, that, and nothing just to keep him occupied while Mother took a towel she'd found somewhere and wrapped it around Dewayne's hand. We managed to get him to stop wallowing around long enough to use his other hand to keep the towel in place.

"Now, you just keep pressure on it and you'll be just fine," Lucille said, standing and walking back toward her chair and purse.

I was proud that my mother was handling things so efficiently because I was still shaking like aspen trees in an autumn wind. I just hoped I didn't look too scared on the outside. "Leroy's going to go call the ambulance now, Dewayne," I said, standing. "I'll help him."

The distinctive metal click of a gun being readied to fire echoed across the bait room.

Instinctively, my head snapped toward my mother. She was back in her chair but she didn't have anything in her hands, specifically her Little Lady. So if she didn't have the Glock out again, and Leroy was just standing there like a tree, then who had cocked a gun?

A loud thundering boom answered my thought. Dewayne Schuman jerked convulsively at my feet. Then I saw a gaping hole in his chest, which was slowly pooling with blood. Oh, God, what now?

My gaze darted around the room.

Lucille had spun around at the sound of the gun, and she was staring toward the front room, her back to the wall. Leroy's head had jerked up, and his eyes were locked in the same general direction as Mother's. I followed their frozen gazes, and turned to stone where I stood.

In the doorway between the rooms was a woman, pointing a huge handgun down at Dewayne.

Susan Schuman Miller had just murdered her own brother.

"Stupid son of a bitch," she said, raising the gun to point it at me. "You had no idea."

No, hell no. About what?

"He was the worst one of them all. My own brother."

What was she talking about? A hundred questions zinged through my head, but not a word came to my lips. I was sucking in little gasps of air and my whole body shaking, but damned if I could control either. This was it. The end. Adios.

Susan laughed. "Cat got your tongue, Jolene? A little surprised at this turn of events, I suppose." She turned toward Leroy. "Give me your gun, asshole."

Leroy did not move, only stared.

Susan sighed heavily and theatrically. "All right, let's try it again. Slide your right hand down to your hip, you stupid prick, lift up the hand grip on the gun in the holster and give the gun to me," she said, as if instructing an imbecile. "Twitch wrong, and you're dead."

Leroy looked dazed, but he did as she asked, floundering every now and then, but eventually he managed to hand Susan his pistol.

Susan stuffed Leroy's pistol into the waistband of her jeans. "I was hoping you'd screw up, not that I need a reason to shoot you. But, I would like to take my time and enjoy it."

Leroy's eyelids fluttered in a fast blink, but he still looked shell-shocked and was probably not going to be of much help, not that there was much he could do now anyway. What could any of us do?

I was trying to get my own petrified brain to function for a half a minute so I could think of exactly what was going on here. I had to keep my eyes on Susan and not on the floor. I had to not think about Dewayne or the blood spreading out from his body in thick pools. And I had to not stand here like an unmoving target. I had to do something.

Susan had shot her brother as if he were a snake in the grass, and I knew we were all just one bullet away from being dead as well. Instantly, life became a highly precious commodity, and I started grasping for a straw that might preserve ours — even temporarily. Something clever would be nice. Panic did not spur my creative juices and the best I could think of was that sometimes killers liked to gloat about what they'd done.

"It's all starting to make sense now," I said, although it wasn't at all. "You were the brains behind the — "

"Everything, sweetcakes," Susan said proudly. "I'm the brains behind everything. The fact that the whole town liked to pretend I was invisible made it all the easier. I didn't waste too much time dabbling in politics, but I did like making little suggestions to the less brilliant types who thought they were in charge."

She laughed, a very evil and unfunny laugh and my whole body shuddered.

"Made them think they were having real ideas for themselves. And it always worked in my favor." She looked right at me. "You people are so easy to manipulate." She kicked a foot out at Dewayne and wiggled his shoulder with her tennis shoe. "Of course, some are too stupid to do what they're told."

What was she insinuating? Had she told Dewayne to hang himself? Oh, God, this was something I would never have imagined — and couldn't even begin to piece together now. I hadn't really thought much about Susan in the whole scheme of things, except to feel sorry for her. Great judge of character I am. Well, I could either berate myself until she killed me, or I could do something. Keeping her talking seemed a good option. I grabbed the first thought that whizzed by. "That was really clever of you to throw everybody off the track by pretending to be at odds with the mayor."

"Who was pretending? The bastard was out to get us — and the money. Stupid Dewayne just couldn't seem to grasp that concept."

I couldn't either. "So why shoot Jerry?"

I knew the answer before she said a word.

"Amy, of course."

"Get rid of the competition?"

She laughed, a wholly evil laugh. "Something like that. He thinks he's perfect, Amy thinks he's perfect, hell, even you think he's perfect. But he's not. And he's surely not invincible, I proved that quite well." She chuckled again and then shrugged. "Oh, I guess if you really must know, it was mostly just convenient. BigJohn had stirred up so much trouble, it was only a matter of time until Jerry got wise to the whole deal. He was supposed to be my second shot. The first was for Granny." She nodded toward Lucille. "I suspected she had the money, even if she didn't know it, and I couldn't very well find it with deputies crawling all over the place. I needed her gone."

Gone as in dead. The woman was fully and completely deranged. "If you knew the money was at the cabin — and somebody had to put that hideaway box in the bathroom — why didn't you just go get it?"

"He put that box in, and I didn't know a damn thing about it until today. He'd been doing entirely too much thinking for himself lately." She scowled and kicked her dead brother again. "And that's not healthy."

"So why did you shoot at me and Leroy?"

Susan laughed, and this time she sounded sincerely amused. "Actually, sweetcakes, I thought you were your mother. How's that for a kick in the teeth?"

The jab hit its mark — and it was a very low one. Okay, Jolene, I told myself, there are worse things than turning into your mother. Yeah, like death, I argued back. I chanced a look at my mother, and what I saw sent my fear hurtling toward hysteria.

Lucille had pure terror written across her pale skin. It was one thing to deal with a known idiot, like Leroy or Dewayne, but Lucille knew serious trouble when she saw it. Susan Schuman Miller was smart and ruthless, and it was scaring the daylights out of my mother.

Lucille pressed her long-nailed fingers against her lips and stared. "You killed BigJohn." Lucille started to cry. "He really did care about me."

"Don't get yourself too worked up, Granny. Bennett's first concern was always for himself. He never even noticed your key missing from his cabinet."

Lucille pressed her fingers to her mouth, but a sob slipped out anyway.

"That wasn't the best part, though. I think the most fun I had was seeing what happened when the gun found its way back home. Everybody thought that slut carving was a zinger at Granny." Susan nodded at me and winked. "But we know better, don't we, Jolene?"

Well, we did now. My father's favorite shotgun had been carved up as a slur against me. Not my mother, but me. Why? Some convoluted thing to do with Jerry and Amy no doubt. And I didn't much care to hear the screwed-up reasoning behind it, because obviously Susan Schuman was seriously screwed up. I kept my eyes away from the floor and Dewayne and the blood. One little glance down and I was likely to crumble. I couldn't think about it, about him, about what she'd done, only what she planned to do, and how I could stop her. How, dammit, how?

I heard Mother sniffling and sucking in little crying gasps, and when I turned to look at her, my heart just broke. Lucille Jackson had tears running down her face and looked absolutely scared to death. I couldn't let her just stand there like that.

"Here, Mother," I said, stepping toward Lucille. "Let me get you a tissue from your purse."

"Hey, there, sweetcakes. I'm not ready to shoot you just yet, so don't make me," Susan said, following me with the gun. "Get away from her."

Susan stood about six feet away from me, and I stood between mother and Susan — and the gun. Mother was semiprotected, but the odds were good that the bullet would keep right on going through me and into her. Gory thought, but true. I didn't have much of a plan, but I knew I had to do something — even if it was wrong. And I had to do it now. Right now.

Leroy was still up against the fish trough, about the same distance away, although I wasn't sure what significance that held. With my back to Susan, I couldn't see what she was doing, or much of what Leroy was doing, but I hoped he was paying attention and might have a jolt of both instinct and ingenuity to help out when I needed it. This was right up there with the pigs sprouting wings theory, but hope springs eternal.

I said, "Either shoot me now or let me get my mother a tissue." I moved my hand toward the purse. "I'm not going to just stand here and not help her. She's an old woman and you're upsetting her. She has a heart condition besides." It was pure bravado talking, but I didn't have anything to lose. I glanced into Mother's face to see if her hackles had raised over my comments, particularly the old woman part. They hadn't. In fact, I didn't even think she'd heard me. And that was a very bad sign.

"Hurry up then," Susan said matter-of-factly. "Clean your sniveling selves up, but knock off the whining. I just hate whiny women."

From the corner of my eye, I could see Leroy watching me. He knew as well as anybody what was in the purse that sat in the chair next to Lucille. What he didn't know was whether I was going to swing it or pull a gun from it. I didn't know either.

Leroy no longer had a gun, so I couldn't expect him to do much, except realize that something was about to happen.

I made eye contact with him, looked down at the purse then kind of jerked my head toward Susan. The gesture wasn't terribly clear, but at least he knew I was about to do something.

"I really hadn't expected you all to show up here together for me," Susan said amicably. "It is rather convenient, but it also rather muddies things up a bit, which is why you're still alive. I will, of course, have to kill you all, but that's not as easy as it sounds."

I did not look around, but knew she was eyeing us one by one.

She laughed. "So many choices. Tying up a neat knot in three murders and a suicide is going to take some doing. If I'd just shot Dewayne in the head, this would all be a piece of cake. As it is, I can't very well just shoot you all here and expect the cops to figure out how you killed one another." She sighed heavily. "I surely do hate doing these things on the spur of the moment. I'm much more effective when I have some time to plan."

While Susan congratulated herself on her intelligence and unfortunate circumstances, I dug in Mother's purse and got the tissue like I'd said I would and wiped away Lucille's tears. It shook me more than I wanted to admit to see my hard-nosed mother so stricken. But then, we very well might be dead in the next two minutes, so I was flying free and loose on the emotional thing. "I love you, Mom."

She blinked a little, tears spilling out from the effort, and sniffed, a ragged sobbing thing. Okay, I'd had enough. No more of this for any of us. If Susan was going to kill us, she just would. Nobody was going to show up to save us so that seemed to leave any saving business up to me.

I knew before I did anything that one of us was going to get shot, and maybe all of us. But I had to do something. I knew there was no way I could get the Glock out of the case and assembled before Susan shot me dead. So, I did the next best thing. I transferred the tissue to my left hand and dabbed Mother's eyes again. With my right hand, I reached down, grabbed the handle of the purse, spun around and flung it toward Susan as hard as I could.

I watched the purse hurtle toward her. I saw her squeeze the trigger. Boom.

I stumbled backward a little.

Leroy lunged toward Susan, knocking her gun arm up.

Another roaring boom.

Another.

Leroy stepped back. He must have grabbed his gun back from Susan because it was still pointing at her chest.

Stunned disbelief on her face, Susan crumpled to the floor, falling across Dewayne.

Leroy stepped over and kicked Susan's gun across the room then looked toward Mother and me. His face got all funny looking and his jaw hung slack, but I couldn't see that he was hurt anywhere.

I glanced at Mother to make sure she was all right. Her eyes were wide and she looked petrified. I could understand that feeling. "Mom, you okay?"

She started sobbing and pointing at me then spun around and ran to the far end of the room. When she came running back with a towel, I knew something was very wrong. "Leroy," she shrieked, seeming to come out of her shock a little. "Get over here!"

But Leroy was already there beside me, although I didn't know exactly why. "Good Lord, Jolene," he said, his voice quivering. "You've been shot."

What? About then I began to notice that I couldn't move my left arm and a searing pain was creeping up through my shoulder. I ventured a look down. Blood. Lots of it. Mine. "Well, damn."

I felt myself sliding down to the floor and saw Leroy's big old hands grabbing for me.

The next thing I knew, I had a towel wrapped tightly around my upper arm, and Leroy and my mother were standing over me, telling me everything was going to be okay.

I knew it wasn't, though, because they were both crying.

———⟫●⟪———

Chapter Twenty

I don't remember that much about the first few days after surgery, except the doctors explaining about the metal rod they had to put in my arm. And the only reason I remember that is because they had a visual aid to enhance their shuddering presentation. A long shiny piece of metal and wicked-looking screws. I would have really preferred not to know.

I had no doubts that my mother had been with me the whole time, even though I hadn't done much except sleep. But every time I woke up, there she was. Nice. I also remembered Jerry being here every now and then, and my kids. Matt and Sarah. I remembered seeing them, too. Were they really here or had I just dreamed it?

I'd been dozing off and on this morning, but I hadn't felt like chatting so I'd just kept my eyes closed. However, in my brief moments of consciousness, I'd felt almost human.

I was in that hazy half-awake place where thoughts race around wildly giving you all sorts of ideas on what you could or should be doing, then like wisps of smoke, they vanish into nothingness. You know darn well they were important thoughts, too, but they're gone. It seemed like I'd had some kind of revelation, an important one, but I couldn't quite reel it back in. Then, I thought I heard my mother talking to me. She'd been doing that a lot these last few days. So had the kids. But Mother was here now, I was sure, because I could see her.

"Wake up, Jolene, somebody's here to see you."

Mother's words registered slowly, and they weren't words I really wanted to hear. I wasn't all that excited about seeing anybody just yet, but I dutifully tried to wedge my eyes open. It took a few blinks, but I finally coaxed my lids to stay halfway open.

Mother was standing beside the bed. And so was Jerry, but he wasn't in his uniform. He was in a hospital robe, with an IV. He stood for a moment then sat back down in a wheelchair. I was trying to make sense of that, when I saw who was holding the back of his chair. Amy. Amy? What was she doing here?

I wasn't sure if I'd died, or if I wished I had. Jerry and Amy. Here. Together. Heaven, it was not. And Jerry was still in the hospital. I thought he'd gone away with Amy. Damn, but this was confusing.

"Hey, how are ya?" Jerry said, his soft Texas drawl a little strained. "We've been really worried about you."

Lucille patted my good shoulder and walked away so the lovely couple could get closer to my hospital bed.

Amy gripped the bed rail and leaned toward me, her perfect blond beauty shimmering out like a delicate light. "I'm just so sorry about all of this, Jolene. I feel so responsible. I thought I knew her. She helped me through some hard times. I'm just so sorry. I can't imagine her being this different person." She blinked and sniffed. "I wish I could undo everything. Oh, Jolene, I'm just so sorry."

So was I. Very, very sorry. "It's okay, Amy. Really." Actually, I didn't know that anything was okay, but it seemed to be the thing to say, especially to Amy. I was the one half-dead and yet I was still compelled to comfort her. And she's here with Jerry besides. It was enough to send my already spinning head completely into orbit. "Jerry, are you okay? Did you have to come back to the hospital?"

He shook his head. "No, Jo, I never left. I did change rooms — and names, however, when Bob found out Dewayne was on the run."

"I came to see you...." I said pitifully.

"I know," he said, a soft smile curving his lips. "I tried to call and tell you what was going on, but that wasn't something I could say on a cell phone. Just not secure. I'm really sorry about that, Jolene. I hope you weren't worried."

Me? Worried? Ha! I scoff at worry and fear and panic. And just what the hell were these two doing here together anyway? I had mustered up enough courage to ask that very question when Jerry stuck his hand through the bed rail and squeezed my arm. "I bet you don't know that you're the talk of the county," he said, grinning like the owner of a first prize pig. "You wouldn't believe the newspaper articles that have been written about your heroism."

I groaned, never happy to have an article written about me, particularly in this place. "Kimberlee Fletcher?"

Jerry chuckled and shifted himself in the wheelchair. "It was all good things this time, Jo. Your mother's keeping a scrapbook. When you get to feeling better, you'll see all the good that's come out of this."

"That's right," Amy chirped, like a soft, little snowy dove. "If it hadn't been for you, Jerry and I might never have resolved our problems. We both owe you so much."

Resolved? Owe me? Oh, that sounded grand, just grand. Me, the marriage counselor. I was so proud.

"Amy and I are going to make things work," Jerry said, still smiling broadly. "For the kids' sake. I mean really, Jolene, this whole thing really makes you think about what's most important in life."

"Yeah, it sure does," I said, keeping the "and it's not me" comment to myself. But while we were analyzing priorities, I figured mine ought to be to get right back to Colorado and away from Jerry Don and the glorious Mrs. Jerry Don lest I interfere with their resolution or reconciliation or whatever. I tried to scrunch down into the hard hospital mattress and disappear, but it didn't seem to be working. Where were those ruby slippers when you really needed them?

"Besides," Jerry continued cheerfully. "You and I have been friends for over thirty years, Jo, and it's worked out just fine."

Fine? Oh, yeah, it was working out just dandy. I was in the hospital with a steel rod and matching screws in my arm and he was back together with his ex-wife. Yes, everything was just great. So help me, if they told me they were going to a marriage counselor I was going to scream.

"Jerry's such a good father," Amy said, sniffing just a little and patting his shoulder. She looked so pretty and fragile I just wanted to choke her.

"I feel so bad about this whole thing," she said softly. "I made some awful mistakes, but there's no reason the kids should suffer for them." She seemed to suck in a new burst of energy and hers eyes sparkled brighter. "Oh, Jolene, you just won't believe what we've worked out. Jerry's going to move back into the house!"

I choked. I coughed. I wanted to cry. Their reconciliation was moving mighty fast and I wasn't taking it well at all. Like a three-year-old to be precise. I tried to suck it up and act mature. "I'm so happy for you both," I said, my teeth clenching reflexively. I'd given it my best shot, really I had, but sincerity did not naturally radiate from the grinding of pearly whites.

"Oh, you're just so sweet," Amy said, natural honey oozing from her voice. "Why, I told Jerry we owe it all to you. And I just want you to know you'll be welcome at our house any time, whether Jerry's there or not. The kids just can't wait for you to tell them about your adventures."

I couldn't see that I'd ever have much of a story to tell, except about the metal spike in my arm, but I nodded and tried to look honored. I had no right to expect anything from Jerry. We were just friends. Had always been just friends. I had to be happy for him. He deserved to be happy. So did Amy. So did his kids. So did everybody in the whole stinking world.

I took a deep breath and tried again. "Your kids are great," I said, thinking of Rachel and Benjamin. They really did seem like great kids and I'd liked them right off. "Tell them I said hi." It was lame, but I wasn't in top form at the moment.

Amy smiled and reached around Jerry to pat my arm. "I'd better run along now. I've got to get my things out of the house by tomorrow since Jerry should be home by then. Oh, my, Jerry, I almost forgot. I'm going to run by this afternoon and get Rachel's soccer shoes for camp so you won't have to worry about that when the time comes. And Benjamin's going to mow the grass this afternoon so that will all be done before you get there." Amy's smile fluttered angelically across her face as she fluttered to the door. "I know the kids are going to be so happy to have Jerry back in the house. He's such a wonderful father."

I tried to smile but it was halfhearted at best. Yes, he was a wonderful father, and they were a wonderful family. Wonderful. Everything was just wonderful.

Amy flipped her blonde hair over her shoulder and shrugged. "Everyone thinks we're crazy, moving in and out of the house instead of just shuffling the kids back and forth between us, but I think it's worth a try. That way, the kids stay put in their own rooms and have what they need. Kind of like having a different nurse every shift. Only it will just be the two of us swapping out. We'll work it around Jerry's schedule, of course."

Of course. Wait a minute, what was she talking about? "I'm confused." It was a serious understatement.

"I know." Jerry chuckled, then gingerly stood up, leaned over the rail and kissed me, on the lips, right in front of Amy. "But you'll figure it out eventually."

"You take care now, Jolene." Amy smiled sweetly, floated to the door and left the room with a dainty little wave.

While I was trying to make sense of the fact that Jerry had kissed me right in front of Amy, and Amy had acted like all was just peachy, a big hulking thing of flowers came through the door followed by a big hulking thing named Leroy. He nodded to Jerry, then set the flowers on the shelf by the window and ambled up to the bed. "How ya doing, Jolene?"

Not too well. Not too well at all. If I wasn't confused enough by Jerry and Amy's deal, Leroy pushed me right over the edge. Something was severely off kilter here. I really didn't have the energy to think through the specifics or to say much, so I sighed and let my eyes fall shut. "I'm okay, Leroy. Just tired. Thanks for the flowers."

"Hey," Leroy said, heartily, "it was the least I could do, after all, you saved my butt." He paused for a minute and then laughed — loudly. "Hey, that's kind of funny. Saved my butt. Heh, heh."

I wasn't laughing. I kept my eyes closed and tried to keep that particular image at bay. Nobody seemed to mind my lack of input to the conversation. Leroy just started in telling Jerry about his various in-the-line-of-duty injuries for what was most likely the seventeenth time.

I needed a nap.

"Jolene, honey," Mother said, straightening my pillow. "The kids had already gone back out to the house this morning. They both stayed the night here, you know, but I just called and talked to Sarah. They're on their way back in right now. You just rest until they get here."

Sarah? My Sarah, and my baby Matt? They were here? For me? I felt the tears well up in my eyes, but I clenched them tight so Mother wouldn't notice.

"I'll be right here if you need me," she said softly. She smoothed the hair back from my forehead just like she had when I was a little girl. It felt really good to be cared for and taken care of for a little while. All this warm, fuzzy stuff was kind of nice for a change.

In fact, considering all that had happened — and where I was — I figured things weren't all that bad, even for Kickapoo, Texas. Things could be worse —

Like Pavlov's dog hearing a bell, I snapped to attention. I knew better than to ever even think things could be worse, because invariably they got that way fast.

True, we were in a hospital, and I had the sheriff and his second-in-command to guard me, if there was any guarding needed, but I still had this pesky insecure feeling. Even in my debilitated state, I felt on edge, like there was something beyond my control that might blow up at any second. My shoulder twitched reflexively, my eyelids sprung open and my eyes darted around the room. "Mother, where's your purse?"

Conversation stopped and Lucille hurried back to my bedside. "Don't you worry, Jolene. You rest. Everything's just fine and I'll be right here if you need me."

I believed her about that — the being there for me part — I really did. It was certain other topics that raised my doubts, namely an inanimate object she lovingly referred to as her Little Lady. Even under the influence of heavy-duty pain killers, I still broke out in a sweat just thinking about the laser-sighted Glock.

It seemed strange to me that I'd spent forty-three years being this woman's daughter, and yet I hadn't even really known her. Maybe never would. But what I knew — had always known — was that she would protect me, her cub, like the fiercest of sow bears. I just hadn't known exactly how all she'd go about that until now. Having the female geriatric version of Dirty Harry for a mother was almost comforting.

Almost.

"Mother, please don't whack anybody with your purse or do any shooting until tomorrow. I'd really like to get some sleep."

"Why, Jolene, whatever are you talking about?" Lucille said, entirely too sweetly. "You get the silliest notions. Why, when you were little you had the biggest imagination. Suppose that's why you never took to reporting, having to tell just the facts and all. You know, if you'd kept up with that, you'd probably be on television by now, giving the six o'clock news. Now that would really be something...."

I smiled and closed my eyes, letting my mother recite her familiar list of could-have-beens, should-have-beens and why-on-earths to herself. It was a sure sign that things were on the road back to normal, or at least as normal as it ever gets in Kickapoo, Texas.

DEAD MAN

FALLS

PAULA BOYD

Diomo
Books

Chapter
One

I can't be sure, of course, but I suspect that for most folks, their mother's birthday is neither an earth-shaking event nor a life-altering one. Oh, if only it were so for me.

When the long summer days begin to shorten and the September chill sweeps across my home in Colorado, there are a few things of which I am pretty much certain: the aspens will turn gold, fresh snow will start to fall, and Jolene Jackson will find herself back in Kickapoo, Texas. Like it or not.

This last little inevitability occurs because my mother is certain she will die on the spot if I don't show up for her annual birthday bash at the town's social center, meaning the local Dairy Queen. She also prefers that I arrive cheerful and perky, but we all know that's a long shot. I make a good effort, really I do, but a body can only take so much St. Johns wort without becoming comatose.

Now, I suspect that the correlation between a big to-do at a Dairy Queen some seven hundred miles south of my home and a personal crisis requiring herbal mood enhancers is not readily apparent, so let me explain.

There are several routine problems associated with my dear mother's birthday extravaganza. To be sure, Lady Lucille's whims and antics are enough to give me an annual case of dread as well as ulcers. However, the really big stomach-churner this year is the fact that September isn't that far removed from July — or my last certifiably painful visit here. The tedious facts and fatalities don't bear repeating, so I'll stick to the more generic personal revelations of my unfortunate sojourn.

To begin with, I found out a whole bunch of things about my seventy-two-year-old mother that I really didn't need to know. For one, she's in the market for another boyfriend, the previous one being a dud even before he was murdered in the aforementioned July fiasco.

For another, she carries a 9mm Glock with a laser sight in her purse. Yes, really.

Both of these things make me a little nervous. Okay, the gun makes me really nervous — twitchy even. Being nearly killed will do that to a person. And no, my mother didn't shoot me, although I had the feeling she thought about it a time or two. The almost-healed bullet hole in my arm — and the resulting steel pin holding the bone together — was the work of a now-deceased local crazy. But let's not dwell on past unpleasantries when there are certainly new ones to be had.

I arrived at my mother's house in Kickapoo, Texas, around nine p.m., which means I had managed to force myself up, up and away by eight. That would be in the morning. As anyone who knows me will attest, I am of the opinion that eight a.m. is a time for sleeping. Ditto for nine. Ten is negotiable.

In spite of the unpleasant early morning departure time, I usually drive down rather than fly. Redwater Falls does have an airport — of sorts — and you can eventually get there from Denver, but it is neither pleasant nor cheap. Besides, driving my own car gives me the illusion that I have control over something. Once I enter the twilight zone, aka Kickapoo, Texas, even that is iffy.

After unloading my one duffel bag and chatting semi-amicably with my mother, I found myself collapsed on the couch in front of the television — just in time for the local news. Not good.

My mother perched herself on the edge of a new grape-colored velvet chair, her gaze intent on the TV screen. The initial news bites that are supposed to keep you watching through the upcoming commercials were definitely doing their job.

"This is the biggest thing that's happened around here since the tornado of '83," she said enthusiastically. Lucille shook her head and clucked her tongue. "I don't much care for that new girl. She spends more time prissing for the camera than she does giving the news."

Please, no, not the "You could've done better than that" speech. I rubbed my road-weary eyes, tucked a stray wave of auburn hair behind my ear and pretended she hadn't said a word. A yawn and stretch emphasized the point.

It is no secret that Lucille Jackson has always wanted to see her only child in the limelight, onstage, front and center. Forty-three years of waiting — and nagging — for it to be so has been hard on her. She'd initially hoped to be a stage mom on the beauty pageant and/or fashion model circuit. Unfortunately, my non-anorexic five-foot-four-inch body — not to mention my budding feminist attitude — put me at a decided disadvantage in both categories.

Once, in a weak teenage moment, I agreed to participate in the high school all-star Greenbelt Bowl — as a potential queen, not a fullback. Suffice it to say that my comment to the judges about moving the pageant proceedings to the feedlot down the road where we could have us a real meat show did not secure me a rhinestone crown — or an amused mother. She didn't even attempt to get over it until I got that journalism scholarship to UT, which spawned a whole new set of maternal dreams. I blew those all to hell, too, of course, but she did have a few brief moments of almost-glory.

To this day Mother has held firm in her belief that I would have made a lovely television news anchor had I not squandered my potential and my journalism degree by running off to Denver, marrying an idiot (I'd give her that one) and starting that silly little card company, which gives me that silly little income, which allows me to drop everything and run to Texas on her every little whim or incarceration — whichever comes first.

Now, I do make a serious effort to try to please my mother — witness my current whereabouts — but living here is above and beyond the call of duty. Besides, I doubt any self-respecting Redwater station would have hired me anyway. I hadn't been meek and mild in high school and I was less so after finishing at the University of Texas in Austin. Geographically speaking, Redwater Falls is nowhere near Austin. Philosophically, we're talking different galaxies. Redwater is, however, about ten minutes north of where I grew up in Kickapoo, and is the "big" town in these parts, meaning its population bloomed to about one hundred thousand thirty years ago and has stayed pretty much the same ever since.

"There it is!" Lucille exclaimed, springing forward in her chair. She waggled a purple acrylic nail at the television screen, her bespangled wrist tinkling like chimes in a breeze. As she wiggled this way and that to punctuate her enthusiasm, her rhinestone-studded sweatshirt shot flashes of light across the room like a disco ball. "Would you just look at that! This is what I've been trying to tell you about. There's our new waterfall!"

She sounded very excited about something, but I wasn't exactly sure what. Did she really say waterfall? I blinked a few times and tried to focus my eyes on the fleeting image of what looked like a large wall of Volkswagen-sized rocks. "A what?"

"Oh, my," Lucille gasped, her attention still riveted to the screen. "Oh, for heaven's sake. Whatever will they do? Why, this is just awful." A gold glittery slipper stomped the floor. "Oh, well, hmmm, fire hoses. Wonderful idea."

Huh? Fire hoses? I scooted myself semi-upright on the couch and made a feeble attempt at paying attention to what the painted lady with the really big cyclone-proof red hair was saying. I suppose I'm also obligated to mention the spandex and cleavage as well, but don't ask me to explain it. This is heavy-duty Bible Belt country, but that belt's known for missing a loop or two when it's convenient.

I was sorely tempted to climb upon my high horse and examine the moral juxtaposition of luscious lips and bulging boobs selling news to the conservative Christian crowd. But since that particular horse has a tendency to run away with me, I reined myself in and focused on what anchor-babe was actually saying.

Mother's running dialog filled in the blanks and I pieced together enough details to determine that the wall of rocks I had just seen was a newly-erected waterfall — only it was built above the river and water didn't flow over it naturally. (No, I was not even a little surprised.) High-powered pumps were required to move water up and over the falls, then back into the river. But the pumps weren't going to be ready for the big opening ceremony tomorrow. Thus the fire truck option. Firefighters with high-pressure hoses would shoot water over the top so, as they say, the show could go on.

I also managed to discover that the big falls dedication was part of the city's sesquicentennial celebration, meaning they were having a big party because the town has been in existence for a really long time. More specifically, it had been 125 years since the first luckless travelers' mule died and they got stranded here for life. I wisely kept my ugly thoughts to myself as Lucille does not find my little asides humorous, and in fact gets rather testy when I say anything the least little bit untoward about her revered hometowns — yes, she claims them both.

Of course, this is home to me, too, and I was slightly embarrassed to admit that in my 18 years of growing up here, never once had I wondered if Redwater Falls actually had a falls. I also never wondered if Mineral Wells had any wells, if you could really "see more" in Seymour, or if Holliday was like a . . . well, you get the idea.

"So, is this an old falls they're making bigger, or a new falls they added just to go with the name?"

"Well, Jolene," Mother said, rather snotty-like, tipping up her aquiline nose for emphasis. "I'm certain there was a falls around here when Redwater was first settled, but where it was or was not located is beside the point. What's important is that we've got one now and everybody in the whole world will know where it is."

Indeed. No doubt travel agents worldwide were fast at work setting up week-long tours at this very moment. I smiled. "That sounds great."

She did not return my smile, just pointed the remote at the TV and clicked it off. "The new falls is built right off the main highway so as to be a showpiece for those coming into town from the north. It's really quite nice. Of national landmark quality. I can't wait for you to see it."

See it? Why would I want to see it? My stomach gurgled, accompanied by an all-too-familiar queasy feeling. That crash course in self-preservation back in July taught me a healthy respect for my internal early warning system and I intended to pay attention. "I'll see the falls one of these days, Mother. I'm sure it's very nice, but I'll just wait until the big crowds die down, you know I just hate crowds."

Lucille stood and patted her fluffed but sturdy pinkish hair. Since I'd last seen her, she'd done a little tweaking to the color of her trademark bouffant and I didn't much like it, not that I was stupid enough to say so.

She gave me a sly glance. "I rather expected you'd want to go to the celebration tomorrow. All of your old friends will be there."

Uh huh, and that was another problem. There was only one old friend I cared anything at all about seeing and she very well knew which one that was.

"Jerry Don Parker's going to be there," she said, right on cue.

I'd seen it coming, but the statement still hit me like a punch to the gut. If the truth be told — and I'd darn well prefer it wasn't — I had been looking forward to getting down here so I could see Jerry again.

Obviously, she knew this and was now using it to get me to do what she wanted. I could turn my back on a 125-year historic event and the unveiling of a brand-new fake waterfall, but I couldn't turn my back on my old high school sweetheart. Or so she thought.

"Sure, Jerry will probably be there, along with ninety-nine thousand other people," I said, putting a little bravado and swagger in my voice. "I'm also sure he'll have his kids with him."

Jerry's children were eight and eleven, good-looking, polite and all around well-behaved. And I didn't want to deal with them.

You see, I've already raised my brood. Yes, I mean raised, like on a farm, in a barn, with the pigs, and so on. Jerry's children, however, are being reared by his sweet ex-wife Amy. He has a good ten years left on his parental sentence, whereas my debts are almost paid off. My little darlings are exactly where kids should be, living in another state with others of their kind.

Okay, I'm kidding. I love my children dearly. We three weathered some tough times together and have moved to the stage where we're almost friends. Matt and Sarah are great people. Both are honor students at their respective universities and I'm very proud of them. They're proud of me too, particularly when they need money.

"Hey, how about my kids, Mother? You haven't asked about them," I said, deftly steering the conversation away from Jerry. "You probably don't know it, but this semester at college has been tough."

Lucille sighed dramatically. "I just talked to them both this morning, Jolene. My little angels are doing just wonderfully and you very well know it."

Yes, I knew it. I knew a lot of things, like the fact that Lucille called her grandchildren often, which was just peachy, but what kind of peeved me was that they called her just as frequently. Weren't eighteen- and twenty-year-olds supposed to be preoccupied with themselves and never call unless they wanted something? Sort of seemed to work that way with me.

I didn't much like where that train of thought was headed so I stood up, ready to retreat to my old bedroom.

"You know," Lucille said, lilting her voice to snag my attention. "Merline's cousin over in Bowman City said it's just a crime the way women are throwing themselves at that Jerry Don Parker these days."

That stopped me in my tracks.

"Why, I guess he just can't go anywhere in peace anymore. And mothers even pushing their nearly teenage daughters on him, if you can imagine," she said, implying that she could very well imagine it. "Suppose it's to be expected, him being the sheriff and available and all, not to mention real good-looking . . ."

Having deftly set the hook, she swiveled around and pranced off to the kitchen.

My mother had no doubts that I would follow her; all catfish are drawn to stink bait. They just can't help themselves and neither could I.

With my heart thundering in my chest and my teeth clenching spasmodically, I watched her fill a glass of water from her special purified jug in the fridge and suddenly decided I could use a little drink myself. Water wasn't my first choice at the moment, but I really don't like liquor and my beloved Dr Pepper would keep me wired all night — no matter how tired I was. Imagining hordes of women slobbering after Jerry wasn't going to help either.

As Mother reeled me in with a knowing smirk, she also grabbed a fresh glass from the cabinet and filled it from the jug. Holding it out to me, she said, "I wasn't implying that Jerry Don was taken with any of the girls or anything, mind you, just that he's being pursued."

I snatched the cold glass of water and was a little surprised it didn't start boiling in my hand. I took a sip. "Nice try, Mother, but I'm not biting. I don't care who's drooling after Jerry. It doesn't have a thing at all to do with me."

It was a lie, of course, and she knew it as well as I did. If indeed women were falling at his feet — and I fully suspected they were — I darn well wanted to know every single one's name and home address — not to mention date of birth and bra size.

Lucille flicked her acrylic claws as if shooing flies. "Well, he is quite a catch, and I'm sure there are plenty of women that would be more than happy to take care of his children if they got Jerry Don in the bargain."

She paused for effect and took another sip of water. When she was darned good and ready, she said, "Really, Jolene, under the unfortunate circumstances, it wouldn't hurt you to befriend his children. Those poor little things could use a good role model."

Me? A role model? This was definitely a new development since I couldn't recall a single time I'd ever made a parenting decision that the queen mother had agreed with. I don't think she'd ever been straightforward in saying so, but it was clearly implied that Matt and Sarah had turned out to be intelligent and decent human beings because of their grandmother's remote influence and in spite of my daily one.

"Jerry's kids have their mother," I said, pointing out the obvious and ignoring the fact that I had to actually have a relationship with Sheriff Parker for any of this to even matter. "Besides, I'm sure you'll cheerfully agree that compared to me, Amy Parker is a saint."

"Well, yes," Lucille said, not even bothering to try to placate me. "Amy's a sweet, good-natured, darling girl." She looked at me and fluttered her eyelashes.

I fluttered back. "What's your point?"

Lucille toyed with a dangly earring of multi-colored beads. "Well, it's just that I heard Amy has herself another girlfriend now . . ."

She left the sentence hanging there, just begging me to pick it up, but I was not about to get into that conversation. No way, no how. I let her stew for a bit as I slowly sipped down the rest of the nice cool water, which had amazingly simmered me down to just barely "hot under the collar" and slipping toward "merely amused."

"Well," I said, setting the glass on the counter. "Sounds like every woman in the county is either after Jerry or his ex-wife. Statistically speaking, that's pretty darned amazing. But, I don't see that Amy's love life is any of my business." *Or yours, Mother*, I conveyed with a pointed look. "Ready for bed?"

Lucille put the jug of water away. "Have you talked to him much?"

Him obviously meaning Sheriff Jerry Don Parker. I like to call him my Texas James Bond, kind of a Pierce Brosnan with a rumbling twang, but not to his face, of course. I couldn't help but smile at the image. And yes, oh yes, I'd talked to him. "He called a few times to see how I was doing."

The truth of the matter was that Jerry and I had talked at least twice a week and sometimes twice a day. We chatted about old times, new times, personal things, family things, and other things, but he hadn't mentioned women falling at his feet, Amy's new girlfriend, the big city celebration or the new waterfall. Probably because he knew I wouldn't care — at least about the falls.

I hadn't made a point of telling him that I'd be in town for my mother's birthday either, for a similar reason. Not that he wouldn't care, exactly, I just didn't want him to feel obligated to see me. A long-distance phone friend was one thing. Showing up back in town as a face-to-face friend was quite another and I wanted to do that privately.

"Well then," Lucille said, rather smugly. "I'm sure he'll be anxious to see for himself that you're doing okay. Why, you absolutely must give him a call in the morning and let him know you'll see him at the falls."

The trap, like a snare around a rabbit's foot, came full circle and yanked shut. Lucille Jackson is very good at this sort of thing, but I'm not that easy to manipulate. She knew I wanted to see Jerry, but I'd chew off my leg before I let her think she could tell me what to do.

"I'll see him later," I said, quite nonchalantly. "Besides, this is such a special event, I wouldn't want to intrude on his time with his kids."

She frowned a little and pursed her lips, but having been trained by the master, I continued on with my rebuttal before she could respond.

"I'll just stay here at the house, out of the way. Merline and Agnes won't know what to do if you're not right there with them, so you just go on and have a good time. Don't worry about me. I need to get things ready for your party anyway, you know, and that's going to take quite a while. Yes, this year's going to be a doozy. I need some time to pull things together, pick up the cake, that sort of thing."

Lucille gave me a stern look, apparently unimpressed by either my enthusiasm for her party or my lame attempts at playing her game. I might have studied at the feet of the passive-aggressive master, but I was not an adept student.

"I'm going to the celebration tomorrow, Jolene, and you're going to take me," she said, cutting to the chase.

I moved my jaw up and down a few times, searching for some really clever refusal-type words, but managed only gurgled moans.

"Now, listen, missy, I've already told Agnes and Merline that I couldn't go with them because you were going to be here and I knew you'd want the two of us to go together. Everyone is expecting you to be there with me and you darn well will be."

Beads of sweat suffused my skin in a mighty hot flash and I swallowed a very undaughterly groan. This was not good. Not good at all. I knew better than to take the upfront approach and "just say no." That would earn me the cold shoulder for the entire time I had to be here. Of course, I could just leave and go back to Colorado — always a lovely idea — but that would earn me a cold shoulder for the rest of my life — yes, I fully expect to be buried first as Lucille will live to be at least 143. Besides, I am an only child and she is my only living relative other than my children. Damn.

With another gurgle of my stomach, inspiration struck. "Well, I suppose I can try to take you to the big event tomorrow, if I'm up to it. That long trip down from Colorado is a killer, you know. I'm really not feeling all that great." I rubbed my temples. "Headache, stom-achache . . ." I wasn't lying either.

"I'm sure you'll feel just fine in the morning," she said, entirely too sure of the matter. "Now, get some sleep. We've got a big day ahead of us."

I tried to smile encouragingly while looking as sickly as I could. "Maybe a good night's rest will help. I just hope I can sleep." I stopped and frowned. That sounded like my mother's voice coming out of my mouth and it did not have a melodious ring to it. Maybe I'd learned more from Mother dear than I'd thought — and that was not a good thing. "See you in the morning," I said, but not with enthusiasm.

Lucille flicked off the kitchen light and trotted to her bedroom, no doubt grinning smugly.

I did my own about-face, turned out the light in the living room and marched back to my corner, giving myself a scathing what-for every step of the way. I was an adult, for godsakes. I didn't have to do what my mother told me to anymore. If I didn't want to go to the stupid fake-rocks-and-fire-hose show tomorrow I darn well didn't have to. And I'd tell her just exactly that first thing in the morning.

I could be sick if I wanted to. So there.

Chapter
Two

It had been a good theory, the one about being an adult and doing whatever I pleased. In practice, however, it left a lot to be desired. The pretending-to-be-sick thing hadn't worked out so well either. I'd given it my best effort, really I had, but I discovered I was no better at playing dead now than when I'd been ten years old. And here I thought I'd learned something in the last thirty years. If I have, it apparently has nothing at all to do with dealing with my mother.

Okay, if you must know the unpleasant details, I might have whined a little, moaned and/or groaned a lot, and even seriously considered writhing on the floor for dramatic effect. I eventually conjured up a pretty good whimper and produced a few real tears as I presented my complaints of sleep deprivation, nausea, headache, diarrhea, and a couple of long shots like kidney stones and an aneurysm.

Lucille was not moved. I'm not even sure she noticed.

Apparently I shouldn't have forewarned her that I was planning to be sick in the morning. But even so, she would have seen right through my semi-fake illness just as she had when I was in grade school. I don't think I ever got away with cutting class even once. I'm not very good at deviousness and deceit. However, compulsive sarcasm and the ability to insert my foot into my mouth at any given moment — I've got those down pat.

Actually, Lucille didn't stomp and rant and demand that I go to the big celebration with her. She just wondered aloud, over and over and over again, what would happen to her if she went alone and had a heat stroke, a frail old woman out there all by herself, alone and at the mercy of strangers. When she began her dramatic interpretation of a mother's heart being ripped from her chest and stomped on — we are a theatrical pair — I gave in, but not gracefully.

Negotiations — and I use the term loosely — for the conditions of the outing were neither subtle nor fair on either side. Despite

Lucille's efforts to shame me into it, I refused to dress as if we were going to a funeral, regardless of how similar the events were expected to be. I opted instead for a comfy pair of denim shorts, a tee shirt and sandals, my standard uniform of choice when sweltering is expected.

I also did not let myself get coerced into putting on a bunch of make-up. Lucille wears enough for both of us. Besides, it's common knowledge that the beauty-queen thing never appealed to me. All the cosmetics I own can fit into a sandwich bag — with the sandwich. My mother's collection, however, requires a tackle box worthy of a pro bass fishing champion. You open the top and all those little trays unfold like bleachers in a gymnasium. But I digress.

The trip into Redwater Falls had been both silent and uneventful, but now that we were on the highway by the falls I could feel the excitement bubbling forth from the passenger seat. In true funeral procession style, we took our place in the queue of cars snaking along the access road at the edge of the river. We could see into the main parking area, which had a bit of a carnival atmosphere. Various food and beverage carts dotted the perimeter of the parking lot, all festooned with bunches of frolicsome balloons and surrounded by lines of people. Finding a close-in place to park was looking highly unlikely.

The city, knowing a hot tourist attraction when it built one, had cleared an ambitious area of trees and grass — and paved and striped it admirably. This grandiose parking area would no doubt hold several thousand cars. Unfortunately, there were about ten times that number trying to get in.

"Park right over there, Jolene," Lucille said, pointing up ahead to a grassy patch under a huge cottonwood tree to the far right of where the big new falls had been erected. "It'll be real cool in the shade there. Just pull up on the grass. It won't hurt anything."

"Nah, won't hurt a thing except that we'll have to call a taxi when my car's towed away for illegal parking."

"Oh, for crying out loud, Jolene, everybody will be parking everywhere. Besides, we know the Bowman County sheriff and that cute little blond Redwater detective. What was his name?"

I did not volunteer his name, although I did remember it. How could I forget? Rick, aka Surfer Dude, was not little, but he was very cute and very blond. Tanned and lean, he looked like he belonged on a beach in California instead of sporting a detective's badge in

Redwater Falls, Texas. He was also a part of a very bad time that I preferred to forget. I shook off a shudder at the still-fresh memories, reflexively rubbed my arm and studied the parking options for a few more seconds.

While Mother's frequent and energetic marathons at the mall are the stuff of legends, I decided it really would be best if she didn't have to walk too far in the impending heat. The temperature had already ripened to ninety-four degrees with a similar number on the humidity scale, and Mother wasn't as young as she used to be. The shade might also prove helpful if perchance I discovered a way to enjoy the festivities from my Tahoe — my dark blue, sun-sucking Tahoe. So, with mostly selfless motivations, I hopped the curb and drove carefully toward the designated tree.

Pulling to a stop under the thickest spot of shade, I glanced around and noticed that my trailblazing had started a trend. Cars and trucks were packing in around us like frogs in a shrinking mud hole. There was some safety in numbers, I supposed, since it was doubtful they could haul us all off. I just hoped none of our new vehicular neighbors were setting up for a rousing tailgate party that would impede my solitude should I actually find a way to escape back here.

Mother unhooked her seatbelt and grabbed her tackle box from the back seat. She set the box on the console, snapped open the latches, and spread out all the little trays. After some deliberation, she selected a long brown pencil, flipped up the passenger side mirror, and expertly began embellishing her brows. That was only the beginning, of course, and I kept the car — and the all-important air conditioner — running while she re-based, re-powered and re-blushed. A swipe of mascara and an artful lip painting completed the cosmetic process. But she wasn't done yet. From the bottom of the tackle box she pulled out an industrial-sized can of hairspray and shook it.

Heat or no heat, I rolled down the windows fast.

"What do you think about my new color, Jolene?" she said, spraying and patting her helmet of pale mauve hair. "I was getting a little tired of Frivolous Fawn and decided to try something new. It's called Reticent Rose."

Painfully Pink would have been my guess. Obviously, I did not verbalize my opinion. Nope, I just smiled, very nicely, mind you, and coughed discreetly at the fog of hairspray engulfing me, then pointed all the air conditioner vents in her direction. "It does have quite a bit of reddish tint to it," I said, tactfully, and with not a hint of sarcasm. Honest.

"That's what I thought." Lucille leaned back from the visor mirror so she could take in the full head view. "Of course, it could just be my natural color coming through. I was auburn like you when I was younger, you know. When I'd get out in the sun, my hair would glow just like the burner on an electric stove."

Lovely visual, just lovely. "Well," I said, still very kindly. "You can keep trying different colors until you find one you really like."

Lucille finished with the spray can, reloaded the tackle box and snapped the visor up, ready to venture out into the masses.

For the festivities, she had chosen a purple pantsuit with matching earrings that dangled in strings of little purple balls, which matched the purple nail polish on her acrylic fingernails and non-acrylic toes. To complete her ensemble, she had opted to wear her favorite gold glitter sandals — presumably to show off the coordinating toe polish. As strange as it sounds, on Lucille, the look worked — very well. She looked rather fetching and certainly blended into the local crowd better than Plain Jane Jolene, who was starting to wish she had dressed for a funeral.

As more and more people flocked past the car, I began to surmise that everyone in Redwater Falls and the surrounding counties was here to see the unveiling of the new fake waterfall — and most, if not all, were dressed in their Sunday best. This does not mean shorts and a tee shirt. People around here dress to be seen, and one's image is not something to be taken lightly. I know this, but I try to pretend it doesn't matter — and it doesn't, shouldn't. But no matter what I tell myself, when I get around this mentality, I start worrying about what other people think of me. It's just plain weird.

"Hurry, up, Jolene." Lucille swung the car door open wide and grabbed the overhead handhold to help herself to the ground. She didn't make any ugly comments about my "monster truck" as she shimmied down, but the tooth marks in her fresh lipstick said she'd surely thought about it. She huffed a little as she smoothed away the wrinkles from her pantsuit. "We'd better hurry if we want to get a good place where we can see the water when it comes over."

I rolled up the windows, killed the engine and covered my mouth to hide my yawn. The heat does that to me, makes me want to just lie right down and take a nap. If I've just had a nice big chicken-fried steak with gravy and a tall glass of iced tea, so much the better. My mother — unlike most of the local populace — did not appear to be afflicted by this problem. As sleek and restless as a caged cougar, Lucille Jackson was neither dreaming of fatty foods nor yawning. She was, in fact, abuzz with energy. Before I could tell her to calm down, that we had plenty of time, a band — I'm guessing the high school marching variety — began to play what I hoped were just warm-up notes.

"Hurry up, Jolene, they're starting the ceremony!" She slammed the car door shut and took off like a shot.

Well, damn. I climbed out of the Tahoe, pointed my clicker behind me to lock the doors and tried to catch up with Lucille Speedwalker, who was zipping through the burgeoning crowd at about thirty miles per hour.

Clusters of people rippled and surged toward the edge of the river, accompanied by exuberant whoops and hollers — and an unhealthy amount of secondhand cigarette smoke. Coughing and muttering, I pushed my way along, trying to keep my eye on the bobbing mass of puffed pink hair. It wasn't as easy as you'd think, and the whole situation was beginning to wear on my good nature. Then, through a break in the sea of humanity, I caught another glimpse of my mother up ahead, elbowing her way to the front of the pack, her big black purse swinging this way and that. My shoulders shook in yet another involuntary shudder.

Blinking away a flood of unsettling flashbacks, I followed Mother at a prudent pace, muttering apologies to the poor souls left swaying in her wake.

"Hey, Jolene!"

It took a few seconds and a few steps for it to sink in that someone had called my name. I took a few more in hopes that the person — a male person whose voice did not ring a bell — was actually calling to someone else as I am not the only Jolene on the planet. When he said my name again, with Jackson added for clarification, I stopped and turned around.

A squinty-eyed guy in a turquoise Hawaiian shirt, cutoff jeans, and a long dangly feather earring waved and called my name again. His hair was now shoulder-length and mostly gray and his eyes weren't quite as vacant, but Russell Clements still looked pretty much like he had in high school. The spaced-out doper and I had been the top contenders for the "most time spent in the office" award, he for obvious reasons, I for trying to convince the superintendent to fire the principal. Russell they knew how to handle, me, not a clue.

People ebbed and flowed around me, closing off my exit path, so I stopped. "Hi, Russell," I said. "How's it going?"

"Hey, you remembered me! Wow." He stuffed his hands in his pockets and shuffled his thong-clad feet. "Man, it's been a long time since high school, but I knew it was you. Wow. High school. Really takes you back, huh?"

Oh, yeah, way back, and it's not a pleasant trip. "Listen, I've got to — "

"Hey, did you know I'm thinking about getting married?"

Uh, no, and why would I?

He jingled some change in his pocket and shrugged a little. "Me, finally getting married at forty-four. Who'da thought?"

Not me, that's for sure. "Congratulations, Russell," I said, and pretty darn politely, too, considering about eighty people around me were alternately blowing smoke and coughing up lung tissue. I'm all for their freedom to kill themselves however they please, I just prefer they not kill me at the same time. "Who's the lucky girl?"

"She's not really a girl, I guess, but she's real good to me. Keeps me lined out on things. I help her too." He shuffled his feet a little more. "Getting married was kind of her idea."

"We all need support, that's for sure." I didn't have any at the moment — unless you counted the three hundred people who'd rammed into my back in the last thirty seconds — but it was a nice thought. And yes, we all know who I'd prefer to have around to do the supporting. "Best of luck with your — "

"She's got stuff to deal with before we get married, about her kid and all." He shook his head, his beaded feather earring slapping against his face. "It gets weird sometimes. I've tried to help, but me not having any myself — kids, that is — it's kind of hard for me to understand, not that he's little or anything."

It was also fairly hard to understand Russell since he'd barbecued his brain as a teenager. Still, I realized he was in need of a sympathetic ear. I'm usually a sucker for such things, but I didn't have time for it at the moment, not with Lucille on the loose. "I'm sorry to have to run, Russell, but my mother is going to be worried if I don't catch up with her." And she might hurt somebody. I fanned a fresh haze of cigarette smoke. "Glad things are going so well for you. Best of luck with the wedding."

He looked a little sad that I wasn't going to stay and listen some more. Before I could find a clear path, however, a stray thought caught hold and his eyes widened a little. "Hey, you won't believe who all's here. I've seen half our class already. Even saw Coach Kelly and Miz Addleman." He whistled. "Man, you ought to see her daughter. What a babe. Long dark hair like you used to have. Wow."

"Listen, Russell — "

"It's really cool that you're here all the way from Colorado for this, especially since you didn't make it to the last reunion. Hey! You know who you gotta say hi to? Rhonda. You won't believe her."

I never did believe her. Rhonda Davenport and I have a long and unpleasant history. We had been friends in grade school, but about the time puberty hit so did our rivalry. Although "rivals" is such a genteel term. Down and dirty mortal enemies was closer to the truth. And yes, the feud revolved mostly around Jerry Don Parker — or any male who happened to take an interest in me. Rhonda made it a contest, and except for Jerry, she always won. Teenage boys are easily swayed.

"Hey, I know you two didn't always get along, but you gotta see her. Talk about changed." He whistled again for emphasis. "She told me once she had a kid to take care of, everything changed. Said it was like being born again."

Oh, no, no, no. We were not going down that road. If Rhonda had seen the light and it changed her from a lying slut into a decent human being, well, good for her. But I didn't want to hear about it. I craned my head this way and that, looking for my mother to save me. I didn't see her, but I waved and hollered anyway. "Here I am, Mother! I'll be right there. Good talking to you, Russell. Gotta run." And run I did.

I managed to dodge and weave through maybe a dozen people when I heard my name again. And no, it still wasn't my mother.

I paused and turned to my left.

A tall woman with silver-streaked black hair waved at me. She wore a long floral dress, autumn colors, standard Laura Ashley issue. And I had no clue who she was.

"You are Jolene Jackson, aren't you?" she asked, stepping up next to me.

I nodded tentatively, not sure whether she considered that a good thing or a bad thing.

"You don't remember me, I suppose." She smiled and clutched her hands to her chest. "I'm your old principal's wife. Well, ex-wife."

Oh, no. Not Mrs. Pollock. I smiled. "Sure, I remember you." Glad to be rid of the pervert? "How are you doing?" And why do you want to talk to me?

"I'm doing just great. I saw you in the crowd and just had to be sure it was you. I'd heard you'd moved away."

I gave her the short version of my move to Colorado several decades ago, and yes, I was just visiting, here for the birthday thing.

"Well, isn't that nice," Mrs. Pollock said. "I'm sure your mother is glad to have you home." She paused and frowned. "Weren't you just here a few months ago? Oh! Now I remember. That unfortunate situation with the mayor. And your friend Jerry Don. How is he doing?"

I smiled and tried to be just as cheerful and perky as I could manage. "He's doing great."

"He's a sheriff somewhere, isn't he?"

"Yes. Bowman County. Seems to really like it."

"Well, you better run along, dear. I saw your mother up near the front rail, just to the left up there. I'm sure she's wondering where you are. Take care, now."

With another wave of her hand, she disappeared into the crowed.

It took a little elbowing and wedging to make it through all the people, but I finally found my mother at the very front of the pack, right up against the decorative iron railing.

"There you are," Lucille said, with minimal enthusiasm. "I figured you stopped to talk with some of your old friends. I told you they'd all be here."

"And you were right." Mother likes hearing this phrase often, particularly from me.

But meeting "old friends" was exactly why I hadn't wanted to come. As I might have mentioned, I don't consider high school the best time in my life — except for some parts involving Jerry Don Parker — and I don't want to fumble through the old hierarchy or establish a new one. I just don't care. I've moved on and I don't want to go back.

"You know, I think I even saw some of your old teachers. You ought to say hello to them too."

"Mmmm," I mumbled noncommittally, figuring I'd already had my share of old home week just walking through the crowd. Still, there were several teachers I'd always wanted to say thank you to, but whether they'd necessarily want to hear from me was another matter. "Maybe another time."

"Now, Jolene, don't you start that foolishness about nobody liking you. You know good and well everybody in that school looked up to you and those teachers thought you just hung the moon. It's not going to hurt you to go say hello."

It might, depending on who I said hello to. True, I had been a leader in the school, and I was respected, but I was not particularly popular. I was what you might call a contradiction.

I had been a model student, never causing any trouble in class, getting good grades, that sort of thing. I'd also believed I could right the wrongs of the world — or at least the school — all by myself, and proceeded accordingly. My popularity peaked and valleyed depending on whether or not the outcome was an improvement to student life, that is, less homework, more privileges. The little scandal involving Miz Addleman and some unread — but graded nonetheless — reports scored a double negative, although it had been entertaining in the short term.

I felt a big thump in my side, in contrast to the continual bumps and nudges from the people around me. I looked down.

A little boy about four years old, holding a rapidly melting chocolate ice-cream cone, wedged himself up to the rail beside me. He dug the toes of his tennis shoes into the bars of the iron fence, pushed himself up as high as he could and screamed like a little demon, flinging melted brown mush all over my arm and tee shirt.

My first thought was to pluck him off the fence and hurl him into the river. My second was to gently help him down and escort him back to his keeper, if indeed he had one.

As it turned out, I didn't have to do either because his screeches began to sound almost like real words, "Look, look!" being the most discernible. So after wiping away the sticky goo as best I could, I did as he commanded.

The new falls was on the opposite side of the river from where we stood — that's the Redwater River, not to be confused with the Red

River which is located a few miles north and protects Texas from Oklahoma or Oklahoma from Texas, depending on your perspective. Here, a four-foot-tall decorative iron fence did the honors, preventing any overly zealous types — such as those on either side of me — from venturing too close to the water's edge.

A braided red cord roped off a small bridge that led to the official presentation area on the far side, directly in front of the falls. Visitors would eventually be allowed to cross the bridge and walk up to the falls for a closer look or a photo shoot if the urge possessed them. But not today. Today we all stayed back from the makeshift stage and hosing area.

As much as I like to make fun of anything and everything around here, I have to give credit where credit is due. Even without water flowing down the front, the manufactured structure that was going to put the falls back in Redwater Falls looked great, almost natural even, and it was impressively huge.

Tons and tons of smooth brown boulders had been carefully cemented into the side of the hill overlooking the river. The rocks were arranged in various steps and staggers of outcroppings where, presumably, the water would form pools, then cascade over and back down into the river. Eventually, when the pumps came on line, water from the river would be pumped up to the top, then flow naturally along the rocks back into the stream.

In truth, the massive falls and surrounding tree-covered park with the lazy river flowing through it made for a darned nice-looking place. I could honestly see why the entire town was brimming with pride.

"Well, Mother, it surely does look like a lot of thought and effort went into this project. It's really very nice. And much bigger than I expected. I'm impressed."

She glanced around at me and glared, kind of uneasy like, probably wondering if I was being a smart ass, which, for once, I was not. "There are plenty of very nice things around here, Jolene. And some plenty smart people too. We're not all idiots like you seem to think."

Idiots? Did I say anything about idiots? Okay, I know I have a little attitude problem regarding this place, but I'd been nice this time, really I had. "I wasn't being sarcastic, Mother. I meant it. The falls is very impressive."

The unsubtle narrowing of her eyes told me that nothing I could say would convince her of my sincerity about liking the waterfall. I had just decided to keep my mouth shut and smile like a fool when a big hairy tattooed arm shot between me and the jungle boy on the fence.

The ice-cream cone went flying forward over the rail and into the grass.

The little kid screeched out an agonized "No!"

"Harley Junior, what the hell you thinking, running off like that?"

A young guy, early twenties, about six-four, with short blond hair, hauled Harley Junior off the fence and held the boy under his arm like a football. "Your grandmother's worried herself sick," he said, sounding pretty upset himself. "I ought to paddle your little butt right here." He caught himself and glanced in my direction. "Pardon me, ma'am. I hope he wasn't bothering you."

I smiled, thinking of my previous evil thoughts — and we all have them, I just admit mine. I was glad I hadn't scolded the boy since the man, presumably Harley Senior, looked quite capable of taking care of that and then some.

"Don't be too hard on him," I said. "He's been having a great time. He sure didn't look lost though or I would have helped him find you."

Harley Senior nodded. "I'm just glad he's safe. You never know these days."

"Look, look!" Junior hung under Harley Senior's arm like a sky diver, waving his hands this way and that. "What's that!"

A bass drum boomed and cymbals crashed, snagging my attention. The band burst into an energetic march, one I vaguely recalled from my high school days.

On the temporary stage across the river and to our left, about a dozen people jockeyed for positions. Several men wearing dark business suits and a buxom young lady wearing a shiny yellow gown and sparkling tiara fanned out across the platform. I turned back to see if the little boy was still excited about the festivities, but the Harleys were both gone.

A little disappointed that I didn't get to put in another good word for Harley Junior, I occupied myself with trying to remember the name of the song the band played — played very well actually. A march. "British" something. About the time I closed in on the name,

Lucille swung her purse around from her elbow, whipped it open and started digging. I sucked in my breath and started shaking. Odds were real good she wasn't looking for a camera.

Flutes trilled and trumpets burst out the high notes, but I was frozen in place, waiting for either the tell-tale chink-chink of a bullet being loaded into the firing chamber or the glimpse of a red squiggly laser beam zipping around like a drunken housefly.

By the time I came out of my temporary shell shock, Lucille had pulled out a compact umbrella, popped it open and held it high above us.

"They should have let us stand over there under those shade trees out of this hot sun," she yelled, oblivious to my little post-traumatic stress episode.

And yes, the umbrella was also purple.

After the obligatory opening prayer and mangling of *The Star Spangled Banner*, the band broke into an authentic piece of Old West-style music, complete with clip-clops, while one of the men gave a glorified history of the city. The mayor stepped up next, without musical accompaniment, and a gave a folksy talk on civic pride and how they'd all worked together, blah, blah, blah.

I was just nodding off when someone rather rudely rammed an elbow into my side. I jumped, then gave that someone a dirty look. She pointedly ignored me and glared straight ahead.

Fine. I turned and glared too, and since I didn't hear any more speechifying, I presumed it was finally time for the main event. Yippee. I covered my mouth with my hand to hide a yawn and then rubbed my face to try to wake up. Given the right circumstances you really can sleep standing up, but not with your mother jabbing her elbow into your ribs. Another jab. "Ouch! Stop that!"

"Look up there," Lucille said gleefully, pointing to the top of the rock wall. "They've got the lights flashing on the tops of the fire trucks. You can just barely see them above the bushes. My word, they must have fifty trucks up there."

Five was more my guess, but the thrill of a light show to go with the shooting of the fire hoses stilled my tongue.

The trucks howled their sirens and the mass of humanity behind and beside me went wild. I stuck my fingers in my ears.

On cue, a squadron of fire hoses sprayed forth and the crowd sucked in its collective breath. I took my fingers out of my ears in time to hear the roar of rushing water rumble down from the top of the hill. The band started playing something that sounded suspiciously like a pep rally song and the fans were immediately whipped back into a frenzy.

A thick mist filled the air and high-velocity gushes ricocheted toward us. The fire engine pumps spewed with such pressure I couldn't help but worry that they'd loosen some of the fake rocks and send the whole mess tumbling down into the river any second. Leaves, twigs, a couple paper cups and a plastic grocery bag flew off in the gush, but eventually the top pools filled and water began trickling, then cascading, out and down to the next level of rocks.

The crowd whooped louder. The band played faster.

The second layer of pools began to fill and flow, all except the center one. I squinted against the sun, trying to see the problem. From my distant vantage point on the opposite side of the river, it looked like a big log or blob of trash had lodged against the rock edge of the upper pool.

This was not an immediate concern — despite the "Don't Mess with Texas" campaign — since Styrofoam ice chests, plastic milk jugs, aluminum cans, and glass bottles are still considered important parts of the ecosystem here, homes for fish and such. There are also economic issues and civic duties to consider. If Bubba don't throw his beer cans out the truck window, them boys in the orange suits won't have nothing to do and widespread unemployment will wreck the whole economy. Oh, yes.

After a few minutes, enough water had built up behind the impromptu dam to push the blockage up and over the edge. The lumpy brown mass — which was looking bigger by the second — plummeted out and down the falls in one long clump, end over end, bouncing off the rocks and landing with a big splash in the river below us.

I didn't gasp, but I did mutter an "Oh, shit." Even through the gush and foam of the water, I knew a dead body when I saw one.

Ordering Information

Available to readers through retail outlets and online booksellers.
Available to the trade through Ingram, Baker & Taylor, Brodart
or Diomo Books at (303) 816-2521, Fax (303) 816-0952.

To order additional retail copies of this book, please use the form
below.

Name: _____

Address: _____

City: _____ State: _____ ZIP: _____

Phone: _____ Email: _____

I would like to order:

_____(#) copies of *Hot Enough to Kill*

    @ $13.95 each = ... $ _____

_____(#) copies of *Dead Man Falls*

    @ $13.95 each = ... $ _____

Shipping: U.S. $4 for the first book and $2

               for each additional book $ _____

Total books & shipping costs . . . . $ _____

Enclose check or money order for above total and mail to:

DIOMO BOOKS
P. O. Box 645
Pine, CO 80470

Allow 1 to 2 weeks for delivery.